Saved by the Belle
The Royal Saboteurs
Book III

Shana Galen

Also by Shana Galen

Acknowledgments

Thank you to Elodie Papon for her advice with the French in this book. Any and all mistakes are mine.

Much gratitude to my team, including Gayle Cochrane, Abby Saul, Kim Killion, Maddee James, and Sarah Rosenbarker.

Chapter One

"It's exquisite, isn't it?" Hew Arundel turned this way then that, admiring the wool superfine coat. The blue was the color Navy men wore. He'd chosen it because he had blue eyes, and blue was his favorite color.

"Exquisite," the tailor at Schweitzer and Davidson's echoed. But Hew was paying the tailor to admire the coat—not that Schweitzer and Davidson would ever create an item of clothing of inferior quality. Hew's gaze met Randall's in the mirror. Randall raised a brow.

"Surely you don't need my approval."

Hew shrugged, liking the way the material of the coat flexed with his movement. "It's been so long since I've worn anything remotely fashionable, I've stooped to relying on your opinion."

Randall snorted good naturedly. "It's exquisite, though for that price, you could buy three coats."

"Not *exquisite* coats." Hew waved the tailor's hands away when he tried to assist in removing the coat. "I'll wear it," he told the man. "Have this coat"—he gestured to the not-Navy blue coat he'd worn in—"sent to the Mivart's."

"Very good, sir. Might I interest you in—"

Hew waved him away.

"Mivart's?" Randall asked as Hew stepped away from the cheval mirror where he'd been admiring the coat. "I assumed you were staying with your parents." Randall rose from one of the dark leather chairs set against the wall of the private dressing room. Schweitzer and Davidson's was an old and respected tailor and catered to the wealthy and privileged. That sort appreciated the dark wood paneling, the sedate lighting, and the comfortable chairs with a decanter of port or sherry within reach. Some of his friends would have said Schweitzer and Davidson's was too traditional and patronized Henry Poole & Co. But after nine months crawling through mud at the training ground he and the other agents called the Farm, Hew wanted his little comforts.

"They're not in Town," Hew said. "They've gone to the country." Most of his friends and all of his family were in the country now that fall had descended. The Season was over, and there was no reason to stay in London. But Hew wasn't looking for dinner parties and balls. This was his first leave since joining the Royal Saboteurs, and he wanted a large slice of civilization.

"You should have said something," Randall said, following Hew out of the curtained dressing room and into Schweitzer and Davidson's showroom. Like the dressing room, it was dark and quiet, smelling of tobacco and cedar. "You might have stayed with Lydia and me."

Hew gave his friend a narrow look as he stepped past the man who held the door open for him and emerged onto Savile Row, which was teeming with people despite the chill in the air. "Your wife, lovely as she is, does not need a house-guest at the moment."

"You're just afraid she'll give birth while you're trying to sleep. But the doctor says she has several weeks yet."

Hew didn't believe that for a moment. He *had* intended to stay with Randall and his wife. Randall was an old friend from Oxford, who had disgraced his family by choosing a life in trade. Randall had a knack for finance and kept the bankers in Threadneedle Street busy managing his investments. But when Hew had stepped off the train and spotted Randall in the station, he'd also spotted his wife. Mrs. Lydia Randall looked ready to burst. Of course, Randall had written to Hew that his wife was expecting. Hew just hadn't thought she would be expecting any moment. He'd allowed the couple to assume he was staying with family as Randall had been correct that he hadn't wanted to be wakened in the middle of the night with the screams of a woman in labor. God knew he was awakened in the wee hours of the morning enough at the Farm.

Now that he'd completed his first mission—a successful mission at that—he wanted rest and relaxation. "I don't want to impose on your marital bliss," Hew said. "Besides, at Mivart's I can sleep until noon and no one accuses me of sloth."

"No one would dare accuse you of sloth. From the little you've told me of your training, it sounds as though you work as hard as three laborers."

Hew doubted the laborers would agree. It was true he spent his days at the Farm crawling through muddy fields, practicing evasive maneuvers; learning how to diffuse explosives; and shooting at targets until his fingers were numb. But there were servants there to cook and clean for him and the other agents, as well as doctors to tend any injuries. Not that training to be a Royal Saboteur had been easy by any stretch of the imagination.

Before he'd been accepted as a Saboteur, Hew had been a diplomatic aide on the Continent. The job, from his experience, involved mingling at dinner parties and collecting state secrets, which he'd passed on to the Foreign Office. He'd been good enough to be considered for the Royal

Saboteurs, an elite group, which he had only heard whispered about before he'd been offered a chance to join.

"It is too bad that your family is not in Town," Randall said. "They'd want to celebrate the successful completion of your first mission. Though I don't suppose you could tell them any more about it than you told me."

"I'll go see them at Christmas." That was assuming he didn't have another mission that kept him away.

"Will you dine with us tonight?" Randall asked.

"If your wife doesn't mind."

"She was the one who suggested it. Let's stop at my club for a drink, and I'll send word."

The two spent an hour in the members' only gentlemen's club to which Randall belonged then made their way through the streets of Mayfair to the Randall town house. Randall owned the house, unlike Hew's family, who leased theirs every Season. The lack of a permanent London residence was another reason he'd reserved rooms at Mivart's.

Lydia Randall, tall and lovely, waddled toward them when they arrived just before the dinner hour. "There you are," she said, taking her husband's arm and smiling up at him. Hew was almost jealous of the look the couple exchanged—until he remembered not every woman was as faithful as Lydia. Some could look at you with adoring eyes while stabbing you in the heart. Lydia smiled at Hew, her expression turning friendly. "Mr. Arundel, I hoped you would join us for dinner. I told the butler to set another place. Darling"—she gazed back at her husband—"shall we go into dinner or do you want a drink first?"

"Arundel and I just had a drink at my club." He was frowning down at his wife. "Are you well? You look tired."

Lydia swatted his shoulder. "Just what every woman wants to hear." She patted his arm. "I'm fine."

The three went into dinner. It was a simple meal, but the food was very good. "What have they been feeding you at this farm?" Lydia asked the third time Hew complimented the fare. "Gruel?"

Hew forced himself to set down his fork. "Not at all. The food is quite decent. Not that I generally care as I'm usually so tired at the end of the day I'm likely to fall asleep with my face in the plate."

"Oh, my. What do you do all day?"

Hew realized he had begun a conversation he probably shouldn't have. Randall must have seen the hesitant look on his face because he chimed in. "I believe that information is top secret, darling."

"Surely you can tell us something," she said. Then, with a glance at the footmen who had cleared the table, she tried to push up. "But I've stayed too long. I should leave you to your port."

"Stay," Randall and Hew said at the same time.

She hadn't yet been able to push out of her chair, and she ceased struggling. "Are you certain?"

"Yes," Hew said. "Have your tea in here. In fact, if you don't mind, I'll have a cup myself."

"You won't regret it," Randall said. His smile stretched from ear to ear. Clearly, he was thrilled to stay at his wife's side. "Lydia's brother married the daughter of a prosperous tea merchant. It's the best I've ever tasted."

"It's almost good enough to make my parents forgive him for lowering himself," Lydia said.

Hew smiled. Neither Randall nor Lydia's family was titled, but they were both children of gentlemen who owned property and lived a life of leisure. To marry into a family involved in trade was quite frowned upon. Hew had often been told any labor at all was beneath him. He'd joined the Foreign Office anyway and with only a bit of muttering from his parents. Diplomatic work was an acceptable pursuit, even if they did remind Hew at every turn that he did not need the salary. He had no idea what his parents thought he did at present. They certainly would not approve of the Royal Saboteurs.

"You were asking about my work at the Farm," Hew said when the footmen had left to fetch the tea service.

"Is there anything you could tell us?" Mrs. Randall leaned forward, her gaze riveted on him. Randall was right. She did look tired. She had dark smudges under her light blue eyes, and she hadn't eaten more than a few bites of the excellent dinner. "Charles says you are a member of the Royal Saboteurs." She lowered her voice on the last two words.

"Darling!" Her husband shot her a quelling look.

Hew waved a hand. "It's fine. I am a member." With the completion of his first mission, he had been asked, formally, to join. He'd been told that six short months as a probationary member was quite impressive, but it had felt like years to Hew. "I'm not allowed to give any details about my mission, but I can tell you a bit about the group in general."

"Please do. I assume since the group has the word *royal* in it, you work for the queen?"

"I suppose that's true, but I've never met her. It's more that our mission is to protect Queen and Country. We're called saboteurs because we sabotage efforts—both foreign and domestic—to harm either the queen or the country."

"Are there people that wish harm to Her Majesty?"

"Of course. There are many individuals and foreign governments who would benefit from the chaos that would result if something were to happen to the queen or if widespread violence or disruption were to befall England. Our task is to sabotage groups and individuals trying to cause harm or disruption, whether that be an assassination attempt or a riot over grain prices."

"Oh, my. I fear asking you questions has only piqued my curiosity and raised many more. I remember last spring reading about the queen being shot at in the park. Were you involved in protecting her?"

Hew touched a spoon on the table, straightening it. "I was not, no." But Hew knew who had been called to the palace to infiltrate the Court and ferret out the assassin. The fact that Willoughby Galloway was able to apprehend the would-be assassin and keep the subsequent attempts on the queen's life from becoming public knowledge spoke of his unsurpassed abilities.

"But I've no doubt the Royal Saboteurs kept her safe," Randall said.

"We're not bodyguards," Hew said, avoiding the topic. "But we are trained in both firearms and hand-to-hand combat."

"And that's what you do at the Farm?" Lydia asked. "Train?"

The conversation ceased as the tea service was brought in and tea poured for all three of them. Hew spoke as he allowed his tea to cool. "We do train in the skills I've mentioned as well as explosives, evasive maneuvers, languages, cyphering..." He sipped his tea then paused and lifted it to his nose to inhale the fragrance.

Lydia was watching him. "I told you the tea was exquisite."

"Quite," he said. "Well worth the scandal of a mesalliance."

"You're making me envious," Randall said, "with all your talk of explosives and evasive maneuvers."

"I promise you there is nothing to envy. Evasive maneuvers involves crawling through mud and brush in the cold hours of the early morning while an instructor yells at you and tells you to crawl faster. And this is before any tea or coffee or a bite to eat."

"Barbaric," Randall said. "And you say there is a waiting list of men wanting to join?"

"Women too," Hew said.

"Women!" Lydia set down her cup. "Really?"

"Absolutely. We have two ladies in training at the moment, as well as one who completed a mission last winter."

"And they crawl about in the mud?"

"They do." He thought of Margaret Vaughn and Lucy Galloway. Neither had been faster than he on the obstacle course, but Margaret could decode anything, speak a dozen languages, and she was a wonder with a knife. Lucy, on the other hand, had no fear and had a love-hate relationship with explosives. She might not be the quickest through the obstacle course, but she could move like a phantom and be at your side before you ever knew she was in the same room. "There's not a man or woman in the Saboteurs who doesn't deserve to be there," Hew said, and he meant it.

"Must you return to the Farm or do you wait in London for your next assignment?" Lydia asked. "I do hope you will stay a few more weeks so you might meet the baby."

Hew smiled. "Unfortunately, I must return north by the end of the week, but Randall knows where to send word. Once the child is born, I will return posthaste." He finished his tea. He considered staying for another cup, but Lydia Randall did look tired and Hew felt a bit melancholy now that he'd mentioned his fellow agents. He wondered what

Duncan, Cal, and Will were up to. For all he knew, Cal and Will might be in London at this very moment.

"Now I shall take my leave," Hew said.

"It's still early," Lydia protested, but Randall gave him a grateful look. Clearly, he was concerned about his wife and wanted to put her to bed.

Randall rose. "Mr. Arundel doesn't leave for a few days yet. We'll see him again."

Hew motioned for Mrs. Randall to stay seated and crossed to her, kissing her hand and thanking her again for the exceptional tea. "I'll send a tin of it back with you," she said.

"I'll be the most popular agent at the Farm," he said, then walked out of the dining room with Randall. But instead of seeing him to the door, Randall accompanied him outside.

"Will you walk?" Randall asked.

Hew looked up at the sky, from which a steady drizzle fell. "I think I will hail a hackney. Knowing my luck, the heavens will open up halfway to the hotel."

Randall motioned to a footman, who moved to the corner to hail any approaching conveyances for hire. "Is it just my imagination," Randall said quietly, "or does she look tired?"

Hew did not have to ask who *she* referred to. "Your wife does look a bit pale and weary, but no more so than any other woman in her condition."

"She ate almost nothing."

Hew wasn't sure what to say. He didn't have any experience with breeding women, and he didn't know what Lydia Randall's lack of appetite might portend. Surely, he could not go wrong by reassuring the father-to-be. "I'm certain it's nothing a night of sleep won't cure."

"I hope so." Randall looked over Hew's shoulder at the sound of an approaching conveyance. "That one is occupied," he said, his tone irritated.

"You needn't wait in the rain with me," Hew said. "Go inside to your—"

He felt the prickle of something off—something wrong—and because he was not expecting it, reacted just a second too late. He turned, swinging his arm up to ward off an attack, but the attacker had already struck. Hew felt the blade of the knife sink into his ribs. Surprisingly, after the initial pain that took his breath away, he felt nothing. He swung out, catching the attacker on the jaw and sending him stumbling away.

"Get him!" Hew yelled. At least he'd tried to yell. His voice came out as little more than a wheeze. But Randall jumped into action, sprinting after the attacker who was now running into the street. Hew watched with annoyance as the approaching hackney slowed, the door opened, and the attacker jumped inside. Randall had to jump out of the way to avoid being trampled by the horses.

"Nicely done," Hew muttered as he sank to his knees. Whoever had planned this attack—and there was no doubt it had been planned—had timed it perfectly. If Hew hadn't turned the second he did, the knife would have plunged straight through his back and punctured his lungs. As it was, the knife had slid into his side, just below his lungs. He tried to rise, found his legs would not cooperate, and then put his hand where pain had begun to radiate. The knife was still there.

"Bloody hell!"

Hew wasn't certain where the voice came from. The streetlights had gone out and the night was closing in.

"Call for a doctor. Hurry!" Someone caught him just as Hew fell over.

"Call for a doctor. He's been stabbed." It was Randall. Hew knew that voice.

"I'm fine."

"You're not fine," Randall argued. "You have a knife sticking out of your side." Randall stiffened. "Lydia, darling, go inside. It's not safe out here."

"But Randall!" Her voice was high and sounded terrified. Hew's vision cleared for long enough to see her coming toward them. The front of her dress was wet as though she'd spilled water in her lap. Except Hew did not think that was water.

"The baby. He's coming!"

"What?"

"I told you it wouldn't be several weeks," Hew croaked. "Go to her."

"Where is that bloody doctor?" Randall demanded, his voice bordering on panic. Lydia made a sound of pain and Hew felt himself lowered to the ground. He reached over to find the hilt of the knife again, and his hand brushed the wetness on his coat. His *new* coat.

"Bloody hell," he muttered. "Not the coat."

The streetlights dimmed again, and the world went black.

Chapter Two

Belle Howard loved this time of the evening. The shop was closed, and the streets were all but empty. Her father had gone upstairs to sit by the fire and read, leaving her alone to close the shop and tidy all for the next day. She straightened and swept all day, so there was very little tidying to do, which meant she had time to indulge in her true passion—tea.

She walked the shelves, her hand reaching out to touch the cakes of oolong, wrapped carefully in paper and tied with twine. Next came the high quality, lighter teas, preferred by the upper classes. These were the Assam and the Ceylon, the Darjeeling and the Earl Grey. There were blends upon blends of each variety, and she knew and loved them all. Belle passed the green teas and the expensive white teas, displayed near the counter where her father and she could keep an eye on them, then moved to the herbal teas. She'd sent her father upstairs with a lavender tea to help with the headache she could see behind his eyes.

Finally, she stood on the side of the door with the darker, less expensive black teas. These were preferred by those who could not afford the lighter teas. It was common to add milk and sugar to these to make them less bitter. But Belle could appreciate the bitterness of a black tea, and rarely added anything to a cup.

She had dusted the teapots, cups, and saucers they sold as well as the tins of biscuits, but she ran a finger over them just to be sure they were free of dust. Having made her rounds, she returned to the counter and opened the lock box with the key she always kept tied at her waist. She emptied it of coins and bills—mostly coins—and placed all but what she would need for change the following day in a cloth bag. Then she locked the box again and carried the bag to the storeroom.

Like the front of the store, the back was ruthlessly organized and clean. Various teas lined the shelves, ready to be placed in the front of the shop should supplies run low. She unlocked a cabinet with another key at her waist then unlocked the padlock of the safe housed in the cabinet. She placed the bag of money next to the proceeds from the day before. Tomorrow she would take a chunk of those profits and pay the landlord as well as go to the docks and visit the warehouses owned by the importers from China and India. Her father said she had a nose like a bloodhound, only she could sniff out the best teas. She had the palate for it too and was able to identify over fifty blends and varieties of teas even with a blindfold. Or at least she had been able to when she'd been younger and her sister and she played what they called the "tasting game."

The days when she visited the warehouse to choose the teas for the shop were her favorite. Most of the time, she found nothing unusual and purchased the usual Darjeeling, Ceylon, and Assam. But occasionally she found something extraordinary.

Her gaze fell on the small package of green tea from China. Howard's Teas & Treats carried Pan Long Yin Hao. It was pricey, as the tea leaves were hand rolled and the tea was very smooth and came all the way from the Zhejiang Province. But never had she tasted a variety of Pan Long Yin Hao like this. The man she had bought it from insisted it was the blend preferred by the Emperor, and that the small quantity he sold her had come straight from the Emperor's Court. He called the tea Curled Dragon Silver Tips, and when she poured the tea leaves into a bowl, she could see why. They did look like tiny sleeping dragons with whitish tails that might look silver in the candlelight. The handful of tea had cost her as much as fifty cakes of oolong, but she had bought it. The scent alone had been hard to resist, but when the merchant brewed her a small cup and she tasted it, she had known she would probably never again taste any tea as smooth and flavorful. Belle could well believe the Emperor drank this tea.

Naturally, her father had been dismayed when he'd seen the tea and the price, but he understood her too well to be angry. He simply remarked that they would need to sell this before purchasing more. That was over a month ago, and Belle had been looking for the perfect buyer ever since. It was unfortunate that most of the *ton* had left London for the country. On occasion a viscountess or baroness came into the shop. More regularly, the cook or housekeeper for a marquess or a duke came in. Those were her targets, but she would have to wait.

In the meantime, the tea tempted her every day. During slow afternoons, she would often stand at the counter and dream of brewing a cup—just a cup—of the Curled Dragon Tips. She was sorely tempted now. What would it hurt? One little cup?

But if she gave in now, what was to stop her from giving in tomorrow or the next night? Soon she'd have none of the Emperor's Pan Long Yin Hao left to sell. She'd instead treat herself to a cup of white tea—perhaps the Pai Mu Tan or the SowMee White, as she had the taste for something sweet tonight.

Belle placed the Pan Long Yin Hao back in its pouch, but before she could replace it in the safe, a loud pounding startled her. She almost dropped the tea, but fumbled and caught it just in time.

"Miss Howard! Mr. Howard!" came a voice and more pounding. Belle's heart had jumped in her throat. She frowned as she replaced the tea in the safe, locked it, closed the cupboard door, and locked it.

The pounding continued. No customer would come this late and demand entrance. Perhaps her sister or a neighbor had come to some harm?

Belle stepped out of the back just as her father descended the steps from their private residence upstairs. "Belle!" he said, out of breath. His hair was disheveled, and his face creased, indicating he had probably fallen asleep in front of the fire. "What is it?"

"I don't know. I was in the back."

The pounding continued, and her father went to the door, pulled back the shade, and said, "Just a moment then."

He patted his coat for his keys, found them, and unlocked the door, saying over his shoulder, "It's one of the Randalls' footmen."

The Randalls? Why on earth would the Randalls send a footman with an urgent message to Belle and her father?

They knew the Randalls, of course, but the acquaintance was only that—an acquaintance. Belle's younger sister, Maggie, had married Lydia's brother, a substantial step up in the world. The Randalls had been welcoming to Maggie, but they had never indicated they wished their association with the Howards to deepen any further. In fact, Belle thought of Lydia Randall as more of a customer than a relation. She sent one of her footmen to purchase tea every month. As Belle recalled, Lydia preferred an expensive blend of English Evening tea.

The door swung open, and the footman, dripping wet from the rain, stepped forward. "I am sorry to intrude, Mr. Howard. There's an emergency at Mr. and Mrs. Randall's residence."

"Has something happened to Maggie—er, Mrs. Dormer?"

The footman peered at Belle, his gaze lingering just a little too long, and Belle felt her face flush. She had forgotten that she'd pulled the curls she wore about her face up and away with a ribbon. The footman looked away, seeming embarrassed, as though he had seen something he was not meant to see. "Not Mr. or Mrs. Dormer, no. To my knowledge, they are still in the country. But the doctor has been summoned to the Randalls' residence, and Mr. Randall has called for you, Mr. Howard."

"Is it the baby?" Belle asked. She couldn't think why Charles or Lydia would want her father at the birth of their first child, but who could understand the minds of the upper classes? In any case, if the baby was coming, she would bring tea—perhaps chamomile or hibiscus?

"I'm not at liberty to say, miss," the footman said, this time not looking at her. "But Mr. Randall did say it was urgent." The footman indicated the Randalls' coach, which was waiting just down the street. Belle hadn't even noticed it until now, though the horses were blowing and stamping impatiently, probably unhappy to be pulled from their warm stalls and their dinner.

"I'll get my coat," her father said. "And your cloak, Belle."

"Thank you. If you could give us a moment?" she said to the footman.

He nodded and stepped away. Belle closed the door to the shop, gave it a last look to make sure all the shades were drawn and all was secure, then she hurried behind the counter and pulled the ribbon out of her hair so the limp ringlets fell about her face. She did not have time to use the curling tongs on it, so this would have to do. By then her father had come down from the upper floor and closed the door to the stairs, locking it as he did so. "Are the profits from today in the safe?" he asked as he held the cloak for Belle.

"Yes. And I locked the safe and the cupboard before coming out to see about the knocking."

"Good girl."

Belle pulled the hood of the cloak up around her face, liking the way it shielded her from view. "We can't be too careful," Belle said. In London there were always thefts and burglaries. A tea shop did not hold as much interest as a jewelry store, grocer, or tobacco shop for a thief or his gang, but the Howards did not like to tempt fate.

A few moments later, Belle and her father were settled in the coach and watching as the shop and Fenchurch Street faded into the distance. The coach traveled west, toward Mayfair, at what seemed to Belle an alarming speed, but then she was not used to traveling by coach. Her usual mode of transport was to walk, but when she needed to accompany a large purchase of tea, she had ridden in a cart or wagon. Those were large and cumbersome, though, not at all like the light, quick conveyance she occupied now.

"Why do you think the Randalls summoned us?" Belle asked. *Summoned* seemed the right word considering the class difference between the families and the way the footman had appeared unexpectedly and all but demanded they accompany him.

"I suppose we'll find out," her father said, sounding tired. And well he should be. They had both been up since dawn and then working in the shop for hours. Belle was suddenly quite angry at the Randalls for asking her father to leave his comfortable chair and fire to come out in the middle of the night. It was one thing for Lydia Randall, who could sleep until noon tomorrow, to go out at all hours, but the Howards had a full day of labor on the morrow.

Her father put his hand over Belle's, ostensibly reading her thoughts. "I'm sure they would not have called for us if it was not important."

"It does rankle a bit," she answered, "to be treated like servants at their beck and call."

"Or perhaps we are more like family, and they must lean on us in a time of need."

What could she say to that? Belle took her father's hand and squeezed it, determining it was best if she kept silent the rest of the way. As they neared Mayfair, the coach slowed as it encountered other carriages. Finally, they were delivered to the Randalls' residence — not to the door, Belle noted — but that might be because a gig was blocking the walk.

Her father nodded to it as they followed the footman to the front door. "That must be the doctor."

The butler must have been watching and waiting for them because the door opened before they had even reached the porch. A great rectangle of light illuminated them, and Belle squinted at the brightly lit foyer. It seemed every light in the house burned.

"Good evening, Mr. Howard. Miss Howard." The butler—Belle had forgotten his name or never known it— nodded to them. "Please wait here a moment."

The butler motioned to three chairs set against a wall then started up the wide staircase. Her father took one of the chairs, but Belle did not feel like sitting. "I would have thought the house was on fire and now he asks us to sit as though there's no emergency at all," she said, looking about her. She'd only been to this house once, and that was for a small family party to celebrate Maggie's engagement. It had been one of about six engagement celebrations. Belle had asked her sister, more than once, if she was certain she wanted to go through with the marriage. All those parties and people were quite intimidating. But the affair at the Randalls' house had been small and intimate, and that's when she had seen how warm the Dormer family was and how much John seemed to love Maggie. She hadn't said another word after that.

A sound from above caught her attention, and Belle looked away from a painting on the wall to see Charles Randall racing down the stairs. He did indeed look like a man in the throes of calamity. His normally perfectly styled brown hair was tousled, his neckcloth askew, and he wore no coat. Spots of red—*was that blood?*—stained his limp white shirt.

Charles Randall was usually quite a handsome man, if one liked thick side whiskers and a ramrod straight posture. "I'm so glad you came," Randall said, going straight to her father and taking his hand in a firm handshake. "I am so sorry for the inconvenience."

"No inconvenience," her father said. Belle went to stand beside her father and Randall gave her an absent nod.

"We've had quite a scare tonight."

"Is it the baby?" Belle asked.

Randall swallowed. "Yes. The baby is coming, and the doctor and midwife are with Mrs. Randall right now. The doctor says she is doing well. That's not why I called for you."

Belle and her father exchanged glances.

"We've had an…incident. A friend of mine from school dined with us tonight. As we stood outside waiting for a hackney to take him to his hotel, a man passed by and stabbed him."

"Oh, my!" Belle put a hand to her heart. "Is he badly hurt? Was it a robbery?"

Randall opened his mouth then closed it again. "We don't know the motive, and yes, he is badly injured." He held up a hand. "The doctor says he has a good chance of recovery if…"

He trailed off and neither Belle nor her father pressed him. It was not difficult to imagine all that might go wrong and lead the man to die — fever, infection, bleeding internally.

"He's treated the wound and given Hew — Mr. Arundel, that is — some laudanum for the pain. He's resting, and the doctor says he must continue to rest if he is to recover. He must have quiet and dedicated care."

A scream echoed from above and startled all three of them. *Good Lord*, Belle thought, *was that Lydia Randall?*

Randall looked at the stairs, clearly wanting to go to his wife, but he did not move. "As you can see, he will not get much rest here. Once the babe is come, all attention will be directed to him."

"And babies are not known for their peace and quiet," her father said, his voice sounding like one who knew of what he spoke. "This is no time for Mrs. Randall to attempt and nurse an injured man."

Randall looked relieved and grasped her father's hand. "Exactly, sir. And Mr. Arundel is a good friend. I cannot trust him to the care of servants."

"You want family."

"Exactly." Randall smiled and Belle could have sworn there were tears in his eyes. "I would not have called for you save everyone else is out of Town. I will send a letter to Mr. Arundel's family, of course, but would you—could you—until they arrive—"

"Of course. We would be honored," her father said.

Randall let out a relieved sigh. "Thank you. I will have Farnsworth ready everything. If you will excuse me? I know it is rude to leave you as such—"

Another scream from above, and Randall looked almost panicked.

"Go. We will be fine. Leave everything to me."

Randall did not wait for another word. He took the stairs two at a time and was gone. Belle looked up at her father. "Did you just agree to care for a stranger who has a mortal knife wound?"

Her father smiled down at her. "It appears I did. And we do not know if the wound is mortal."

"What if he dies? We could be blamed."

"We will simply have to make sure he doesn't die."

"I'm not a nurse," Belle objected. "I know nothing about knife wounds."

"We will figure it out together. Did you bring the tea?"

Belle had almost forgotten about the hibiscus tea she had tucked in her reticule. She withdrew it now and placed it on the table in the foyer. "Do you think that was blood on Mr. Randall's shirt?" she asked with a shudder.

"Better not to think about it," her father said.

The next half hour was a blur of activity. The housekeeper appeared with an armful of clean linen and a piece of paper with instructions from the doctor. Belle took the linen, her father took the instructions, and the housekeeper took the tea. Belle flinched every time Mrs. Randall screamed. The screams came at regular intervals, which, fortunately were not close together yet. Finally, just as Belle was certain her nerves could not take any more, four footmen came down the stairs with a man on a pallet.

Her first view of Mr. Arundel was not impressive. He was a limp, pale form whose limbs dangled off the pallet. She caught a glimpse of dark hair and a long face and then he was being carried out the door and to the waiting carriage. Belle looked at her father. "I suppose we follow?"

"One moment!" An older man in black came down the stairs. His spectacles were askew and his neckcloth loosened. Belle could only assume this was the doctor at last. "You are Mr. and Miss Howard, yes?" He had an upper-class accent and a stiff way of walking.

"We are," Belle's father said, coming forward to shake the doctor's hand at the base of the stairs. "We have received your instructions."

"Good. You can read?"

Belle bristled, but her father just smiled. "Both my daughter and I read and write." He unfurled one of the hands clasped behind his back and made a gesture for her to hold her tongue. Not that she had anything to say to this doctor. He'd obviously judged them right away by their dress and speech.

"Follow my instructions to the letter. I will call on you tomorrow—God willing." His gaze lifted to the ceiling and the upper floors where Mrs. Randall labored. "I've bandaged and stitched the wound, but it's impossible to tell if there's irreparable internal injury. For now we try to keep him comfortable and stave off infection. When he develops a fever, and he most certainly will, you will need to keep him cool. An ice bath is best."

Belle covered her mouth to keep from laughing. An ice bath! As though they were made of money and could purchase enough ice at this time of year to put in a bathtub!

The doctor stepped closer to her father, ostensibly so Belle would not hear his next words. He murmured something and her father nodded gravely. "We will do our best, sir."

Another scream sounded, followed by a curse, and the doctor looked up. "I had better go back. I think we've some time before the babe comes, but I can provide comfort with my presence." He started back up the stairs without a by-your-leave.

Belle snorted. "As though he would be any comfort." She took her father's proffered arm. "Poor Mrs. Randall. She may be screaming for hours to come."

"Your own mother had mercifully brief labors," he told her as they left the house and walked through the steady rain to the waiting carriage. "And yet it seemed as though she was in pain for days. Those were the best and worst two days of my life," he said, giving her a smile.

He didn't speak of her mother often, but when he did it always made Belle's heart clench. It was so obvious he had loved Isabelle Howard, her mother and namesake. Belle wished she had known her mother more. She'd been seven when her mother had died, and now, eighteen years later, her memories were vague and fuzzy.

A footman held the door to the carriage open. The pallet had been laid vertically so that the man's head was on one seat and his feet on the other. He was a tall man, and his legs were bent to accommodate his length on the pallet. Belle climbed in and took the empty spot on one side of the coach, and her father took that across from her.

"John Coachman will drive slowly," the footman said. "Good night, Miss. Sir." He closed the door and the coach started away slowly, as promised. Even with the slow, careful pace, the carriage bumped over the streets, jouncing the pallet. The man seemed to be unconscious, but he made small sounds of pain, his brow furrowing. Belle told herself not to care. His care had been thrust upon them and would certainly interfere with the daily work of running the shop. She hadn't bothered to point out the inconvenience taking this injured man on would be because she knew her father would hear none of it and insist it was their Christian and familial duty. As far as Belle was concerned, she didn't owe anything to Lydia or Charles Randall, but she supposed she would be truly heartless if she refused to take an injured man in for a couple of days. Surely, his family would ride hell for leather to reach London and take over his care.

She just couldn't let him die before they arrived.

The man moaned in pain, and Belle reached over and took his hand in hers. She had only thought to offer him some comfort, but she heard her father clear his throat. "Do not become attached to him, Belle," he said.

Ha! As though she would ever become attached to some man unceremoniously thrust into her care. Of course, her father had said the same thing when she'd been about nine and brought home a sickly kitten. That kitten had not lived, and she'd cried so much her father had given her another, a healthy kitten, a few weeks later. But if this man died, he would not be so easy to replace. Belle narrowed her eyes. "What was it the doctor said to you before we left?"

Her father sighed. "I was afraid you'd ask about that."

"Go on then."

Her father glanced at Mr. Arundel and lowered his voice. "He said the man would be fortunate to live through the week. He gave him a fifty percent chance of survival."

Belle glanced at Mr. Arundel. Squeezing his hand, she said, "I hope you're a fighter."

Chapter Three

Arundel did prove to be something of a fighter as he made it through the trip across London in the coach and through being carried upstairs by the footmen. Unfortunately, the Howards' stairs were narrow and steep, and the footmen had to dispense with the pallet and carry the man bodily. Belle thought it was fortunate he was unconscious because with his injury, the jostling could not have been comfortable.

Finally, they had the man upstairs, in the tiny flat. The stairs led to a small living area and the bed chambers opened off opposite sides. "This way," her father said, gesturing to the footmen to bring Mr. Arundel into his chamber.

"Absolutely not," Belle said, jumping to block their path. "Put him in my chamber."

"That hardly seems appropriate, my dear."

"You are not giving up your bed. I can sleep in the chair in the parlor."

"You need your privacy," her father objected.

"And you need your rest."

The footmen were looking from one to the other, the injured man suspended between them. "This way," Belle said, using the voice she employed when negotiating at St. Katharine Docks with the tea sellers. "Follow me."

The footmen followed, and Belle stripped back the bedclothes then instructed them to lay Arundel on her bed. She removed his shoes, wondered if she should remove any other garments, but decided to cover him instead. The fire in the parlor had gone out, and she hadn't been upstairs to start a fire in her chamber, so she did that now. Just as she had it going, her father came in with a chair from the dining table.

"Good idea," Belle said, replacing the fire poker. "I can sit here and watch over him tonight."

"You have been on your feet all day. I will watch over him."

Belle shook her head, but she stopped short of flatly telling him no. He was still her father, and if he insisted on sitting up with Arundel, she would not be able to dissuade him. She tried another tactic. "Why don't we take shifts? All of this excitement has me wide awake, but I'm sure in an hour or so I will not be able to keep my eyes open. I'll take the first watch and wake you when I tire."

"Oh, no. I know you, Belle. You won't wake me to relieve you." He did know her too well.

"I will. Don't forget I have a shop to manage in the morning. We both do, and we must rest if we are to muddle through. I'll wake you."

He gave her a dubious look.

"I promise," she said. Wonderful. Now she would have to wake him…but she hadn't promised *when* she'd wake him.

"Very well," her father said. He pulled the slip of instructions from his pocket. "This says we must keep the wound clean. I'll need to remove his shirt as he was stabbed on the side of his chest."

"I'll help," Belle said.

"I suppose you must," her father said, clearly not liking the idea of his maiden daughter undressing a strange man. For her part, Belle was rather intrigued. Not that she would ogle an injured, unconscious man, but she was curious about the male body. She had only ever seen it in books with illustrations of art from the British Museum.

"I'll unfasten his cuffs. You deal with the fastenings at his neck."

Belle did as she was instructed. The man's neckcloth had been removed already and the buttons at his throat loosed, but she undid the remaining ones so that his shirt was open halfway down his chest. He had a smattering of dark hair on his chest and that was as much as she dared look.

"How should we do this?" her father mused aloud. "The best way is probably for me to push him up from behind and for you to pull his arms out of the shirt and the garment over his head. Carefully, yes?"

"Very well."

Her father went to the head of the bed and propped Arundel up slightly. He groaned in pain, but he didn't open his eyes. Belle concentrated on extracting his hands from the sleeve and then tugged the shirt up. Whoever had dressed him after the doctor had tended him had not tucked the shirt into the waistband of his trousers, so at least she needn't deal with those. She pushed the shirt up his abdomen, trying not to notice that that part of his body was flat and muscled. Though he was wealthy and upper class—he must be if he and Randall went to school together—he obviously did some sort of physical labor. Her mouth went dry at the sight of those muscles and the broad expanse of his chest. Belle swallowed and tried to avert her eyes as she maneuvered the shirt higher. But then there was a new obstacle. With her gaze averted, she had to feel her way up his body, up the smooth, taut, warm skin of his chest. It was lightly furred with hair that tickled and intrigued. She bit her lip, scolding herself for drooling over an injured man in her care, and attempted to focus.

Finally, the shirt was over his head and away, and her father had laid him back down.

Belle's gaze strayed to her patient's chest again, and she hissed in a breath. "The bandage is soaked with blood."

"Not surprising considering how much he's been moved about. I'll fetch the clean linen, and we will change it."

Changing a bloody bandage was about the last thing Belle wanted to do at midnight after she'd been up at six that morning and would need to be awake again in six hours. Her father left to fetch the linen the housekeeper had sent, and Belle set about unknotting the linen wrapped around the man's upper chest, which held the bandage in place. She tugged the wrapping off so she would not have to move him, then held the bloody bandage in place, waiting for her father to return. She told herself her actions were completely necessary, but it felt strangely intimate to lean across the man's body this way, even if it was only to hold a bandage to his wound. He was half naked, and the warmth of his flesh made her belly tighten and her breath come quicker.

Her sleeves were three-quarter length so as not to interfere with her work or become dusty with tea. It was sweet torture to feel the heat and smoothness of his chest against her wrists and the tender flesh of her inner forearms. She tried not to react to her forced proximity, tried to slow her breathing, tried to think of tea or chores or anything but the man she touched. It was impossible, though, and as her father still did not return, Belle gave in and turned her head to study her patient's face.

He was closely shaven, only the barest hint of dark stubble having grown back since his last encounter with a razor. His jaw was square, as was his face. He had a nice nose, not too long or short. It was crooked, though, and she assumed that meant it had been broken at some point. His eyes were closed, so she could not see their color. He had dark lashes and brows that matched the dark hair on his head. That hair, still damp from the drizzle outside, had a bit of curl and wave to it, though she would never have said it was unruly. Still, she felt another shiver of attraction flit up her spine. She had to find a way to quash that attraction. She was supposed to be a chaste, proper woman, not a panting wanton.

The world—her world of Fenchurch Street—saw her as a virtuous spinster, but little did her neighbors know her virtue was not by choice. She had desires and urges like any other woman. She'd learned to disguise them, knowing she would only be pitied for wanting what she could not have. But now, alone with a flesh-and-blood man who was undeniably attractive, she was finding it very hard to control her body's feelings of desire.

What would Mr. Arundel think if he knew the direction of her thoughts? If he knew she imagined him recovered so she could run her fingers over his muscles and kiss that flat abdomen. Perhaps he would wake up and repay the favor...

Or would he?

Except for the crooked nose, the man looked like the perfect gentleman. Most likely he was a gentleman. Why else would he be dining in the Randalls' home? And Randall had said the two had gone to school together. When he woke—if he woke—he would probably be appalled to find himself in a flat above a tea shop on Fenchurch Street. He would be disgusted by the pockmarked woman tending him. The last thing he would want to do was touch her. She could only pray his family would arrive and take him home before he awoke. If their country estate was not far, they might arrive tomorrow afternoon or evening.

"Here we are," her father said as he pushed open her bed chamber door. Belle let out a breath of relief. He carried the linen and a tray with a teapot.

"Spearmint?" she asked.

"I thought it might help with the excitement of the evening."

Belle nodded, though she would have preferred a black tea that would help her stay awake. Her father set down the tea tray and handed her an empty bowl. She removed the bloodied bandage while he fetched her washbasin and ewer. He poured water in the washbasin, and she dipped clean linen in the cool water, cleaned the bloody wound, and, trying not to look at the blood, held out a hand for a fresh bandage.

"Oh, dear," her father said. He stood over her and looked down at the wound.

Belle looked at him instead of the injury. Her stomach felt queasy just thinking of the thread holding the pieces of skin together. She had to make an effort not to shudder. "What is it?"

"One of the stitches has torn. That must be why he is bleeding."

Belle kept her gaze firmly on her father. "The doctor can repair it when he returns tomorrow." She certainly could not do it. She was no seamstress, and she would most definitely retch if she had to pierce skin with a needle. "The bandage," she said, her voice hoarse as she tried to swallow the rising bile.

Her father gave her the thick piece of linen, and she placed it over the wound. Relieved that it was covered, she took a breath and held out a hand for the long strip of linen to wrap him. Her father handed it to her then helped gently lift the man so they could wind it about his body. Belle waited a moment, praying blood would not immediately seep through the bandage, but the cloth remained white. She pulled the covers back over him and sat back.

Her chamber felt cold now without the heat of the man against her, but that was nothing tea wouldn't solve. She poured a cup and stood with her hands curled around it. Her father was seated in the chair he'd brought. Her chamber had been small before, but now she could hardly move with the chair taking up more space.

"I don't like leaving you alone," her father said, his gaze on Mr. Arundel.

"I'll call for you if I need any help," she said. "And I'll wake you in a couple of hours."

He nodded then rose. "I don't like this."

"Neither do I," she said. "I don't know how we might have avoided it, though. A home with a new baby is no place for a man to convalesce."

"I hardly think a tea shop the best location either."

"It's not so loud up here," she said. "And it's only until his family can be notified and return to take him in."

"Let's hope that is sooner rather than later."

Belle agreed. The last thing they needed was a dead man in the tea shop.

***

She drank her spearmint tea then brewed some of her best English Evening tea. She was no great reader as there was no time for such pursuits, but her father had a few books in the flat. She tried to read one but ended up unable to focus. Instead, she sipped endless cups of tea and stood at her window, looking down on Fenchurch Street. The street was dark and barely visible through the streaks of rain on the window. Her chamber boasted the only window in the flat, and in the summer they filled a window box with flowers to make the shop look more inviting. Now the box was empty save for the rainwater pooling in it and slowly draining out through the small holes in the base.

The fire had finally taken hold in her hearth, and she was warm in her cloak. She removed it then decided she would change into her nightclothes and robe. Since this was her private chamber, she did not have a screen or curtain, so she changed quickly, casting furtive glances over her shoulder at Arundel. He hadn't moved or made a sound other than breathing shallowly. He looked paler. The last time she had checked, he did not feel overly warm to the touch, but she would check again in the next hour and had water and clean linen at the ready to make a cool compress.

After she'd changed and knotted her robe in place, she went to her dresser to deal with her hair. She pulled out a small stool and sat, unpinning her hair and brushing it out. There was no mirror here, and she preferred it that way. She did not want to look at her face. She braided her hair by rote, tucking the annoying side sections that she curled—or at least attempted to—into the braid so she was finally free of the hair brushing against her face.

She felt sleepy now, but she was determined not to wake her father. He would scold her in the morning, but he needed his rest much more than she. Besides, if the rain continued like this into the morning, business at the shop would be slow.

Belle took a seat beside Arundel again and reached out to place the back of her hand on his forehead. Belle closed her eyes in frustration. He'd felt warm earlier but not feverish. Now there was no doubt he had a fever. His skin was hot to the touch, and she could see the beginnings of an unnatural flush on his pale cheeks. It was four in the morning, too early for the doctor to come. The Randalls' baby might not even have been born yet. Belle told herself to remain calm and dipped a strip of clean linen in the cool water and pressed it to his forehead.

Should she give him more laudanum? She spent the next few minutes searching for the doctor's orders and finally found them on a chair in the salon. When she returned, Arundel had tossed off his covers and thrown the arm on his uninjured side up and over his head. The sight of his bare chest startled her. He'd been so still for hours that she'd almost forgotten her earlier attraction.

Almost.

He must be in pain and discomfort, and surely the laudanum had worn off. She held the paper close to her lamp and read, realizing she should have given him another dose of the medicine some time ago.

She would give it now, but how was she to accomplish that? She'd have to raise his head and at the same time balance a spoon with laudanum and guide it into his mouth. She'd had laudanum before, and the taste was extremely bitter, even though the opium was mixed with alcohol and spices. She might have put a drop or two in tea and delivered it that way, but Arundel was not awake enough for a cup of tea.

Belle took the laudanum and spoon to the bedside, set the bottle on the chair, and uncorked it. Then she gently placed the man's arm back at his side and covered him again. She took the discarded compress, replaced it in the washbasin, and then placed herself in the small space on the bed between the man and the chair. The plan was to ease him into a sitting position with his head on her shoulder or chest. Then she could reach over to the chair, pour the medicine, and spoon it into his mouth.

She curled a leg under herself and levered him up slowly and gently. He moaned, and she paused. Finally, he was quiet again and she began to raise his torso. He was hotter than he'd been earlier. She could feel the heat burning off him and penetrating her robe and nightgown. She would have opened the window to allow cool air in, but it was raining steadily now. After she gave him the medicine, she'd bank the fire. He must feel stuffy under the covers in the warm room.

Finally, she had him in position, and she was ready to administer the laudanum. She tried for the bottle, but it was just out of reach. Good Lord, could one thing not go right this evening? She hated nursing with a passion. She could remember nursing Maggie when she'd been ill, and Belle had been awful at it then. She preferred working in the shop any day to sitting at the sickbed. Give her a broom or a dust rag. She'd even be happy to move shelving or clean the storeroom. Anything but this.

She leaned a bit further, doing her best to balance Arundel on her chest and not jostle him too much. Her fingers grazed the bottle when she felt his head turn. She glanced down and locked eyes with him. His eyes were incredibly blue, quite lovely, and clear. This time there was more than a shiver of attraction up her spine; it was a full blown bolt of lightning hitting her.

"What are you doing?" he asked.

Belle froze. She hadn't expected him to wake up. She hadn't expected his voice to be so deep when he spoke. He had an upper-class accent, as she'd expected, but it suited him. She tried to answer his question, to say something reassuring, but her voice caught in her suddenly very dry throat. It wasn't dry only because of those blue eyes or the deep voice or even because he was incredibly close to her at the moment—though none of that helped—her voice had left her because that was what always happened when she tried to talk to a man.

Not any man. Belle could talk to her father, of course, and she generally managed with her brother-in-law. She'd also learned to manage with men who came into the shop. She could talk about tea with anyone. But even the flavors and varieties of tea could not save her if the man showed any interest in her. Then she became self-conscious and shy, and since she hated herself for blushing and stammering, she countered the behavior by becoming loud, brassy, and impudent.

That was her father's sign to come to her rescue, and if her father wasn't available, it was the man's sign to retreat. It always worked because men liked compliments and ladies who fluttered their lashes. They didn't like pock-marked girls who gave them what-for. They often told her so.

But Mr. Arundel wasn't her father or brother-in-law. He wasn't a customer. And he wasn't a misguided lothario. She had no idea how to behave with him, especially when her heart was beating so hard at their closeness.

"I-I'm nursing you," she said finally, answering his question and cringing at the way she'd stammered.

He stared at her, his brow furrowed in confusion and his eyes never leaving hers. "I'm injured?"

Belle took a deep breath. He was injured and confused and vulnerable, rather like a small child—though he looked nothing like a child and certainly didn't feel like one, pressed up against her. But she could try to think of him as she might a vulnerable child.

"Yes, you are injured," she said patiently. "You were stabbed. Do you recall?"

Belle remembered she'd wanted to give him more laudanum and wondered if she should lie him back on the bed. They were much too close, their faces just inches apart. Now that he was awake, she could prop up the pillows and order him to take the tincture.

"Came out of nowhere," he said, his eyes taking on a far-away look that told her he was slowly remembering. His eyes looked softer, like velvet, when his look was less intent. "You are a nurse?"

"Not exactly. I..." How to explain who she was. Technically, she was no relation to the Randalls. Her sister was married to Lydia's brother. The relationship was distant to say the least.

"You're far too pretty to be a nurse," he said.

Belle jolted. She hadn't expected the compliment, but of course, he was looking at her right side, her good side. She felt her cheeks heat with color and had the urge to put him in his place. Then she reminded herself the man was wracked with fever. He did not know what he was saying. "It's time for your medicine," she said, trying for a firm tone she imagined a nursemaid might use. "I'll lie you down and—"

"I rather like it here," he said. "You're soft."

"Belle?"

Belle jolted again at her father's voice. She felt suddenly guilty, as though she had been doing something untoward. But her father couldn't read her thoughts and her actions had been appropriate. A moment later her father pushed the door fully open and stood frowning at her from the entry. "What are you doing?"

Arundel turned his head. "And who is this? The husband?"

Belle ignored Arundel. "He was asleep until a moment ago," she said, hoping her father couldn't see her blush in the faint lamplight. "I was attempting to give him the laudanum."

"Like this?" Her father held out a hand, and Belle realized that if anyone besides her father had come upon them like this, the situation might look compromising.

"I didn't know how else to manage."

"Why not wake him?"

"I didn't think I should." What was that saying? Never wake a sleeping…oh, that was for infants, not men with fever. "He has a fever," she said abruptly. "Could you help me?" Now she indicated the heavy form of Mr. Arundel, and her father immediately crossed to her and held Arundel up while she extricated herself.

"That's not nearly as nice," Arundel said, once she had moved away.

"I imagine not," her father said. "And this will be worse yet." He gestured for Belle to prop up the pillow. She did so then poured the laudanum onto the spoon. Her father took it and said, "Open up."

To Belle's surprise, the man did as he was instructed. But then her father had raised two children almost entirely on his own when her mother had passed away. He had experience nursing.

Arundel grimaced slightly at the taste of the laudanum but swallowed without protest. "Awful stuff."

"I agree, but without it that wound of yours will become unbearable."

"That must be the burning pain in my side."

Her father placed a hand on Arundel's forehead and then glanced at Belle. She realized she'd been standing there, staring at Arundel like a ninny. Immediately, she grasped the ewer, sloshed water into the basin, and dipped a cloth into it. After wringing it out, she handed it to her father, who placed it on Arundel's hot forehead. "Better?" he asked.

Arundel grunted faintly. His eyes had closed, and he didn't speak again for a few moments. Belle thought perhaps he had fallen asleep as he didn't stir when her father turned the compress over. Belle dipped another cloth in the cool water and handed it to her father, taking the used compress in exchange. It was far too warm, which was a bad sign. Fever meant infection and infection usually meant death. Belle glanced at Arundel. *Please don't die here*, she thought.

Not only would his family have questions, but it also couldn't be good for business for their patrons to know there had been a dead body lying just a floor above their biscuits and Earl Grey. And on Fenchurch Street, there was no keeping of any secrets. Tomorrow morning, every neighbor would be talking about the man lying in Belle's bed.

Her father pressed the cool compress on Arundel's forehead, and his eyes opened again. They were more velvet blue now, foggy with the effects of the laudanum. "And who are you again?" he asked. It was a surprisingly coherent question for a man in his condition.

"We are friends of Mr. Randall," her father answered.

"Charles," Arundel said, before closing his eyes again. "Need to contact Baron," he mumbled.

Her father looked at Belle, and she shrugged.

"Expecting me. Need to tell…danger." Arundel was falling in and out of consciousness now, and Belle would have left him to it.

"Which baron is this then?" her father asked. "I'll send him word that you are here."

"Farm," Arundel muttered.

"Baron Farm?" Belle whispered. There were probably hundreds of barons in the country, but she doubted any were Baron Farm. Still, what did she know? She could try and find out, but it wasn't as though they had a copy of Debrett's lying about. Perhaps they could ask the doctor when he came to call or Arundel's family. If only the rain would stop it would mean travel would be faster and easier and Arundel could die somewhere else.

Then feeling guilty at the thought, she amended—he could recover somewhere else.

"He's resting now," her father said, standing and stretching his back. "You were supposed to come and wake me."

"I planned to give him the laudanum and then wake you," Belle lied.

Her father gave her a long look. She didn't know why she even tried to lie. She wasn't any good at it, and even a stranger could usually tell when she wasn't being truthful. Her father most certainly could. "I am awake now and will take over. You should go and rest."

"We should both rest. He's asleep and not likely to wake any time soon."

"Someone needs to keep him cool," her father said. "I don't have any ice, but I can keep changing the compress."

He glanced at the window. "If this infernal downpour would cease, I'd open the window."

"At least the rain will keep most people indoors. We shouldn't have a rush of customers," Belle said.

Her father laughed. "That's the first time you've ever seemed pleased about losing business. Now, go and rest, Isabelle. No arguments."

The fact that he'd used her full name indicated he meant what he said. There was no point in arguing now. Belle took a wrapper from a hook on a wall, then, with a last look at the injured man, carried it to the parlor. He certainly was handsome. Her body tingled at the memory of the feel of his weight against her chest. Belle settled into a chair and pulled the warm wrapper around her. She hadn't intended to sleep, but she must have, because when she opened her eyes again, her father was calling for her.

And his tone was one of panic that made her jump to her feet and run.

Chapter Four

Jumping to her feet might not have been the best idea. Forgetting to eat dinner probably wasn't a good plan either, though to be fair, she hadn't planned not to eat. She had just forgotten with all that had happened last night.

Belle swayed unsteadily then took a deep breath. The parlor came into focus. "Belle, come quickly!" her father called again. Her heart thudded hard against her chest. His tone was unusual. He was always so calm and collected, even when the shop was full of customers demanding this tea or that biscuit. Now her father sounded alarmed.

"Coming!" Belle rushed across the parlor and pushed open the bed chamber door. She saw immediately why her father had sounded panicked. Arundel was standing in the middle of the room, stumbling about drunkenly. Her father was attempting to take hold of his arm and guide him back to bed, but every time her father managed to grab onto him, Arundel shook him off.

Her father was not a large man, but he was taller than she, and Arundel seemed to dwarf her father. She'd known he was a large man. It had taken three footmen to carry him up the stairs and his feet hung off the edge of her bed. But seeing him in the middle of her room, bare-chested and broad-shouldered, he looked like a giant. A well-built, powerful giant. Belle bit her lip as her eyes took him in.

She should stop ogling him and try to help. "What happened?" she managed to say.

"He's burning with fever," her father said, moving so as to avoid Arundel's waving arm. "He insisted on rising from bed. I couldn't convince him otherwise."

"I imagine not." Belle winced as Arundel bumped into her dresser, causing the contents on top to topple over and fall to the floor.

"Where is it?" Arundel asked, his speech slurred. He turned again—a veritable bull in a china shop—and knocked over the ewer, causing it to shatter. The sound must have caused him to focus because he stared down at the floor then stooped and lifted the washbasin. "Here it is."

Then to Belle's shock, he loosed the fall of his trousers. She realized what he was about and hastily turned and stumbled out of the bed chamber. She heard the sound of Arundel relieving himself. It went on for some time, which had explained why he'd been rather desperate to find a chamber pot.

Finally, there was silence and then the murmur of her father trying to coax Arundel back into bed. "Belle!"

She poked her head into the chamber. Arundel was seated on the bed, one hand cupped over his bandage, which was again tinged red with seeping blood.

"Laudanum," her father said, indicating the bottle, which had fallen to the floor but mercifully not broken. She went to retrieve it as her father took the washbasin to the window, opened it, and tossed the contents out on the street. She glanced over at the sound of the rain. It was still coming down in sheets and, though it must be nearly dawn, the sky was as dark as night.

"Lie back, Mr. Arundel," she said, focusing back on her patient. Thank God he had fastened his trousers again. She would never have been able to keep her gaze from that part of his anatomy. She was too curious. "This will help with the pain."

"No," he said through clenched teeth. "I won't become an opium addict."

"I hardly think a spoonful of laudanum will cause you to start down that road."

He gave her a narrow look, and his eyes were clear blue. He looked completely lucid, and the directness of his gaze made her swallow hard and want to duck her head to hide her scars. "And how would you know? Friendly with scores of opium-eaters, are you?"

"No, but—"

Her father snapped the window shut, muting the sound of the rain. "How about some medicinal sherry then?" he asked. Belle glanced up at him. She hadn't known he kept any sherry—medicinal or otherwise.

"I wouldn't say no," Arundel said in a tone that was more like a growl. He was obviously in pain and also obviously quite unwilling to take the laudanum.

"I'll fetch it, but you must do as Belle tells you."

Arundel's gaze went from her father to her. "Belle?" he asked.

Her cheeks felt hot, and the urge to turn her face so he would only see the right side all but overwhelmed her. She resisted, feeling defiant. Why should she care if this man thought her ugly or not? She might admire his beauty, but that was all.

Liar, a voice inside her said. *You want him so much you all but pant every time you're in the same room.*

"Short for Isabelle," she said, ignoring her rogue thoughts. "Obviously not a sobriquet I was given for my beauty. Now, lie back. You're bleeding through the linen, and I'd rather not have to change the sheets in addition to the bandage."

To her surprise, he did as she asked and laid down. As soon as he did lie flat, he seemed to deflate like one of the hot air balloons she'd seen in Hyde Park a few summers ago. He closed his eyes and went still, making a small sound of pain as she began to unwrap the linen from about his chest.

Knowing he was in pain quashed any sort of lecherous thoughts. She noted his skin was hot and dry to the touch. With such a high fever, she was surprised he was not delirious. But he was a large, strong man, and it would take more than a few hours of fever to fell him. "You are burning with fever," she said as she unwrapped the linen that held the bandage in place. She hadn't intended to speak, but she needed to say something to avoid the awkward silence. Had he seen her face? He hadn't commented on it. Was he recoiling at her touch, even as she watched his muscles flex when she ran her fingertips over them in the course of her work? She wondered, if she wasn't so disfigured and if he wasn't injured, if he would have been aroused.

And then she wondered what the devil was wrong with her. Why was she thinking of arousing the man? Even if he wasn't burning with fever and likely to die, she was a pockmarked spinster virgin of five and twenty. Her hopes of arousing a man were long past.

"Tell me something I don't know," Arundel said.

Belle looked up at him in confusion and then remembered that before she'd been distracted by his chest, she'd remarked that he was burning with fever. "Very well. You've opened your stitches and your wound is bleeding."

"That must be why my side feels as though someone is holding a hot poker to it."

"I'm sorry," she said as she removed the last of the wrapping and tossed it aside. She had to take a deep breath before touching the scarlet bandage. Belle felt the nausea rise in her throat and preoccupied herself by mentally inventorying the shop.

"You have nothing to be sorry for. You didn't stab me," Arundel said.

She nodded, still focused on her mental inventory. Holding the bandage in place with one hand, she reached for a clean piece of linen. She would do this quickly—swap one for the other and discard the bloodied linen so fast she would barely touch it.

Belle removed the bloody bandage and moved to quickly cover the wound with the clean linen when Arundel grasped her wrist, stopping her. "Let go," she protested.

"I want to see it."

"No, you do not," she said.

"Yes, I do." He was maneuvering himself into a half-sitting position so he could view the injury. The action caused his chest to all but push into her face, and she caught the scent of him. She'd expected him to smell of fever and sickness, but he smelled faintly of bergamot and… hmmm, what was that? Cardamom? Belle leaned closer to sniff again and bumped her nose into his ribs.

"Are you feeling faint?" he asked.

"No." She withdrew, not feeling faint but definitely experiencing a bit of dizziness. She'd never been so close to an attractive man who not only had an extremely nice chest but a scent almost as intoxicating as tea. She felt all but compelled to discover all the components of the scent that was uniquely him but managed to restrain herself, especially when she saw he was twisting to view the damage to his side.

Belle hastily averted her eyes.

"This hurts worse than it looks," he said.

"It's bad enough," she remarked, opting not to point out that the doctor had been less than confident in Arundel's chances of recovery, especially if he developed a fever.

He made a sound of agreement. "Two stitches are torn. Do you sew?"

Belle made a gagging sound. "No!"

He gave her a look she could only describe as dubious.

"Just because I'm a woman, you think I sew?"

"It has nothing to do with your sex. Most people know how to sew, else they wouldn't have any clothing."

He had a point. It was quite expensive to buy ready-made attire, and even when one did, it often had to be repaired or altered after long days of wear.

"I don't sew...people." She swallowed, trying to keep the bile down.

"Oh, I see."

Belle stood and glared down at him. "See what? What does that mean?"

"You're scared of blood."

"I'm not!" She had no idea why she said she was not as she very much feared blood. It made her want to retch just thinking about it. "I simply don't want to stick a needle through your torn flesh and piece it together with another bit of torn flesh."

"Then fetch me a needle and thread."

"You can't possibly think to—"

"The doctor is with Mrs. Randall. Her labor could last all day. Not to mention, the rain is coming down in sheets. While I'm still up to it, I'd better do what I can to tend to this injury." He gestured to the wound, and Belle made the mistake of looking at it. Her gaze caught on the angry red gash, oozing dark, thick blood. Black thread held the top of the jagged flesh together, but it had ripped through at the bottom, leaving the skin ragged and raw.

"Damn," she murmured as the room spun and she fell back. Thankfully, she had been kneeling beside the bed, so she did not have very far to fall. That was her last thought before her head hit the wooden floor with a thunk.

***

Hew stared at the woman who had been arguing with him a moment before. Suddenly, she had gone as pale as the moon and fallen over. What had she been saying about having no fear of blood?

"Sir!" Hew called. He couldn't remember the father's surname. He only remembered the woman was called Belle. The name suited her as she was a pretty thing—a bit thin with big brown eyes and wispy honey-blond hair. Pretty in a delicate way, though it had taken him only thirty seconds with her to realize she was not delicate at all.

Except, apparently, when it came to knife wounds.

"Sir!"

Footsteps sounded and the man appeared in the doorway. Hew noticed he didn't hold a bottle of sherry, which meant he hadn't found it yet. His eyes widened as he saw Belle sprawled on the floor.

"Belle!" He ran to his daughter and knelt beside her, cradling her head in his lap and patting her white cheek softly. "What happened?"

"She saw my wound and fell over. She denies it, but I think she's afraid of blood."

"She would deny it."

"Here." Hew handed him a pillow, and the man placed it under his daughter's head. Hew put the man at about fifty. He had light brown hair, thinning on top and made lighter with the gray threaded through it. His face was thin and long, as was his body. If he was twelve stone, Hew would have been surprised. But like his daughter, he seemed to possess an inner strength. He moved with assurance and calm. In fact, as soon as he'd returned to the room, Hew had felt much of his anxiety fade away. It wasn't that he didn't have any worries—after all, as Belle had pointed out, he was burning with fever and had a bleeding knife wound. He had seen enough in his time in the field to know he might very likely die. He also knew this lucidity of thought would not last. The longer he burned with fever, the more likely he'd succumb to delirium. He had to act quickly in the time he had.

"I made the mistake of asking if she could sew." Hew indicated his wound.

The man looked over at it and nodded. His eyes expressed concern but not revulsion or panic. "We were waiting for the doctor."

Hew flicked a glance at the window, where the rain pelted against the glass. "I think he might be some time yet. If you fetch me a needle and thread—"

"I can do it," the man said. "I've sewn my share of hems and buttons, made a stitch or two in a minor cut on occasion." He brushed his daughter's hair back from her forehead and rose. "I'll fetch the needle and my thickest thread."

"Perhaps some smelling salts?" Hew suggested with a nod at Belle.

"After we patch you up," her father said. "And then I have just the trick."

He left again, and Hew lay back on the bed, missing the pillow now under Belle's head. He turned and looked down at her, noting her breathing was steady. His gaze traveled from her abdomen to the curve of her breasts. She wore a loose robe, so they were not exactly outlined, but he could make out enough of their shape to want to see more. He'd been trained to observe, but he shouldn't allow his thoughts to stray to the personal. That was the male part of him intruding on the agent part.

Trying to be more objective now, his gaze traveled down the length of her slim body. Her robe more than covered her, but it had pulled up slightly on one side, revealing a sliver of pale ankle and one foot which had lost its slipper.

She had a small foot, and he thought he could have closed his hand around her ankle or at least come close. Her toes were blunt, the big toe the longest and the others a bit shorter and in neat succession. The nails were neatly trimmed showing that she took some care, though her calluses—those he'd seen on her hands and now on her feet—proved she worked very hard at whatever it was she did.

She was clearly not a seamstress. She'd bristled at that suggestion. Considering her bedside manner was somewhat lacking, he didn't think she was a nanny or teacher either. What other sorts of professions did women have?

The father entered again this time with the sherry in one hand and a needle and thread in the other. "I think you'll need this. Unless"—he looked hopeful—"you want to try the laudanum?"

"No laudanum," Hew said. He'd seen too many men—and women—take laudanum for a minor ailment and then develop a craving for it that necessitated daily dosing. Hew had no intention of living his life in a stupor.

The man poured Hew a large glass of sherry and handed it to him. Hew drank, looked at the glass in confusion as this was the worst sherry he'd ever had, but then drank again.

"It's cooking sherry," the man said. "I'm sure you are used to better quality."

"No matter." Hew drank another sip. It was weak, but it was something.

The man was drying his hands on a cloth after pouring water over them. "Ready?" He set down the cloth and held up a needle he had threaded with a thick black material.

No, Hew thought. He said, "Of course." He turned on his uninjured side, ignoring the pain the movement caused him, and presented his wound. The man moved closer and raised the needle. Hew knew this would hurt. He'd been stitched up before. Still, he hissed in a breath, attempting to mute his gasp, when the needle entered his battered flesh. He forced himself to remain still even as his every instinct was to pull away from this unimaginable pain.

"I'm sorry," the man said. "I know this hurts."

"It's fine," Hew lied. Then because he needed to do something other than dig his nails into his palm or scream, he clenched his teeth and gritted out, "What is your name, sir?"

"George Howard." Howard glanced at Hew's face. He had brown eyes like his daughter, but his were full of concern.

"And Belle is your daughter?" Hew asked, closing his eyes against the pain and making a monumental effort not to scream.

"Isabelle Howard, yes. My other daughter is married to Mr. Dormer, Mrs. Randall's brother."

For a long moment, the string of names meant nothing to him. The pain blotted out everything else, and Hew struggled to focus on something—anything—but the needle poking through him. "Ah. I see now," he said. "I wasn't certain of the connection before."

"Rather a distant connection, I know," Howard said, "but under the circumstances the best Mr. Randall could do, I think."

Hew tried to reply, but he couldn't do anything other than grip the mattress and force air into his lungs.

"Almost done," Howard said.

Thank God for small mercies. After what seemed months of agony, Howard snipped the thread and moved away. Hew peered down at the wound and nodded. The stitches were not neat, but they would do the job. "More sherry?" Howard asked.

"God, yes," Hew said. He sat gingerly, fighting through the wave of pain the action caused him, and downed another glass of the weak stuff.

"Should I put sherry on the wound?" Howard asked. "I've seen doctors do it, but I don't know if sherry cleans as well as what they use."

"It couldn't hurt," Hew said. He'd been wrong about that. The sherry burned like the devil's pitchfork. He spat an expletive or two before he managed to restrain himself again. "I beg your pardon," he said a moment later. He was panting and sweat streaked down his temples.

"No need," Howard said. He nodded at his daughter. "Fortunately, she is still unaware, though I venture to guess she has heard it all. I had better brew some tea and attempt to revive her."

"If you don't mind, Mr. Howard," Hew said. "I will just lie here and try not to weep."

Howard smiled. "You are a stronger man than I." He took the needle and thread and—to Hew's disappointment— the bottle of sherry. Hew could hear him rattling something in another room, but the pain was coming in waves, and he couldn't really focus on anything but breathing through the next rise of agony.

Perhaps bleeding to death would not have been such a bad way to go. It would have hurt less than the remedy, that was certain.

After what seemed hours but was probably only a few minutes, Mr. Howard returned, carrying a tea tray. Hew desperately needed something stronger than tea. Something as strong as, say, gin. Hew wasn't usually a gin drinker, but at that moment, he would have drunk it down. He desperately wanted something strong that burned his throat and gave him a few moments of pain-free oblivion. Of course, there was always the laudanum, but that was a last resort. Hew did not like losing control of his dreams or his ability to wake. He'd rather the pain than the feeling of drowning in sleep. It was unnerving to know one was asleep but to feel as though one was submerged in a deep pond and unable to swim to the top and take a breath.

Howard set down the tea tray and knelt beside Miss Howard. Hew almost hated to see him wake her. She looked so peaceful lying there. Through a pain-filled haze, Hew watched as Howard lifted the teapot and poured a half cup of tea. Then he moved the cup near her face and wafted the scent of the tea under her nose.

"Smelling salts would have been more effective," Hew rasped.

"Belle has a very delicate nose," Mr. Howard said, not looking up from his task. "This will do the trick."

Hew doubted it, but he was in no condition to argue. Earlier he'd felt as though he were burning up. Now it was as though someone had packed him in snow. He shivered and his teeth chattered, and he rubbed his arms to keep from shaking. If he hadn't been in so much pain, he would have pulled the covers over his shivering body, but any movement sent waves of pain through him.

The teacup had been under her nose for no more than fifteen seconds, when Miss Howard opened her eyes. "Black Currant," she said.

Her father nodded. "I knew it would wake you."

"I could have smelled it a block away."

Hew inhaled experimentally, but he was only a few feet away and could barely smell the tea.

She put a hand out to her father.

"Now, Belle, take your time. You fainted." He helped her to sit, and he lowered her head onto her knees.

"I never faint," she muttered. "It was the blood." Then, as though remembering him, she raised her head and met his gaze. Her eyes were dark brown now and a bit hazy. "You're awake," she said.

"I closed the wound and replaced the bandage," her father said.

Hew could see the shudder travel through her slim body. "Thank you." She took the teacup from him and sipped. "No doctor yet?"

"It's still raining and still early."

"Not so early. I should go down and ready the shop to open."

Hew thought it strange that her voice sounded as though it were fading. She looked to be fading as well, as though she were falling down a tunnel and disappearing from view.

"There's time." Howard's voice was faint as well.

Hew must have closed his eyes because when he opened them again, Belle was standing over him.

"He's still shivering," she was saying.

He tried to raise an arm to indicate he needed the blanket, but when he moved his elbow, he realized someone had already covered him. And yet, he was still deathly cold.

Hew heard Mr. Howard say something, but he couldn't make sense of the words. All he could do was stare up at Belle's lovely brown eyes, lighter now that she was recovered. They reminded him of the eyes of a fawn. He'd seen his share of deer, admired the quiet way they moved and the gentle way they raised their head and looked at a passerby as though he were some sort of new creature. She had those same curious but gentle, large brown eyes.

"You look like a deer," he said. Her brow creased, and he realized that had come out wrong. "I mean—"

"Shh." She put a hand on his forehead, and though his body was frozen, somehow her hand was cool against his flesh. "Close your eyes and rest."

"Stay," he said.

"I'm right here." Her hand was replaced by a cloth and that was cool as well. Hew closed his eyes and the world spun. He dreamed of a street, a carriage, and a man with a knife

Chapter Five

Belle loved opening the shop in the morning. There were usually three or four people waiting outside to buy a breakfast tea, having not realized until the last moment they were low. Today the rain had kept everyone inside, and when she unlocked the door, opened the shades, and turned the sign, no one stopped in to shop.

Belle looked up at the ceiling and wondered how her father was getting on. He'd shooed her out of her bed chamber, telling her he would take a shift with the patient. Belle had thought she'd be relieved to get away, but then Arundel had asked her to stay. Now she felt guilty for having left him.

Not that he had any idea what was happening around him. Her father said he'd refused more laudanum, but he was talking as though he'd had a half bottle. He kept saying she was a deer. She might have thought he was calling her *dear*, except that he was insistent that she looked like a deer, and she understood he meant the animal. Belle had not spent much time in the country, but she'd seen one or two deer in the park. She didn't think she looked anything like a deer.

But then why was she puzzling over what a semi-conscious man, who would probably be dead by evening, said? Of course, he didn't make sense. He was delirious with pain.

The bell above the door tinkled as it opened, admitting a woman who was closing her black umbrella and shaking water off her hat. Belle smiled, "Good morning, Mrs. Tipps."

"What's good about it?" Mrs. Tipps grumbled. She always grumbled. She'd been coming in once a week for years, and not once had she ever smiled or answered Belle's greeting with anything other than a grumpy acknow-ledgment. Belle didn't mind. It was rather comforting in a way, and she could appreciate the return to routine after the unusual night she'd passed.

"I see the rain hasn't let up," Belle said, when Mrs. Tipps stowed her umbrella in the stand and removed her wet wrap and hung it on the rack.

"If this continues, we'll all be drowned."

Belle was unfazed by the negativity. She was too tired to try and infuse some cheer into Mrs. Tipps. "I was about to brew some Hot Cinnamon Spice tea. It's a lovely blend, perfect for days like this. Would you like a cup?"

Mrs. Tipps halted midway to the counter. "Hot Cinnamon Spice?" she said as though the words were another language.

"Yes." Belle lifted the little packet of tea. "This blend features three types of cinnamon, and they are combined with clove." She sniffed at the leaves. "Orange rind as well, I think. It has a bit of spice and is said to be good for the circulation."

"There's nothing wrong with my circulation.

"I didn't mean to imply—"

"And what is wrong with Darjeeling? Mr. Tipps and I always drink Darjeeling."

Belle let out a small sigh. What had she been thinking? She knew better than to offer anything new to Mrs. Tipps. "Darjeeling is wonderful. It's one of our most popular teas."

"I should think so," Mrs. Tipps said, coming to stand at the counter. "It's tradition, and there is nothing wrong with tradition."

The bell on the door tinkled again, and both women turned to see Mrs. Price enter. She was not carrying an umbrella but held her wrap over her head, ostensibly to keep off the rain. As the rain had slowed from a deluge to a mere stream, she was reasonably dry. "Good morning, Belle. Mrs.

Tipps," she said, hanging her wrap on the rack beside Mrs. Tipps's damp wrap.

"What's good about it?" Mrs. Tipps said again.

Mrs. Price—Belle didn't know why they called her missus, as she'd never mentioned a husband in all the time Belle had known her—paused to consider that question. "The rain is good for the flowers," she said with a decisive nod. She came forward to join Mrs. Tipps on the other side of the counter. By now, Belle had warmed the pot, spooned the Hot Cinnamon Spice into the teapot, and was pouring the water she'd boiled on the small stove into the pot to steep the tea. Several years ago, she'd suggested to her father they take the unusual step of adding a stove behind the counter so they might brew tea during the day and offer samples to customers. Mrs. Tipps might not appreciate a sample, unless it was Darjeeling, but Belle suspected Mrs. Price stopped in daily because she always hoped for a complimentary cup.

Mrs. Price rarely bought tea and then only the cheapest blends, but Belle didn't mind. Mrs. Price was always pleasant company.

"Flowers!" Mrs. Tipps scoffed. "It's November. What flowers?"

"Oh, all the flowers waiting to bloom in spring," Mrs. Price said airily. "What is that scent, dear? It smells wonderful."

"Hot Cinnamon Spice."

"Ooh!" She clapped her hands together. "Might I try it?"

"Of course."

Mrs. Price threw a look at Mrs. Tipps. "I suppose you will stick with your Darjeeling."

"It is a classic," Mrs. Tipps said.

"I love to try something new." Mrs. Price leaned on the counter. "Speaking of all things new, I noticed you had some commotion at your door last night, Belle."

Belle bit her tongue in an effort to stifle a curse. She'd hoped that with the dark and the rain, her neighbors would not have spotted the Randalls' coach or the footmen carrying Mr. Arundel inside.

"Did we?" she said, pretending to rummage about under the counter for the teacups. Of course, she knew exactly where they were. They were right where they always were.

"Yes," Mrs. Price went on, seemingly unaware that Belle wished to avoid the topic. "Quite a grand carriage too. At least it looked like it from my window."

Mrs. Price would know as she was almost always looking out her window, keeping a watchful eye on

Fenchurch Street. She didn't have a direct view of the shop as her flat was on the same side as the tea shop, but she could see the street well enough. Belle was usually appreciative of her neighbor's vigilance. The shop had been vandalized a time or two and no shop in London was safe from urchins who ran in to snatch and grab.

At the moment, however, Belle wished Mrs. Price had been in bed last night. "It was Mr. and Mrs. Randall's carriage," she said. "Mrs. Randall is a family relation."

"Of course," Mrs. Price said. "Her brother is married to dear Margaret. How is Margaret?"

"Might I have my tea now?" Mrs. Tipps asked, impatiently. Clearly, she was in no mood for chitchat.

"Of course." Belle held out the tea and took the coin Mrs. Tipps offered. "Margaret is well. She is with Mr. Dormer at his country house."

Mrs. Tipps gathered her tea and started back toward the door and the rack holding her wrap.

"Then it was not she who was carried out of the carriage last night," Mrs. Price said. Mrs. Tipps halted, turned, and started back for the counter.

Belle pretended to remember her Hot Cinnamon Spice. "I think this has steeped long enough. Let me drain the leaves and pour you a cup."

"None for me, thank you," Mrs. Tipps said. "Who was carried inside last night?"

Belle took her time with the tea, trying to decide what or how much to say. But really, what was the point in hiding the truth or dissembling? Everyone knew the business of everyone else on Fenchurch Street, and it would all come out eventually.

Belle turned with a teacup in each hand. She set the cups on the counter. "It is a man called Mr. Arundel. He was stabbed."

Mrs. Price made an O with her mouth, and Mrs. Tipps's eyes widened. She took one of the cups of tea—the tea she had not wanted—and sipped.

"Stabbed?" Mrs. Price said, finally recovering her voice.

Belle nodded. "I don't know the details, but he is good friends with Mr. Randall. Apparently, he was accosted right outside their home."

"And how do you know this man?" Mrs. Tipps asked, eyes narrowed.

"I don't."

"He is acquainted with Mr. Howard then?"

Belle shook her head. "No. Neither of us had met the man before last night." She might drag this conversation out by offering only tidbits of information here and there, but that would only mean she would be asked about it all day from one neighbor or another who would find an excuse to stop in. She could avoid some of that if she just told Mrs. Price. Mrs. Price would be certain to inform the rest of the street. Mrs. Price picked up the other cup of Hot Cinnamon Spice and seemed to settle in for a tale.

"The Randalls were quite at sixes and sevens," she said. "Mrs. Randall is with child, and it seemed the shock of Mr. Arundel's injury sent her into labor."

"Oh, dear." Mrs. Price put a hand to her cheek.

"The poor woman." That from Mrs. Tipps, who was still drinking Belle's cup of Hot Cinnamon Spice.

"Yes, well, the Randalls called the surgeon, and he stitched Mr. Arundel, but the doctor who came could hardly care for Mr. Arundel and Mrs. Randall."

"Does he not have people of his own?" asked Mrs. Tipps.

"He does, but they are in the countryside. Mr. Randall asked if we would care for him until his family could be notified and return."

Mrs. Tipps looked at the front windows and the steady rain. "I should think that might be several days."

Belle sincerely hoped not. Arundel's burst of strength and coherence a few hours ago had been short-lived, as she'd expected. Now he was delirious and burning with fever.

"But who is caring for the poor man now?" Mrs. Price asked.

"My father," Belle said. "Though there is not much to be done. The patient is rather ill."

"Oh, I do hope he will not die!" Mrs. Price's eyes were wide with worry, and Belle thought there was probably a glint of delight there as well. After all, today had begun as rather dreary and the older woman had been unlikely to spot anything of interest from her window. Now, an injured man dying above Howard's Teas & Treats had been plopped in her lap.

"Of course, he will not die," Belle said. "The doctor will arrive any moment."

"He could very well die," Mrs. Tipps said, unhelpfully. "If he has a stab wound and a fever, there's not much a doctor can do."

Belle bit her lip to keep from saying what she thought of that dire pronouncement. "Well, we are certainly doing all we can."

"Of course, you are," Mrs. Price said, patting Belle's hand. "But do you think your father is up to this task? I understand why he has taken over. You are a young, unmarried woman. You cannot tend a man alone."

"Neither should she be left to tend the shop alone," Mrs. Tipps said.

"I tend the shop alone all the time," Belle said. Not only that but she handled the banking, the importers, and the delivery boys—all without needing help from her father. Who did they think had taught her to handle all of it by herself?

Mrs. Price looked at Mrs. Tipps, and Mrs. Tipps looked at Mrs. Price. Belle instantly narrowed her eyes. The two ladies had never shared a look like that, not since the last time they had attempted to play matchmaker. That attempt had been with Mrs. Price's nephew and Belle. When, like the others, he'd taken one look at her and hastily found a reason to run away, they had abandoned matchmaking.

At least, she hoped they had.

But now here was the conspiratorial look again. How was it these two ladies who barely seemed to tolerate each other most days could so quickly become allies?

"I think we had better see if Mr. Howard needs any assistance," said Mrs. Tipps, setting down her empty cup of what had been Belle's tea.

"Yes, we should, indeed. After all, we ladies are much more skilled at nursing."

"My father is quite capable—"

"Just until the doctor arrives, Belle," said Mrs. Tipps. "When he does, send him upstairs directly."

Belle didn't even bother arguing. She simply watched as the two women went to the door leading to the Howards' personal apartments and started up the stairs. "Helloooo, Mr. Howard!" Mrs. Price called as the door closed behind her.

Belle sighed and put her head down on the counter. She should be glad the two ladies had taken over. It certainly relieved her of the burden of caring for the man. But for some reason she was not relieved. In fact, she felt a slight sense of envy. She wished she could go back upstairs and care for Arundel. She didn't know why she would want to do such a thing. Her last attempt at caring for him had been a disaster, but it seemed there was something about him that drew her. There was his obvious physical attractiveness, but it wasn't only that he was handsome. She tapped her short fingernails on the counter and decided it was the way he looked at her. He seemed to look right through her, right past her physical flaws and to really *see* her. Which was ridiculous. He didn't even know her.

But she wanted him to know her. If there was any man who might be able to fight his way past her hard exterior and to do what no man had done—find the soft, vulnerable parts of her—it was the Arundel. He'd proved himself a fighter already by surviving this long. Belle shook her head at such fanciful thoughts.

She began to clear away the teacups and started a new pot of Cinnamon Hot Spice. This time she would actually drink a cup. By the time this was done, she heard her father's footsteps on the stairs. He emerged into the shop, looking tired and unshaven but otherwise presentable.

"Hot Cinnamon Spice?" he asked, closing the door behind him.

"It seemed a good choice for a day like this."

"The perfect choice, as usual." He went to the window and peered out onto the street. Belle followed. The rain had turned to a drizzle, but the streets were covered with an inch or two of water from the heavy rains. Heavy rain always left standing water on Fenchurch Street. Now customers would drag mud into the shop for days.

"I am sorry about Mrs. Price and Mrs. Tipps."

Her father waved a hand, his gaze still on the street. "I know how they are. I am glad for the respite, though I think they came more to gawk than nurse. If the doctor does not come soon, one of us will need to tend Arundel's wound again."

"I'll go," Belle said. She'd spoken too quickly, too eagerly, and her father turned and gave her a curious look. "It is my turn. You had to repair the stitches," she said. She felt weak in the knees just saying the words. "Tea?" Belle returned to the stove and busied herself preparing two cups.

When her father stayed at the window, she brought him a cup and stood beside him. A few people had ventured outside, but most were hurrying to work, not looking to shop. "I knew we could not keep Arundel's presence here a secret," her father said, sipping his tea and nodding in appreciation. "But I do think we must find a way to keep our neighbors from gossiping too much."

"Why?" Belle asked. She might have asked *how*, but she doubted her father knew any better than she.

"The man was stabbed in public. In front of a town house in Mayfair, its owner, and a half dozen of his staff. That's a rather brazen act, and one, I think, that must have been planned out."

Belle hadn't considered that the stabbing might not have been a random act of violence. Those were common in London, even in the better areas of Town like Mayfair.

"You think someone wanted to kill Mr. Arundel?" Belle asked. "And if he learns his attempt failed, he might try again?"

Her father turned from the window. "You always were quick and clever. Yes, Belle, that's exactly what I think. And I don't want to be in the way when the assassin returns."

"But surely whoever wants Mr. Arundel dead won't think to look for him in a tea shop on Fenchurch Street."

"I hope not, but it won't help us if Mrs. Price and Mrs. Tipps tell everyone in the area that the man is here with us."

"I don't see how we can prevent it. If we ask them to keep quiet, it will only make the telling all the more exciting."

"Which means, we need his family to arrive sooner rather than later. Either that or we must move him somewhere safer."

Belle could see the wisdom of the suggestion, but it was impossible. "Father, he is not well enough to be moved, even if his family did show up on our stoop. And with the weather as it is, that is highly unlikely. The Randalls will send a footman to contact his people, but even a seasoned rider wouldn't start out in weather like that of last night. A rider might try and go now that it's morning and the rain's abated, but the roads will be awful."

"It could be days before he reaches Arundel's people and then days before they are able to make the journey back."

Belle slumped, and her father put an arm about her. She did not often let anyone touch her. She didn't care much for hugs and hand holding, but she could use the comfort this morning. "We will figure something out. We always do."

She leaned her head against his shoulder. "In the meantime, we must keep him alive."

"Well, Mrs. Price and Mrs. Tipps are hard at it this morning, and if I know you, you will bully him into recovery."

She smiled. "I will do my best."

A man in clerkish black paused in front of the window, shook out his umbrella, and opened the door. Belle straightened, but her father patted her shoulder. "I have it. You go have that cup of tea you brewed." He moved forward. "Good morning, sir. Staying dry, I hope?"

Belle went back to the counter and sipped her own cup of tea. She offered a cup to their customer, and he ended up buying Hot Cinnamon Spice as well as the standard Darjeeling. A few more customers stopped by between bouts of heavy rain, but by midday, it was clear they would not turn a profit this day. Belle could hardly blame the city for staying inside. She had no desire to visit the landlord to pay the rent and the tea warehouses were out of the question. Unfortunately, though she could put off the tea warehouses, she could not put off the landlord. A glance at the windows told her the rain had slowed to a steady drip. She looked about for her cloak and realized she'd left it in the flat.

"The landlord must be paid," Belle told her father, who was standing at the window, presumably willing customers to come inside. "I'll go up and fetch my cloak."

"I'll not let you go out in this weather," her father said. "I'll pay the landlord. I want to stretch my legs a bit anyway."

Belle fetched the rent money from the safe in the back, and when she returned, her father had donned his coat and hat. He tucked the money inside, close to his chest, kissed her cheek, and went out.

Belle considered brewing another cup of tea. Today would have been a good day to go over the shop ledgers, but she was so tired, she couldn't trust herself to add two and two, much less any greater numbers. Perhaps she should run upstairs and check on the patient and Mrs. Tipps and Mrs. Price. As though the two ladies had been summoned, the door to the private quarters opened, and the ladies stepped into the shop. They were smiling and murmuring but both went stiff when they spotted Belle.

"How is Mr. Arundel?" she asked.

"Resting comfortably," Mrs. Tipps said. "But that fever is concerning."

Belle looked out the window again in vain hope the doctor might make an appearance. "The doctor has still not come, and I don't know what to do."

"We gave him a bit of water," Mrs. Price said, "and I think you might try a bit of broth."

Belle raised her brows. "*I* might try?"

"I am sorry to leave you, dear," Mrs. Tipps said, "but Mr. Tipps will be wondering what has become of me."

Belle looked at Mrs. Price hopefully. She knew there was no Mr. Price. "I had thought to stop in for tea to have with my toast. As it is, I've eaten nothing all day."

Neither had Belle, and the mention of toast made her stomach growl.

"Of course. You both have been such a help. My father or I will take over from here."

"Where is Mr. Howard?" Mrs. Price asked.

"He went out for a moment. He should be back shortly." That was not quite true. The landlord lived about a fifteen-minute walk from Fenchurch Street, but her father would not be gone long.

"Would you like us to stay until he returns?" That was Mrs. Price again. Mrs. Tipps looked as though she had no intention of staying, but Belle had always supposed Mrs. Price had a bit of a soft spot for her father.

"No, no. I'll be fine." Belle tried to think how she might be subtle in the suggestion that the ladies not mention their injured guest, but nothing came to mind, so she pushed on with her characteristic bluntness. "I do have a favor to ask of the two of you."

Mrs. Price's brows went up with interest, but Mrs. Tipps put a hand on her hip. "What's that?"

"Would you mind keeping Mr. Arundel's presence here to yourself? He was stabbed, and I'm sure Mr. Randall has notified the authorities, but we don't know why he was stabbed or if he is still in danger, and until we speak with a Constable, it might be best to keep the man's presence here to ourselves."

"You can count on me, dearie," Mrs. Price said in a tone so laced with excitement that Belle knew she was right to assume she would have had more success keeping Mr. Arundel's presence quiet if she herself had stayed quiet.

"I'm no gossip, Isabelle Howard," Mrs. Tipps said, clearly offended. "Now, you have more important matters to worry about. Best not to leave him alone too long." Mrs. Tipps pointed to the ceiling in the general vicinity of Belle's bed chamber.

"I won't."

The two ladies gathered their umbrellas and wraps and set out. Belle closed the door behind them, struggling a bit as the wind had kicked up. It was strong enough to blow Mrs. Tipps's umbrella back.

Belle looked out the window for her father, but even if she had been able to see past the rain, it was too early for him to return. She made the decision to lock the door and turn the sign to CLOSED.

Then she went upstairs to see the patient.

Chapter Six

The flat was strangely quiet and dark as no lamps had been lit or windows opened. Belle made her way to the open door of her bed chamber, and then stopped and stared. Mr. Arundel had been tucked neatly under the covers, which were straight and tucked tightly under his arms, which lay pin-straight at his sides. His face was still flushed with fever, but he looked relatively peaceful, even gentlemanly with the shirt the ladies had put on him to help warm him. Belle narrowed her eyes. Had the ladies brushed his hair?

Looking past the patient, she saw her room had been put to rights. In fact, it was neater than she had left it before Mr. Arundel had shown up. She suspected the ladies had wanted to snoop through her things more than they wanted to tidy her chamber, but as Belle had nothing to hide, she didn't mind.

A glass half full of water sat on the bedside table, and Belle thought she had better take the advice of the ladies and attempt to get him to take some liquid. One benefit of the rain was that at least neither lady would meet anyone on the street to whisper to about Mr. Arundel. Still, she couldn't hope that they would keep it to themselves for long. Belle moved the chair beside the bed out of her way and sat on the edge of the mattress with the cup in hand. Gently, she lifted Mr. Arundel's head. He was still far too warm, and it concerned her how still he was.

She put the glass to his mouth, but his lips wouldn't open. "Come now, Mr. Arundel," she said. "You must drink something." She attempted to force his lips open, but once she had them parted and tried to make him sip, the water just ran down his chin.

Belle mopped up the spill and then jumped when she heard a pounding on the shop door. She gathered her skirts and hurried down the steps. It couldn't be her father, as he had a key. She expected a customer and all but collapsed with joy when she saw the doctor. She opened the door and held on so it would not blow back, and the doctor came in on a whoosh of rain and cold. He removed his hat and nodded to her, looking even wearier than she felt. "Miss Howard, was it?"

"Yes," she said. "Thank you for coming, Dr. Mayhew. Would you like some tea?"

"If it's not too much trouble."

"It's none at all," she said. The doctor seemed like an Earl Grey man, and she hastily set water to boil.

"How is the patient?" Mayhew asked.

"He is resting at the moment, but his fever is quite high."

"Did you place him in ice as I instructed?"

Belle spooned tea into the warm pot. "No, sir. I'm not sure who your usual patients are, but we have no ice nor means to obtain it." She poured the boiling water into the pot.

"I see. Too bad he couldn't stay with Randall."

Belle nodded. It was indeed too bad as that would have been best for everyone. "Did Mrs. Randall deliver her baby?"

"She did," the doctor said, giving Belle a faint smile. "A healthy boy, though a bit on the small side. He has a healthy set of lungs on him, though."

"That's very good news." She wasn't sure what else to say, and the tea had not yet steeped long enough to pour it.

"Was it smallpox?" Mayhew asked, indicating the left side of her face. She hadn't had time to curl the hair she usually styled to cover most of her scars, and the stringy tresses she'd left down were not adequate. Surprisingly, with all that had happened last night and this morning, she'd actually forgotten about her face. Mrs. Tipps and Mrs. Price were used to her and everyone who had stopped in had been far too concerned about the rain to look at her.

Belle resisted the urge to touch the ruined side of her face. "Yes, when I was four, it swept through our house. My father said I almost died."

"Looks to have been a severe case. Curious that only one side of your face bears the marks."

Belle might have pointed out one or two pockmarks on her right side. As it was, she wished he would stop staring at her. Finally, the doctor remarked, "Your scars are quite desirable as they indicate you won't infect anyone else with the disease. You cannot contract it twice." The doctor nodded his head in approval.

Belle had heard every platitude about her scars a dozen or more times before and didn't bother to retort that she would have rather people worry she would give them the disease than suffer the unsightly scars. Instead, she poured the tea and handed the doctor a cup. "If you'll follow me, I'll take you to see Mr. Arundel. I was just trying to persuade him to drink a bit of water."

Mayhew seemed surprised that she'd started away so abruptly, but he gathered his teacup and followed her up the stairs and into her bed chamber. "And where is your father?"

"He's gone to pay the rent," she said.

"You've left the patient alone?" the doctor said.

"I had no choice if I was to answer the door."

"And why is he all wet?"

Belle sighed. "He wouldn't swallow the water."

The doctor shook his head in disappointment. He made no move to do anything to help, however. "Take a cloth and dip it in the water," he directed. "Then you can squeeze small amounts of water onto his lips and in his mouth." He sipped the tea, looked at the cup, and sipped again. "This is very good," he said, sounding surprised.

"I know," Belle said. "Any other suggestions?" She indicated Arundel in case the doctor had forgotten the reason he was here.

"Keep giving him the laudanum and keep him quiet and still. To be honest, Miss Howard, I do not expect that he will live. But I have seen God work miracles before." He sipped the tea again. "Really, very excellent tea. I must purchase some before I go."

As the doctor seemed to have no other advice, save to rely on God, Belle sold him the Earl Grey then showed him out. She looked out the window again, hoping to spot her father, and when she didn't see him, she locked the door. She turned to go upstairs when she heard a loud thump and a crash.

Belle lifted her skirts and raced up the stairs, burst into the flat, and stared at the man swaying in her bed chamber doorway. How could he possibly be up and out of bed? He'd been lying still and half-dead to the world a moment ago. "Mr. Arundel!" Belle closed the door behind her and cautiously crossed the floor toward him. "You should not be out of bed, sir."

"I'm fine," he said, grabbing hold of the door jamb to steady himself. "I only need to find my bearings."

"You are not fine." She approached him slowly, holding her hands out. "You have a fever and a knife wound." She put her hands on his arms and patted him awkwardly. "You need to go back to bed."

"I will live," he said, his blue eyes fixing on hers with a clarity she didn't expect. "I'm not going to die."

"Oh, no." He'd heard Doctor Mayhew's dire predictions. They'd both thought Arundel was asleep, but they should never have assumed. Except she hadn't assumed. That had all been the doctor.

"I agree," she said, holding his gaze, though it made her uncomfortable. "You will not die. I have no intention of allowing that to happen. That doctor is an idiot."

"They usually are." To her surprise, Arundel grinned. It was a rather roguish grin that made her belly feel fluttery inside. That and the fact that she was still touching his arms. His hard, sinewy, muscled arms…

"He was more interested in the tea I gave him than tending to you."

"What sort of tea was it?"

An off question, all things considered, but she would humor him. "Earl Grey."

"Now I'm even more offended." His tone was light, but it was edged with pain.

"To be fair, it was a very good Earl Grey." Belle had a sudden inspiration. "Would you like a cup?"

"Yes," he said. "I'd like to see what the doctor found more interesting than keeping me alive."

"Get back in bed, and I'll bring it."

He turned his head and swayed again. Belle caught him, this time putting her arms about his waist. If she'd been uncomfortable touching his arms, this was even more unnerving and enjoyable. But she couldn't exactly allow him to fall.

His body was still burning with fever. She could feel the heat through the layer of linen covering his chest. She could also feel his slim waist and the broadening of his chest as it expanded to his shoulders. But she would try not to think about the image of him shirtless. She was supposed to be nursing him. Lusting after her patient was another reason she made a poor nurse.

They moved slowly back toward her bed, her hip brushing against his in an intimacy she hadn't sought and was enjoying far too much.

"Have I been having fever dreams, or were there two women here earlier?"

"That was Mrs. Price and Mrs. Tipps. They were sitting with you while we tended the shop."

They reached the bed, and he sat down hard, making the bed creak. "We're above a shop?"

"Yes, Howard's Teas & Treats. My father owns it."

He looked up at her suddenly, and she had to jerk back to prevent their noses from colliding. "Mrs. Randall served your tea at dinner."

"Did she?" Belle asked to be polite. "Go ahead and lie down now."

He obeyed, his bare feet and calves making him look strangely vulnerable. She pulled the covers up to his waist.

"And Mrs. Price and Mrs. Tipps are…?"

Belle opened her mouth then closed it again. "I'll brew the tea." She started to move away, but he grasped her wrist with his hot hand. Despite how weak he'd appeared a few moments before, his grip was surprisingly strong, and his fingers easily encircled her wrist. Belle had always been rather small and slight, but she'd never *felt* small or slight. Until now.

"They are your aunts? Your mother-in-law?"

"I'm not married, and my aunts do not live in London."

He gave her an expectant look, and she wanted to squirm. The longer he looked at her, the more conscious she was of her smallpox scars. She had tried all of her life not to care what people thought of them. She only hid them with her hair so as not to have to listen to comments about how it was too bad she was scarred because she could have been a true beauty. But for some reason, she did not want Mr. Arundel to see her scars. She turned her face slightly and ducked her head, hiding her left side from view as best she could. "They are neighbors."

His grip on her wrist tightened, not painfully but almost as though he'd been given an unwelcome surprise. "Your neighbors know I am here."

"Not exactly," she said. "It's not as though we told any of them, but Mrs. Price is always looking out of her window and saw the Randalls' carriage arrive." She glanced up at him. "Would you release my wrist, please?"

"No. Why didn't you tell her some sort of fabrication?"

"I suppose because I didn't realize your presence here was a secret." She shook her hand, trying to free her wrist.

"You realize that now?"

She took a breath. "My father pointed out that since you had been stabbed, rather deliberately, the man who stabbed you might be looking for you. Unfortunately, that was only after Mrs. Price and Mrs. Tipps had come into the shop and insisted on helping my father with your care."

Arundel abruptly dropped her hand. "Are you saying the ladies here earlier today were…customers?"

Belle had the distinct impression that she shouldn't confirm that. And now she was feeling defensive. "That's right. We're selling tea, biscuits, or a peek at the injured man upstairs. We hope you will bring in a sixpence a week."

He said nothing for a long moment. "I should think I could bring in at least a crown."

"Someone has a high opinion of himself. Only pistol ball injuries are worth that much."

He barked out a short laugh. The sound of it warmed her. She didn't delude herself that the moment of levity meant he was past the worst of his recovery. His fever could spike again, and most likely would. The infection raging inside him could spread. He might still die. But, by God, she would get some tea in him first.

"I'll be back in a few minutes with the tea. Try not to kill yourself while I'm out."

She put water on to boil, the familiar ritual of making tea soothing her. While the water heated, she sliced a piece of bread and found a bit of cheese, eating it standing over the stove. Once the water boiled, she rinsed the teapot and warmed it with the hot water. Then she dumped out the water, put the water back on the flame, and filled the pot with tea leaves. She poured the now boiling water over the leaves and allowed the tea to steep. Belle had an innate sense of how long to allow a tea to steep. Some blends should steep longer than others. Her father often lifted the lid of the teapot and checked the color or aroma of the tea, but Belle never had to do so. She simply knew when the tea was ready.

While she waited, she sliced another piece of bread and put it on a plate to bring in with the tea. Mr. Arundel might not eat it, but if he could stomach it, it would help him regain some of his strength.

Finally, the tea was ready, and she brought the tray into her chamber. Arundel was still lying where she'd left him, his eyes open and looking about her room. When she stepped in, he smiled at her, and Belle almost looked over her shoulder to see who he might be smiling at. Ridiculous. Of course, he was smiling at her.

"Here we are."

"It smells good."

"I've brought you some bread too, if you're up to eating something."

"I'll try." She helped prop him up on the pillow then stood uncertainly beside the bed. Should she hold the teacup to his lips or allow him to drink on his own? He made the decision for her, taking the cup from her hands. The cup shook on the saucer, making a rattling sound, but he seemed to have a grip on it. Belle didn't want to stare at him, so she stepped to the window and looked out. The rain seemed to have stopped for the moment, and she opened the window and leaned out, looking up and down Fenchurch Street. The dark clouds in the distance promised more rain. She stretched, peering down Fenchurch Street as far as she could in the direction her father had taken and wondered, again, when he would return.

"What's the matter?" Arundel asked.

"Nothing," she said. "It looks like more rain is coming."

"You're not a very good liar, Miss Howard."

Belle rounded on him. "Come see for yourself then. Or just wait an hour. It will be raining again for certain."

"That's not what I meant. Something is wrong. I've been trained to observe people and note small gestures and expressions. You're worried about something."

Interesting how he said he had been *trained* to observe. If she was a curious sort of person, she might have asked more about that, but she had learned it was better not to be too curious. Sometimes one discovered information one would rather not know. Belle waved a hand. "I don't think it takes much training to read someone. I can tell the moment someone enters my shop what sort of tea they want."

"I imagine you can judge the quality of their clothing and steer them toward tea they can afford."

"There's that." She nodded. "But it's more than that. Some people are keen to try something new and others want what's comfortable. That sort will never stray from their Darjeeling or their Earl Grey." She gestured to the cup he held.

"I must say, it's very good. Probably the best Earl Grey I've tasted."

"I know," she said. He grinned and sipped again.

"For those people, the ones who want comfort, I'll never sway them," she continued. "They might be willing to try an Assam or an Irish Breakfast, but a Jasmine or a Pai Mu Tan? Out of the question."

"What's Pai Mu Tan?"

"A sweet white tea. It's not something you'd enjoy."

One dark eyebrow winged up. "How do you know?"

"Because it's sweet and subtle, and you are anything but."

"I might say the same of you."

"I hope so. I'd hate to be called sweet or subtle. Still, I enjoy a Pai Mu Tan from time to time."

"But it's not your favorite."

"No, it's not. Like you, I enjoy something stronger and bolder."

"I don't like bitter teas," he said.

Belle folded her arms. "I didn't say bitter. My point is, if you came into the shop, I would know the type of tea to present to you."

"I'm sure it would be expensive."

"The best teas are worth the cost."

"Like everything in life, I suppose. So you can recognize a customer who is not adventurous and a customer who is, and you think that by changing the topic, I'll forget something is bothering you."

Oh, so he was clever. How she wished that made him unattractive, "I think I liked you better when you were unconscious."

"I'm sure I'll oblige you soon enough." He paused. "Where is your father?"

Belle turned to close the window.

Behind her, she heard him make a sound of affirmation. "That's what it is."

Annoying that he was observant too.

"How long has he been gone?" Arundel asked.

"I'm sure he will be back momentarily."

"Miss Howard."

At the note of alarm in his voice, she gave him a sharp look.

"How long has he been gone?"

"An hour and a half? Perhaps two hours now? I'm sure it's nothing to worry about."

But he didn't reassure her. "Where did he go?"

"To pay the rent. Usually I go, but he said to stay here since it was raining, and the streets are muddy."

"How long a walk to reach the landlord?"

His barrage of questions was making her more ill at ease. "Perhaps a quarter hour. Maybe a little more with the mud and water."

"Then even being generous, he should have been back an hour ago."

"Perhaps the landlord invited him in and—"

"Miss Howard, I don't know your landlord, but if he is anything like others I have encountered, he's not friendly with the tenants. No one wants to evict a friend."

Belle sighed. He was right. The landlord was an old man who usually opened the door, took the money, and made her wait outside while he counted it. Once satisfied, he sent her off with a wave until the next month. "I should go out and look for him."

"No." The determination in his voice made her pause.

"I am five and twenty, sir. I can make my own decisions."

"This isn't about your age—"

She opened her mouth, but he interrupted before she could speak "—or your sex. This is about me. If something has happened—and I'm not saying it has—it almost certainly has to do with me."

"It's *your* fault my father hasn't returned?"

"It might be."

"If he's in trouble, then I must look for him. I won't stay here and do nothing." She grasped a hat from a hook and started for the door. Arundel was surprisingly quick for an injured man and caught her about the waist before she could reach it.

"Let go of me." She twisted against his hold.

Chapter Seven

Her large brown eyes met his. If looks could maim or injure, he would be on the floor, writhing in pain. He might end up there at any rate as his head was swimming due to his sudden rise. If he allowed himself to feel the pain of his injury, he'd probably sink to his knees. One item they had not told him during training at the Farm was how bloody much it hurt to be stabbed.

And how much it continued to hurt.

"Drastic measures?" Miss Howard said, her lips barely moving. She must have clenched her jaw tightly. Thank God she had stopped squirming.

"I can't fight you, but I outweigh you by at least four stone, probably five." The woman couldn't have weighed more than eight stone. Hew could practically feel her ribs through her dress. He should be the one feeding her tea and bread. "I can sit on you and keep you here."

"And what will you do when I poke at your injury?" She twisted, almost escaping his hold this time. "I wager you will allow me up quick enough."

119

Hew narrowed his eyes. "You wouldn't do that, Miss Howard. And you will cease fighting me and sit down." He caught the faintest flicker of capitulation in her eyes and, as a show of good faith, released her waist. She stepped back, sliding the fabric of her dress down as though he'd hurt her, even though he had been gentle—firm, but gentle.

"You had better sit down yourself," she said. "Before you fall down."

He had hoped that the swaying had been the building, but buildings in this part of the world didn't sway. He also didn't think Belle Howard was the sort of woman to give up so easily. She'd wait until he passed out again and then walk right out the door and into danger. Hew did what any agent in his condition would—he sank down in front of the door.

"Not there, you oaf," Miss Howard said, her voice filled with irritation. "In the bed." She offered a hand to help him rise and move to the bed, which, he could admit, would have been a sight more comfortable, but he waved her hand away.

"I like it here."

She stood and stared down at him. "You think blocking the door will keep me here?"

"I don't think you're foolish enough to go out the window, but I could be mistaken. Perhaps you want to break your neck."

The look in her eyes said she wanted to break someone's neck. It also said she was worried enough about her father to do just about anything. Fortunately, the rain chose that moment to begin again. It was a light spattering on the window, but if her weather forecasting skills were one-tenth of her skill with tea, then it would be raining more heavily soon. Even a headstrong woman without an ounce of sense wouldn't try and climb out a window in the rain.

Miss Howard glanced at the window, giving it a look of loathing she had heretofore reserved for him. Then she walked deliberately to the chair, grasped it with both hands, dragged it to the end of the bed, and set it to face him. She sat, arms crossed and staring at him. Hew was fairly certain this was one of the most unusual situations he'd ever been in. He was in bare feet and shirtsleeves, sitting in front of a door, keeping an unmarried, unchaperoned woman hostage. He had a moment to wonder what had become of his new coat from Schweitzer and Davidson's then decided it was best not to know.

"I am not a curious person, Mr. Arundel. I mind my business and leave others to their own. If I go to St. Katharine Docks and a man approaches me and whispers he has a SowMee White or Yin Chen and will give me a good price, I don't ask questions. If the tea is good quality, I buy it and let him worry about customs fees and import taxes."

Hew rubbed his forehead, attempting to ease the pounding that had begun there. All this talk of tea made him wish he'd had the forethought to grasp the cup she'd given him before sinking down in front of the door. "I don't think your ignorance will shield you from prosecution, should you be discovered with smuggled tea."

She lifted a shoulder. "That example was purely hypothetical."

"Sure it was." His gaze flicked to the still half-full cup of Earl Grey. He hoped she hadn't acquired that from smugglers, but even if she had, he would have drunk it. It truly was the best he'd ever had.

She rose, as though hearing his thoughts, fetched the tea and saucer, and handed it to him before taking her place in the chair again. "My point," she said after he'd had a long sip, "is that I don't ask unnecessary questions. I don't want to know more than I need to. But I find that as much as I wish *not* to know, I must ask who you are and why you were stabbed."

Truth be told, Hew had been expecting the questions much sooner than this. Mrs. Price and Mrs. Tipps had peppered him with questions for the few minutes he'd been conscious in their presence. He'd pretended to go to sleep to avoid them. Even Mr. Howard had asked him questions. Hew had evaded them all. He didn't want to involve this family any more than he had, but at this point, their involvement couldn't be avoided. He'd put Miss Howard and her father in danger, however unintentionally.

Hew sipped the tea again and leaned his head back against the door. "Who am I?" he said. "That's a complicated question for anyone."

"Not really."

He smiled. She was abrasive, but he liked her for that. She reminded him of Lucy Galloway, one of the agents with the Royal Saboteurs. Lucy was bold to the point of rudeness, though she always asked her pointed questions and made her sharp remarks with a dimpled smile.

"My name is Hew Arundel. I come from a family with a long lineage."

"A wealthy one with ties to the upper class, if the name is any indication."

He didn't deny it. His father had married the daughter of the Duke of Ely, and though his father hadn't had a title, he'd had money enough to mean his lack of a *Lord* before his surname could be overlooked. His uncle Ernest, the brother his mother called *Blue* because of his piercing blue eyes, had taken an interest in Hew when he'd been ten or eleven.

Hew was not in the habit of using the Ely title to his advantage, so he left it out now. "My mother was born to a family of some renown," he said. "Her younger brother, my Uncle Ernest, liked to tell me stories about his days as a soldier. He fought against Napoleon during the Peninsular Wars. According to my uncle, he was captured three times and escaped three times—freeing his comrades-in-arms with him. He was good at extricating himself from difficult situations.

"I like to think he saw something of himself in me as he encouraged me to become a diplomat."

She took his empty teacup and set it on the floor. He'd forgotten about it, and his hand had gone slack. His body felt slack.

"You'll think me ignorant, but what does a diplomat do? I thought those were the men who traveled to France or Austria and negotiated treaties no one cares about."

Hew gave her a faint smile, about as much as he could manage through the pain. "I imagine you care about those treaties and negotiations having to do with tariffs and taxes on your precious tea."

Her eyes narrowed. "You had something to do with the taxes on tea?"

Hew held up both hands. "No. I promise I never took any part in those sorts of dealings. I was more of a messenger, a courier, if you will. I might be sent to Spain as an assistant to the ambassador, and while he met with the Queen's advisors, I would meet with a friend to the Crown and receive information. Occasionally, I was asked to pass on information or a package of some significance."

She cocked her head, her honey blond hair falling forward. His gaze followed it, and he remembered that he'd smelled something clean and like cinnamon when she'd leaned over him before. Had it seeped into her hair from tea or a spice in the kitchen? Was it on her clothes? Would she think it odd if he tried to sniff her? Yes, he decided. She would object.

"I thought men of your station found spying beneath their dignity and rank."

"I wouldn't call my work *spying*—"

She snorted.

"—but even if it was, I'm not the sort to crave battlefield glory. I'm not the sort who needs to charge into the fray with raised sword, though I have done my share of fighting when necessary."

Miss Howard looked as though she had more questions, but true to form, she refrained from asking them. "How does your *diplomatic* work put you here?" she asked.

The sound of the rain against the thick windows grew louder. Hew hoped Mr. Howard was not caught in it. He hoped the man wasn't lying dead in the street. If he hadn't been half-delirious with fever, he would have warned the man. As it was, he needed to fight that delirium now. He could all but feel the surge of fever rising in him again and gnawing at the fringes of his lucidity. Hew wanted badly to close his eyes and surrender. Instead, he focused on Miss Howard's deep brown eyes. He'd always liked brown eyes on a woman. This woman met his gaze with a level stare, and he liked that too.

"I'm not a diplomat anymore. I was recommended for another position with a group called the Royal Saboteurs." And there he could thank his Uncle Ernest again. His uncle had worked with the Saboteurs' leader, Baron, years ago. Uncle Ernest had put in a good word for Hew, and a few months later, he'd been on a train to northern England and the training camp known as the Farm.

"And this group undoubtedly wanted you for your so-called skills in observation."

He gave her a faint smile, deciding to ignore her slight. "Among other reasons. I've been training with them since January, honing my skills in surveillance and various other arts. The mission of the Royal Saboteurs is to protect Queen and Country. It may surprise you to know that there are forces, both domestic and foreign, who wish harm to England and Queen Victoria. It's our mission to sabotage their efforts."

"Sir, at this point, the only efforts I see sabotaged are yours."

He gave her the best glare he could manage when his head was pounding. "I was ambushed, but, to be fair, I was not in London for a mission. I just finished a mission and came to visit friends and enjoy a brief holiday."

"We are a tourist attraction now." She gestured to her chamber and the building at large.

"Yes," he grumbled. "You could charge sixpence a week."

"For you, a crown," she shot back, echoing their earlier conversation.

"I'd laugh, but it would hurt too much."

"I know the feeling because, if I understand correctly, you are some sort of spy who was attacked by some other spy, and when Mr. Randall sent you here to convalesce, he was involving us in an international incident."

"It might be a domestic incident. My mission before I came to London was investigating a bridge collapse. You've probably heard about it."

She blinked at him.

"A train traveling near Carlisle went over a bridge. Midway across, the bridge crumbled and a section collapsed. Ten people were injured and three killed."

"I hadn't heard. I'm sorry for them."

Hew stared at her. He didn't expect her to know of the investigation—at least not his part in it—but the accident had been in all of the papers. The agents at the Farm had even heard about it. "How have you not read of this?" And then he realized she might not be literate. He shouldn't have assumed. "Or perhaps heard of it?"

"I work for my bread," she said, "and not the sort of work that allows me to *relax* with friends on holiday. We are open every day except Christmas, Easter, and the queen's birthday. If I'm not at the shop selling tea, I'm at the docks buying tea. I don't have time to read about train accidents on the other side of the world."

"Cumbria is hardly the other side—" He waved a hand. "You're right. This doesn't concern you." He closed his eyes out of frustration and pain.

"Except it does now. Clearly, whatever you did in your investigation angered someone."

Hew's eyes snapped open. "It's not a given that my stabbing and the train investigation are related." It was a possibility but not a certainty.

"What other conclusion is there? I presume the train accident was no accident, and when you uncovered the sabotage—that is your mission, yes?—you became a target of the...what word did you use? Saboteurs?" She stumbled a bit over the pronunciation, her London accent making it seem far less French. "Yes, you became a target of the saboteurs"—she almost had it now—"who followed you to London and decided to kill you before you could..." She glanced at the ceiling and put a hand to her chin as though thinking. "I don't know what they were trying to prevent. Surely you have sent your findings or you would not be at leisure to visit friends in London."

Hew stared at her. If his stabbing was related to the train investigation—and she made a good argument that it was— she was smarter than his attackers. She'd easily found the flaw in their plan. But she didn't know all the details, though he imagined if he gave her one or two, she'd have the entire thing solved, despite never having seen the train, the wreck, or even knowing where Carlisle was.

"I've sent preliminary findings along with my theories about who might have a motive for the sabotage."

"You said it wasn't an international incident, so it must be someone in that area. Do they have farms in that part of the country? Perhaps the train tracks were cutting through fields the farmer might cultivate, and he thought an accident might cause the train company to alter the route of the tracks."

He held up a hand. She was far too astute for her own good. Hew's suspect was not a farmer at all but a local landowner by the name of Pennywhistle. The gentleman previously owned the land where the tracks had been laid. Hew discovered that recently he'd had surveyors on the area adjacent to the land he'd sold to the railroads. Those men had been looking for minerals—valuable deposits of copper and iron ore. It wasn't yet clear to Hew whether the surveyors had found mineral deposits, but if they had, the land was worth a fortune. It would be enough to go to great lengths in order to buy it back. That being impossible, Pennywhistle—the landowner—might be able to sneak men on to the land to excavate the mineral deposits, if the railroad was incapacitated for some time. It would take a little bribery, but a few hundred pounds paid to railroad officials was a small price compared to the riches the gentleman might uncover.

Hew couldn't prove any of this—not yet. It was a theory that needed more investigation, but after the attempt on his life, Hew was beginning to think his theory might have some merit.

Pennywhistle almost certainly was not in London, but if he'd killed three innocent people on a train in order to have his way, he wouldn't balk at sending men to kill one agent of the Royal Saboteurs.

The question was whether those men would stop at Hew's death or kill anyone associated with him. Right now they had no reason to kill the Howards, but if Miss Howard or her father got in their way, that could change.

"It might be better if we don't discuss this further," Hew said. "The less you know, the better."

"I'd agree with you," she said, "except that my father is missing. I can't protect myself if I don't know what to watch for."

"I'll protect you," he said.

She laughed. "Right now you are one stiff breeze away from falling over. You can't even stand."

Hew knew a challenge when he heard one. "Can't I?" With determination and sheer tenacity, Hew pushed himself up from the floor, using the door at his back for support. Slowly, sweat running down his face and his injury throbbing, he made it to his feet. He took a step forward, putting the bed behind him in case he fell. But she didn't need to know he might fall at any instant. He'd more than proved himself.

Hew liked to think there was a glimmer of appreciation in her gaze. But he'd have had to look past the smugness in order to see it. She had a face he could read far too easily, which made him more the fool for giving her exactly what she wanted—access to the door and the exit. Hew groaned as his legs gave out, and he sank onto the bed.

"Very impressive," she said. "But you should rest and conserve your strength."

"Don't patronize me." He tried to push her hands away as she eased him onto the mattress. He was weak now, and his efforts made no impact. The room spun as he looked up at the ceiling. Miss Howard arranged the covers about him and adjusted his head on the pillow. At least she hadn't run straight out the door. He knew she wouldn't listen, but he had to try. "Miss Howard." No, he needed to make her listen. "Belle."

Her brown eyes snapped to his face. She was so pretty, her honey-blond hair falling out of its confines, her pink mouth, whose lips made the shape of a bow, and, who could forget those intelligent eyes? It was the intelligence that got to him. He'd known dozens of beautiful women, but the sheer vacuousness behind their eyes made a great many of them lack appeal. The problem was that intelligent women were dangerous. Look at the female agents for the Saboteurs—Bridget Kelly or Lucy Galloway. Both were beautiful and deadly.

Of course, they weren't a danger to him because he had no interest beyond friendship with either lady. And after what had happened with his late wife—an exceptionally beautiful and intelligent woman—Hew had vowed never to allow any woman to elicit anything stronger than friendship in him again. If a woman stirred anything deeper in him, Hew ran the other way.

Belle Howard was stirring those feelings inside him, but he couldn't run. He told himself it didn't matter. She obviously had no interest in him. He was safe.

Except he was not.

She had that face he could read, and when he'd said her name, when he'd said *Belle*, something in her eyes had flickered. There was a softness there, one she didn't want him to see, and one that told him she was not impervious to his charms. That shouldn't matter—that little chink in her armor. He didn't need to know that she had a weakness for him because he did not intend to seduce her. Hell, he couldn't seduce her even if he wanted to. He could barely stay conscious.

Still, Hew wished he hadn't seen that flicker because now not only was she lovely and intelligent, she was dangerous.

"Belle," he said again, and this time he didn't look at her eyes. "Listen to me. You only put yourself in more danger if you go out."

"I won't—"

He grasped her hand and pulled her down. He must have some strength remaining because she lowered to the bed, close enough that he could see the gold flecks in her eyes. Ah. That was what made them so pretty. They weren't just brown, but they were flecked with honey-gold, like her hair. "I told you," he said, trying not to stare at those eyes. Trying not to lose himself in the gold flecks or the lure of unconsciousness. "I'm a trained observer. I know exactly what you're thinking."

"Do you? You might be taking more care if you knew *exactly* what I was thinking."

He would have grinned if he hadn't been fighting so hard to stay awake. Clearly, she was annoyed with him. "Besides wanting to hit me over the head, you plan to run out the door as soon as I release you. Don't do it. You can't help your father by racing into danger. And when he returns and finds you gone, you'll only cause him to worry. Stay, Belle."

"Close your eyes now, Mr. Arundel," she said. "I'll get a cool compress."

The suggestions sounded so good, he didn't even try to resist. He closed his eyes, and his hand must have released her because a few moments later he felt a cool cloth on his forehead. He was so hot. It was as though he were on a spit, and a fire had been lit beneath him. Except the fire came from inside, originating from his wound, which insisted on pulsing with pain.

The compress was removed and replaced, the coolness barely penetrating the heat. Before he succumbed to the darkness, he heard the sound of the rain on the window, her footsteps as she walked out of the room, and then the silence of an empty flat.

Chapter Eight

Belle closed the bed chamber door and leaned on it, gulping for breath. She'd gathered the tea things before she'd left, and she could hear them clinking together as her hands shook. She told herself she was acting this way because she was afraid for her father, but if she was honest, Arundel's murmured words had rattled her. He probably hadn't even meant them for her. He had been barely conscious.

Or he had been thinking of another woman.

He must have been.

Except. He'd said *her* name.

Belle closed her eyes, and in her mind she saw his eyes open, blue velvet with pain and fever. His gaze fastened on her. "Belle," he'd said. "So beautiful. That's what makes you dangerous."

Now that she thought about it, she didn't suppose it had been a compliment to call her *dangerous*. But he'd also said she was beautiful. How could she take that in any way other than a compliment, especially since it was the first time anyone had ever called her beautiful without a qualifier, such as *you'd be such a beauty if not for those scars*?

Belle put the tea things in the pail they used for dirty dishes. It was almost full, and she should really draw some clean water, heat it, and wash the dishes. She should also go down and open up the shop, though with the rain coming down in waves again, it was unlikely anyone would come in.

More important than the dishes or the shop was her father. He should have been home by now. Something was wrong. He would never have left her for hours to tend the shop and the injured man alone.

Arundel had tried to keep her from going after her father, but she'd won in the end. She couldn't sit in the warm, dry flat while her father needed her. She pulled on her cloak and went to the door, making it all the way to the shop window before she paused.

Though it was midday, the sky was dark and the rain meant the lamps hadn't been lit. Rain was coming down quite heavily and had turned the streets into mud. She'd be soaked and up to her knees in mud as soon as she stepped outside. That didn't matter to her. She'd do anything for her father.

As she stood at the door, her mind conjured all sorts of horrible scenarios. Her father had fallen and broken a leg. He had been swept away by high water in the streets. Arundel's train-hating farmer had found him and stabbed him. Thieves had set upon him, stolen the rent money, and left him for dead.

None of these, except for the last, seemed plausible. But even if he had been set upon by thieves, how would she find him? She knew the path she took to the landlord's home, but how would her father travel?

She might trudge about in the dark, pouring rain for hours to no avail. And what if her father came home while she was out and couldn't find her? Belle leaned her head against the shop windowpane. Arundel was right. She should stay here and wait. It wouldn't help her father if she went wandering about London, catching her death in the cold rain.

Or catching her death from the knife of a farmer who detested trains.

She'd give her father another hour, and if he wasn't back by then and the rain had abated, she'd go out after him. There. She could be reasonable. Her plan made sense.

It also made sense to close the shop. She hated to do it, but she told herself she wasn't turning away business. No one was coming in this weather. Besides, she couldn't leave Arundel alone. She was an awful nurse, but his fever had spiked. Even a bad nurse knew he must be cooled down.

Belle closed the shop's shades, made sure the door was still locked, then blew out the lamps and went upstairs. She peeked in on Arundel, changed his cool compress, and made herself a cup of Earl Grey. It was simple and fortifying, and that was what she needed. She brought it with her into her chamber, sipping it between changing the compress and staring out the window overlooking the empty street.

An hour passed, her father did not return, and the rain continued. Arundel was hot to the touch and hadn't opened his eyes since she'd gotten him back into bed. Belle slumped down beside the bed, having placed a new compress on his hot forehead. She drew her knees up and placed her forehead on them, allowing silent tears to fall.

She knew she was jumping to conclusions, but how could she not assume the worst after her father had been gone so much longer than he ought? What would she do without her father? Would she have to give up the shop? Go live with her sister? She loved Maggie, but it would be humiliating to have to ask her younger sister to support her. John Dormer seemed a nice enough man, but he probably didn't want to share his home with Maggie's spinster sister.

The hot tears trailed down her cheeks, and she used her sleeve to swipe them away. There was no use crying, but she couldn't hold it in any longer.

She felt something warm and heavy on her shoulder. For a moment, she stopped sniffling and enjoyed the comfort. Then Belle stiffened, realizing there was only one person who might be comforting her right now. She spun around, rising on her knees, and faced Arundel.

"I didn't mean to startle you," he croaked.

"I thought you were—" She sniffed, knowing her eyes were red and she disguised nothing.

"Dead?" he said, his voice raspy and dry.

"Asleep," she said. "Here." She offered the last of her tea, and he struggled to rise enough to sip it. She supported his head, and when he'd finished, he lay back and tried to catch his breath.

"Thank you. It's rather humbling to be weak as a kitten."

"I can imagine."

"Your father?"

She shook her head, a lump rising in her throat so that she could not speak. He didn't say a word, merely opened his arms in a gesture that was universal. Belle resisted for a moment and was proud of herself for that mere hesitation. But she wanted comfort. She was afraid and feeling so alone.

Belle expected to feel odd about falling into Arundel's arms, but it felt natural to allow him to hold her. She didn't usually enjoy physical affection, but now she rested her head on his warm shoulder and allowed the tears to fall as he patted and rubbed her back. He murmured things like, "Everything will be fine" and "It will all work out."

He couldn't know if anything he said was true, but somehow hearing him say it made her feel better. She finally stopped crying and lay, eyes stinging, against him. He was stroking her hair, and she closed her eyes and allowed it. It wasn't the sensual caresses she'd imagined earlier, but it was what she needed and that was a gift.

Feeling safe and calm, Belle did something she hadn't done in a long time. She prayed.

When she opened her eyes, she saw the window to her bedroom. The rain had stopped, and the sky was streaked gray with dusk. She wasn't certain what had made her start awake. Perhaps it was a cramp in her leg, which was trapped beneath Arundel's leg. Or the heat of his chest pressed against her back.

Belle started, realizing she had fallen asleep in Arundel's arms. Literally. She was using one of his arms as a pillow, and he'd draped the other over her waist. He must have felt her start, even in his sleep, and that arm tightened on her. She tried to sit and made no progress. "Let me up," she said, pushing against his arm. It didn't move.

Belle wiggled, turning her body until she faced Arundel and her back was to the window. This had the effect of ruching up her skirts and twisting her bodice uncomfortably, but now she was facing him. His eyes were closed, dark lashes stark against his pale skin. She took a moment to appreciate that his skin wasn't flushed with fever, though he still felt warm.

"Mr. Arundel."

His eyes fluttered but didn't open.

Belle poked him in the chest, well above the injury on the side not stuck to her. "*Mr. Arundel.*"

He opened his eyes, velvet blue in the dim room, and blinked at her. Their faces were inches apart, and Belle hadn't realized what it would feel like to be pressed intimately against a man and then to have him looking down at her, sleepily. It seemed he drew her closer, tightening his leg over hers and gathering her to his chest with his arm. He closed his eyes again then nuzzled into her neck.

Belle's heart thudded then rammed against her ribs. Were those his lips on her neck? His breath was warm on her skin as he inhaled then released. "You smell"—he inhaled again—"like cinnamon."

He still smelled of bergamot and she realized now the other scent she hadn't been able to place before was probably just him, the smell of a man. Her body was reacting to his, even as her mind struggled to catch up. His lips brushed her neck again, and she inhaled sharply at the pang of pleasure that shot through her. She wanted to run her hands over him, to kiss him back.

She shouldn't be allowing this, and yet, what could it hurt if she allowed one more brush of his lips?

But his head jerked up, and when she looked at him, his gaze was intent and focused on something else. "Someone is here," he said. "In the building."

"No—" But then she heard it too. The sound of feet on the stairs and the rattle of the door to the flat. "My father!" she said. That must have been what had woken her. She'd heard the door to the shop open and close. Joy rose in her and then horror as she realized where she was and what she was doing. Arundel must have realized it too because he removed his arm, lifted his leg, and drew away from her as though she were a viper.

Belle jumped up, smoothed her skirts, and would have raced to the door, but Arundel grabbed her hand. He was slower to rise, obviously feeling pain when he moved. "Wait. Belle!" He hissed her name as she tried to free herself. "It might not be him. I'll go."

This was the second or third time he'd tried to protect her. She wasn't used to it or the way it made her feel.

"Of course it's him," she said. "No one else has a key."

Arundel's grip on her wrist tightened, and she thought she might have to wrest free.

"Belle?" That was her father's voice. She would have done anything to be free at that moment, but Arundel released her. She ran to the bed chamber door, threw it wide, and raced into the parlor. Her father was just closing the door behind him. He turned from the lock in time to catch her as she threw herself into his arms. "What's this?" he said with a laugh.

Belle could imagine he was surprised as she rarely showed any affection and probably hadn't hugged him like this since she'd been a small child. "Where were you?" She pulled away. "What took you so long?"

"I'll tell you everything," he said, cupping her cheek. She felt his gaze travel over her and wondered if she looked as disheveled as she felt, but he didn't say anything. "First, tell me about Mr. Arundel. How is he?"

"Still alive," came a voice from the bed chamber door. Arundel stood in the doorway, leaning heavily against the wooden frame. He looked as rumpled as she. Belle tried to control her gaze, but it traveled from the arms that had held her to the lips that had kissed her neck. He'd pulled a blanket over his shoulders so at least she couldn't gawk at him.

Her father set Belle aside and went straight to Arundel. "You look as though you're about to fall over."

"I'll manage. What happened?"

Her father glanced over his shoulder, and Belle shook her head. "You cannot think to keep this from me. What happened, Father?"

Her father looked back at Arundel. "I believe I met some of your friends."

***

"No friends of mine," Hew said, meeting George Howard's angry gaze. Hew didn't blame the man for being angry. He hadn't asked to be dragged into this. Moreover, he certainly didn't want his daughter placed in danger.

Hew didn't want that either, but it was too late now. The Howards had been pulled into this nightmare the moment Randall had sent for them. All Hew could do now was protect them as best he could. But to do that, he needed information.

"Do you mind if I take a seat?" He gestured to the small table and chairs. Mr. Howard pulled one of the chairs out and indicated his daughter should take the other. Then he disappeared into her bed chamber and returned with a third chair. Hew sat gratefully, but Miss Howard stood behind her chair, her hands on the crest rail. She was watching her father, a mix of relief and concern in her gaze.

"I would stand," Hew said, realizing he was violating good manners by sitting while she stood, "but I'd probably fall over."

Miss Howard blinked at him then nodded in understanding. "Both of you sit. I'll make tea."

"Hibiscus, I think," her father said. "We've all had something of a scare."

"Of course. I'll go down and fetch some." She was out the door and her footfalls on the steps before Hew realized what she was about. Apparently, there was no hibiscus tea in the flat. Personally, Hew would have preferred the Earl Grey again, but then she would remove him from the adventurous tea drinkers category, and for some reason, he didn't want that.

"She's pretty, isn't she?" Mr. Howard asked.

"Very," Hew said before thinking. Then he looked away from the door where Miss Howard had retreated. "I mean no disrespect, sir."

"Oh, don't worry. If you were disrespectful, she would give you what for. She's not afraid to speak her mind."

"No, she's not. She's frightfully clever too."

"You've noticed that."

"I'm in awe of her powers of deduction."

Mr. Howard smiled then looked toward the door again. Miss Howard was still in the shop. "She uses words as a shield. She's had to develop a tough exterior. Most people never see her softer side. She doesn't trust easily."

"That's a trait we share, though for me it's due to my work."

"I certainly didn't think you'd been mocked for your appearance."

Hew cocked his head.

Mr. Howard touched the side of his face. "The scars from smallpox," he explained. "She was teased about them mercilessly as a child, and now she's routinely pitied."

Hew had to think for a moment, to imagine her face.

"You won't pretend you hadn't noticed them," her father said.

"I notice everything," Hew said, and this was true and part of his training. "But I can't say I particularly noted the scars. They certainly don't take away from her beauty." Hew was aware that sounded like false flattery, but he'd been sincere. Yes, he'd seen the smallpox scars, but they hadn't stood out to him. She was beautiful, and the scars didn't make her less so. But her father's words did unlock several questions he'd had about her—the way she tilted her head down when she spoke to him and how she brushed her hair over the left side of her face. He had wanted to push it back behind her ear several times but resisted as the gesture would have been overly familiar.

She was hiding her scars from him.

She probably didn't even realize she had those habits. He imagined hiding one side of her face had become habit to her.

Hew supposed many people felt sorry for her, but pity wasn't an emotion he could conjure toward her. Not when lust was so easily at hand. And there was definite lust after he'd had her in bed beside him. He'd meant only to comfort her, but waking with a woman in his arms, one that was so lovely and receptive to his touch—better not to tell her father that bit of information. Hew wished he hadn't recognized the feeling himself, but as an agent, he couldn't afford to ignore his emotions. He'd been trained to confront them, to use them if possible, and to understand how they might be used against him.

Hew hadn't intended on having any feelings toward either of the Howards. But it was difficult not to admire Miss Howard's beauty and cleverness. In his fever-ridden state, admiration might have been the extent of it, but then he'd heard her crying. At first, he'd thought he'd been dreaming.

His fever dreams were strange and nonsensical. But when he opened his bleary eyes, she'd been sitting next to the bed, head in her hands, weeping. In that moment, he'd felt a dozen emotions. First, he was grateful she hadn't gone after her father. He'd known she had sense, and she'd proved it. Secondly, he felt empathy. Of course, she was worried about her father. Hew wished he could tell her the man was not in any danger, but they both knew that wasn't true.

All Hew could do was offer comfort. It had started innocently enough when he'd put a hand on her shoulder. But the next thing he knew, he was pulling her into his arms and holding her against his chest as she shook with weeping. She didn't go into his arms easily. She didn't fit there as though she was always meant to be there. She'd been stiff and awkward and clearly hadn't wanted to want his comfort. But in the end, she'd given into it and cried herself into exhaustion. In sleep, her body relaxed, and Hew had been forced to lie there and feel her soft curves against him.

It had been years since a woman had slept in his arms. Years since he had gathered a woman close, inhaled the scent of her hair, kissed her temple. These were intimacies he didn't want. He supposed Miss Howard didn't want them either, but perhaps in that moment, they both needed each other. Hew thanked God for the first, and last, time that he was injured. If he hadn't been, he might have taken advantage of the situation. Or at least tried.

Fortunately, all he could do was *imagine* taking advantage of the situation. He'd imagined that in detail until her warmth and softness had finally lulled him back to sleep.

Hew looked at Mr. Howard now and wondered how much he suspected. Nothing had happened between the two of them, but clearly her father had seen something of Hew's interest as he'd baited Hew with a comment about his daughter's attractiveness. Hew would have to guard his thoughts and expressions from now on.

"Of course, Miss Howard's appearance is neither here nor there," he said dismissively. "The more important issue is the matter of the man or men trying to kill me."

Miss Howard chose that moment to return to the flat, and she stopped just inside the doorway. "You could at least wait for me to brew the tea before starting to talk of murder."

"We've only just begun," her father said. "You haven't missed anything."

She made a sound that indicated she doubted that very much then began the routine of brewing the tea. And it was a routine. She moved quickly and efficiently, as though she had boiled the water and prepared the tea a thousand times. And Hew supposed she had, but though her movements were economical, they were also graceful. He could have watched her all day. But considering her father was watching *him*, Hew looked away.

"Now that we're all here," Hew said, "tell us what happened."

"First, I have a question," Mr. Howard said to Hew. "Did Randall know he was putting us in danger when he sent you here?"

"I don't think so," Hew said. "If his wife hadn't gone into labor at almost the same moment I was attacked, he might have put the pieces together, but I believe he assumed the attack was random. Regardless, I don't want to be there anymore than I want to be here. I'm not eager to put either of you in danger, especially not Mrs. Randall, when she is attempting to deliver a child."

"The babe has been born," Miss Howard said, pouring hot water into the teapot. "The doctor came by while you were sleeping and said the Randalls have a new baby boy. He is a bit small but doing well."

Hew smiled. "That is good news." He rubbed his temple. "I don't seem to remember the doctor visiting."

She looked up at him. "I'm not surprised. You were rather feverish at the time. The doctor didn't examine him," she said to her father, taking cups and saucers from cupboards. "He said to give Mr. Arundel more laudanum and that he'd probably die. That was the extent of his visit."

Hew laughed. "That sounds like most doctors I know. I can't even argue with him. I feel like I'm about to die."

Miss Howard gave him a sharp look. "Perhaps you should go lie down."

"Not until I try this hibiscus tea."

"Too late," she said, pouring a cup of tea from a second pot he hadn't noticed before. "I made you the Earl Grey."

Hew opened his mouth to ask how she'd known then closed it again. Clearly, she possessed some sort of witchcraft when it came to tea. She placed the steaming cup before him, and Hew made himself wait before sipping it. He'd rather not have both a burnt tongue and a knife wound.

"Putting aside the doctor's incompetence," Mr. Howard said, "clearly, someone wants you dead, Mr. Arundel. Any idea who?"

"I have some idea, yes. But I'm sure the man has sent lackeys to do his bidding. I assume that's who you met when you were out."

Belle put the hibiscus tea before her father. It smelled somewhat flowery but also slightly medicinal. He was glad he had his Earl Grey.

"I wouldn't say I met them, exactly," Howard said. "But as I walked to the landlord's house, I became aware I was being followed."

"I knew I should have gone," Belle muttered.

"So they could follow you?" Her father shook his head. "I don't think so." He looked back at Hew. "At first, I thought I might be imagining it. After all, it was raining lightly and the few people out were all skulking about, trying to stay dry. But after I paid the landlord and started home, I saw the same two men, and that's when I knew."

"But why were they following you?" Belle asked.

"I imagine they know Mr. Arundel is here with us."

"How? Surely Mrs. Price hasn't had the opportunity to spread the news yet."

"They aren't relying on gossip," Hew said. "They won't be paid unless I'm dead. After they attacked, they regrouped and came back to watch the Randalls' home. They undoubtedly saw you arrive, saw me loaded into the carriage, and followed us here. Or perhaps with all the rain, they couldn't follow and had to make an attempt to discover who you were. They might be following you to discover whether or not I am here, and if I am, if I'm still alive."

"Then I suppose all of my efforts to avoid being followed home were for naught," Howard said. "I led them on a merry chase through London. In and out of shops and pubs, finally managing to lose them after hours of pursuit. Only then did I return."

"I applaud your efforts, but they probably know where you live. Their question is whether or not I am here, and as they didn't discover that following you, they'll try another way."

"I don't like the sound of that," Belle said.

"And I don't like having to be the bearer of ill tidings, but I don't have time to sweeten the truth. It's almost nightfall," Hew said, glancing at Mr. Howard for confirmation. The older man nodded. Hew continued, "They'll strike when it's dark. Perhaps tonight. Perhaps tomorrow. We can't wait. We have to leave. Now."

Chapter Nine

"Leave?" Belle set her teacup back on the table and stared at Arundel. He was pale, his dark hair disheveled, and it was clear he was holding onto the table in an effort to remain upright. "We can't leave. Even if my father and I were willing to abandon the shop, you are in no condition to go anywhere."

"I'm stronger than you think."

"I think you quite strong," she said, "but you are not a god. It's clear you have reached your limit. Father?" Belle gave her father a pointed look.

Her father took a deep breath then let it out again. "It may kill you to travel now," he said to Arundel.

"It may kill all of us if we stay here."

"This is madness," Belle said. "Where would we go?"

"Leave that to me." Arundel looked about. "I need a pen and paper."

"You need to lie down," her father said. "You dictate, and I will write."

"I will write," Belle said. "Father, you have been away all day and out in the rain. I insist you put on warm, dry clothes and rest. I'll take care of what needs to be done."

Her father shook his head and then seemed to think better of objecting. "You're right. I won't be of any use to you if I am falling over from exhaustion or catch a chill. Belle, are you certain—"

"Yes. Please, go lie down. I'll help Mr. Arundel back to bed."

She watched her father rise slowly then walk stiffly to his bed chamber and close the door. Then she ignored her own exhaustion and turned to Mr. Arundel. "Let's get you to bed."

He waved off her offer of assistance and rose on his own. His face betrayed nothing, but he must have been in pain. She could see the fever rising in him again too. His face was once again flushed. Clearly these Royal Saboteurs had known what they were about choosing a man like Arundel to be one of them. Not only was he unnervingly observant and unfailingly astute, he seemed to have untapped strength and an instinct to protect. If she had wanted to devise a hero out of thin air, she imagined Arundel would come very close.

Belle went ahead of him, pushing her bed chamber door wide, closing the curtains over the dark window, and pulling back the bedclothes for him. For a moment, she looked at her bed with longing, but she couldn't allow herself to feel the weariness. If she did, she would collapse, and she had to stay strong.

Arundel paused in the doorway, leaning against it for support. Belle raised a brow. "Are we still pretending you do not need assistance?"

"We are," he said and stumbled to the bed. He fell on it clumsily, and she waited until he'd pulled himself onto the pillow—this time his face showing the pain—before she covered him.

"I'll get a lamp and writing instruments. That is, if you are still up to dictating a letter."

"I'll push through," he said.

When she returned a few moments later, his breathing was labored and his eyes had the glassy look of the sea after a storm. She had no desk, so she set paper and ink on the floor and lay down as she had when she was a child. She looked up. "Shall I date it?"

"Yes. The salutation is *Madam*."

Her handwriting might have been finer, but it was legible and in her mind, that was what counted. Generally, she only wrote out receipts and noted purchases and expenses in the ledger. But her father had taught both Maggie and Belle to read and write, knowing it was a skill they would need if they hoped to find a good position when they grew older. As it turned out, Maggie had married well and had no need of work and Belle had stayed at the shop and used her skills to help her father.

She wrote the salutation then looked up expectantly. Mr. Arundel was staring at the ceiling, his face pale except for two patches of color in his cheeks. "Ready?"

"Yes." She held her pen aloft.

"Write this: Please forgive my impudence in writing to you uninvited. Although we have not met, your reputation precedes you."

"Slow down," Belle said. "I'm trying to work out how to spell *impudence*."

He spelled it for her and then *precedes* as well, which was a good thing because she had been certain the word had an *O* and apparently it was all *E*s.

"Ready?" he asked, and she made a sound of assent. "I am a special friend of your husband and find myself in need of—no, put desperate need of assistance. *Assistance* is spelled—"

"That one I know." But she was never certain where to double the *S*es. Still, she had *some* pride.

"You may find me at"—he glanced at Belle—"put the name of your shop here and the number on Fenchurch Street. When you've done that, let me have it."

Belle finished, waited for the ink to dry, then handed him the paper. He squinted and read it over. If he thought her handwriting poor, he made no comment. "Close it with *Your servant* and then *Arundel*."

"Do you want to sign it?"

"No. I need to close my eyes for a moment." His voice trailed off on the last word.

"Mr. Arundel, where do I send it?"

"I don't know the street, but address it to *The Right Honorable Lady Keating*."

He closed his eyes then and was quiet. Belle finished the letter then while it dried, she opened the window, collected water in the washbasin from the still falling rain, and set it aside. When she moved to close the window again, she thought she saw a movement in the doorway across the street. That shop had once been an apothecary, but the owner's son had gone to seek his fortune in Canada and apparently found it as he'd sent for his parents to join him. The space was presently unoccupied. Belle stared at the shop but now saw no sign of anyone. She closed the window and the curtains then blew out the lamp and parted the curtains a sliver again. She watched the shop for several moments and saw nothing.

With a shake of her head, she decided she was seeing things. She gathered the letter and the writing supplies and carried them out of the bed chamber, leaving Arundel with a cool cloth on his forehead. Then she tucked the letter in her pocket, donned her cloak, and went downstairs. She almost went to the front of the shop but still had an uneasy feeling about that movement at the apothecary. Instead, she went into the back room and out the door into a narrow walkway. The walkway was usually packed dirt, but after the hard rains, the mud and water rose to her ankles. She ignored it and trudged through until she arrived at the gate of the church. Though there was not a cemetery, that she knew of, in the church yard, she had an uneasy feeling about cutting through. Still, she couldn't stand out here in the cold and the wet all night. If she stayed out too long, her clothes would become soaked. She'd placed the letter in an empty tea tin, keeping it relatively safe, but now she needed to find a lad to search out Lady Keating in this awful weather. Belle could only hope the lady was sensible and had stayed home this evening.

Hurrying, Belle made her way through the dark church yard and emerged on the other side. She hurried past the church, down the street, and crossed to another street. She was well and truly soaked now, the water making squishing sounds in her boots. Ahead she saw the yellow lights of a public house where she and her father sometimes dined and was glad to see the owner had stayed open. But then she supposed even in rainstorms, men wanted their beer and ale.

Belle pushed inside, noting the dining room was less crowded than usual. She shoved her dripping hood off her head and went straight to the bar. The publican, a Mr. Plumkins, gaped at her. "Miss Howard! You are soaking wet. Is anything amiss?"

"No, Mr. Plumkins. My father and I are both well. But I wondered if I could ask for a favor."

"Let me get you a cider. You look chilled clear through."

"No thank you, sir," she said firmly. "My father is waiting anxiously for my return. But I wondered if you have a boy you trust to deliver a tin of tea for me."

"I have a boy, but surely the tea delivery can wait. The rain has eased for the moment, but it could come down in sheets again like this." He snapped for effect.

"This is a special order," Belle said and leaned close so that the men standing nearby would not hear. "For a baroness. If I keep her waiting, we may lose her business."

"I see. I see. Very well. Jacob!"

A boy of perhaps ten rose from the stool he'd occupied behind Mr. Plumkins and doffed his hat. Belle produced the tin of tea. "I need you to deliver this to Lady Keating. I don't know the street, but it's somewhere in Mayfair. You'll know how to find her?"

The boy nodded. He need only find a tavern near Mayfair with servants from the wealthy houses, and they would point him in the right direction. Now came the part Belle disliked—the parting of coin. She pulled a penny from her skirts. She'd thought of paying less but knew the penny would be a strong enticement. "This is for your trouble," she said. "The baroness will give you tuppence when you deliver the tea." Belle had no idea if this was true or not, but Jacob would demand it, and then the lady could make up her own mind. In any case, her calculations had worked because the boy's eyes lit up. In a blink, the penny and the tea tin were gone from her hands, and the boy was pulling his cap over his ears and tucking his treasures into his shirt.

Then he was gone, out into the dark, wet night. Belle turned to Plumkins. "Thank you, sir. I'd best get back to my father."

"Be careful, Miss Howard."

"I will."

Belle heaved a sigh of relief when she stepped back into the shop. She locked the door and shed the cloak, heavy now with water. She went through the shop, checking all was as it should be, then upstairs to the flat. There she laid the cloak on a chair before the fire, where it began to steam. She sat on the floor and removed her boots and stockings then took her hair down as well. Feet bare, she padded into her bed chamber to fetch dry clothing. Though she was wet and cold, she paused at Arundel's bedside and felt his forehead. It was burning hot, and she dipped the now hot cloth in cool water and pressed it to his face then laid it on his forehead.

Finally, she gathered dry clothing and went into the parlor to change. When her wet clothes were strewn before the fire and she wore a clean shift, she went to lie down on the couch. Her eyes were so heavy she could barely keep them open. In a half hour she would go down and hope Jacob returned with a reply. But she could spare a few minutes to rest. Unfortunately, as soon as she lay down, she heard a moan and pushed herself up. She returned to her bed chamber to find Arundel had thrown off the bedclothes. His arms were over his face, and when she went to him and tried to return his arms to his side, he resisted. He was, as always, amazingly strong for a man radiating heat like a furnace.

Belle considered leaving him as he was, but the fire was low and she had no dry wood to add to it. The room would soon be cold. "Mr. Arundel," she said, bending over him. "You must keep the blanket on. You'll catch a chill."

"Hot," he said. "So bloody hot."

She ignored the strong language and pulled the covers up and over him. Gently, she tried to push his hands down to his sides, but he caught her wrists, and when she looked down at him, his gaze was fixed on her face. She couldn't see his expression clearly in the firelight, and she doubted he could see her at all, given her back was to the fire, but he pulled her down to him until her face was just a few inches from his.

"Let me go, Mr. Arundel."

"Go then," he said but didn't release her. "Go, if that's what you want."

Belle ceased tugging her wrists for a moment, realizing Arundel wasn't speaking to her. She didn't know to whom he spoke, but he must be in the depths of some sort of dream.

"Mr. Arundel. It's Belle Howard."

"Go, if that's what you want," he said again, seeming not to hear Belle. "Go, Clara. Away with you. But don't come back to me. Don't come crying back."

Belle felt a shiver of ice race up her back. Who was Arundel speaking to? Who was Clara and what had she done?

Whatever it was, he'd warned her not to come back. Had she? Or had she left him and never looked back?

Belle had the fleeting thought that if Arundel had been hers, she would not have left him. If a man like that loved her—and surely what she heard in his voice was love or at least the last vestiges of it—she would never walk away.

"Mr. Arundel," Belle said, her voice gentle now. "Release me. You're not well."

"Clara." His voice was anguished, and his grip unrelenting. His eyes opened slowly, and though they were unfocused, they settled on her. She waited for him to realize she was not this Clara and release her, but instead his gaze traveled from her eyes to her mouth. He lingered there, lingered so long her mouth went dry and she felt the need to wet her lips. At this gesture, he gave a low chuckle that sent a shiver up her back. It was not a shiver of fear but of desire. Belle had never had a beaux, but she had felt the stirrings of longing before. Years ago a young man had begun to come into the shop every week. He had been attending Cambridge but in London for the summer. She'd waited all week for him to come in and buy his tea. Sometimes she didn't even wait on him, leaving Maggie to do it. He always smiled at Maggie appreciatively, and Belle had pretended, when she was alone, he had looked at her that way.

The shiver she'd felt now, with Arundel, was that same feeling she had when she'd see the young gentleman at the door of the shop. But this time it was not an unattainable desire. This time a fevered man—but still a man—lay in her bed and held her close. She wanted him, and he wanted her too. It was the middle of the night and, she realized now, as his gaze dropped to her neck, that she wore only her shift. If her father should find them together...

Belle watched as Arundel's eyes traveled lower and his lips parted with pleasure. She looked down, following his gaze, and gasped when she saw the neck of her shift was loose enough to give him a view of her breasts. Not that she thought he could see much in the dim light, but clearly he saw something as evidenced by the low timbre of his voice when he spoke. "Come here," he said.

Heat flooded Belle at the low note of yearning in his tone. Warmth spread from her cheeks down to her neck, her breasts, and then seemed to coil like a lazy serpent in her belly.

"Mr. Arundel," Belle said, making a last attempt to rouse him from whatever dream his fevered mind had conjured. "You must release me." Her voice was low and husky, and she did not even recognize it as hers. He didn't release her, and she hardly blamed him. She didn't sound at all like a woman who wanted to be set free.

Then to her surprise, he did release one wrist. Before she could pull back, though, he reached for her waist, his hot hand all but searing her through the thin fabric of her shift. With a gentle pressure, he pulled her closer, so close she could smell the scent of tea on his breath.

"Belle," he murmured. His use of her name shocked her enough, but then his hand slid from her waist up her ribs to cup her small breast through the thin linen of the shift. She gasped, and he took that opportunity to catch her lower lip between his teeth.

The bite was gentle, not even a bite at all, just a tug to keep her mouth near his. It worked. Belle froze, and then she did something she never thought she would do. When Arundel released her lip and opened the hand on her breast, clearly giving her the option to refuse him, Belle leaned closer and pressed her lips to his. She didn't know why she did it. Perhaps because her unsated desire finally got the best of her. Perhaps because though Arundel was fevered and clearly not in his right mind, he was a handsome man who made her head spin. Perhaps because she was a spinster and didn't want to cross into becoming a thornback—the term society liked to use to refer to women approaching thirty—without kissing at least one man who truly desired her.

She hadn't considered he would kiss her back. She pressed her lips to his, unsure what to do next, and then shocked when his mouth moved beneath hers. He returned her slight pressure and gave it back to her, moving his lips to brush them along hers. At the same time, his hand returned to her breast, his thumb finding her nipple, hard now and straining, and caressed it with that same lazy stroke.

Belle felt as though she might combust from the heat engulfing her now. Every part of her was too hot. No wonder people disrobed when they went to bed together. She was unbearably warm and undeniably aware of the tingling between her legs. She wanted to press her hand there, to ease that tension.

A crack of thunder some miles away finally broke through the stupor that had come over her. Lightning flashed, again distant, but close enough that she could see Arundel's face. His eyes were bright with fever, and not at all focused. He probably wouldn't even remember this in the morning. Whereas she—she would remember it the rest of her life. But it was probably best if this kiss was all there was to remember.

Belle pulled back, forcing her body away from his touch and his heat. Everything in her resisted. She wanted to move closer, to crawl into the bed beside him and press bare flesh against him. But she was supposed to be nursing him. She was supposed to be caring for him, and instead she was taking advantage—or at least allowing him to take liberties.

"Wait," he said, but this time she was firm and managed to extricate her wrist from his grasp.

"Rest now, Mr. Arundel," she said as she straightened and pulled her shift higher to preserve her modesty. "Close your eyes."

He obeyed, and a moment later was breathing deeply. *Asleep*, she thought as she dipped the cloth in cold water and laid it on his fever brow again. In the morning, he'd think all that happened a dream—if he remembered at all. It seemed somehow fitting that her first kiss should be from a man at death's door who wouldn't even remember it. Or if he did, he'd think he'd been dreaming about another woman. Clara—whoever she was—had meant something to Arundel.

Except...

Had she imagined it or had Arundel said *her* name at one point? Hadn't he said *Belle* before he cupped her breast and nipped her lip? So had he known he was touching her or had he just been muttering and she thought he'd said her name? Maybe she'd *wanted* to hear her name.

No, she had certainly heard it. But she wanted his use of her name to mean something, and that was where she must be careful. It meant nothing. Their kiss meant nothing. He was injured and delirious and she shouldn't have allowed it to happen.

Except she wasn't sorry at all. She'd never forget their encounter.

And wasn't that pathetic?

Still, a pockmarked shopgirl must have something to keep her warm at night.

Thinking of warmth, she stoked the fire in the hearth in an attempt to keep it from going out then returned to the parlor, which had a similarly banked fire. She wished she or her father had thought to bring in more wood this morning. It might be dry enough by now to burn. As it was, she must shiver on the couch in only her shift and threadbare wrap.

She heard her father's quiet snores coming from his dark room and was glad someone was resting. She should be sleeping herself. She was exhausted but had pushed herself so long and so hard that her mind wouldn't quiet. Who was this Lady Keating she had sent a missive to? Was she a Royal Saboteur? How would she lend Arundel assistance? Clearly, from what Arundel had had her write in the letter, he wasn't actually acquainted with the lady and only knew her by reputation.

It fascinated Belle that women could be agents for the Crown. She didn't know why she hadn't ever thought such a thing possible before. The idea was ingenious. No one would ever suspect a woman, most especially not a man. Belle had learned long ago when dealing with her men customers to allow them to think her suggestions or recommendations came from her father. It was easier if her male patrons believed her father sought out exotic teas and bought them from the exporters at St. Katharine Docks.

Belle allowed her eyelids to flutter shut, grateful that sleep finally closed its grasp on her. She felt the slow slide into oblivion just as a clink registered in the back of her mind. Her mind, overly tired and desperate for respite, tried to push that clink aside. But Belle opened her eyes and stared at the dark room, listening.

She didn't hear the clink again, but she heard something else—the telltale sound of someone moving in the shop below. It was dark and whoever it was did not know their way about. They were quiet, and yet she heard the shuffle of feet and a small thud as the thieves bumped into a shelf.

Her father's snores continued uninterrupted, and Belle hoped for a moment that she was dreaming or imagining she heard bumps in the night. But she knew that clink. It was the sound the bell above the door made when someone grasped it to keep it from tinkling. She'd caught that bell herself a thousand times when she'd wanted to enter the shop quietly.

Fear made her heart thud harder and made her limbs cold. Her skin prickled with awareness, and she had the urge to find somewhere to hide. Instead, she drew herself up and took a breath. There would be no hiding, no allowing some thief to take her tea or her coin. She didn't think it likely any thief would be able to breach the safe with their meager profits or her special Pan Long Yin Hao. Truth be told, she was more concerned about losing the Pan Long Yin Hao.

Belle rose, tiptoed to the hearth, and grasped the fire poker. She would brandish it at the thieves and scare them away. Most thieves fled at the first sign of trouble.

She started for the door to the flat then stopped dead. What if these were not thieves but the men who had tried to kill Arundel? What if they had come to finish what they'd started? Belle, poker in hand, hesitated long enough that she heard the footfall behind her.

The intruder was not downstairs, but inside the flat.

Chapter Ten

"My head is already pounding," Hew said, swerving back to avoid having his brains bashed in by the poker Miss Howard swung at him. "Don't make it worse."

"I thought you were—"

"Shh," he said, putting a finger to his lips. He could hear the men's low murmurs downstairs, which meant they could hear their voices above—if they listened. The room swayed and Hew moved with it, causing Miss Howard to rush to his side. She put a hand on his bare back, and her touch felt cold against his hot flesh.

"Go back to bed," she hissed.

"I'd rather die standing," he muttered, though he was likely to fall over at any moment. "Those men downstairs are here for me."

"I was afraid of that." She lifted the poker again. "I'm ready."

Hew stared at her. "You are—no. You are not going down there."

"They are in *my* shop." She narrowed her eyes. "You certainly cannot defend us."

"Give me the poker." He snatched it out of her hand and had to refrain from rolling his eyes. She thought she would defend them this way? He'd even warned her before he'd taken the weapon from her. "Now go lock yourself in your father's bed chamber and don't come out until I—"

"Until you fall over and they finish you off?" If there was such a thing as a whispered shout, Miss Howard had perfected it. "Sir, I did not spend all this time nursing you to have you murdered in my tea shop."

"I want to believe you care, but I think you are more concerned about your customers not wanting to buy their tea where a dead body lay just hours before."

"It's certainly not good for business." She grabbed a small broom with a long metal handle from beside the hearth. "I'm ready."

She'd sweep them to death, apparently. He didn't have time to argue any further. The men sent to kill him would finish searching the shop and be on their way to the flat any moment. Cautiously, Hew opened the door leading down the steps. The staircase was steep, and he'd be at a disadvantage on the way down. But strangely enough, the men hadn't opened the door at the bottom of the stairs. "This might be an ambush," he said to Miss Howard over his shoulder. If the men had heard them arguing above, they might decide to simply lie in wait below. "Wait for my signal before opening the door to the shop."

She nodded and started down behind him, broom at the ready. He held his poker in one hand, his other hand clamped firmly on the railing. He didn't know why his legs should feel so wobbly when it was his side that had been stabbed.

Behind him, Miss Howard inhaled sharply. "No!"

"What's—" Before he could even ask the matter, she pushed past him, almost causing him to lose his precarious balance, and raced for the door. "No!" he cried before she could open it. "The am—"

She flung the door open and swung her broom wildly as two men jumped out at her.

"—bush," Hew finished. "Damn it all to hell." He raced down the stairs to rescue her, his nose finally registering what she must have smelled moments before.

Something was burning.

At the base of the stairs, Miss Howard batted the broom and waved it about, keeping the attackers at bay. She'd surprised them, which was why the ploy had worked, but there were two of them and one of her. Any moment, one would grab her and the other do away with her. Hew chose the man slightly behind her and lunged, his poker wielded like a sword his ancestors might have used at Agincourt. His would-be assailant, a large man in a wet coat and dripping hat, was armed with a knife. Little use against a poker.

The man didn't waste any effort trying to fight. He backed up and then ran, toppling over shelves of tea with a crash as he raced for the door. He flung it open and disappeared into the darkness. The door open now, the scent of wet earth mingled with the smell of smoke and bergamot. Hew rounded on the other attacker. That man, short and slim, saw him coming and began to retreat from Miss Howard's slashing broom. Hew recognized the man as the one who had stabbed him. He couldn't see the man's eyes as he wore a tricorn pulled low, but he could see the dark bruise on the man's jaw where Hew had struck him during the attack.

"You!" Hew lunged for him, but the attacker saw him coming and pushed a tea set off a shelf, causing the porcelain to shatter on the floor and Hew to throw up his arms to shield his face from flying shards.

"How dare you!" Miss Howard yelled, bringing the broom down on the attacker's shoulder. Hew heard the soft thud, and though the broom didn't do much damage, he imagined it still hurt.

Covering his head to protect it from further blows, that man fled through the open door too. Miss Howard rounded on Hew. "You should have left *me* with the poker."

Perhaps he should have.

"Over there!" she said, pointing to a small fire creeping its way up a far wall. "We need water."

"There's plenty of water to be had outside." Indeed, it was still raining.

"I'll fetch a bucket."

She started for the door behind the counter, paused to pat where pockets might be if she was wearing a gown instead of only a shift and wrapper, then swore. "The keys are upstairs."

"I have them," came a voice from the stairway. Hew recognized it as Mr. Howard. He turned in time to see the man take a faltering step, miss, and tumble down the last half dozen stairs.

"Father!"

Hew cursed the fever burning through him. It made him slow and sluggish. He had lunged for the stairs but was too late to catch Mr. Howard. The man landed in a heap at the base of the steps. Hew fell to his knees, quickly assessing injuries. Howard lifted a hand to his head, where Hew could already see a large lump rising. "Don't move," he ordered.

Miss Howard fell on her knees beside Hew and her father, she reached to take his head, but Hew grabbed her hands. "Don't move him."

"I'm fine," Howard said. "Just bumped my head. Belle—" He held out a hand with the keys, and she looked at the keys, glanced at her father, then snatched the keys and raced to the back room.

"Lie still," Hew ordered, but Howard waved him off and sat up.

"I'm fine. Where are the deuced fellows?"

Hew glanced at the open shop door. "Gone." At least he hoped they were gone. Miss Howard rushed back into the shop, dragging a bucket with water sloshing over the rim to the growing fire. Hew struggled to his feet, but by the time he'd reached her, Miss Howard was racing out the front door. "Wait—" he called, but she was outside.

Hew wasn't entirely certain the attackers weren't waiting outside for them. He'd thought Miss Howard would fetch water out the back door again, but she had probably wanted to go to the nearest source. He made it to the door just as she returned, lugging the bucket. "I'll take it," he said.

She looked up at him. "And rip open your stitches again? I think not." She shouldered past him and doused the fire again.

"Oh, my eyes!" came a high female voice. An older woman in a froth of ruffles and a white cap over her hair stepped in from the drizzle and stared, open-mouthed at Hew, who realized he wore only his trousers and was bare-chested.

"Mrs. Price!" Miss Howard said on her way back to the door. "Thank you for coming. Would you see to my father?"

"Mr. Howard?" She dragged her gaze away from Hew. "Oh, dear." She must have spotted him, still sitting on the floor with his hand to his head. She went to him, the lace and ruffles of her nightclothes undulating like waves on a sea as she moved.

"One more bucket, I think," Miss Howard said as she pushed past Hew and back into the night. Hew followed her this time, his eyes darting around for any sign of the attackers. Fenchurch Street was dark, but a few lights shone in windows and one or two people had opened their doors to peer outside and call to ask if assistance was needed. Miss Howard declined, saying the fire was all but out. The onlookers stayed where they were. Hew knew a fire at one shop could easily spread to other homes and businesses. Even with everything soaked through as it was, the danger of fire made everyone nervous.

Miss Howard dipped the bucket in the water standing on the street and then lugged it back into the shop. Hew felt momentarily helpless, a feeling he did not enjoy and had not been enjoying for what seemed days and days now. He didn't see the attackers, but that didn't mean they weren't there. And they would certainly come back, targeting this shop until they'd accomplished their mission. Hew couldn't let that happen to the Howards. He had no choice but to leave or they could lose everything, and that would be the worst way to repay their kindness to him. He stumbled away from the shop. If he could flag a hackney, he could be driven to Mivart's. It would be harder and easier, in some ways, for the assassins to kill him there.

Hew took a few more steps, didn't see the curb as it was covered with water, and splashed down into the street. He all but fell over just as a large vehicle rolled into view, the horses' hooves heading right for his head.

"Wait!" Miss Howard called, holding a hand up and racing in front of the coach. Hew couldn't tell if the coach slowed or not, but Miss Howard grasped his shoulder and pulled him back from the street.

"Stop saving me," he said, glowering up at her.

"Stop trying to get yourself killed."

The door to the coach opened, and both of them turned to look as an elegant woman stepped out. She wore a pelisse with a hood that placed her face in shadow, but she moved with authority and grace. "Which one of you is Arundel?" she said. Hew stiffened and her head turned toward him. "You?"

He waited, making no move to either confirm or deny her question.

She moved through the high water toward him, heedless of her clothing. "I am Lady Keating," she said. "You wrote?"

"My lady," Hew said, relief flooding through him like a thousand rainstorms. "You came."

"He's injured," Miss Howard said immediately. "Knife wound. The attackers came back tonight and tried to burn down my shop."

Lady Keating glanced at Miss Howard then back at Hew. "Then I suppose we should be on our way. Robert!" At the name, an outrider jumped down and sloshed toward Hew and Miss Howard. The man offered Miss Howard his arm, and she waved it off and pointed to Hew.

"I am staying."

"No, you're not," came her father's voice. He stood in the shop doorway, the light from the carriage lamps flickering over him. Mrs. Price stood at his side, supporting him, while he leaned his other shoulder on the shop doorway. "This has gone far enough. I won't have you murdered in your bed or among the tea tins."

Miss Howard took the outrider's hand and stood. "Nor I you. Once Arundel is gone, so is the danger."

"Not necessarily," Lady Keating said. "I suggest all of you come with me."

Miss Howard rounded on her. "And leave my shop? I think not madam—er, lady."

"I will stay with the shop," Howard said.

"No," Hew and Miss Howard said together. They glanced at each other in shock, and Miss Howard gave Hew a fierce scowl.

"He can stay with me," Mrs. Price said. "He has a nasty bump on his head. I'll tend it."

"Perfect." Hew struggled to his feet with the help of Robert the outrider. "Keep out of sight and send word if you have any trouble. Miss Howard, take this man's hand and get in the coach."

She looked at her father, then at the coach.

"Go," her father said. "This is not up for discussion."

Hew thought Miss Howard might just stomp her foot in a show of petulance. Instead, she sloshed past the outrider, ignoring his help, and climbed into the coach. Hew wished he could have done the same, but he would have ended up face down in the muddy water. Instead, he allowed the outrider to help him into the coach, where he sank into the squabs beside Miss Howard. She gave him a look that stabbed almost as deep as his wound and turned her back to him.

Lady Keating climbed in last, taking a seat across from them. A moment later, the coach lurched away, leaving Mr. Howard slumped in the doorway of Howard's Teas & Treats with Mrs. Price at his side.

***

Mrs. Price had been waiting for this moment for years. Belle knew the thought was uncharitable, but it was true. Mrs. Price had been trying to sink her claws into Belle's father for as long as she could remember. Maggie had always thought it was sweet. She'd even tried to play matchmaker, but Belle had been glad her father showed little interest. In fact, he'd seemed oblivious to Mrs. Price's efforts at flirtation.

Now, he was in her clutches.

Oh, very well, she thought as the carriage moved slowly away from Fenchurch Street and toward Mayfair. That characterization was a bit dramatic. Still, Belle would like to have cared for her father herself. And that was just selfishness because even this afternoon Mrs. Price had demonstrated she was a better nurse than Belle. Besides, Belle would not be away long. She'd see Mr. Arundel settled then return to Fenchurch Street to help repair the damage from the fire to the shop and they'd be open again in just a few days.

She sighed with impatience at the slow-moving conveyance. The rain had made the roads worse than usual and standing water impeded their progress further. She glanced at Arundel. Lady Keating had given them both blankets to ward off the chill from their damp clothing, but Arundel was still shivering, and his hands were white knuckled on his knees. Clearly, the journey was causing him pain. Belle couldn't even fathom how he was still upright.

First, he had shocked her by appearing in the flat when she'd heard the intruders. How could he have possibly heard them and known they were a danger? She'd not even been injured and almost slept through their break-in. Then he had fought them off—with her help, of course—and insisted on working with her to douse the fire. All of this while battling a life-threatening injury and fever.

Who was this man?

Belle glanced at Lady Keating, who was also watching Arundel fighting his pain. The two women exchanged a look then Lady Keating opened a compartment in her seat and withdrew a dark bottle. She uncorked it and handed it to Arundel. "Drink this."

He took the bottle, sniffed, then drank a large sip and handed it back.

"He has seen a doctor?" Lady Keating asked.

"Yes, and a surgeon who stitched the wound before he came to stay with us," Belle answered.

"They gave him laudanum, I assume," Lady Keating said.

"He won't take any." Belle realized she'd left the laudanum in the flat, so even if Arundel had agreed to a dose, she had none to offer.

"I have something that will help with the pain. I'll need to take a look at what we're dealing with first, though."

"*You* need to take a look?" Arundel said. "No."

Lady Keating didn't argue, but Belle saw the tightening around her mouth and doubted the conversation was over. Though the woman had white hair and her face showed the lines of age, she carried herself with an authority that indicated she was used to being obeyed. "I don't think I caught your name," Lady Keating said to Belle, which was a polite way of indicating they hadn't been introduced.

Arundel waved a hand. "Lady Keating, might I present Miss Belle Howard."

"It's Isabelle Howard," Belle said. "But my friends call me Belle."

"Miss *Isabelle* Howard," Arundel said, "the Baroness Keating."

"I'd curtsey," Belle said, "but I'm not sure how one does that in a coach." Or even outside of a coach.

"It's not necessary, Miss Howard. The shop where there was a small fire—was that your family's shop?"

"Yes, my father's tea shop. The two ruffians who stabbed Mr. Arundel set it on fire."

"The fire was contained?"

"Yes. I did not have a chance to assess the damage, but once Mr. Arundel is settled, I will return and do so."

"Hmm." Lady Keating pursed her lips. She offered the bottle to Arundel again, but he shook his head. Lady Keating replaced it in the seat compartment and closed it. "Are you in London on a mission for my husband?" Lady Keating asked.

Her husband? Her husband was part of Arundel's secret group?

"No. I just finished a mission and am in London on holiday."

"I think perhaps your mission followed you here." She gave him a rueful smile.

"It does appear that way. I haven't been able to write to Baron and explain—"

"I'll take care of that. I can give him the basic details. I want no specifics, and it's best if we don't commit them to paper at any rate. Winn can put two and two together easily enough." The carriage seemed to slow. "Ah, here we are."

Belle peered out the window. A man with an umbrella had opened an iron gate, wide enough to allow the carriage to pass through. The gate itself was very tall and designed to block the view of the house from the street. In fact, the house was set back far enough that the coach had to continue for another minute before pausing in front of the house. The door opened, and a footman offered a hand to Lady Keating. She took it and Belle followed. Once out of the coach, Belle turned back. "He needs assistance."

"Fetch a pallet," Lady Keating said.

"No," Arundel argued, waving away the footman's help. "I can walk."

Lady Keating gave Belle a look of quiet exasperation, and Belle smiled. It was comforting to know she was no longer alone in this. "Did you prepare the room?" Lady Keating asked a woman who came forward.

"Yes, my lady. The maids are finishing now."

Lady Keating gave orders to her staff and started inside. Belle knew she was meant to follow, but she looked behind her at the short drive and the gate she'd passed through. The entire property appeared to be surrounded by the iron fence. Vines and bushes grew along it, making the grounds difficult to see from the outside. She turned back to the house and looked about, trying to keep her mouth from dropping open. She'd never been in a house like this. How wealthy must Baron Keating be to afford a house in Mayfair—not a town house and not a terraced property, but a freestanding home with grounds?

The drizzle was beginning to soak through her blanket, and she followed the staff inside a large foyer. Except for the lamps the servants carried, the house was dark, and Belle noted that some of the furnishings were covered with white sheets that gave the place an eerie feeling. Belle did not know much about the upper classes—save their preferences with regard to tea—but she did know they covered couches and chairs when they traveled to avoid the accumulation of dust. "Have you just returned from a trip?" she asked Lady Keating, who led the small party up the stairs. She moved very slowly, which Belle assumed had to do with the way Arundel was struggling. The lady herself looked quite healthy and spry.

"No, I am preparing to embark. In fact, if not for the rain, I would have already departed. It's fortunate your letter reached me," she said to Arundel. "Are you quite certain you don't want any assistance? The stairs do continue." She gestured to a generous curve in the stairs as they led to the second floor.

"I have it," he panted.

Belle hoped he didn't topple down the steps or rip out his stitches. Fortunately, someone else was here to sew them. She'd leave his care to those more qualified.

"I'm sorry if I have forced you to postpone your trip," Arundel said, leaning against the wide stair railing. "I didn't know who else to contact."

"You were right to send for me," Lady Keating said. "You'll be much safer here than above a shop, especially since whoever wants you dead had tracked you there. They'll not be able to track you here, and if they do, they won't be able to get in. And you haven't delayed me at all. As I said, that was the rain's doing. We'll have you fixed up and then I will be on my way."

"But…" Belle all but tripped on a step. "But you cannot leave. He needs someone to nurse him."

"I'm afraid I must leave. But not to worry, you may stay and nurse him. I'm sure he will be well in a few days."

Belle looked at Arundel, whose face was white as a ghost and who was struggling to climb the next step. Blood had seeped through the blanket he held against his chest, meaning his stitches had opened again.

"Thomas," Lady Keating said calmly. "Catch him before he falls."

The footman behind Arundel stepped forward and caught the man as his eyes rolled back and he fell. Another footman joined Thomas and the two hefted Arundel between them and carried him the rest of the way.

Belle stood at the top of the staircase and wondered if she could make a run for it. If she didn't leave now, she might never get away.

"Are you coming, Isabelle Howard?" Lady Keating asked.

Belle met the other woman's eyes. It seemed to Belle that the baroness knew exactly what she'd been thinking and wouldn't stop her if she ran. Belle was tempted. Her shop was in a shambles and her father injured. The desire to return to Fenchurch Street was strong. But then so was the desire to stay here. Something pulled at her when she thought of Arundel. Responsibility?

Perhaps.

Duty?

That was part of it.

The memory of the kiss they'd shared?

Belle sighed. She was in trouble, and she knew it. Worse, she wasn't going anywhere.

Chapter Eleven

"This is my friend, er—" Lady Keating made a vague gesture to a man standing near the windows of the chamber they'd just entered. Belle was looking about the chamber, which was obviously a hastily prepared guest chamber. It was large, the size of half her flat. A hearth with a crackling fire was situated on one wall and a large bed with four posts was on the opposite wall. A maid was folding the Holland covers and Arundel was laid on the large bed even as another maid was still tucking the fresh sheets under the mattress.

Belle's gaze traveled over several other furnishings—chairs, couch, rug, dressing table—before it returned to the man stepping away from one of the windows. He was dressed in black and was small in stature for a man, perhaps only a few inches taller than Belle. He had brown skin that looked weathered and lined from age or sun, and his black hair was worn close to his head. He had a long nose that reminded her of the masks she'd seen people wear as part of a costume to represent plague doctors of the past.

"Er—let's call him Smith," Lady Keating said, indicating the man who had gone to Arundel's side.

"Smith?" Belle raised her brows. This man was not a Smith. The man-who-was-not-Smith raised Arundel's wrist and pressed two fingers to the inside. At the same time, he lifted Arundel's closed eyes, to look at the whites under the lids. "Is he a doctor?" Belle asked.

"Something like that," Lady Keating said. "I trust him with my life. He's traveled the world studying medicine and has an unparalleled knowledge of medicines and treatments. Shall we leave him to it?"

Belle, who had wanted to escape nursing the moment it had been thrust upon her found that she now wanted to stay. But Lady Keating's suggestion to leave had really been more of a directive. No doubt not-Smith would need to strip Arundel in order to see the wound, and it wouldn't be seemly for ladies to be present. Of course, she'd seen his wound and was quite familiar with his bare chest by now, but that wasn't the point.

"Would you like some tea?" Lady Keating asked, and those were powerful words.

"Yes," Belle said firmly. "Yes, I would."

She patted her pocket, where she had slipped the Pan Long Yin Hao from the safe before she'd found the bucket in the back room. The fire was her priority, but she would never have left the Pan Long Yin Hao at risk of destruction from the fire. It was too valuable—and too delicious.

She followed Lady Keating to another chamber, surprised to find it was not the drawing room but an antechamber to what was most likely her bed chamber. A fire burned here, and a small grouping of chairs had been arranged before the hearth. A maid stood at the ready, and Lady Keating asked her to bring tea.

"If you don't mind, I brought my own tea."

Lady Keating gave Belle a startled look and the maid lifted her brows in affront. Belle raised her hands in supplication. "I am certain your tea is of the best quality, but I brought a very special tea with me, and it would calm me to drink it."

"Very well." Lady Keating glanced at the maid. "Bring the tea things, and Miss Howard will prepare her tea."

"I would be happy to make you a cup as well," Belle offered.

Lady Keating inclined her head. "Very well." She gestured to her maid who left the two alone. Belle stood awkwardly, taking in this small, cozy room.

"Please sit." Lady Keating indicated the grouping of chairs and Belle sat gratefully, feeling the exhaustion wash over her as soon as she had a moment to feel the heat of the fire and the softness of the chair. "Do you always carry tea with you?"

Belle snapped her eyes open. She must stay awake. "I confess I do."

"I imagine when you own a tea shop you become quite particular."

"My father says I was born particular. From a very young age I had an ability to taste and smell the best blends of tea. We are a small shop on Fenchurch Street, but I like to think we have a reputation for selling the best tea in London."

"And how do you find such exquisite tea? I confess that though I am a copious tea drinker, I know little about the business."

"I go to the St. Katharine Docks and inspect the tea myself. I only buy the best."

Lady Keating raised a brow. "*You* go to the docks? Is that not dangerous?"

Belle knew how to be careful. "I know who to trust and have friends there who look out for me."

"It's good to have friends," Lady Keating said, glancing at the door as the maid entered with the tea tray. Belle had the feeling the baroness would have said more if her servant hadn't come in at that moment.

"Anything else, my lady?" the maid asked.

"No. You may retire. It will be an early morning, Flanners."

Belle did not wait for permission but began the process of preparing the Pan Long Yin Hao. She was aware Lady Keating watched her and heard the woman's intake of breath when she revealed the tea leaves. "Those are beautiful," Lady Keating said.

"This is the tea of the Emperor of China. I'm told it's hand rolled by royal servants."

"It's lovely. What is it called?"

"The man I bought it from called it Curled Dragon Silver Tips, but it's more commonly known as Pan Long Yin Hao."

"Commonly known? I have never heard of that."

Belle was in her element now. "It's a green tea. Green tea is harvested and prepared in a very special way. The leaves are plucked and then fired in a pan to make them soft. Next the leaves are rolled over heat. The farmers use their fingers, palms, and forearms to roll the tea. The process is quite intensive, I must say."

"It does sound so."

"Lastly, the tea is fired, blended, and ready to be consumed—or in our case, shipped."

"Fascinating. I usually drink—"

Belle held up a hand. It was probably rude to do this to a baroness, but she was curious to know if she had guessed the woman's preferences. "You prefer Irish Breakfast in the morning."

Lady Keating's eyes widened. "How do you know that?"

Belle felt her cheeks heat with pleasure and a little awkwardness. "It's a guess."

"A very good one. Do you know what I drink in the afternoon and evening?"

Belle tapped her forehead. "In the afternoon, I imagine it's an Earl Grey Cream. I think you like the vanilla."

Lady Keating's mouth dropped open.

"In the evening, you would drink a white tea." White tea was composed of only the tips of the leaves. This made it expensive and considered a delicacy, so naturally only members of the upper class consumed it with any regularity. "A Mutan White?"

"Sometimes."

She was close. She studied Lady Keating. "You want something slightly sweet," she said slowly. "A Yin Chen," she decided, smiling with victory.

"You are amazing," Lady Keating said.

"It's my profession." She shrugged.

"You are very good at it. Will I like the Curled Dragon Silver Tips?"

Belle peered at the tea and decided it had steeped long enough. "Shall we try it?"

She lifted the delicate china cups from the tray, silently admiring the craftsmanship. This was the sort of vessel meant for the Pan Long Yin Hao.

She handed one cup to Lady Keating and took the other, taking time to let the aroma of the tea bathe her senses before she tasted it. Lady Keating merely gave the tea time to cool then took a small sip. "Hmm," she said. "It's very smooth."

"Do you like the flavor? It's not for everyone."

"It's not what I am used to, but it's very good. I feel quite special, knowing I am drinking the same tea as the Chinese Emperor." She took another sip. "You sell this in your shop?"

"This blend? No. I had been saving it in my safe for the right customer. I'm afraid I may drink it all before I ever sell it."

"I'm sure that's a hazard of your work." She set down her teacup, and Belle knew the pleasantries were at an end. "I imagine having your shop attacked and a wounded man to care for is a hazard to which you are not accustomed. How is it Mr. Arundel came to be in your care?"

Belle told Lady Keating the events of the past twenty-four hours. The baroness did not interrupt, just nodded encouragement. Finally, she sat back in her chair. "I'm surprised he told you about his work for the Royal Saboteurs."

"He did not tell me very much. Perhaps I shouldn't have mentioned them to you. I assumed you knew of them, which was why he wrote to you."

"That is an astute assumption. I am quite familiar with the Royal Saboteurs. My husband is their leader."

Belle set down her empty teacup. "Then Mr. Arundel is exactly where he needs to be. Your husband can take custody of him. When you said you were leaving, I worried I would have to stay here with Arundel."

"No one can make you stay," Lady Keating said, "but you were not mistaken."

"I don't understand. If your husband—"

"My husband is not in London. He's at the Saboteurs' training camp. He's been training new agents and won't be returning to London for several more months."

"And what of Mr. Arundel?"

"I will send the baron word, of course, but even if he were here, there would be little he could do. Lord Keating is awful at a sick bed. He always likes to be doing something, you see. He does not like to be idle."

Belle thought that tending an injured man left little time for idleness. Perhaps the baron had been tending the sickbed incorrectly.

"I would stay with Mr. Arundel, of course, but I'm afraid I have another emergency. I mentioned before that I planned to leave? My granddaughter suffered a fall recently. She broke her wrist, which would be unfortunate enough, but she has two small children to care for. Her mother is on the Continent as her husband is the ambassador for Portugal, so she has asked me to come and help for a few weeks."

"I see."

"Yes. I hate to leave you with Mr. Arundel. I would take him with me, but I fear moving him."

"He should not be moved."

"You certainly do not have to stay with him. I can pay Mr.—er...What did I say his name was?"

"Smith."

"Right. I can pay Mr. Smith to tend him, and of course I will leave staff here. You can return to your shop, but I would advise you against that."

"Why?"

Lady Keating leaned toward her, seeming to impart a piece of wisdom. "The men after Arundel found you there once. It's unlikely they tracked us here, but even if they did, they cannot get onto the grounds or in the house. We have excellent security. Your shop is a different matter. These men can and will hurt you if they think they can use you or your father to get to Arundel."

"I need to write to my father immediately."

"I agree. You should both stay away from the shop and in hiding until Mr. Arundel recovers and can sort this out."

Belle didn't want to ask what would happen if Arundel didn't recover. Instead, she said, "All of this over a sabotaged railway."

"It's not about the railway. It's never about the obvious. In my experience it's almost always about money or power. Mr. Arundel discovered something that will cost someone dearly in money or power. Arundel may not even know what it is he's learned that's so dangerous. But he's a good agent. He will settle this matter."

"You seem to have a lot of faith in a man you've never met before."

"My husband chose him for the Royal Saboteurs. That means he's the best." Lady Keating rose. "Now, if you don't mind my saying so, you look exhausted. I asked my housekeeper to prepare another chamber. May I show you to it so you can rest?"

"What about Mr. Arundel?"

"He will be my concern tonight. And Mr. Smith will care for him as well. You need only sleep. You can make a decision about whether to stay here or return to your shop in the morning."

Once in the chamber she'd been given, Belle slumped against the door. She'd refused the offer of a maid but was relieved to find hot water and clean linens waiting for her. She stripped out of her bed clothes and resisted the urge to toss them all in the fire. Instead, she scrubbed her skin clean of the smell of smoke and the flecks of ash then put on a clean nightrail provided for her. If she hadn't been so weary, she might have explored the room. It was not as large as the one where they'd put Arundel, but it was still more luxurious than any room she'd ever slept in. Even Maggie's home didn't have rugs so plush or curtains so heavy. Belle climbed into the bed and pulled the mound of covers over her until she was buried under them.

She wondered where her father was sleeping right now. She wondered if Arundel was still alive. She wondered how her life had been turned so topsy-turvy.

And then she wondered nothing else because sleep descended on her, and she gratefully succumbed.

***

Every muscle in his body ached, including a few he hadn't known he possessed. For a long while, Hew lay still, assessing his injuries. His side still hurt as though someone had pressed a hot poker to it. His head pounded, which made his eyes throb in turn. His arms, legs, hands, feet, even his hair felt raw and wounded. But he was alive.

He was also clean. He caught the scent of soap and his skin felt free of the sweaty grime from the days of fever.

He opened his eyes and stared at the unfamiliar ceiling. Then he stared at the unfamiliar man who peered down at him. "Good morning, sir," the man said in accented English. Hew couldn't place the accent at the moment, not with all the pounding and aching distracting him.

"Feeling better?" the man asked.

"No," Hew croaked.

That didn't seem to deter the man, who lifted Hew's eyelids, one by one, then prepared a tincture from a liquid in a blue glass jar, which he unceremoniously dumped down Hew's throat. Hew would have objected, but the task was accomplished before he'd even realized what was about to happen.

This man had to be a quack. No one else would have been so efficient and skilled. "Your fever has broken, and I imagine you are hungry," the quack said.

Hew was hungry. He was starving, in fact.

"I think you might eat a little broth. I'll have some sent up. You can manage that?"

"Yes," came a feminine voice Hew recognized. He turned his head and found Miss Howard curled in a chair near the fire. She was watching him, her brown eyes calm.

"Good. Keep him quiet and still. I will return in the morning." The quack departed through a door, and Miss Howard took her lamp from the table and carried it to the bedside. Not only did she look less harried, she looked rested. Gone were the purple bruises under her eyes and the lines of strain. Her honey-blond hair looked clean and neatly secured at her nape with a ribbon. She wore a gown of some expensive material that didn't quite fit her, being too long and a bit too large.

He noticed she approached with her head tilted so her right side was visible and her left shielded. She was hiding her smallpox scars. Hew could imagine the teasing and pain she'd experienced because of them over the years. And yet, she was beautiful. It wouldn't be the first time people couldn't see past a small imperfection to the beauty beneath.

Good God, what had been in that tincture? Next he'd be writing a treatise on injustice in the world.

She paused and gave him a wary look. He'd been staring at her, and now she probably felt uneasy. "What is it?" she asked, and her hand went to her scarred cheek.

"What was in that tincture?" he said. "It's making me philosophical."

"That's an impressive word. You must be feeling better."

"Yes, when I dredge up the five syllable words, that's always the first sign of healing. You look rested."

She dipped her head again, and Hew wished he could put a finger under her chin and nudge her to look directly at him. She would doubtless not appreciate that gesture. She'd look at him directly when she trusted him, and now that he was feeling better—at least that's what everyone told him— he wouldn't be in her presence much longer. Certainly not long enough to develop any sort of relationship. That was a good thing.

"I should look rested," she said. "I slept for fourteen hours."

He tried to sit at that revelation, but pain seared through him. So apparently, he wasn't feeling *that* much better. "Have I been asleep fourteen hours?"

"No."

Thank God.

"Much longer than that."

"What?" He could have sworn she smiled at his dismay.

"You've been asleep two days."

"Lady Keating—"

"Has long since departed."

"What do you mean?" He'd come here to solicit her help. Had she gone to summon reinforcements?

"She had a family matter to attend to and took advantage of a break in the rain to leave Town. She left the morning after we arrived."

Hew squinted at the room, but with the curtains drawn, it was impossible to know what time of day it was. "And what morning is it now?" he asked.

"It's night. This will be our third night here."

He really had slept for days. With that much rest, he should feel better than he did, but then he probably hadn't eaten anything other than that awful tincture. He'd been right to send to Lady Keating. She'd have written to Baron of his state. Hew only wished he might have spoken to her and explained his theory of who was behind the attack on him. But now he could go to Baron himself, provided he wouldn't pass out on the train.

"What are you doing?" Miss Howard asked when he pushed the covers off. Hew looked down and discovered he wore a shirt and no trousers.

"Standing up. You should probably avert your gaze."

"You cannot stand up. Mr. Not-Smith said you had to stay in bed."

"Who?"

"The doctor. Lady Keating said his name was Smith."

"His name probably isn't Smith."

"Clearly."

"The quack also said my fever had broken," Hew continued. His head was pounding a little, but it was nothing he couldn't manage. "That means I can get out of bed."

The bed chamber door opened, and a maid entered with a tray. "Oh, dear," she said, eyes widening at the sight of Hew's bare legs. "Sir, you are not to get out of bed."

"Help me get him settled again, Mary," Miss Howard said. Together the two women managed to cajole his legs back under the covers and to prop him up on the pillows so Miss Howard could feed him broth. Hew immediately took the spoon and fed himself. The broth tasted amazing, which told him he must be starving. Whatever was in that tincture had begun to work its magic as well. He was indeed feeling better.

"Would you bring tea, Mary?" Miss Howard asked. "I think a chamomile would be soothing for Mr. Arundel."

"Yes, missus, I'll be right back. Would you like the tea you had last night?"

"The Mutan White? I can make it."

"No, no. It's no trouble for me. You stay here with Mr. Arundel." And she was gone. Hew wondered if she was the one who had bathed him or whether one of the male servants had done it. Humiliating to be so weak as to need a sponge bath, but he was grateful to be clean.

Hew sipped his broth and studied Miss Howard. "You're not used to servants."

"I don't like being waited on when I'm perfectly capable of doing things myself."

He ate more broth. "This isn't your house, and it would be more trouble to show you where everything is than just to do it for you. Besides, I imagine the servants want you out of the way."

Her eyes widened with affront. "Why? I'm no nob."

"You're not one of them either." His spoon scraped the bottom of the bowl, and she took the tray from him. "I'm surprised you stayed. I would have thought you'd have gone directly back to your shop."

She glanced sideways, and he recognized that he'd hit close to the mark. "That was your plan then?"

"Lady Keating said it wasn't safe to return, and I'd only put myself and my father in danger."

Hew knew it was her father that had mattered to her. Miss Howard didn't seem to worry overly much about herself. "She sent a footman and told my father to stay out of sight. We're hoping in all the confusion that your attackers didn't see him leave with Mrs. Price."

"Did Lady Keating think they tracked us here?"

"Possibly, but she said they can't get to us here."

"No, she'd have excellent security." Hew tried to push away the feeling of disappointment that washed over him. Miss Howard obviously hadn't stayed because she cared about him. He didn't even know why he should want her to stay for that reason or why he should want her to care. "This is all the more reason for me to get back on my feet."

She frowned at him. "I think I've just explained that we are very safe here."

"Yes, but you won't want to be trapped here. I need to find the men who attacked me, determine who hired them, and send him before a magistrate." And he'd have to do it quietly too. No need for the whole country to ask questions about who Hew Arundel was and what sort of business he had that made him a target. Baron would not welcome journalists sniffing about for information on the Royal Saboteurs.

"It's already past nine," she said, looking at a clock. "Perhaps you should start fresh in the morning."

He gave her a narrow look. He had the feeling she was humoring him because she thought him too weak to stand up much less track down attackers. He could prove her wrong, but he'd be cutting off his nose to spite his face. No doubt she was right that starting off in the dark of night with nothing but broth in his belly wouldn't be the best strategy.

"Fine. I'll go in the morning."

Her brows lifted in surprise. "Fine. I'll leave you to rest."

Hew was suddenly aware that he didn't want her to leave. "Stay," he said. She turned back. "We—er, haven't had our tea yet."

"I can take mine in my chamber."

"Where's the fun in that?"

She gave him a look that said where-is-the-fun-in-anything-to-do-with-you? He could hardly blame her. He'd come into her life and completely upended it. No doubt she'd be glad to see him go. He was not of the same mind. It was more than the fact that she was a beautiful woman, though that didn't hurt. Hew had been born curious. There was much more to Isabelle Howard than he knew, and he wanted to unwrap some of those layers. He'd have to engage her, find a way to open her up.

The chamber door opened again, and the maid entered with the tea tray this time. Hew smiled. "Tell me about your love of tea. When did you realize you—how shall we say it—had a discerning palate?"

"I'm sure there are other things you'd rather discuss. Thank you, Mary."

The maid bobbed a curtsy and left the room, closing the door with a knowing smile on her face. Hew supposed he wasn't being very clever, but he wasn't feeling quite himself either. And perhaps that's why he said the next thing that came into his head. "I don't care what we discuss. I just don't want you to leave."

Chapter Twelve

How was she supposed to react to a statement like that? It was bad enough that she hadn't stopped thinking about the kiss they'd shared the other night. The kiss…not only the kiss but also the way he'd touched her. It was humiliating to think that she couldn't seem to block that moment from her thoughts when Arundel probably had no memory of it. How his teasing now stung. Was she supposed to find it amusing when he pretended to have an interest in her?

"Yes, I'm sure you are fascinated by a spinster who works in a tea shop. Good night, Mr. Arundel." She started for the door then realized she'd left her tea. She went back and lifted her cup and teapot from the tray.

"Belle."

Her head snapped up at Arundel's use of her family's pet name.

"I do want you to stay. If you'd rather not talk about tea, we could speak of something else."

Belle opened her mouth to tell him not to call her Belle. She would have told him a half dozen other things as well, but then she looked into his eyes. They were such a pretty shade of blue and filled with what truly looked like sincerity. Was it possible he was not merely pretending to have an interest? It was dangerous to allow herself to hope. She had walled off that part of herself—the warm, soft part that wanted a man to look at her like she was the most important thing in the world. Like her scars didn't matter. Like he couldn't live without her.

Belle knew that would never happen. She'd been teased and humiliated too many times. And yet...

She was a flesh and blood woman, and Arundel was an attractive man. She'd liked his touch and his kiss. She wanted more. That was all the more reason to toss him a sarcastic rejoinder and be on her way. But how was she supposed to walk away from a man who looked at her the way Arundel was looking at her now? Men had looked at her with lust before. Men had looked at her with curiosity. But no man save her father had looked at her with the sort of warm affection she saw in Arundel's gaze.

She would be sorry if she stayed. She knew it. She already liked him far too much, and the more time she spent with him the more she would come to like him. But she set down her tea anyway, pulled the chair Mr. Not-Smith had been using earlier closer to the bed, and sat.

"Fine. I'll stay." And then because she felt awkward, she lifted his teapot. "Shall I pour your chamomile?"

He made a face. "Do you really think I will like chamomile?"

She couldn't stop the smile. "No, but it will be good for you." She poured him a cup and handed it to him. He looked at the cup as though it were filled with scorpions. Belle poured her own tea and held the warm china in her hands. She could appreciate fine china almost as much as fine tea.

"Won't you even try your tea?" Belle raised her brows.

"If I drink it, do I receive something more than broth to eat?"

"I didn't think to ask."

"Then he didn't forbid it. I'm starving."

That had to be a good sign, Belle thought. His fever had broken, and his appetite returned. "Start with the tea," she said.

With a sigh that indicated he felt he was long-suffering, Arundel drank the tea. He did not sip. He drank about half the cup down.

"Well?" she asked.

"Tolerable. It needs toast. With beans. And perhaps some mushrooms and tomatoes."

"And eggs and sausage—yes, I know what is served with breakfast. With the staff abed, you're unlikely to have all of that. I'm sure I can make some toast, though."

His eyes widened with interest. "Let's make a foray to the kitchens."

"Oh, no. You cannot go anywhere."

"I'm fine. Whatever that quack did, he did well. I feel a thousand times better. I'm tired of lying about."

"Yes, well, it wasn't long ago that we arrived, and you fainted on the stairs. I'd rather not watch you tumble down a flight and break your neck. Lady Keating's servants will not appreciate the extra chore of cleaning up your broken body."

"Your concern overwhelms me. I won't faint. In fact, it's widely known that men never faint."

Belle eyed him over the rim of her tea. "It looked like fainting to me."

"I lost consciousness. That is what men do. When you looked at my wound the other day, and I asked if you could sew, *that* was fainting."

"That was lack of sleep and nourishment. I'm much stronger now." She did not like the look in his eyes.

"If that's true, then help me with this bandage. I want to see the wound."

"*Why?*" She hadn't meant it to come out quite so forcefully, but the last thing she wanted to do was see that wound. She wouldn't mind seeing his chest again, but she'd forego the pleasure if it meant not having to see those awful stitches.

"I'd like to see if it looks as good as it feels. It still hurts like the devil, but the hurt is different, if that makes sense. Help me remove my shirt."

"Sir!"

"Don't go all missish on me now. You've seen me without my shirt. If it offends you, don't look."

"That's not it. Before—and now—" She watched in horror as he pushed the covers back again. "And you haven't any trousers on."

He looked down. "I see your objection there. I'll wrap the sheet about my waist." He began to rise to do just that, but Belle waved him down.

"Give me a moment." She set down her tea and went to the wardrobe. She pulled it open and found his trousers, cleaned and pressed, inside. "Here you are."

She carried them back to the bed and handed them to him. "Will you be able to don them on your own?" Apparently, he would not be swayed from the idea of getting out of bed. Belle knew a lost cause when she met it.

"Of course." He took the trousers and gestured for her to turn around. She gave him her back and heard him rustling about. She stared at the wall, her gaze fixed hard on the pale green vines of the paper on the other side of the room. Belle tried desperately not to think about what Arundel was doing in that moment.

And then his hand came down hard on her shoulder, pulling her back and off balance. "Oh!"

"I'm sorry," he said. "Bit of dizziness."

She swung around, grasping his arm and holding him tightly. "Get back into bed, Mr. Arundel. I told you I didn't want you to faint."

"Men don't—"

"Very well. I don't want you to lose consciousness."

"I'm fine." He gave her a direct look, and his gaze was clear. "I stood too quickly, and since I haven't had anything but broth, I lost my balance. I'll be better once I have that toast. You can turn back around."

Belle wanted nothing more than to turn her back to him again, but if she took her eyes off him, would he fall over? "If you still insist on doing this, I'd better help you."

"But your delicate sensibilities."

He was definitely teasing her now. "I promise nothing you have will interest those *delicate sensibilities*." This was an outright lie. Her heart was already pounding just from touching his arm. She did not dare think about the fact that he stood beside her in nothing more than a longish shirt.

"You're in no danger from fainting at the sight of my bare calf then?"

"It would take more than one of your puny legs to make me faint, sir." But she'd made the mistake of looking down at his legs, and they were not puny. In fact, he had nicely shaped calves, covered with fine dark fair. Then came rounded knees and a good portion of thigh. Thick thighs that seemed corded with muscle.

Her gaze shot back to his. "Let's get this over with." She didn't wait for him to answer, but snatched the trousers from his hands, knelt before him, and gestured to one of his bare feet. He had rather large feet, but they were narrow and finely boned. Apparently, nobs even had expensive-looking toes. He didn't offer one of those feet right away, and she looked up at him. Too late, she realized she was kneeling at the level of his waist. Well, just below his waist. Apparently, this fact hasn't escaped him.

Belle was not an experienced spinster. She hadn't had love affairs and romantic rendezvous. She'd either been too busy in the shop or too wary of men who professed an interest in her. She'd learned early that men might say sweet words to her face and mock that same face behind her back. When she'd been about sixteen, she'd been wooed by a boy of about the same age who worked at one of the tea warehouses. He'd flirted and given her small gifts and made a point to speak to her whenever she came to the warehouses. She'd made excuses to go more often, and he'd taken the liberty of kissing her once and hinted he'd like to do so again—perhaps do more than kiss her.

Belle had been curious and flattered by the attention. She'd returned to the warehouse the next day, even though a new shipment of tea was not expected for another week or so. She'd wanted to surprise the boy. She remembered his name perfectly, but chose never to use it, much less think it. She'd surprised him. She'd come upon him talking to his friends. They hadn't seen her, and she'd overheard their conversation.

"A face like that would make my prick shrivel up," one of the men was saying.

"I just turn the ugly side away and I can stomach it alright," the boy had answered.

Heat had flamed in her cheeks because she'd known they were speaking of her.

"Besides, once I have her skirt tossed up, I don't need to look at her face."

"Ye can toss it *over* her face!" one of the men said to raucous laughter.

Belle had sidled away, shame and humiliation washing over her. She'd never felt so ugly or so much the fool. She'd never spoken to the boy again, though she'd had to go back to that warehouse again. And because the docks were full of sailors, who inevitably attracted prostitutes, over the years, Belle saw plenty of what men and women did with a woman's skirts tossed up. Once she'd even seen a woman on her knees, her mouth engaged in pleasuring a man. Belle had been so surprised to come across the scene that she hadn't realized, until the man met her gaze and smiled, that the prostitute's client was none other than the boy.

And now, here she was, in that same position as the prostitute.

Arundel offered her his hand. "Stand up, Miss Howard. I can manage."

Belle had the urge to push him over so that he fell on the bed, but this was not that boy. This was Hew Arundel, and he'd done nothing to her. Well, nothing she hadn't wanted. He'd been nothing but respectful and kind, even in his most delirious moments. She supposed in one of those moments he had been less than respectful, but she could hardly blame a man who was out of his head with pain and fever. And because he was out of his head, she could have stopped it. He hadn't forced his attentions on her.

And he wasn't forcing them on her now. She looked at his outstretched hand then shook out the trousers in her hands. "Give me your foot, Mr. Arundel." Belle would not let that stupid boy from the past affect her now. This moment had nothing to do with anything from before.

"Are you certain?"

"I've dressed children before. I can certainly dress you."

"You do have a way of putting things," he said, and offered a foot. She eased one trouser leg over it and up about the ankle and then asked for the other foot. She felt a sense of accomplishment when the trousers were secure about the ankles. "Now we just need pull them up," she said, taking hold.

"I have it," he said, but when he bent, he hissed in a breath of pain.

"Of course you do," she muttered, taking hold of the trousers and pulling them up his calves. "And you still think you won't faint on the stairs."

"I told you—" His voice cut off, and she realized she'd reached his thighs and was sliding the trousers higher. Her bare fingers had brushed the back of one of his thighs, and she felt the skin pebble with gooseflesh. That wasn't his only reaction. After all, she was at eye level with his nether regions, and she saw a definite stirring there. Had she caused his manly part to do that?

Arundel took hold of the trousers and pushed her hands away. "I have it now," he said and turned. He pulled the trousers over his buttocks, inadvertently lifting the shirt as he did so, and giving her a nice view of his bare arse. For some reason, Belle had wanted to reach out and stroke it. Or bite it. He had nicely rounded cheeks.

Belle abruptly stood and stepped away from him. What was the matter with her? She was a pockmarked spinster. Practically a thornback. She had given up on men. Why was she doing this to herself? She grasped the china teacup and drank down her tea in one swallow. It was an awful waste of the lovely white tea, but the hot liquid on her throat burned some sense into her. Arundel was *not* interested in her as a woman. He'd had a perfectly normal male reaction to a woman's hand on his thigh. He would have had the same reaction if any woman had touched him there.

Wouldn't he?

"I think I have it now," he said. "You can turn around."

She turned, keeping her gaze firmly above his waist. Unfortunately, that meant she watched him unfasten the buttons at his throat, revealing the V of skin there. The buttons at his wrist were not fastened, so he began to draw the shirt over his head. She heard the hiss as he lifted his arms and took hold of the shirt. "I'll do it. If you open those stitches again, *I* will stab you."

Carefully, she drew the shirt up his chest, pausing to help him extricate his arms. Belle tried very hard not to touch his skin, but she kept inadvertently brushing against his chest and feeling the soft hair and the hard muscles. Though the work wasn't difficult, she felt a trickle of perspiration roll down her back, and she could feel that her cheeks were burning with heat. Finally, she pulled the shirt over Arundel's head and stepped back. She had the urge to fan herself, but that would only draw more attention to her state.

He smiled at her. "Bit warm in here, isn't it?"

"It's perfectly comfortable," she snapped. The man noticed everything! That was advantageous when he was working for the Crown but annoying when she wanted to hide her reaction to him. But he wasn't looking at her any longer. He crossed to a cheval mirror beside a washstand and a changing screen and studied his wound. Belle averted her eyes, but she'd already taken in his broad shoulders and the way his body tapered to a slim waist. She wanted to trace that lovely line and clenched her hands together to stop them tingling.

"It does look better," he said, his voice low as though he spoke to himself. "Clean. No infection. Bit of redness here but that's to be expected."

"I suppose this means you will live." Her tone was mocking, but the words gave her a sense of relief. A knot of tension in her belly unfurled, and for the first time in days, she felt as though she could lower her shoulders and take a deep breath. Arundel would live. This nightmare was almost over.

"I won't live long if I don't find something to eat. Help me with the shirt?"

She rolled her eyes. "I think I liked you better when you were wracked with fever and insensible. You made fewer demands."

He lifted the shirt from the bed and handed it to her. "I think you like me fine now, Miss Howard. You have a sharp tongue, but you don't mean half of what you say."

"Ten minutes of consciousness and you think you know me."

He ducked his head so she could put the shirt over it. "I would never presume to claim to know you, but I am beginning to understand you."

She draped the shirt over his head, but he didn't straighten. He continued to look her directly in the eye. His face was only inches from hers, and she could smell the chamomile on his breath. She had the strange urge to lean forward and kiss him. He was close enough that they might kiss. Instead, she made a show of tugging the shirt down and then taking his arms and none-too-gently forcing them in the sleeves.

"Thank you," he said with a wince.

"Are you still determined to go to the kitchens?"

"I think I must, or I'll wither away."

"You really are ridiculous. You do know that."

He draped an arm over her shoulders in a manner that was far too familiar. "I know you like me more than you let on."

"You don't know anything." She removed his arm and crossed to the door, not waiting to see if he followed. This door opened into a narrow corridor. The staff had gone to bed and the lights were out. Of course, Arundel stopped behind her a moment later, carrying a lamp. Dratted man thought of everything. "I'll carry that," she said, taking it from him. "You had better hold on to the wall."

"Your concern is touching."

She moved slower than she would have liked so he could take his time. Her concern *was* touching, after all. At the landing to the stairway, she paused. This part of the house was open so one might stand at the gallery railing and look down into the foyer. A footman sat by the door, his head lolling on his shoulder. Other than that, they were alone. Belle turned to Arundel. "Put one arm about my waist and use the other to hold onto the railing."

"No need. I'm fine."

She narrowed her eyes at him. "Do not make me mention how you fainted the last time you tried these stairs."

"I rather think you just mentioned it."

"If you don't want me to take this lamp and march right back to my chamber then do as I say."

"I think you were a schoolmaster in another life." He put his arm around her waist, and she tried not to notice how warm he was. He wasn't overly warm. The heat of fever had left him. Now he felt comfortingly warm and solid. It seemed absurd to think she would be the one to support him.

"I don't believe we have other lives. That's blasphemy."

"It's more like heresy than blasphemy." He gripped the railing, and they started down the steps. "But unless there's a clergyman lurking nearby, I think we're safe from rebuke."

He really was making good progress on the stairs. He probably hadn't needed her assistance, but she told herself it was best to be safe. She told herself she'd wanted his arm about her waist only to keep him steady, not because she liked it when he touched her. And how pathetic to think that the only way a man would touch her was if he was compelled because he was too ill to make it down the stairs himself.

At the base of the steps, he released her, and Belle tried not to think about how eager he was to be free of her. Of course, there was another set of stairs to the kitchens. At the top, he reached for her again, but she sidestepped. "I think you're fine on your own."

"Do you really think we should risk it?"

Belle stared at him. She had to be imagining that he wanted to touch her. She had the urge to go on ahead and force him to make his way to the kitchens alone, but if he did fall, she would never forgive herself.

"You're right. You might faint at any moment."

He put his arm around her waist and squeezed her, making her yelp when he touched a ticklish spot. "I told you," he said near her ear. "I don't faint."

Belle shivered at the feel of his breath on the sensitive skin of her neck. She struggled to control her breathing, struggled more to keep from turning in his arms, pushing him against the wall, and kissing him. What was the matter with her?

"Let's go," she said, her voice sounding far harsher than she'd intended.

He drew back, grasping the plain wooden railing and moving down the stairs with her. At the bottom, they stepped into the kitchen. She set the lamp on the large preparation table in the center and looked about at the hanging copper pots and tidy counters.

"Here's the larder," Arundel said, trying a large door. He stepped inside and reappeared with a plate covered with a cloth. "What have we here?" His eyebrows went up and down comically, and she couldn't stop herself from smiling.

He set the plate on the table near the lamp and withdrew the napkin with a flourish. Belle peered down at the plate. "Scones," she said. "Probably intended for the staff."

He lifted one and bit into it. "Sorry staff," he said, mouth full. He took another bite, and she looked about, wondering where the tea stores might be. She'd had enough for tonight, but she was curious to see which teas the baroness kept on hand. But instead of finding the tea, she caught her reflection in the window glass. A window above the sink looked out upon the yard, and as it was night, her lamp turned the window into something of a mirror. She could see Arundel starting on yet another scone and herself, small and looking stiff and proper beside him. Normally, she didn't like looking into mirrors, but the lovely thing about a reflection in a window was that it was poor quality and didn't show her pockmarked skin.

She looked almost pretty in the window reflection.

"This one is lemon," Arundel said, holding half a scone out. She turned to look at him. "Best one yet. Have a bite."

Belle was about to say she wasn't hungry, but her stomach chose that moment to growl. His brows rose. "Don't say you don't want it. You're as hungry as I am."

"I doubt that," she said, eyeing the all but empty plate.

"Taste this," he said, holding it out to her. She tried to take it, but he pulled it back. "If I give it to you, I'll not get it back."

"I'll not be fed like a child."

"Fine." He broke off a piece of the pastry and she took it, popping it in her mouth. It was very good, the lemon tart and pairing nicely with the mild sweetness of the bread. She didn't often put lemon in her tea. She couldn't afford to buy fresh lemons and she was too much of a purist to adulterate her tea with additions, but she could see how someone might find a slice of lemon in a Darjeeling refreshing.

"You have a crumb just here." Arundel gestured to her mouth, and Belle put her tongue out to catch the crumb.

"That's not it. Here." His hand caught her chin and swiped at a spot just below her lip. She felt the crumb fall away, but he didn't move his hand. Instead, one finger slid upward to trail over her bottom lip, tracing the shape of it.

Belle couldn't move. His touch seemed to hold her captive. She looked up and into his face and inhaled at what she saw in his blue velvet eyes. He was staring at her like he'd looked at the plate of scones a moment before.

"If I kiss you," he said, "will you break this plate over my head?"

"I don't know," she said truthfully. She couldn't think. She was sinking into his eyes, floating on the soft caress of his finger on her lips.

"I'll take my chances," he said. "You're worth the risk." And leaning forward, he brushed his lips gently over hers.

Chapter Thirteen

Hew felt the change in Belle immediately. She seemed to melt into him as soon as he brushed his lips over hers. He reached out, put an arm about her, and pulled her close, pressing her body against his chest. She felt boneless, offering no resistance.

His mouth moved on hers gently, learning its curves and dips. He'd been wanting to do this ever since he'd first opened his eyes, looked into her face, and she'd told him she was nursing him. He'd been delirious and drugged with laudanum, but he'd wished he could kiss her. Now he was kissing her, and to his surprise, she was kissing him back.

Hew knew she wanted him. He'd been married and knew a little—a very little—about women. He didn't believe the current mythology that women didn't have the same lusts men had. His wife had enjoyed their bedsport as much as he. Hew knew what desire and arousal and appreciation looked like. Even if Belle Howard hadn't wanted to feel any of those things toward him, he'd seen them in her face.

She wanted him, and now she was showing him how much. She made a sound of frustrated need, and Hew deepened the kiss. She opened to him, tasting him as he tasted her. He caught the flavors of the tea she'd been drinking, light and sweet. Her arms went around him, her fingers digging into his back, pulling him closer. So perhaps she was not so sweet. Hew turned and pushed her against the preparation table. She broke the kiss, levered herself onto the table, then pulled his mouth back down to hers. When her legs wrapped about his waist, he felt his own desire heighten.

He'd intended to satisfy his curiosity with a long kiss, but now he found himself even more curious. A kiss would not satisfy—either of them, it seemed.

Hew allowed her to take the lead, her kisses fumbling but passionate. He tilted her head back, loosed her hair, and let the soft tresses fall over his hand. His other hand was at the small of her back, and he was conscious of the need to cup the swell of her hip or the curve of her buttocks, but he held that hand firmly in place. As much as he wanted to toss her skirts up and take her on the kitchen table, he was still a gentleman. Belle was more than a vessel to satisfy his lust. She'd saved his life, and he wouldn't repay her by rogering her on a hard wooden table.

Her legs tightened on his waist, drawing him closer to the heat at the center of her. His hand on her back tightened as he attempted to control his baser urges. She was making that more and more difficult by the minute as her sweet tongue slid into his mouth and tangled with his. Erotic thoughts flitted through his mind, acts Hew was pretty certain he wasn't yet strong enough to attempt. But, oh, how she made him want to try all of them and more, even if it killed him.

He was pretty sure her kisses were further weakening his resolve, and he pulled back, trailing his mouth over her right cheek, along her jaw, and then underneath to place delicate kisses on the soft skin of her neck. She inhaled sharply and made a sound that sent heat right into the pit of his belly. He continued the trail of kisses, tasting his way to the small lobe of her ear and kissing her just behind it.

She must have bathed and washed while he slept as she smelled faintly of soap and the cinnamon scent he always associated with her. He had the vague impression he'd kissed her like this before, but certainly that had only been fever dreams. Now he had her in the flesh.

His lips trailed back down, brushed over her exposed collarbone, then moved back up again—despite the fact that he desperately wanted to move his mouth down and place hands and mouth over her small, rounded breasts. Instead, he kissed her neck, moving up to her jaw, and then to her cheek with the intention of reclaiming her mouth.

Until she shoved him back.

"No," she said.

Hew had to grab the table to keep from falling backward. For a moment, he thought he would fall on his arse, but he steadied himself and, after one look at her, lifted his hands in a gesture of peace. "Forgive me," he said, not sure what he'd done to warrant her forgiveness as she seemed to be rather enjoying herself only a moment before. Her hand was on her cheek, her face tilted down, and he had the thought that perhaps he'd hurt her. Were her scars sensitive? His mouth had been gentle.

"I won't forgive you," she said, her gaze fixed on the table.

Hew was still trying to catch his breath and gather the thoughts swirling about his head. "That's your right, of course." He paused. "I confess, I'm not certain what I did to offend. You seemed receptive—"

"I'm sure this is all some sort of game to you," she said, her eyes finally meeting his. Gone was the softness he'd come to expect, replaced by a hardness that reminded him of a jewel he'd seen once. It had been placed in a necklace, and the woman who'd worn it had told him it was jasper. "I don't want your pity."

What the devil? "My pity? Why would I pity you? If anything, I should think you kissed *me* out of pity." After all, he couldn't even walk down a set of steps unaided.

She shook her head, her cheeks red with anger. "Stop. I'm not a fool. I forgot myself for a moment."

"I don't think you're a fool. I think you're clever and talented and beautiful—"

"Now you're lying to me?"

Hew knew when he'd dug a hole and when to stop digging. "What exactly are you angry about? And do not say that I should know because, as much as it pains me to admit this, I am but an ignorant man, and my understanding is limited."

"You're making fun of me."

"I'm being sincere. I truly do not understand." He tried to move forward, to take her hand, but she gave him a look that sent him out of striking range again. "I apologize for whatever I did, but it would be helpful if I knew what it was so I don't repeat it."

"You'll never have the chance."

"That's what I'm afraid of," he muttered, but she wasn't listening. She was cursing, shaking her head and seeming to berate herself.

"I'm such an idiot," she was saying. "Why don't I ever learn?"

Hew knelt before her, partly as an act of supplication and partly because the thrill of arousal was wearing off and he found himself feeling weaker than he'd expected. Clearly, he had another day or so before his strength would be fully returned. "You are one of the least foolish persons I know, Belle. If I have behaved as anything less than a gentleman—"

But, of course, he had. He shouldn't have kissed her. He shouldn't have let her wrap her legs around him in the kitchen of Lady Keating's home. He shouldn't have been traipsing about with her in the middle of the night. These circumstances might not be ordinary, but he knew how he ought to behave.

"Oh, don't be ridiculous. You're far too much a gentleman," she said.

Hew frowned. He wasn't about to gainsay her, not when she was already angry with him. He tried to think what to reply to her—was it an accusation of being too much a gentleman?—but failing to conjure any good rejoinders, shook his head in bewilderment. He had forgotten how completely confounding women could be. He was used to interacting with agents for the Saboteurs, and generally that meant attempting to shoot better or decipher a code faster. He'd forgotten what it was to be tossed into the churning whirlpool of female emotions.

She finally sighed at him in exasperation, perhaps realizing—one could only hope—that he really was entirely ignorant. "I know what I look like," she said. "And I'm not beautiful. I know what people say about me behind my back and even to my face. I suppose I can't blame you. No doubt you were curious, and that's why you put your mouth on this." She touched the left side of her face, the side bearing the scars from a smallpox infection.

Hew refrained from speaking for a long moment, taking in what she'd said, turning it over, and then using all of his training to decode it. "This is about your scars?" he said.

The daggers she shot him with her gaze would have felled a small child. Hew barely managed to keep upright. He really was a dolt. He understood now and understood completely. He jumped to his feet, swayed a bit with the poor judgment of rising so quickly, but managed to keep her from jumping down and running away. "I'm sorry," he said, putting both hands out in a gesture for her to stay. "It's I who am the idiot. But, if you'll forgive me for saying so, you are an idiot as well."

Her eyes narrowed, and Hew thought that a smarter man would have moved a safe distance away. "Listen to me," he said quickly, before she could bash him over the head with a blunt object. "I don't care about your scars. You're beautiful with or without them."

She shook her head and made to protest, but he cut her off. "I'll admit in my youth I kissed plenty of women, but I'm far more selective these days. If I kiss a woman, hold a woman, it's because I like her. And I like you, Belle. Not just because you're beautiful, but because you're loyal and kind—"

She snorted at that, and Hew smiled. "Very well, you're not *unkind*. But you're definitely unpretentious and brave and—"

"How can you not care about my scars? Look at you."

Hew looked down at himself, seeing the wrinkled shirt and trousers. He didn't have a coat or shoes, and he could only imagine how his hair looked, or his unshaven face. "I've looked better."

"Even half dead with fever you are the most handsome man I've ever seen."

"Am I?" Well, this was a not unwelcome turn of events.

She put a hand on his chest, pushing him back. "I know better than to think you'd ever want more from me than a tumble in bed."

Hew didn't know what he wanted from her, but it was more than that. Still, he thought it best not to point out, again, that he was a dolt who was ignorant of what he wanted. "Perhaps that's all *you* want from *me*," he said. "Forgive me for pointing out that you kissed me with as much enthusiasm as I kissed you."

"A gentleman would not point that out."

"A gentleman would also not have a five-inch knife wound in his side, but perhaps once you see my scar, you won't want me any longer."

"That's different," she shot back.

"How?"

"My scars are on my face."

"All that means is mine can be hidden. Does it change how you think of me?" He'd made his point, but he could see that she couldn't quite trust him. Not yet. Someone had hurt her. Knowing people as he did, knowing his own sex as he did, he could imagine she'd suffered a barrage of unkind remarks and been made to feel ugly and unworthy. His heart ached for her, but he didn't pity her. How could he when, smallpox scars or no, she was one of the most desirable women he'd ever met?

"It's late," she said. "And you shouldn't even be out of bed."

"We'll speak more of this tomorrow."

She hopped off the table. "No, we won't. We will not ever speak of this again. Tomorrow we need to make a plan. I can't stay here much longer. I have a tea shop to manage."

Hew contented himself with the fact she'd agreed to speak in the morning. "Shall I bid you good night here? I think I can find my way back to my chambers alone."

"And when you faint on the stairs and tumble to your death, then I'll feel guilty for the rest of my life. No, Arundel. I'll help you to your room. Just keep your hands to yourself."

"Fine, but I want one thing clear."

She glared up at him, obviously ready to be done with their conversation for the night.

"I didn't faint."

***

Belle insisted on staying close to Arundel as they made their way up the servants' stairs, past the dozing footman, and then up the main stairway. She wanted to be near to him only in part because she was worried for his safety. Simply put, she liked being near him, liked the way he touched her, liked the way his body felt pressed against hers.

She knew she shouldn't think such things. They weren't married, and even the idea of a nobleman marrying a shopkeeper was preposterous. She didn't know why the thought of marriage had entered her head, except that she'd believed him when he said her scars didn't matter to him. It seemed impossible that he shouldn't find them grotesque and disfiguring. When she looked at herself in a mirror—something she tried not to do very often—the scars were all she could see. But Arundel had been right when he'd said that his knife wound didn't make him any less attractive to her. Could it be possible that her scars didn't make her less appealing?

They reached the top of the stairway, and she forced herself to release his waist and step away from him. She didn't have any reason to keep touching him now that the danger of falling to his death had passed. The man really was a gentleman—in every sense of the word. He had kept his hands to himself, and Belle suspected he wouldn't attempt to kiss her again unless she gave him permission. In writing.

"I can make it from here," he said, inclining his head toward his bed chamber. Hers was on the other side of the landing. Belle knew this was her cue to part from him. She would just have to content herself with the memory of the embraces they'd shared. Why had she cared so much that he'd kissed her scars? Why had she stopped him?

"You take the lamp," he said, holding it out to her.

She took it. "Good night," she said, turning toward her chamber, and holding the lamp up. The flickering light reminded her of the fire in her hearth. She hoped it had not burned too low as the house was chilly. "My wrap!" She turned back to Arundel who was frowning at her. "I left my wrap in your chamber."

His gaze traveled past her to the doors in the shadows just beyond the landing. She knew he was thinking that she could certainly walk a few feet without catching a chill. Nevertheless, he gestured for her to go ahead, and she led the way to his chamber. She opened the door, entering the chamber, which was filled with warmth. She spotted her wrap—Lady Keating's wrap, actually—draped over the chair where she'd been sitting. She snatched it up and pulled it like a shield about the dress she wore. Lady Keating said it had been one of her daughter's dresses, and she was welcome to keep it. Belle would have never presumed. The dress was the finest thing she had ever worn, save the dress she and Maggie had sewed for her to wear to Maggie's wedding. Belle had every intention of returning it as soon as she was able to return to her flat on Fenchurch Street and put on one of her own dresses. She just couldn't walk around the baroness's home in her shift, which was what she'd been wearing when the men broke into the shop.

"Before I go, do you need any help?" Belle asked. Arundel looked tired. The short walk to the kitchens and back seemed to have taken a toll.

"It's probably best if I undress myself," he said.

Belle felt her cheeks flame.

"Much easier to shed clothing than put it on, I think," he added. "And judging by the color in your cheeks, just the idea of removing my clothing is shocking."

"Don't be ridiculous," she said, ducking her head to hide the redness of her face. "I've been nursing you for days, and dressing and undressing a patient is all part of nursing."

He smiled at her. "Considering you fainted at the sight of my wound, my suggestion is that you stick to tea."

Belle put her hands on her hips. "That was one time. Besides, I didn't faint. I just closed my eyes for a moment." There. Two could play at his game of words. She dropped the wrap on the chair again and reached for him. "I'll just help you remove these trousers."

He caught her hands before they could reach the waistband. "I don't think that's a good idea."

She looked up at him, into his blue velvet eyes. "Why not?"

"You know why not. Wait—don't duck your head like that. You don't have to hide your face from me."

Belle realized she had tilted the left side of her face down, instinctively attempting to hide the scars. "It's a habit," she whispered.

"Not one you need when you're with me." He didn't release her hands, and yet he made no move to close the distance between them. Belle raised her face to give him a full view. She saw the way his throat worked as he swallowed. This was no act. He really did seem affected by her. He really did seem to want her. She saw in his gaze then that her scars didn't matter to him, and that seemed to change everything. She felt as though a part of her was abruptly unlocked and the tension released.

It was such a novel sensation to feel safe with a man. To feel as though she didn't have to fear he'd point out her flaws or ridicule her scars.

One more kiss. That was all she wanted, and then she would go to her chamber. "If I kiss you," she said, "would that make me a terrible nurse?"

He grinned. "You're already a terrible nurse. I'd much rather you kiss me than tend me."

She moved closer. "I think I should be offended," she whispered, "but I like that suggestion." She leaned into him, waiting for him to object, to show any sign of reluctance. Instead, his hands tightened on hers as though he was struggling to control the urge to pull her close. She wished he wouldn't control that urge.

Finally, she pressed her mouth lightly against his, and again there was the sensation of pleasure rippling through her. How could she feel it so keenly at just the merest meeting of their flesh? The desire coiled in her belly from earlier unfurled and sent heat radiating through her. She moved closer, wrapped her arms about his neck, and kissed him.

He groaned, the sound one of primal pleasure. It gave her confidence to deepen the kiss. His arms went about her waist, pulling her against his warm, solid body. Quite suddenly, she wanted to touch his body. Not as a nurse might touch his chest, but as a lover. She reached for the shirt he wore untucked and slid her hands underneath. She felt the waistband of his trousers and then the heated flesh of his belly. It wasn't the heat of fever. It was the comforting heat of life.

And yet touching him was anything but comforting. Her heart had begun to pound, and her throat went dry. The heat radiating through her body began to burn as she slid her hands upward, careful to avoid the area of his wound. She wanted to touch all of him like this. To see if the flesh of his legs was as firm and muscled as that of his abdomen.

Arundel's hands flexed on her waist, and then he gently broke the kiss and pushed her back. "It's probably best if you go to your chamber now."

Belle stared at him, uncomprehending, then felt a lump rise in her throat. She'd gone too far. She'd misunderstood his reactions. "I'm sorry," she said, stepping away and groping blindly for her wrap. "Of course, I'll go."

Arundel caught her arm, pulling her close again. "Don't look like that."

"Like what?"

"Like you've done something wrong. I'm sending you away because I want you, and because if this goes much further, we may both do things we regret in the morning."

Belle hadn't thought of that. She hadn't thought of anything except the feel of his skin under her fingertips. But there was one thing she thought she knew perfectly well by now. "I wouldn't regret anything with you."

He closed his eyes as though in pain. "You don't know how much I want you."

Belle thought that if it was half as much as she wanted him, she *did* know.

"If I wasn't injured, I would have taken this too far already."

Belle would have liked to ask what *too far* meant. What exactly would he have done? Would he have touched her as she'd been touching him a few minutes before? "I think I want you to take it too far," she admitted, then felt her cheeks heat again. But she didn't duck her head, and she didn't look away. She was a woman of almost six and twenty, old enough to know what she wanted.

He shook his head. "No, you don't. Too much further, and I'll feel obligated to marry you. That isn't possible."

The part of her that had been unlocked retreated again, and the lump was back in her throat. This time the heat in her cheeks was not from desire or embarrassment but from indignation. She straightened her shoulders. "I'm aware a gentleman like you would never marry a woman of my position, but I'm not one of your ladies of the *ton*. If we were discovered together, no one would expect you to marry me."

"And am I some sort of rake who jumps into bed with unmarried young women? *I'd* feel obligated to marry you."

"Because I'm a virgin?"

His mouth dropped open. She'd spoken too plainly, that much was clear. But she couldn't take it back now. "I hadn't thought of that, but it does rather make my point. I'm not in the habit of deflowering young ladies."

"I'm not young, and at this point, I hardly need save myself for marriage. I'm a spinster. Everyone will be calling me a thornback when I do turn six and twenty."

"Arbitrary terms that mean nothing. You're a young woman, and I won't take advantage of you." He didn't say *you're a young woman of a lower social class*, but he didn't have to. She knew he felt the power differential between them even if it meant little or nothing to her. She was no fair lady who needed saving. She took a step closer to him, and he gave her a wary look but resisted taking a cautious step back.

"Do you really think I'd allow you to take advantage of me?"

He lifted his brows. "Do you really think you could stop me if that's what I wanted?"

She moved her gaze deliberately to the area of his side that was wounded. "Yes."

"Let's not test it, shall we?"

"Let's not," she said, her tone mocking his upper-class accent. "I wouldn't want you to feel obligated to marry a peasant like me, much less one who's so disfigured she's destined to be an old maid." She whirled on her heel and marched for the door, realizing too late she'd forgotten the lamp. She'd rather dump all the tea in her shop into the Thames—like those colonists in the Americas had done to their harbor—than go back for the lamp. Anything but having to spend another moment in Arundel's presence.

This settled it. Tomorrow she would return to Fenchurch Street, Arundel and the thugs who were after him be damned.

Chapter Fourteen

Hew was aware of the knocking. He'd decided it was part of a dream and ignored it. What he couldn't ignore was being shaken like a rag doll. He opened his eyes and stared blearily at the figure looming above him. His heart leaped into his throat, and he would have moved into a defensive posture except he realized, belatedly, that assassins didn't wake one before murdering them.

The figure set down a lamp, and in the lamplight Hew saw her. "Belle?"

"I'm sorry," she said.

He pushed up on his elbows. "What time is it?" He might have asked what day it was, but he was reasonably sure he'd only slept for a few hours.

"Very early morning. I'm sorry."

Hew narrowed his eyes. Belle was not one to apologize—especially not after the way she'd left last night. He felt he owed *her* an apology. Except he was damned if he would apologize for not bedding her. He was protecting her virtue, damn it. "Why are you apologizing? I'd like to think it is for the slander you lobbed at me when we parted last night, but for some reason I doubt that."

The pleading in her eyes darkened, and she scowled. "I am *not* apologizing for that. I'm apologizing because I left Lady Keating's home and returned to Fenchurch Street."

"You what?" Hew sat up straight, wincing at the slight twinge in his side. Only a slight twinge, though. He was healing.

"You are on the mend." Her gaze dropped to his chest and then hastily rose again. "I felt it was time I returned home. I have no idea how the shop has fared after that fire, and some of us must work for our bread."

"I told you to stay away. You're in danger. Returning there put your father in danger."

"Too late for that."

Hew cut short his tirade. The tone of her voice alarmed him. "What's happened?"

"My father—"

To Hew's shock, she crumpled on the bed beside him and began to weep. He hadn't imagined she might weep at this. She always seemed so strong. He dropped his legs off the side of the bed to give her room, belatedly realizing he'd stripped before returning to bed last night. The only thing he wore was the linen bandage over his wound. He pulled the bedclothes up on his hips, but Belle's limp figure had trapped them.

Hew put a hand on her back, attempting to comfort her. "What's happened to your father?" he asked.

"He…Mrs. Price…she said…"

He couldn't understand her between the sobs. "Belle." He turned her head so she looked up at him. "Say it quick."

"Mrs. Price said he's been taken." She threw herself at him, wrapping her arms about Hew's chest. His bare chest. But he would not think about that now. Hew drew her back, despite his inclination to pull her closer, and looked her directly in the eye.

"Tell me exactly what was said."

"She said—"

"No tears now. You won't help him by blubbering."

The look she gave him was full of venom, but his words had the intended effect. She stopped crying and took a breath. "I went to the shop, and he wasn't there. I knew he'd been there because it was locked and the shelves had been restored to rights—mostly. But he wasn't in the shop or in the flat. So I went to Mrs. Price's flat and knocked on the door. She answered, and when she saw me, she burst into tears." Belle's own eyes began to water again, and Hew gave her a stern look.

"Go on."

"She said, well, the short version is that they'd been watching the shop and noted no one suspicious. My father went back to clean up and didn't return for supper. Mrs. Price went to fetch him, and the shop door was open, and he was not to be found."

"Was there a note at the shop? Or some sort of communication?"

"I didn't see anything."

"Then we don't know if this is related to my stabbing."

"Don't we? He's never disappeared before. Come to think of it, our shop has never been set on fire before. I would say all of this has to do with you."

Hew winced. He was painfully aware that the Howards had taken him in, without even a real option to say no, and had done their best to tend him. All he had done was bring them pain and misfortune. He'd set things to right. He was a Royal Saboteur. He could sabotage the assassins' plan—even if it involved his own demise. "I need to see the shop and speak to Mrs. Price."

"I told you what she—oh!"

Hew had thrown the bedclothes back and walked across the room to the chair where he'd left his clothing. His mind on his mission, he'd forgotten he was naked. He glanced over his shoulder to find Belle staring at him, mouth open. He raised a brow, and she turned pink and looked away.

"I told you what she—what she—"

"Yes, you told me what she said." Hew found his trousers and pulled them on, careful not to twist his side or move too sharply. "But I need to see for myself and ask a few questions." He lifted his shirt and tried to put it over his head, but he couldn't raise the arm on his wounded side far enough. "Help me with this shirt, will you?"

"Do you have your, er—trousers on?"

"Yes."

She peeked over her shoulder, and when she saw him, nodded and went to help him with the shirt. "This seems rather improper," she commented, helping him get his arm through.

"If you think this improper, you have no idea what I wanted to do to you last night. Which, might I remind you, I declined to do. Because it was improper."

"You may not remind me," she said pulling the sleeve down his arm rather fiercely. It was his uninjured side, thank God. "And you needn't worry you will ever have the opportunity again. I just want to find my father and be rid of you."

"Then we are in agreement."

She glared at him then stomped away, stopping before an armoire and throwing the doors open. "Lady Keating said you might need a coat." She tossed out several garments. "Let's hurry and put these on."

Hew reluctantly accepted her assistance. It would have been counterproductive to refuse. He did reject the waistcoat, though. He didn't want anything pressing on his wound. He took the coat, allowed Belle to tie his neckcloth in a manner that would have appalled his friends and acquaintances, and then shoved his feet into boots she produced that were a bit too small but would have to do. Hew took one look in the mirror and turned away. Just days ago he'd been wearing a fine coat from Schweitzer and Davidson's. Now he looked as though a blind valet had dressed him.

What had happened to that coat? It had probably been covered in blood and cut off by the surgeon. He should have had it sent to Mivart's instead of wearing it out of the shop. What he wouldn't give to stop by his room there now and dress in his own clothing. No time for that at present.

The charwoman came in and informed them it was almost six in the morning. Hew sent her to tell the footman they needed a hackney. Thus, by the time he'd managed to cram his feet in the boots, the hackney waited outside.

Lady Keating's butler intercepted them on the way out the door. "Mr. Smith will return in just a few hours, sir. He did say to make sure you stayed in bed."

"Tell him I'm feeling much better, thanks to him. Sorry to have missed him."

"Will you return for dinner?" the butler asked.

"I wouldn't count on it." Hew had no idea what the day would bring, but the less the servants knew of his plans, the better. Obviously, the men seeking him either didn't know where he was or couldn't reach him, but that didn't mean they couldn't reach one of the servants.

Puddles still stood on the streets, indicating the rain hadn't moved on completely. Hew stepped over a large puddle and handed Belle over it and into the waiting hackney. He climbed in behind her. "Fenchurch Street," he told the jarvey. Then he closed the curtains and sat back, trying not to inhale too deeply the smells of wet straw and damp wool that lingered from recent customers.

Belle reached for the curtains, presumably to open them and look out, but Hew caught her hand. She tore her fingers from his then cradled her hand as though it were scorched. "Keep them closed," he said. "If anyone is watching for us, I'd rather not be easy to spot." He cocked his head. "How did you go to the shop this morning?"

"I walked," she said.

Hew stifled a groan. She was fortunate she had not been the one abducted. She'd have been an easy target for the assassins or for any ruffian out and about in the early hours. "Don't do that again," he ordered. "A woman out alone in the wee hours of the morning is not safe."

"I've been taking care of myself for almost twenty-six years. I don't need your help."

"If you insist on making idiotic choices, I beg to differ."

She glared at him—he was becoming accustomed to her glares—and didn't speak again until they turned onto Fenchurch Street and her shop came into view. Hew knocked on the roof of the hackney. Belle barely waited for the conveyance to stop before she was out and walking to her shop. Hew paid the driver then followed her. She called a greeting to another shopkeeper sweeping his front stoop, then pulled a key out of her skirts, and opened the door to the tea shop.

Hew stepped inside, feeling strangely comforted by the scents of tea and biscuits. And yet, the scent of smoke still lingered and made the hairs on the back of his neck rise in warning. Everything was as she'd described. The overturned shelves had been righted and the goods put back in their place. Glass and porcelain that had littered the floor had been swept up, and the burnt shades had been pulled down, the water mopped up, and the charred plaster scraped off the wall of the shop. Hew saw no sign of struggle. "Let me see the back room and the flat."

She took him through, but he saw no indication of a fight. The back room was clean and orderly and the flat looked exactly as it had the night they'd been attacked. He'd made one last pass, looking for anything he'd missed. "We'd better speak to Mrs. Price."

Hew could see Belle had a thousand questions, but she kept them to herself, staying quiet and out of the way as he studied the scene. Now she led him down the street, which was waking up as more shops opened and carts passed by. She entered a building, took a flight of stairs, then knocked on a door at the top. "Mrs. Price, it's Belle Howard."

The door opened immediately, and Mrs. Price beckoned them to enter. No sooner had she closed the door and bolted it then she pulled Belle into her arms. "Thank God you returned. I worried something might have happened to you as well."

"Mrs. Price," Belle said, voice muffled, "you remember Mr. Arundel."

"Good morning, Mrs. Price." Hew went to the front of the small room, where the curtains were pulled back from a window overlooking the street. Mrs. Price had a good view of all that went on, including who went in and out of the tea shop.

"Mr. Arundel! I would hardly have known you, sir. You look much recovered."

"Thanks to you, Mrs. Price," Hew said, turning and smiling. Belle snorted, obviously not appreciating his attempt at charm. "We have just been at the tea shop," he informed her. "I saw no sign of struggle. Did you happen to see anyone go in or out when Mr. Howard disappeared?" Hew gestured out the window.

"Poor Mr. Howard!" Mrs. Price dabbed at her red eyes with a handkerchief. "I've been worried sick."

"Sit down, Mrs. Price," Belle said, leading the woman to a chair. "This is upsetting to all of us."

Strange to see Belle comforting Mrs. Price, when Belle should have been the one receiving comfort. Hew had watched her dissolve into tears just hours before, but she'd managed to find a core of strength. Hew didn't have time to coddle the woman. "Tell me what happened. I need every detail, no matter how innocuous," Hew said.

Mrs. Price's eyes widened. "Of course, if you think it will help. Will you search for Mr. Howard? Are you from Bow Street?"

"Something like that."

Mrs. Price jumped up. "Oh, but where are my manners? I haven't even offered you refreshment. You must be famished."

Hew was famished, and normally he would have ignored the hunger and pushed onward, but he was acutely aware that he'd only just recovered his strength. Now was not the time to test it. He allowed Mrs. Price to bustle about and set out several cold dishes as well as hot tea.

"We're wasting time," Belle said, leaning close enough that he caught the scent of cinnamon. Was that her or the Hot Cinnamon Spice tea?

"I'm as eager as you to begin searching," Hew said, "but I've learned to gather all the facts before beginning an investigation. It saves time in the end."

She took the chair beside him. "And what if that's time my father doesn't have right now?"

"Then we save time by not making false starts and chasing dead ends." He grasped her hand. "I know it's difficult to be patient, but they have no reason to harm your father. It's me they want."

She pulled her hand away. "And why is that? You still haven't told me what this is all about."

She had a point, and now that she was more involved than he would have ever imagined, he owed her some explanation. "You're right. I will tell you everything." He inclined his head toward Mrs. Price. "Later."

Mrs. Price finally took a seat across from them, pushing the dishes she'd set out closer to Hew. He tried to make himself eat slowly, noting Belle ate very little at all.

"I told him not to go," Mrs. Price began. "We were tucked up here, snug as could be, while the rains poured."

Belle's teacup clattered as she set it on the saucer.

Mrs. Price went on, seemingly oblivious. "I made sure George was fed and dry—"

"George?"

"Your father, dear."

Belle gave her a look that Hew knew well as he'd been on the wrong side of it too many times.

"But when the rains stopped, he insisted on returning to the shop. I told him not to," Mrs. Price said. "But his mind was made up. And you know your father when his mind is made up."

Belle's hands were gripping the table hard, and Hew reached over and patted them, which earned him a fierce scowl. He moved his hands away slowly; best not to make any sudden movements.

"He set off for the shop," Mrs. Price said with a sigh. "I watched him walk away through the window there. But he didn't return."

"When was this?" Hew asked, grasping information he could use. "When was the last time you saw him?"

"It must have been about midday yesterday. It was after the rains stopped."

"How long was he gone before you became concerned?"

"I didn't expect him to hurry back, but I thought he'd return for supper. He said he liked my cooking. "

Belle made a sound like a growl in her throat.

"I cooked all afternoon, but he didn't come home."

"He *was* home," Belle said. "The flat above the shop is his home."

"Of course, dear. More tea, Mr. Arundel?"

"No, thank you. When he didn't return, what did you do? Did you go to look for him?"

"Of course. It was almost dark by then, but I walked to the shop and had a look about inside. The shop and the flat were empty."

"Wait a moment." Hew held up a hand. "When we stopped there just now, the door was closed and locked. How did you gain access?"

"How did I—"

"Get inside?" Belle said.

"The door was standing wide open," Mrs. Price said. "I thought that strange as George isn't in the habit of leaving the shop door open."

Belle was gripping the table again.

"But I thought he might be trying to clear the shop of the smell of the smoke. Such a shame, that smell. The shop always smelled so comforting."

"Mrs. Price," Hew interrupted, "if the shop door was open yesterday evening then how did it come to be closed and locked when we arrived this morning."

"I closed and locked it. Gangs of ruffians and thieves roam about the city at night. I don't like to think they'd come to Fenchurch Street, but one can't be too careful."

"Do you have a key to the shop?" Hew asked.

"No," Belle said at the same time Mrs. Price said, "Yes."

Hew looked from Belle to Mrs. Price. Mrs. Price cleared her throat. "That is to say, I found the keys on the floor just inside the shop door. George must have dropped them when he was abducted."

Until now Hew hadn't been sure he believed George Howard *had* been abducted. The man could have gone on a walkabout, say to look for his daughter. But it was unlikely he'd leave his keys on the floor to his shop. He would have locked the door before setting out.

"Did you see anyone you didn't recognize loitering near the shop or on the street?"

Mrs. Price considered. "The street was mostly empty by then. It was growing dark and time for supper."

"What about when you were watching him walk to the shop?" Belle asked. That had been Hew's next question. "You said you watched him through the window."

"Oh, I can't see much through the window."

Hew rose and went to the window again. She had a very good view from her window, but she was right that she couldn't see much of the shop front as it was on the same side of the street as her flat. She would have been able to see the street before it or the buildings across. He turned back to the table. "No one was standing about across from the shop, perhaps watching it?"

"Oh, not that I noticed. I wish I had known to pay more attention."

Belle rose and came to stand with him at the window. "Mrs. Price doesn't have a clear view of the shop, but I know who does."

Hew looked at her.

"Mrs. Tipps," she said. "We should call on her."

"We'll go now." Hew turned back to Mrs. Price. "Thank you for your help."

She rose, her hands fisted in her skirts. "You will find George? You will bring him back?"

Hew put a hand on Belle's shoulder before she could pounce on Mrs. Price and rip her to shreds.

"We will, Mrs. Price. In the meantime, if you think of anything or remember anything, send a note to Mivart's. That's where I am staying now."

"Oh." Her mouth made a round O. "No longer with the fine lady who came in the coach?"

"No. I'm at Mivart's," he said, deciding he would make certain to mention it to Mrs. Tipps as well. With any luck, the ladies would spread that news about and the assassins would search for him there. If he didn't find them first.

Mrs. Price's gaze slid to Belle. "Where will you stay, my dear? You are welcome to stay with me, of course. I think that's what your father would have wanted."

"I'll stay in my own home," she said.

Hew wasn't about to let that happen. The last thing he needed was the men after him abducting her as well. Hew was smart enough to keep his mouth shut and save that conversation for another time. Mrs. Price was not quite so clever.

"But you can't possibly think to stay alone. You're a young, unmarried woman."

"Oh, I see. I'm so old I'm called a spinster, and yet I am too young to live in my own home without a guardian."

"Well, I hadn't thought of it like that," Mrs. Price sputtered.

Hew moved away from the window and toward the door. Belle had her hands on her hips and looked as though she had much more to say, but if she saw him leaving, she would most likely cut her tirade short. But Hew halted before the door then bent to scoop up the slip of parchment that had been tucked beneath it. The paper had not been there when they'd entered. Surely, he would have seen it.

"What is that?" Mrs. Price asked.

"It's not yours?"

"No, sir."

Hew opened it.

Serpentine Bridge in Hyde Park. Tomorrow. Midnight.

He crumpled the paper and raced back to the window, looking up and down the street. A man in a dark coat and hat moved away at a brisk pace, but then there were other men and women walking about as well. There was no way to know if the person who'd delivered the note had just done so or a quarter hour before.

"Let me see." Belle took the note and read it. "I don't understand," she said.

"They want a meeting. Probably to exchange your father for me."

Now she was staring through the window as well. "Did they slide this under the door now? While we were speaking? We could have caught them, could have made them tell us where they have my father."

Hew turned to her and took her shoulders. "It could have been them, but they might have given a boy a penny to slide it under the door as well. Our best hope is to find them before midnight tomorrow."

"And if we can't?"

"Then I'll go with them, and you'll have your father back."

Chapter Fifteen

The lump in Belle's throat at the thought of losing Arundel wouldn't go away. She wanted her father back—desperately—but that didn't mean she wanted to sacrifice Arundel. Not that he was hers to sacrifice. No doubt he could take care of himself. He could defend himself. They probably taught him that in the Royal Saboteurs just as they'd taught him how to ask questions and think on his feet. She didn't know how she would have managed the last few hours without him. Her thoughts were all jumbled, and she felt on the verge of tears, but he was calm and collected, methodical and meticulous.

He'd had to be if he was to squeeze any useful information out of Mrs. Price. "I hope Mrs. Tipps is more helpful than Mrs. Price," she told Hew as they walked down Fenchurch Street to Mr. and Mrs. Tipps's flat.

"Mrs. Price is upset. Emotions do tend to interfere with clear thought."

"I don't know why she should be upset. He's *my* father. But as I'm sure you noticed she wants to make him her husband."

Hew didn't respond.

"That's why she was so eager to take him in, you know. She wants him for herself."

"And you want to keep him for yourself?" He gave her a sidelong look.

"No! That's not what I said. I meant—" But what had she meant? And what did it matter? She didn't have to defend herself to Hew Arundel. Thankfully, they were only steps away from the ground floor of a residential building where the Tipps lived. They had a large window overlooking the street with a clear view of Howard's Teas & Treats. Belle had often waved at her when she opened the shades of the shop in the morning as Mrs. Tipps was inevitably cleaning her window or bustling about in her front room. Mrs. Tipps had remarked more than once that Mr. Tipps liked a tidy home.

Arundel paused in front of the Tipps's window and looked across Fenchurch Street to the shop. To Belle it looked strange and sad. Except for Christmas and Sundays, the shop was never closed. Would their customers find other shops to patronize if they came for tea and found the shop closed? How would she pay to repair the damage to the store if they didn't open again soon?

"If anyone saw what happened, it was Mrs. Tipps," Arundel said, hands on hips. "She has a perfect view. I was somewhat delirious when I met her, but if I recall, she is not as forthcoming as Mrs. Price."

"If by forthcoming you mean she is cranky and set in her ways, then you were not at all delirious."

Arundel gave her a sidelong look. "Perhaps you should let me do the talking."

"Gladly."

The door opened before they had a chance to knock, and Mrs. Tipps stood in the doorway, frowning. "This is a fine state of affairs," she said, gesturing to the shop. "Where am I to buy my tea?"

Belle opened her mouth to retort that she had just been in to buy her Darjeeling and should have plenty, but Arundel reached over and put a hand on her arm. She supposed it was meant to look like a comforting gesture.

"Miss Howard and her father plan to open the shop again as soon as possible," Arundel said. "Perhaps you could help with that."

She narrowed her eyes. "You are taller than I imagined. Better looking too when you're not at death's door."

"Thanks to your skill with nursing, I am recovering."

Mrs. Tipps raised her brows. "Charming too."

Belle was growing impatient standing on the street. She might have been impatient of Arundel charming everyone as well. "Might we speak to you inside for a moment?"

Mrs. Tipps shook her head. "Mr. Tipps is out. I don't allow men into the house when he is away."

Belle hardly thought Arundel had any intention of attacking her and beating her with her cane, but another press of Arundel's hand kept her quiet. She didn't like being shushed, though, and she gave his arm a pinch.

"I understand," Arundel was saying. "I'm sure it's been a trying few days for you with the fire and all the commotion of the other night. Thieves in London have become quite brazen."

"Thieves." Mrs. Tipps sounded doubtful. "I see."

"While Miss Howard and I were being treated for injuries sustained during the fire, Mrs. Price was kind enough to look after Mr. Howard."

"Trying to sink her claws in him, was she?"

Belle's eyes widened. Ah-ha! Now Arundel would see what she had meant. Mrs. Tipps saw it too.

"I'm sure Mrs. Price was trying to be a good neighbor."

Belle rolled her eyes, and Mrs. Tipps gave him a thin smile. "But she lost him, didn't she?"

"Why do you say that?" Belle asked, ignoring the quelling look Arundel sent her.

"Because I saw him go into the shop, and I didn't see him come out."

"What else did you see?" she asked. "Did any—"

Arundel pressed her arm again. He cleared his throat. "Did you see anyone else go into the shop after him?"

Belle scowled at him. That had been the exact question she had planned to ask. He might be an agent for the Crown, but she wasn't a dolt. To repay him for cutting her off, she pinched his arm again. Harder.

No response. She'd have to pinch elsewhere.

"Or perhaps some men were loitering about across the—ah!"

Belle bit her lip to keep from smiling. She'd given his bum a sharp pinch. That had gotten his attention.

"What was that?" Mrs. Tipps asked.

Arundel, professional that he was, never even glanced back at Belle, but before she could pinch him again, he caught her wrist and held it.

"Across the street," he said. "In front of your window or just down the street a ways."

"I didn't notice anyone loitering, and I don't tolerate anyone loitering in front of my stoop," she said. Belle could attest to that. She'd seen Mrs. Tipps shoo away more than one group of young boys and girls playing in front of the door to the building. And some of those children lived in the flats above her. "But I did see two men go into the shop."

Belle wrenched her wrist free from Arundel's grip. "When? While my father was inside?"

"Calm yourself, Belle. I don't sit in front of the window and spy all day like some." She cast a gaze in the direction of Mrs. Price's flat. But Belle knew that if Mr. Tipps was not at home that was exactly what Mrs. Tipps did.

"Surely you have other tasks to attend to," Arundel said smoothly. "But you happened to pass by your window and saw the men enter the shop."

"Exactly. I glanced out the window and saw the men enter the shop about a half hour after Mr. Howard went inside. I thought it strange since the sign on the door still read CLOSED and the shades were drawn."

"Did you see them come out again?"

"I was quite busy," Mrs. Tipps said, and Belle wanted to grab her by the shoulders and shake her. "But I didn't notice anyone leaving. Of course, I only have a view of the front of the shop, not the back. Really, I didn't think anything of it until Mrs. Price came knocking a few hours later and asked if I'd seen Mr. Howard. She was quite distraught. She'd gone into the shop and found it empty."

"But by that time, Mr. Howard had been gone for some time—if we assume the men who went in after him took him out the back."

"Well, as I said, I was very busy, so I have no idea how much time might have passed."

"Yes, you do. You were—"

Arundel put his arm about Belle's shoulders and pulled her face into his chest. "Miss Howard is quite distraught. We're almost done, Miss Howard," he said, his voice soothing as he patted her shoulder. But his grip was iron. She fought it, but he held steady.

"How much time would you estimate?" Arundel asked. Belle ceased struggling and turned her head. Arundel continued, "Just an approximation."

"Two hours. Perhaps three."

"Thank you, Mrs. Tipps. Might I ask you one more question?"

"Of course." Mrs. Tipps glanced at Belle. She realized she was still pressed against Arundel's uninjured side. She'd forgotten to try and free herself. He was warm and smelled like the tea they'd enjoyed at Mrs. Price's. But underneath that scent was the scent of *him*. Something about that scent, something about his touch, seemed to have the effect of causing her to forget herself.

"Could you describe the men who went into the shop?" Arundel asked. Pressed against him, his voice sounded deep and resonant.

"I didn't really see them…"

"Anything you might remember," Arundel said. "Color of their hats or coats? Tall or short?"

"Let me think." Mrs. Tipps closed her eyes and put her fingers to her temples. Belle looked up at Arundel who rolled his eyes. She smiled. He was not taken in by Mrs. Tipps's act either. It felt good to know he saw through her too.

"They were both rather short and stocky. Broad shoulders. Thick about the waist. I'm no fashion critic. They wore black or brown coats and hats. Nothing fancy. They weren't from London."

"Why do you say that?" Arundel interrupted.

Mrs. Tipps paused. "I don't know. I just…I had a sense of them being from somewhere else."

"The countryside?"

"Yes. They looked as though they belonged on a farm. Perhaps it was the boots they wore. Mr. Tipps and I don't travel often, but we once toured the Lake District. I remember men working the fields we passed wearing boots like that." She waved her hand. "But that's just an impression. I didn't really see."

"I understand," Arundel said. "But I'm thankful you were at home and happened to glance out your window. Your observations have been most helpful."

Belle realized suddenly that Arundel was no longer holding her against him. Yet, she was still leaning against him. She straightened and stepped away from him.

"Do you know where Mr. Howard has gone?" Mrs. Tipps asked.

"Not yet. But I'll find him and bring him back." He winked. "Preferably before your stock of tea runs out."

Mrs. Tipps smiled, and Belle was loath to admit that Arundel did have a way with people. If he could charm Mrs. Tipps, he could charm anyone. "Good day," Arundel said.

Belle echoed him and they moved away as Mrs. Tipps closed the door. A moment later, Belle saw her at the window.

"Did her spying really help you?" Belle asked when they'd moved down the street a bit.

"Yes. It's exactly as I'd thought."

"Then perhaps you will let me in on your thoughts."

He looked at her, seemed to consider, then nodded. "I believe I owe that to you, yes. But not here." He raised his hand as the approached the corner.

"What are you doing? Why are you flagging a hackney?"

"I'll tell you at the hotel."

"Hotel? I am not going to a hotel with you." Even if the notion made her belly flutter and her knees give way like clotted cream.

"Well, we can't stay here. Ho, there!" He called to the driver. "Mivart's Hotel, please."

"Alright, Guvner."

Arundel opened the door and gestured for Belle to climb in. Belle hesitated, looked back at the shop, and then at Arundel. She had a choice. She could sit at home and hope her father returned soon or she could go with Arundel and help find him.

Belle climbed into the hackney.

Arundel climbed after her then closed the door and tapped on the roof. "I'm really not at liberty to tell you anything about my work," he said once they were underway.

Belle crossed her arms. "And I would hate to throw you out of a moving coach, but if you don't tell me something, I'll open this door and toss you on your head."

***

Hew couldn't help but smile at her. She couldn't have thrown him out of the coach if she'd tried for a year. He had a foot of height on her and probably three or four stone. But he didn't doubt she would attempt to toss him out on his ear. She had a temper and plenty of spirit.

"What have I told you already?" he asked. It was a ploy to give himself time to think, but he also wasn't exactly sure, being that he'd spent much of his time with her previously in and out of consciousness.

"Well, the last time my father was missing"—her tone was accusatory—"you said you have been investigating a bridge collapse. The bridge crumbled as the train was midway across. Ten people were injured and...five killed?"

"Three killed."

"You suspected there was sabotage involved in the accident. Or—well, I suppose if there was sabotage then it was no accident."

"It was not an accident. I can't prove it yet, but I have my theories."

"So you said. And what are your theories?"

This was the part Hew was not at liberty to discuss. Baron would have his head, but Hew couldn't justify keeping her in the dark. She'd lost her father—twice, as she pointed out—had her shop vandalized, and now he couldn't allow her to go home else she might become a target of the men after him as well. Safer to keep her with him at this point, though he had debated that point at least a dozen times.

"Do not make me open this door," Belle said, a warning in her voice. "What are your theories?"

"If I tell you, you must never repeat any of this to anyone."

She gave him a look of disdain. "And who would I tell? The clerk who comes in for his Irish Breakfast tea? No, the seamstress who needs a new teapot because her mother-in-law is coming to visit." She shook her head. "Most people have no time to worry about sabotaged bridges. Most people have never so much as traveled outside of London, much less been on a train."

Hew raised his brows. "Have you been out of London?"

"I've been to Wapping."

That hardly counted as outside of London. "Then you've never been on a train."

"No."

It seemed incredible to him that she should never have left this city, and he was seized with the sudden desire to show her the world. He'd like to see Paris, Rome, and Constantinople through her eyes.

"From what you've said," she continued, "I don't think I'm missing much."

He wanted to say that she was missing everything. There was so much more to the world than Fenchurch Street. But he couldn't say that, of course. Even if she believed him, what difference did it make? He couldn't be the one to take her away. He'd have to marry her for that. And he would never marry again. He would never trust a woman again—not even a woman like Belle.

"Arundel?"

He blinked, aware that she must have been speaking to him.

"Your theories, Arundel."

And he'd just been thinking that he wouldn't trust her. He'd have to trust her somewhat now if he gave her this information. Grudgingly, Hew admitted she had earned some of his trust. "Earlier you mentioned the bridge sabotage might have something to do with the train tracks cutting through a farmer's land. You weren't far off. My suspect—and remember I can't prove this, at least not yet—is a local landowner named Pennywhistle. Pennywhistle was the previous owner of the land where the tracks had been laid."

"He sold the land to the railroads and then regretted the sale. Is that what you think?"

As usual, she had grasped the salient point immediately. "That's my suspicion, yes. I found out Pennywhistle had hired surveyors to map the land adjacent to the land now owned by the railroads. They were searching for deposits of copper and iron ore."

"And I assume copper and iron are valuable."

"Depending on the size of the deposit, they could be worth a fortune."

"So this Pennywhistle probably wonders if the deposits extend onto the land he sold the railroad. Did he try to buy the land back?"

That was Hew's question as well. "The railroad hasn't provided me with that information yet. But that's my assumption, yes. I also know the railroad. That track is built, and they've gone to the expense to build a bridge. They won't sell the land back."

Belle sat back and looked out the window of the hackney. "If he sabotages the bridge, the railroad men will only repair it. How does that serve Pennywhistle?"

Hew gave her a level look. She was so pretty, sitting across from him with her honeyed hair coming out of its confines and her brown eyes large with interest. Hew looked away. He could not entertain these feelings for her. He was not the sort of man to seduce a young woman—and she was young and inexperienced, no matter what she claimed—and then walk away. Hew doubted Belle was the sort of woman he *could* walk away from once he'd had a real taste of her. The kiss they'd shared the night before had only made him want more. But he had been married once and that was more than enough. Let other men take up the mantle of husband and father. Hew was a devoted bachelor.

"There is always a purpose to sabotage," Hew said. "That's the first thing I learned in the Royal Saboteurs. Know your endgame. Sometimes that's easy—sabotaging an attempt on the life of the queen or violence against British citizens saves lives. In this case, I was not the saboteur, but investigating the act—and, of course, hoping to sabotage future efforts. But if Pennywhistle did sabotage the bridge—and someone did as the engineers assured me the damage that resulted in the collapse was deliberate and man-made—then the most likely reason was to give him time."

"Time to search for the mineral deposits? It could take weeks or months for the railroad to repair the bridge."

"Exactly. But I think he found the deposits and needed time to excavate them. He could assemble a group of men on the land to remove as much of the deposits as possible while the train was out of commission."

"And no one would notice men digging up the railroad's land?"

"Bribery," Hew said. "A few hundred pounds paid to railroad officials is a small price compared to the riches Pennywhistle would gain. I had submitted these theories to my director—Baron Keating. He will determine the next steps. Usually the local officials are notified and take action."

"But if Pennywhistle is a prominent man in the area then he might have them in his pocket."

"Astute observation."

She shrugged. "It's not so different than some of the leaders of those criminal gangs who try and extort payment from shopkeepers. They don't usually venture into Fenchurch Street, but I've known tea merchants in other parts of the city who have had to pay."

"And here I thought all you did was sell tea and dust shelves."

She smiled. "That *is* all I do. I live a quiet life."

Until you came along was implied.

"Do you think Baron Keating will send you back to catch Pennywhistle trespassing and digging for minerals? Pennywhistle must think so or he wouldn't have sent men to kill you."

"If he wanted to deflect suspicion, he's certainly gone about it the wrong way. I can't rule out the possibility that the men after me aren't Pennywhistle's, but it seems rather convenient timing. Ah, there is Mivart's Hotel."

She didn't look out the window but instead leaned forward and grasped the hand he'd laid on his knee. Hew raised his brows. "These men are killers. They've already killed three people on the train, and if they'd had their way, you would be dead too. Now they're using my father to get to you. If you meet them tomorrow night, they'll kill you."

"They will certainly try." He grinned at her. "I won't make it easy for them."

The hackney slowed and the doorman from Mivart's stepped forward to open the door. Belle put her hand on it to keep it closed. "I can't allow you to risk your life. Again."

Hew put his hand over hers. "Belle, I can't allow an innocent man like your father to be harmed. It's against the vow I took to protect Queen and Country. I can handle myself."

She snorted. "You are still recovering from an injury that almost took your life."

"It's a good thing I have another day to build up my strength then." He reached for her hand on the door, removing it so the doorman could open it.

"You won't need it," she said as the door swung open, "because I intend to trade myself for my father."

Chapter Sixteen

Belle had never been to Mivart's Hotel, or any hotel, before. Until the last few nights at Lady Keating's, she couldn't recall ever having slept anywhere but her own bed. She'd walked away from the hackney quickly, leaving Arundel to pay the jarvey, and hoping to avoid further discussion of her plan. She'd made up her mind. She would trade herself for her father. She was young and healthy and could endure captivity much better than he.

Her thoughts about her upcoming sacrifice faded as she entered the lobby of the grand hotel. The black and white marble floors and soaring ceilings left her momentarily breathless. She looked about, staring at the footmen in their dark livery and white gloves, carrying silver trays under the glittering lights of the crystal chandeliers. Fresh flowers sat on heavy tables with gilded claw feet and guests wandered through archways to recline on velvet couches. Belle stared at the art on the walls, the sculptures, and then focused on one lady sipping tea in a room just off the main foyer. If she could supply the tea for this establishment, that would be a true accomplishment.

"I hope you don't think that's the end of the conversation," Arundel said, coming up behind her.

Belle turned and grasped his sleeve. "What sort of tea do they serve here? Where do they buy it?"

Arundel stared at her. "I have no idea. And don't think you can change the subject. You are to have nothing to do with Pennywhistle's thugs."

"Fine," she said, not really listening to him. She had always known there was grandeur behind the grand facades of the mansions in Mayfair. She'd seen a glimpse of that at Lady Keating's residence. But for some reason, Belle had thought that sort of opulence only for private residences. But now here was a public place, where anyone could stay in luxury. Well, she supposed anyone who could afford it.

She narrowed her eyes at Arundel. Just how wealthy was he? She didn't believe that an employee of Her Majesty's government had a salary large enough to afford a place like this.

"That agreement came far too quickly. This conversation is not over. For now, keep your mouth closed and follow my lead." He offered his arm, and she stared at it for a moment until he lifted her hand and placed it on his forearm. "Where are your gloves?"

"What gloves?"

"God help us because we will need it." He led her toward a long counter where a short man with a highly starched neckcloth peered at them from over the spectacles perched on his nose.

"Good day, sir. Welcome back."

"Thank you, Mr. Andrews. Do you have any letters or packages for me?"

"Yes, sir. In fact, I do. One moment while I fetch them." He turned sharply, opened a door behind him, and disappeared.

"You receive correspondence here? Is this where you live?" Belle hissed.

"No, but Baron knows I'm staying here and assuming he received the report I sent before I came to London, he would send a reply here. Of course, with the weather so bad and the roads being what they are, I don't have any expectations."

"I had no idea places like this even existed," she murmured.

Andrews returned, with two letters on a silver tray. Belle wanted to ask why he needed the tray when his gloved hands looked to be in perfectly good order, but she'd sold tea to the servants of enough wealthy customers to know that one couldn't begin to understand the foibles of the upper classes. Arundel took the letters and pocketed them in his coat without looking at them.

"Would you like your key, sir?" Andrews asked, holding out a large golden key with a black velvet ribbon tied to it.

"Thank you, Andrews. I would like to show my sister my rooms."

Belle started to be referred to as his sister, but she supposed it was all for show. No doubt Andrews didn't believe she was his sister, but for propriety's sake, they would all pretend.

"Very good, sir. Anything else?"

Arundel glanced at her. "Send a maid with a selection of your teas. All of your teas. My sister is quite particular." He nodded at Belle. "She will want to peruse all the offerings of the hotel."

"Of course, sir. I will send Jenny to you right away."

Belle waited until Arundel had opened the door to his chamber and they were inside before she turned to him. "Thank you!" She didn't think, merely threw her arms about him and hugged him.

He stiffened, but she didn't care. She squeezed him as hard as she could. "What's this for?" he said, voice muffled.

"The tea. You knew I was curious."

"Right." He disentangled himself and set her apart from him. "Try any tea you like. Try all of them if you wish. One of these letters is from Baron. I'll need a little time to decode it."

She didn't know what he meant by *decode*, but then she doubted he would tell her either. "Who is the other one from?"

"My mother," he said and moved to a cream-colored chair in front of a polished wooden desk. *His mother*. For some reason Belle hadn't imagined Arundel had a mother.

"Who is your mother?" she asked, looking about the opulent chamber. "A duchess?" Thick rugs covered the floor so that her thin shoes sunk with every step she took. Large windows overlooked the busy street below, their heavy curtains drawn back to allow daylight to bathe the room. A grouping of chairs and a couch had been placed near the hearth, and on the other side of the room was a small table and two chairs. Behind her, Arundel sat at the desk. A door behind the table was closed but must have led to the bed chamber. She could only imagine how the bed chamber looked. Perhaps it held one of those enormous beds with curtains—the sort of bed a duchess would sleep in.

"My mother is not a duchess," Arundel said from the desk. Then more quietly, "Her mother was the late Duchess of Ely, though."

If his mother was the daughter of a duke and duchess... "Your grandfather is a duke!" She whirled on him. "I didn't think people like you so much as spoke to people like me."

He turned in his chair. "People like you?"

"Lowly shopkeepers."

"There's little difference between us," he said, turning back to his letter. "I work and you work. I am not titled; you are not titled."

Oh, there was an ocean of difference between them, Belle thought, and it wasn't only the fact that he could afford a room like this. Belle went to the window and stared down at the people and coaches moving along Brook Street. Her little corner of Fenchurch Street seemed small, but she need only venture a few blocks away to remember that London was enormous and filled with people. Somewhere, out in the warren of streets and shadow of buildings, was her father. Was he safe? Warm? Hungry? What if Pennywhistle's men had beaten him? What if he was dead, and the meeting in

Hyde Park was an ambush? What if she never saw her dear Papa again?

A hand touched her shoulder, and she turned her head from the window to see Arundel behind her. "You were banging your fist on the glass," he said.

She looked at her hand, which was indeed curled into a fist and resting on the glass. "Sorry."

"Is it your father? Are you worried about him?"

"I…" Her throat seemed to close, and to her horror, tears welled in her eyes. She never cried, especially not in front of men. Now she was doing it again. What was the matter with her?

"Come here," he said and gathered her into his arms. And to her amazement, she went willingly, pressing her wet cheek against his soft coat and feeling his solid chest beneath the layers of fabric. "I will find him," Arundel said. "You'll be together again, and all of this will be a bad dream. You can go back to the way things were before I was dropped into your life."

No doubt his words were intended to soothe her, but they were having the opposite effect. Of course, she wanted her father returned safely, but she didn't want Arundel to go away. She should hate him after all the upheaval he had caused the past few days. And she did think she would come to hate him because once he was gone, her life would go back to the way it had been, and she hadn't realized how small it had been. It was as though Arundel's arrival had swept back the heavy curtain of her life, and the light showed her there was more to existence than dusting tea shelves and dreaming about sneaking another cup of the special Pan Long Yin Hao.

Not that she didn't still dream about the Pan Long Yin Hao. She had a little of what she'd taken from the safe in the shop left, and it was secure in her pocket.

But like Arundel, soon it would be gone, and the curtain would close again, leaving her in the shadows. Funny how with her scarred face, she'd always preferred those shadows. But she hadn't even thought about her scars the past day. Arundel made her forget to be self-conscious about them.

"Do you think they've hurt him?" she asked Arundel when she had control of herself again. He handed her a handkerchief, and she wiped her nose and eyes. He was probably used to ladies who delicately dabbed at their tears, but when she peeked at him, the expression on his face only reflected concern.

"They have no reason to hurt him."

"No, but…" She swallowed. "They have no reason to keep him alive. What if they've killed him? If they only plan to kill you, why bother with exchanging my father? Once you are in the park, they'll kill you."

"First of all, I don't give these men much credit, but the most basic tenet of a prisoner swap is that you produce the prisoner. They must know I'll want to see him before agreeing to anything. Secondly, I'm not so easy to kill. They haven't managed it yet, and I won't be an easy target."

"But—"

"Belle, you will drive yourself mad if you imagine every possible scenario and every small thing that might go wrong. Let me handle that. It's my job."

"Oh, yes." She scowled at him. "As though I can simply stop worrying at the snap of your fingers."

"You're right," he said. "You need a distraction."

She might have asked him what sort of distraction, but he chose that moment to drag a hand from her waist to trace her backbone. His light touch sent shivers through her, and she realized he was still holding her.

The realization sent a shock through her—Arundel was holding her. They were alone in this beautiful chamber.

And she was very much not his sister.

Her eyes met his, and those lovely eyes of his had turned the shade of velvet blue she found fascinating. She couldn't help but drag her gaze down his slightly crooked nose and to his lips. She liked his lips too. They were full and soft, and when he smiled, his mouth curved in the most adorable way.

She didn't know how to play games of seduction, didn't know what to do next, but she knew what she wanted to do. She knew she wanted him to kiss her. She slid a hand up his chest and behind his head, tugging on his neck to lower it so she might reach it. Then, instead of kissing his lips, she brushed a quick kiss over his nose.

He laughed. "Why did you do that?"

"Did I surprise you?"

"Always." He was smiling, and she was drawn by that curve at the corners of his mouth. *That* was where she wanted to kiss.

"How did you break your nose?" she asked.

"That's a long story."

"And you have a letter to decode."

"And I want to do this." He lowered his mouth to hers, kissing her lightly. Belle's heart immediately began to pound, and she felt a sense of dizziness sweep over her. It was the good kind of dizziness. The kind she felt when she tasted a new tea that was unlike any she'd tasted before.

"This is a good distraction," she said against his lips.

"I think I can do better."

His arms tightened around her, lifting her so that she was on tiptoes. His mouth met hers again, this time with more pressure, his tongue sliding between her lips, coaxing her to open for him. Belle gasped at the pleasure that shot through her when his tongue swept into her mouth. His kiss was slow and persuasive, inviting her to join him. And she accepted the invitation, stroking his tongue with hers and stoking the heat that had begun to simmer between them. Belle was painfully aware of the feel of his body against hers, the scent of him, the fact that he'd all but lifted her off the ground as though she weighed nothing. She had a moment to worry about his wound. Should he be lifting her? But then his tongue slid along hers, and she couldn't think of anything except that she wanted him.

And he wanted her. That was the miracle of it. He really did not care that half of her face was scarred and ugly. This was no act. She could feel the evidence of his arousal. He was attracted to her. He desired her.

And then suddenly his mouth dragged away from hers, and he set her back on the floor. She might have stumbled if he hadn't grasped her elbow. She blinked, the room too bright and too warm. "What—"

She heard the tapping on the door. It was a bit insistent, as though the person at the door had tapped already and was making a second attempt.

"The maid with the tea," Arundel said.

She'd forgotten all about the tea. She'd forgotten about everything except his mouth.

"One moment!" he called. Then to Belle he said, "You'd better stand with your back to the room. Look out the window." He turned her to face it. "Take a moment to compose yourself."

Belle realized she must look something like how she felt. Her face felt flushed, and her head was spinning. She touched her lips. They felt swollen and sensitive.

Arundel went to the door and opened it. Belle heard a cheery greeting from the maid and the sounds of her wheeling a tray into the chamber. Belle didn't comprehend a word the maid said. She was still trying to catch her breath. She smoothed her skirts, closed her eyes, and tried to slow her breathing. Finally, by the time the maid had set up the tea service on the small table, she was able to turn and stride across the room to study the selections. The maid handed her a handwritten list of the teas available, presumably that was what the boxes on the lower shelves of the cart held.

Belle perused the selections, noting the favorites—the Earl Grey, Darjeeling, and Ceylon teas. Quite a selection of white teas as well, but her gaze was drawn to the Sencha Kyoto, which was a green tea composed of cherry blossoms. She had recently bought a shipment of what she considered some of the best Sencha Kyoto she'd ever sampled. She wondered how this compared.

"I will have the Sencha Kyoto," she said, "and Mr. Arundel will have the Assam." She glanced at Arundel who merely raised a brow at her presumptuousness.

The maid looked at Arundel as well. "Sir?"

"My sister knows me well. Assam is my favorite."

Of course it was. He hadn't even needed to tell her, but she knew he was the sort who liked a bold flavor, and the malty taste of the Assam added richness. Arundel went back to his letter, though Belle had no idea how he could concentrate on it after the kiss they'd just shared. She could barely keep her attention on watching the maid brew the tea. But she managed. After all, she was quite particular as to how her tea was brewed, and she gave the maid a few suggestions during the process. Finally, the tea was poured, and the maid took the tray away. Belle took one of the chairs at the table, inhaled the fragrant steam of the tea, and took a sip.

"Well?" Arundel asked. She opened her eyes to see he was watching her.

"It's delicious," she said. "But not as good as mine."

"I don't doubt that."

"Do you want me to bring yours to the desk?"

"No. I'm done here." He lifted the letter and carried it to the table with him, taking the seat across from her. He sipped his tea, nodded, and sipped again. "I've decoded the letter."

Belle watched him over the rim of the teacup. Apparently, they were pretending that the kiss from a few minutes before hadn't happened.

"And what does Baron Keating say?"

"He says he agrees with my theory regarding Pennywhistle, and he's sent another agent to poke around Carlisle and the surrounding area of Cumbria and find out more about him. He's also written to the railroad to expedite the release of their correspondence and records concerning Pennywhistle."

Belle sipped her tea again. "What else?"

"As soon as I finish here, I'm to return to Carlisle and continue my investigation. Baron has charged me with catching Pennywhistle in the act of trespassing on the railroad's land, perhaps even catching him in an act of sabotage."

"And my father?"

Arundel met her gaze over his teacup. "Nothing, not even an order from the queen, comes before returning your father to you."

"And once he is safe, you'll be gone."

Slowly, he sipped his tea again, his gaze never leaving her face. "Your life can return to the way it was."

She nodded. "That's all I wanted."

"I won't trouble you any longer."

"You have been quite a lot of trouble."

"Then you'll be glad to see me go."

"Very glad." She set her teacup on the table. "And I'm sure you will be happy to return to your life."

"I won't have to hear lectures on tea."

"You won't miss that, I'm sure."

"Not at all," he said, but his tone said otherwise. Belle wanted to ask the obvious question—was he lying as much as she was? Would he miss her as much as she feared she'd miss him?

"Arundel—"

A tap on the door had them both jumping. Arundel waved a hand. "That must be the bath I ordered."

"Bath? When did you order that?"

"I believe it was when you were engaged with the tea selections." He rose and went to the door, opening it for a pair of footmen, who carried in a large tub. Four more followed, each with two large buckets of water. "Put that one in the bed chamber," Arundel ordered, crossing to open the door for them. Belle gaped as she watched the parade of servants carry the tub into the other room and fill it with water. Their task completed, the men filed out and a maid entered, arms full of white towels and a basket of soaps and other toiletries on her arm. Arundel directed her to the bed chamber, and then she too marched out, leaving them alone.

"The doctor said not to get your stitches wet," she told him, feeling rather stupid at having nothing better to say.

"I'll have them fill the tub only halfway when it's my turn."

"Your turn?"

"You should go before the water turns cold."

"I should—the bath is for me?" For some odd reason, Belle felt her cheeks heat. "But I didn't ask—"

"Well, if you don't want it, I'll tell them not to bring the second tub and use it myself."

"Second tub?"

"A shallow one for me. I thought I'd have it put in here and let you have the bed chamber."

"That's thoughtful."

"Hmm. But if you don't want it—"

"I do." She rose. A bath like this one was a rare treat as it was a serious undertaking to fetch, carry, and heat enough water for a bath. She and her father usually made do with cold water and a rough towel. She'd been given warm water at Lady Keating's, but not enough to submerge herself or to wash her hair. Belle looked at the bed chamber then back at Arundel.

"I assure you I will not disturb you. The key to the door is on the dresser. Lock it if that makes you feel better." Another knock interrupted them. "That will be my bath."

"Excuse me then." And Belle went into the bed chamber and closed the door. She leaned against it and stared at the tub, steam rising from the warm water. She crossed to the tub, dipped a hand in it, and smiled at the temperature. This would be a true luxury. The basket of toiletries was at her feet, and she saw she had a choice of soaps in a variety of fragrances, as well as hair washes. How lovely not to freeze her head while she washed her hair.

She slipped off her shoes and began to unfasten her gown when she remembered the key on the dresser. She could hear the footmen taking their leave from the salon on the other side of the door. That meant Arundel would undress and take his own bath. Meanwhile, she would be naked in this room.

She went to the dresser, lifted the key, then set it down again, leaving the door unlocked as she finished undressing and stepped into the steaming water.

Chapter Seventeen

Hew would have liked to have made use of the large tub in the bed chamber, but he contented himself with the hip bath. The water reached his waist and kept his stitches dry. Careful of his wound, he used soap and a cloth to clean his chest, arms, and shoulders. Then he dried off and utilized a basin to wash his hair. By the time the barber arrived, a quarter hour later, he was dry and dressed in trousers and a bathrobe. He'd forgotten to fetch clean clothing from his bed chamber before Belle had gone inside and closed the door. He could hear the sounds of water sloshing about on the other side of the door, and he was trying very hard not to imagine her naked and in the bathtub.

He was actually grateful for the barber's appearance and even more grateful for the man's conversation while he shaved Hew. For a few minutes, Hew was able to think about something other than what he would have liked to do to Miss Howard.

Hew was not the sort of man to chase after women or take strangers to his bed. He'd gone to his marriage bed a virgin, and he'd fully embraced the pleasures he'd found there. When his wife had left—such an innocuous way to put it—Hew hadn't thought about that aspect of his life for some time. He'd been too angry, too humiliated, and then too devastated. He had sometimes thought about finding a lover, but he didn't want a courtesan or a married woman—definitely not a married woman. He would have considered a widow, but his work as a diplomat and then with the Royal Saboteurs had meant he was too often traveling or training to cultivate any special friendships with women. No doubt this was why he couldn't seem to stop thinking about taking Belle Howard to bed. It had been a long time since he'd been with a woman, and Belle was undeniably attractive. It wasn't just her appearance, though that was appealing. He liked the way she spoke, the way she went a bit dreamy when she spoke of tea, and the look of ecstasy on her face when she tasted a blend she approved of.

He wondered if she looked like that in bed.

And he didn't think he would ever find out. It was best if he never found out.

The barber finished, and Hew gave him a coin and bid him good day. Alone now, he didn't hear any sounds from the bed chamber, and the silence only made his imagination more active.

Hew tried to remind himself that right now he was free to walk away from Belle as soon as he returned her father to her safe and sound. He had kissed her and nothing more. He had no obligations. That was what he wanted. He'd vowed never to marry again. He knew what women were, and he wanted no part of another marriage.

And yet, the lure of Belle Howard was almost irresistible. Before he knew what he was about, he had risen and walked, barefoot, to the bed chamber door. He didn't know what he intended. Perhaps he wanted to listen at the door or just ensure she had locked it. But when his hand touched the latch, it lifted and swung open to reveal Belle, wrapped only in a towel, standing near the fire.

She turned to him, not seeming surprised that he had intruded upon her. Her hair was slick and wet. She held a brush and had obviously been combing the tangles from her hair after washing it. The ends of her hair dripped onto her bare shoulders and down her back, pooling in the cloth from the towel that covered her from chest to knees. Below the knees, her legs were slim, and her small feet looked pink and clean in the firelight.

"How was your bath?" she asked. Hew drew in a breath. He should turn around and walk out now. She should tell him to go.

"Good. And yours?" He closed the door behind him, and she took a step to the mantel and set the brush there.

"Perfect."

Hew leaned against the dresser. "You didn't lock the door."

"You said you wouldn't disturb me."

"Am I disturbing you?" he asked.

One word.

One cross look and he would go. He could still walk away.

"Not yet." And with those cryptic words, she dropped her towel. It was like a punch in the chest to watch the white cloth slip down her body and pool at the floor. His heart clenched, and he couldn't seem to draw in a breath. But his eyes knew what to do. They feasted on the sight of her, all exposed flesh and lovely curves. She was petite and slim, her breasts small and high. Her waist was tiny, and her hips flared briefly before the heart-shaped roundness of her bottom.

"Am I disturbing you?" she asked.

"Very much." And then he was walking across the room, walking to her, seemingly powerless to stop himself from reaching out and putting his hands on her waist. Her skin was warm, but she'd be cold in a moment if she stood naked much longer. The subtle scent of citrus floated up from her hair and her skin, and underneath it the scent he always associated with her. He looked down into her eyes, so large and brown. There was a question in those eyes, and he imagined his own held a question as well.

"Are you sure?" he asked.

"I've been sure," she said. "Are *you* sure?"

"No." But he pushed the doubts from his mind because her skin was soft and warm, and his hands traveled down and over her firm bottom, cupping her cheeks and drawing her against him. He was hard, and the heat of her made his cock ache with need. She put her arms about him and pressed her lips to his, and through his robe he felt the hard points of her nipples against his chest.

How in God's name was he supposed to resist this?

She made a small sound of pleasure as one hand left her bottom and cupped a pert breast. He slid his thumb over her nipple, and she gasped, her mouth opening and her head falling back. Hew took the opportunity to kiss her throat and then to slide the hand on her bottom between her legs. She jerked in surprise, and he paused until she opened her eyes again and met his gaze.

"Do you want me to stop?" he asked.

She shook her head. "No." She glanced at the bed. "Would you think me too forward if I suggested we go to the bed? My knees are a bit wobbly."

Hew almost laughed. Dropping her towel was fine, but asking him to join her on the bed—that was too much? In answer, he picked her up and carried her to the bed. "Stop!" She struggled to make him put her down. "Your injury."

"I don't feel anything but your heat right now," he said. He lowered her to the bed and came down on top of her. "And that's all I want to feel."

Hew lowered his mouth to Belle's and took hers softly and slowly. He wanted to savor the feel of her lips and the way she responded to him. Her reaction was instantaneous. She kissed him back with a fever and intensity that tested his willpower. But before he could slide his hand between her legs again, she pushed against his chest. Hew raised his head, going still. "I'm crushing you," he said, looking down into her dark eyes. "Or do you want me to stop? I'll stop."

She grasped his arms. "I don't want you to stop."

Thank God. The idea of walking away now was torture.

"I do worry about your wound."

"It's fine—"

She put a finger on his lips. "Lie on your back."

Hew was about to object then wondered why the hell he'd do that. He rolled off her and lay on his back. Much as he hated to admit it, that did take the strain off his wound. It also gave him a view of her lovely body. The sun filtered through the pale material of the curtains in the bed chamber. Between that and the light from the fire, Hew's gaze took in the blushing tips of her breasts and the honey-colored hair between her legs. She lowered to her side, propping her head on her elbow and reached over to smooth the hair back from his face. He usually wore his hair shorter, but between his work on the railroad accident and the extended time in London, it had grown past what he liked.

Belle's fingers slid down his cheek to trace his smooth jaw. "I like how you look freshly shaven."

"I like how you look naked."

She smiled at him, bent, and kissed his jaw. Her lips traced the line of his jaw, making him shiver. Heat infused him as her breasts slid against the fabric of his shirt. As her lips met his mouth and the kiss deepened, Hew took hold of her waist and pulled her on top of him. She broke away and stared down at him, shocked. He grinned, liking the view of her above him. "You wanted me on my back."

His hands cupped her hips and slid around to her bottom. When she moved in response, he almost groaned at the feel.

He was still dressed, thank God, but he could feel her heat through the clothing. His hands slid up her back then down over her shoulders and skated over the tops of her breasts. Belle's head fell back as he fondled her but snapped back when his hand slid to her belly. His fingers curled in her soft pubic hair, and her gaze met his.

"May I touch you here?" he asked, his fingers sliding lower.

"Do you want to?" she asked, voice quite breathless.

"Very much. You'll like it, but if you don't, say the word and I'll stop."

She nodded and he nudged her hips so she arched back slightly. The view that gave him made him slightly lightheaded. He placed one hand on her waist, anchoring her, and slid the other between them to stroke her sleek folds. She was damp and pink and slightly swollen. He moved slowly and deliberately, allowing her to adjust to the feel of his fingers on her before moving one finger to her entrance. He hovered there, circling it, until she opened her eyes and gave him a look that was a mixture of confusion and wanting. Her brown eyes were impossibly large and so dark as to be almost mahogany.

Hew pushed up and into her tight channel, feeling her grip him almost immediately. She gasped quietly then stared at him accusingly as he withdrew his finger. He entered her again and this time he slid his thumb over the small nub buried in her folds and stroked it gently as he plunged deeper. "Oh!" she said, and her head dropped back. Hew took his time, sliding in and out of her and teasing that nub until her breathing came heavy and she opened enough that he could insert two fingers. She moaned then and thrust her hips toward him. She was tight and her muscles gripped him as she neared climax.

Hew slid his fingers out again then gently inserted them, this time circling her using the wetness from her body. But instead of teasing her, he continued to circle and flick. She began to shake and her hips bucked. "Please," she said, though she sounded confused as to what she wanted.

Hew knew what she wanted, and with a last stroke, he gave it to her. She cried out and her inner muscles clenched his fingers as her hips bucked and rolled. And then she fell forward to lay her head on his chest, her breaths coming fast and short. He withdrew his hand and stroked her, feeling the way her entire body vibrated. He could feel the thundering of her heart against his chest.

He'd missed this—this feeling of connection, of closeness. He wanted to further it by opening the placket of his trousers and filling her with his cock. But he was still in possession of some of his senses.

With regret, he resisted.

"What we just did," she said, sliding off him and lying on her side. "Am I still a virgin?"

He turned to look at her. "You are. I touched you, gave you pleasure. Nothing you couldn't do with your own hands."

Her cheeks turned pink, but she didn't look away. "Could I do the same to you?"

"You could." She reached for his trousers, but he caught her hand. "But I can't let you."

"Why not?" Her tone was demanding.

"Because if you take these trousers off, I don't trust what might happen next."

"And what if what happens next is what I want?"

"Belle—"

"Listen to me, Arundel. I'm almost six and twenty. I'll never marry. I want this with you—with someone I care about."

He wanted this too. He dared not allow himself to think about how much he wanted her. "I care about you, Belle. And that's why I won't take your virginity. You could become with child, and even if you don't, I'm obligated to marry you if I compromise you."

"Compromise me? I'm not a duke's daughter. I'm a shopgirl. No one on Fenchurch Street cares about such things."

"*I* care. You're worth so much more than you credit."

"I'm a pock-marked spinster. No one has ever wanted me, and no one ever will." She jerked up, and he caught her just before she could run. "Let me go."

"In a moment." Hew wrapped his arms about her from behind, knowing she had to be chilled now. "Let me explain."

"There's nothing to explain." Her voice sounded resigned. "You have your principles."

"It's more than that," he said, not knowing why he went on. He did have his principles. She wasn't wrong. He didn't have to explain further, but for some reason he wanted to. "I was married once," he said.

She stiffened. "Once?" she asked.

He understood her confusion. Marriage was rather a permanent state. "She's dead," he said.

Her face fell. "I'm so sorry."

"I'm not."

At that she tore away from him and walked across the room. He didn't watch her, didn't want to see the disgust in her eyes. What kind of person was glad his wife was dead? After a time, her feet appeared before him again, and he looked up and saw she had slipped on a robe—his robe. One he had left draped over a chair the last time he was here. He liked her in the dark blue and gold silk robe. The sleeves hung down past her hands.

"Did you kill her?" Belle asked.

Hew was still admiring her in the robe, and her words penetrated his mind slowly. When they did, he jumped hard enough that a lance of pain slid through his side. "No. I didn't kill her. She died in childbirth."

Belle took a step back. "Then you have a child."

Hew shook his head. "The child died as well, and in any case, it wasn't my child."

She stared at him for a long moment and then she moved to sit beside him on the bed. "Oh, Arundel." She took his hand.

He turned his head to look at her. "You should probably call me Hew. At least in private."

"Hew," she said, seeming to test it. "Tell me about your wife."

He didn't want to talk about Clara. He didn't want to think about her, but he owed some sort of explanation to Belle. "Her name was Clara," he said. "The marriage was arranged by our parents, but I didn't mind. She was beautiful and charming, very charming, and I think I was half in love with her the first time I met her. She had that effect on men. It should have been a warning."

Belle squeezed his hand, and Hew closed his eyes, hoping to block out the memory of Clara's dark curls and pretty green eyes. "At first we were happy." He massaged the bridge of his nose. "I supposed I always thought we were happy. I never knew what was happening until she was telling me good-bye. I was such a fool."

"I doubt that."

"I was trained as a spy, and I didn't even see what was happening in my own house."

"You shouldn't have had to be a spy in your own house."

"I should have paid more attention. She didn't like being the wife of a diplomat. I think the idea sounded romantic in London, but once we were on the Continent, and she was away from friends and family, the reality was not so exciting. I was away often and the other British women of our circle were older. Clara loved music, balls, the theater. She loved men, especially their admiration. I didn't care that she had a dozen admirers. I didn't have the time or the inclination to chaperone her to every event she wanted to attend."

"And she fell in love with one of those admirers?"

"Love or lust, yes. The Comte du Guitreau became her lover. One night I came home from work early and found her packing her bags. She was leaving me to go to France with him. I was…"

Hew didn't know how to describe what he'd been. *Shocked* seemed too mild a word. He'd simply stood there and watched her pack, watched her walk out the door and spring into the waiting coach. He'd stood rooted in place for hours, not knowing what to do or to say or to feel.

"Angry," Hew finally finished. Because of all the emotions he'd felt, that had been the one he'd clung to. His anger had helped him get out of bed in the morning, had forced him to work, had fueled the rage-filled letters he'd written to her family.

"She betrayed you," Belle said. "Of course, you were angry." She still held his hand, but she didn't try to embrace him. And when he looked at her, he didn't see the pity he'd seen in the eyes of so many others during that time.

"You don't understand," he said, wanting to see the pity in her eyes, so he could find a reason to distance himself from her. "Even after she left me—even after I found out she was carrying his child—I would have taken her back. Her parents wrote to her, urging her to return to me."

Belle only nodded, her gaze concerned but not patronizing. "You loved her."

"Christ." Hew lowered his head and ran his hands through his hair. "I did love her. But I hated her too. She made me look like a fool. I was the same age you are now, five and twenty, and I couldn't walk into a room without people whispering and looking at me as though they were attending my funeral. When she died, I was glad of it."

"No, you weren't."

Hew's head jerked up. "I threw a dinner party and drank until I passed out. I toasted her descent to hell."

"You didn't mean it. You were hurt. You were humiliated."

"I was done," he said. "Done with marriage and women and my career as a diplomat. I returned to London and began working for the Foreign Office. When I heard of the Royal Saboteurs, I made it my mission to become a member.

"Don't say it." Hew held up a finger. "My mother has told me enough times that I worked so hard to forget the pain."

"I wasn't about to say that."

"Then you were about to say that not all women are like her. That may be, but I would have sworn on my grandfather's grave that Clara would be honest and true. But her head, and heart, were easily turned. I'll never trust another woman again."

He saw her rear back as though slapped and reached to take her in his arms again. She thrust a hand between them. "Don't."

"Let me explain. Belle—"

"You mean, you would like to add milk and sugar to your words and make them taste sweeter. I have a secret for you, *Arundel*." He didn't miss the fact that she called him by his surname, not his given name, as he'd asked. "No amount of milk or sugar will sweeten your words, but I'm not sorry you said them because now I understand."

Hew didn't want to ask, but he felt compelled. "What do you understand?"

"That no matter how many times I tell you I'm not trying to trap you into marriage, it won't make a difference. You'll never trust me. You'll never trust any woman."

"I do trust you, Belle. I've never told anyone the things I just told you."

"And I've never allowed a man to touch me the way you have, but I can't let it happen again. I can't allow myself to fall deeper in love with you."

Hew felt his throat tighten and close. He tried to take a breath and couldn't. His chest wouldn't expand. She didn't love him. She simply thought she loved him. And it was his fault—all of it. The last thing he'd wanted to do was hurt Belle or her father, and he'd done exactly that.

"Belle—" Hew somehow managed to croak her name.

"Get out," she said, pointing to the door. "I'm exhausted and want to rest. Alone."

"Let me explain."

"And tell me more about how women will lie and cheat and trick men? About how we can't be trusted? I've heard enough, thank you."

Hew stood, his ears ringing as though he'd had them boxed. And now she was evicting him from his own bed chamber. He supposed he deserved it—the harsh words and the exile. He'd crossed a line with her he hadn't wanted to cross, had known it would come to this, and now he would have to walk away from her.

"I'll leave you," he said and padded across the room. He half hoped, half prayed she would call him back. He still wanted her. He could still taste her on his lips, but when he passed through the doorway, it closed behind him.

When he turned back, he heard it lock.

Chapter Eighteen

Belle had heard other women denigrate men as fools. She hadn't ever shared that opinion. Her father was no fool. He was the most wonderful, caring, loving person in the world. Maggie's husband, Mr. Dormer, was no fool. He was kind and funny and the way he looked at Maggie made Belle's heart clench. She'd known other men—tea merchants and importers, warehouse managers and chefs for wealthy peers. Most of those men were no fools. They knew a good tea and a good bargain.

But now she thought she understood what the women she'd half-listened to all these years were talking about. Men like Hew Arundel were clever and brave and canny. Hew was a perfectly intelligent man—even more intelligent than most men she knew. He was a fighter and a tenacious one at that.

And then she'd kissed him—or he'd kissed her.

Belle rolled over on the bed and tried not to think about the kiss. She tried not to remember the feel of his hands on her flesh. Tried not to wish he would touch her again. Because something happened when Arundel's emotions became involved. He closed up shop and shut her out. She understood it better now. He'd been hurt, badly. He didn't want to expose himself to that sort of pain again. Belle thought she should probably be honored that he felt enough for her to think she could hurt him like that. If he hadn't cared for her, he wouldn't have felt he was at risk.

But if he hadn't cared for her, she wouldn't have allowed him to touch her, kiss her, carry her to bed, give her pleasure.

Belle closed her eyes.

It was difficult not to see his rejection of her as personal. It wasn't that he didn't want her or didn't find her pretty enough, or that he thought her pockmarked face made her unworthy of his attentions. *It's not you*, she told herself, as though repetition would convince her. Arundel would not trust any woman, ever. It didn't matter what she did, how she proved herself. He would always look at her and wonder how she would betray him, *when* she would betray him.

And that did make him a fool. Because if he was hers, she would have done anything for him.

Belle knew the kind of woman Clara Arundel had been, even if Arundel didn't see it. She'd seen women like her in the shop thousands of times. She'd watched them and studied them, never even drawing their notice because with her scars and her unassuming manner, she was beneath their notice.

A woman like Clara had been spoiled and petted her entire life. She'd relied on her pretty face and had gotten whatever she'd wanted just by batting her eyelashes.

She was overly flirtatious and used to being the center of attention. Arundel had mistaken this for charm, and perhaps Clara Arundel did have charm. But once she was away from London and her circle of admirers, she had begun to doubt herself. No doubt Arundel still admired her, but he was off doing diplomat things all day. He couldn't give her attention every hour and moment, and Clara had needed that constant validation. She needed to be petted and flattered and to feel beautiful and desired. No doubt Austria or Saxony or wherever Arundel had been stationed possessed plenty of men willing to give a needy young Englishwoman attention.

Belle could have told Arundel the truth of the matter— it wasn't that women couldn't be trusted. He'd just trusted the wrong one. She told herself the same thing about men many times. Only she'd never thought she would find a man she could trust.

And maybe she was wrong to think she had because clearly Hew Arundel could never give her the only thing she wanted from him—his heart.

She should cut her losses. It was like the Pan Long Yin Hao. She'd paid an exorbitant amount for it, knowing it was worth every shilling. But only another tea connoisseur, like she, would ever pay that for the blend. She'd never recover her investment in it. And the truth was, she'd never expected to because she'd bought it for herself. So time to own up to her mistake and move on. First chance she had, she would drink her last portion of Pan Long Yin Hao, savor it, and bid it good-bye.

Time to bid Arundel good-bye as well.

As soon as she had her father back.

If she hadn't thought of her father right then, she might have been able to sleep. But once she thought of him, she began to wonder where he was and if he was in pain or discomfort. There was no sleeping after that. There was only cursing of Arundel because not only had he claimed part of her heart, he'd upended her life and was the reason her beloved father had been taken from her.

A tap on the door made Belle sit up in bed and push her hair back. "Go away, Arundel."

"I know you're not sleeping," he said. "I can hear you tossing and turning and *thinking*."

Ridiculous. He couldn't hear her thinking. She didn't even think he could hear her tossing and turning through a closed door.

"I'm not thinking about you." Not only about him, anyway. "Leave me alone."

"If you're not sleeping, I thought you might want something to eat. I've ordered a tray to be brought up. The maid should bring it within the half hour."

Belle had half a mind to tell him she didn't want his food or anything from him. She just wanted her father back and to never see or hear of Hew Arundel again. But her stomach gurgled and growled, and declining food when she was hungry wouldn't hurt Arundel.

"Fine," she said, falling back onto the bed and wishing she could sleep. Her eyes stung and her body ached with exhaustion.

"Does that mean you will join me in a meal?"

"I'll think about it," she said. But of course, she would join him.

Some twenty minutes later, she heard the outer door open and the squeak of wheels as a tray was rolled in. She also heard the soft murmuring of voices and then the door closing again. Belle heard the clink of china and silver, and that was when the scent of freshly baked bread wafted into the bed chamber. Her mouth began to water, and her belly gave a demanding growl.

Belle climbed out of the enormous bed, stomped to the door, flung it open, and stared at Arundel. He was seated at the small table just outside the bed chamber. The tray had been rolled beside the table and the food was set out, covered with silver domes. He had been reading a paper but looked up at her when she tore the door open. Belle wanted to hit him. He looked so impossibly handsome with his cleanly shaven jaw and his bright blue eyes. How did he manage it when he was still recovering from near death? Belle could only imagine what she looked like. She should have brushed her hair when she'd risen from bed.

Arundel stood, as though she were some sort of lady. "I didn't know what you liked," he said, going to the other chair and pulling it out for her. "So I ordered a bit of everything."

Belle had the urge to tell him that wasn't necessary. She'd be happy with a bit of bread and cheese, but she clamped her mouth shut and nodded. And she took the seat he proffered too. Why not begin to behave as though she deserved this sort of treatment? She'd be back to her real life soon enough.

She lifted the dome over her plate and stared at the enormous plate of food. There was so much, it had begun to fall off the plate when she'd removed the dome.

"Do you want tea?" Arundel asked. "I ordered the Sencha Kyoto from earlier."

Why the deuce did he have to be so thoughtful? It made it difficult to hate him. "I'll have tea after I eat," she said. She'd need to fetch her Pan Long Yin Hao from the pocket of her skirt in the bed chamber.

She lifted her fork and began to eat, barely tasting the food but too hungry to reject it simply because sitting here with Arundel was uncomfortable. For a long time, there was only the clink of silver on china and awkward silence.

"Belle," Arundel said when it seemed as though the silence had gone on for years. "I feel as though I should apologize."

She gave him a look from under her lashes.

"I—er—*know* I should apologize," he amended. "But I can't, for the life of me, think what I should apologize for."

Belle sat back and gave him a direct look. "Can't you?"

"Should I apologize for being honest with you?"

Belle blinked, slowly.

"Should I apologize for refusing to lead you on? I could take you to bed and then tell you I can't marry you. Instead, I preserved your virginity and told you the truth."

Belle clapped once. Then again. Then again. "You are quite the hero."

Arundel crossed his arms over his chest. "What should I have done? I know. I know." He held up his hands defensively. "I never should have opened that door. Never should have walked into the bed chamber."

"Wrong." She dropped her fork, letting it clatter sharply on the plate. "Do you want to know what you did wrong? What you've done wrong? What you are *doing* wrong?" She stood and glared down at him. Arundel gave her a wary look and slid backward in his chair.

"Where do I even begin? Oh, I know." She came around the table. "You are an idiot."

He furrowed his brow. "I beg to differ."

"Don't." She held up a finger. "You married an unfaithful woman. I'm sorry about that. You're not the first cuckold and you won't be the last. But you're an idiot if you think that because one woman betrayed you, every woman will." She wagged the upraised finger. "We're not interchangeable, *Hew*."

"I see, but—"

"No, you don't. That's the problem. Because that's not the only reason you're an idiot." His expression darkened. Belle ignored it and held up another finger. "For some reason, you have the idea that I want to marry you lodged in your skull." She reached over and poked him in the head. "You think if you"—she made a sweeping gesture with her hands and changed her voice to imitate his accent—"*compromise* me, I'll try and trap you into marriage. Idiot!"

"You can stop saying that."

"No, I can't! Have you ever considered that perhaps I *don't* want to marry you any more than you want to marry me? Are you too much of an idiot to realize that not every woman wants to trap a man into matrimony?"

Arundel opened his mouth then closed it again. Belle wasn't sure if he'd thought better of what he'd been about to say or feared she'd call him an idiot again.

She lifted another finger.

"Don't say it," Arundel warned.

"There's a third reason you're—"

"Don't say it."

"An idiot," she said. He was on his feet before she could blink and had her hand closed in his, effectively lowering her fingers.

"I'm not an idiot." He walked her backward until he had her pressed against the wall.

"No, you're a Royal Saboteur. You've taken all the training classes. But you must have been absent the day they taught you how to know when to trust someone. And if you don't trust me by now—after all I have done for you and all we have been through—then you really are an—"

His mouth came down on hers before she could say the word. This kiss was nothing like the sweet, teasing kisses they'd shared before. This kiss was that of a conqueror, seeking to subjugate. But Belle was not so easy to vanquish. She kissed him back with equal passion, nipping at his lip until he pulled back and glared at her.

"I didn't want this," he panted. "I didn't want to want you."

"Then walk away," she said between gulps of air. "You think I want a man who doesn't trust me?"

His hand still gripped her wrist, trapping it against the wall, even as his body pressed against hers intimately. She could feel the hard planes of his muscles, the core of steel underneath it all. How had she ever worried he might die of a simple knife wound? In this moment, he seemed invincible.

"I think you want me as much as I want you—even against our better judgment."

Oh, no. He would not get away with questioning her judgment. She'd proven without a doubt that he was the idiot.

"Oh, really?" She yanked her wrist free of him. "Watch me use my better judgment and walk away." But she couldn't walk away, not with him trapping her against the wall. "Move back."

He lowered his head and slid his lips over her temple. "Are you sure that's what you want?" he whispered in her ear, his breath making her shiver. His lips slid over her ear and his tongue darted out to nip at her earlobe. Belle gasped, heat flooding her and making her knees weak.

His mouth—that mouth she'd known was skilled but hadn't expected to completely vanquish her every sense—skated down her neck, kissing a path of fire in its wake. His hands, meanwhile, had not been idle. They pushed the shoulders of the robe off to allow his lips to tease and tantalize the skin there.

"I'll stop whenever you want," he whispered against her skin. "Just say the word."

She would say the word. She would say it—oh! His hand cupped her breast, fondling the nipple through the thin fabric.

"You can say it now or you can wait." He parted the robe, revealing her breast. "Until I take your breast into my mouth."

How could she stop him, knowing what he was about to do? She bit her lip, letting her head rest against the wall as he sucked and teased her nipple with his tongue.

"Do you want to say anything?" he asked as his hand slid over her belly and toward her center.

She did. She would tell him to stop. Her head was saying *stop* but her mouth wouldn't seem to obey. And her body— her body was in full on revolt. It wanted Hew's touches, his kisses, *him*.

"You called me an idiot." He slid to his knees, pressed his mouth to her bare belly, and made her gasp. He looked up at her. "But you are an idiot as well."

She shook her head.

"Oh, yes you are." His mouth traveled lower, and he slid a hand between her legs opening them wider. "Because you don't realize how beautiful you are. You don't think you deserve this." He bent and pressed his mouth to the curls at her center. "You don't think you're worthy." His breath tickled her, made her shiver. "You don't think any man will ever love you." He licked her then, making her cry out as his tongue rasped against her most sensitive parts. "You're wrong."

She wanted to ask what he meant by that. What was he saying? It couldn't be—he couldn't be saying—but in the next moment every coherent thought was robbed from her mind. He spread her wider and pressed his mouth to her, licking and teasing until her hips were bucking and her whole body seemed to thrum in time to his strokes. She should tell him to stop. She should be embarrassed by what she was allowing him to do, but she liked it. She was glad she was not some high-born lady who couldn't cry out as the pleasure rose within her. She was happy she'd been born in a flat over a shop on Fenchurch Street so she could pound her fist against the wall as his tongue slid over her and her entire body tightened in response. Belle didn't think she could stand any more, and just as she had the thought she slid over the precipice, bowing away from the wall and making a sound she had never known she could make. It was something between a moan and a scream.

When she finally came back to herself, she was shaking, her knees weak, and Arundel had a hand pressed against her belly to keep her upright. He was still on his knees before her, and she rather liked how that looked. She would have told him that too if he hadn't loosened the pressure of his hand so that she slid to her knees before him.

"Tell me you didn't want that," he murmured, voice husky.

"Go to hell," she said.

"Oh, I'll go to hell." He grinned. "And I'll take you with me."

She couldn't resist that grin, and when he reached for her, she went with him, allowing him to press her to the floor and cover her body with his. One of his legs slid between hers, opening her. Belle kissed him, pressing her center against his leg to ease the ache rising there again. He would think her completely insatiable. Perhaps she was. But this time she would not be the only one naked. Her robe was still on her arms, but completely open to reveal her body. Now she slid his shirt up, unfastened the buttons, and tore it over his head. Her hands slid up the wide expanse of his back, careful to avoid the bandaged area of his wound. His mouth had claimed hers, but she broke away and kissed his neck, his shoulders. She wanted to move lower, to kiss his chest, his belly, but he took her lips again.

Pressed so tightly together, she couldn't fail to be aware of him, thick and hard against her belly. Once when she'd been waiting on the docks to meet with an importer, she had heard two whores talking. They'd been sitting on two barrels, sharing a bottle of gin between them. They either hadn't known or hadn't cared that Belle was there. One of them was recounting the first time she'd had carnal relations. "There's a reason they call it a prick," she said. "It hurt like the devil."

Belle, who had been all of fifteen, had felt her cheeks heat and ducked her head. The whores had laughed and passed the bottle.

Now, a decade later, Belle remembered that conversation and wondered if Hew's prick would hurt her. She couldn't imagine him hurting her, couldn't imagine that his touch would ever be anything but pleasurable.

Belle slid her hand between them and down over his belly. When she reached the waistband of his trousers, he jerked his head up, breaking off their kiss. "Belle—"

"I want to touch you," she said.

"Not a good idea." But he didn't stop her hand from moving lower.

"Fair is fair," she said, and slid her hand over the wool material of his trousers. He was thick and hard and hot. As her hand passed over him, gripped him, she felt his member jump. "Did that hurt?" she asked.

"It's the best sort of torture," he said through a jaw clenched tight.

She wanted to feel his skin, wanted to know if it was as hot as she thought it would be. She reached for the buttons of his trousers, undid one.

The loud knock at the door made them both jump. Belle looked up at Hew, who looked back down at her, his expression mirroring her confusion.

"The maid coming for the dinner tray?" she suggested.

"Yes." Then he turned to the door. "Go away. We're not finished." He lowered his mouth to hers. "Not finished at all," he murmured against her lips.

"I'm not the staff, Arundel," said a male voice with an upper-class accent. "Open the bloody door before I knock it down."

Chapter Nineteen

Hew knew that voice. He knew that tone, and it didn't bode well. There was only one reason another agent of the Royal Saboteurs would seek him out here and now, and that was to end his mission. Belle scrambled out from under him and collected the ends of her robe, wrapping it around her body. Hew might have been angry at the interruption, but it had probably saved Belle Howard's virtue. He certainly didn't have the willpower to wrap her back up after having her naked.

"Arundel!" The pounding on the door started again.

"One moment!" Hew called. Then he lowered his voice. "Go into the bed chamber and close the door."

Belle blinked at him, her dark eyes huge in her face. Hew tried not to notice her pink cheeks and her swollen lips. He tried not to think about how he wanted to lay her back down on the rug and finish what they'd started.

"You know this person?" she asked.

"He's a friend."

She nodded and hurried past the dining table to the bed chamber, closing the door with a soft click.

"Sometime this century, Arundel," came the voice through the door. Still, Hew took a moment to lift his shirt from the floor and drop it over his head. On the way to the door, he combed his hair back into place with his fingers. He unfastened the bolt and opened the door to Willoughby Galloway—friend and fellow Saboteur.

Will pushed his way into the suite. "Took you long enough. The lady down the hall threatened to call the footmen and have me thrown out."

"Perhaps standing in the corridor and yelling for me to open up was not your best tactic."

Will grinned. "Perhaps not." His gaze swept over Hew, and his grin faded. "You look...different."

Hew resisted the temptation to look over his shoulder at the closed door of the bed chamber. Will couldn't have any idea what he was doing just a few moments before or with whom. "I'm still recovering," he said.

"Ah, that's right. You were wounded."

"How the devil do you know that?"

"Baron sent a courier with a missive. The man looked ready to drop dead from exhaustion. He'd received no reply from you and a disturbing message from Lady Keating, and since I was in London, here I am." Will's light brown eyes narrowed. "What exactly *were* you doing when I knocked on that door? Who is here with you?" Will walked to the dining room table, studied the meal set for two, and gave Hew an inquisitive look. "A woman?"

Hew didn't ask how Will knew that. He'd trained in surveillance as well. Belle had hardly touched her plate of food, and the bites she'd taken had been small and dainty.

"When I was mulling over marriage to Emily, you said women were fickle and not to be trusted."

"It's not like that. Miss Howard and her father took me in and nursed me back to health. Now her father has been taken and is being used as bait for me."

"Yes, I know something about Mr. Howard's abduction."

The bed chamber door swung open, revealing Belle, dressed now in the borrowed clothes she'd been wearing earlier. "What do you know about my father?"

Will seemed completely unsurprised to be confronted by a woman he hadn't known was in the suite a moment before—but then he probably had known. Will was extremely perceptive. "Miss Howard, I take it?"

"Where is he? Is my father well?" she demanded.

"I don't know, and I don't know," Will said, then turned to Hew and gave him a look. His expression said, so-this-is-what-you-were-doing. Hew cleared his throat.

"Miss Isabelle Howard, might I present Mr. Willoughby Galloway."

"I don't care who he is. You have information on my father?"

"Yes, miss, but the information I have is privileged."

Her brow furrowed. "What does that mean?"

"It means he can't share it with you," Hew said. "Go back into the bed chamber and try to rest—"

"Bollocks to that!"

Will raised a brow, looking from Belle to Hew and back again.

"If this is about my father, I want to know."

"I'll tell you later," Hew began.

"He can tell me now." She pointed at Will.

Hew started to move toward her, thinking he might have to carry her from the room, but Will raised a hand. "Let her stay. I know that look. I've seen it on my wife's face often enough. There's no point arguing." He looked about the chamber then strode to a chair near the hearth. "Might we at least sit?"

"Of course," Hew said. "Would you care for tea?"

"This isn't a garden party!" Belle erupted. "Where is my father?"

"I don't know," Will said again, glancing at Hew, who took Belle's hand and pulled her down on a couch across from Will. He sat beside her, keeping his arm about her. Will finally sat in the chair opposite. "I wish I could tell you more, but I don't have any specifics about your father. The courier arrived in the wee hours of the morning, and I immediately set out to find Arundel. I learned about Mr. Howard's disappearance while searching for you." He gestured to Hew.

"We were asking questions on Fenchurch Street as well," Hew said. "You must have been right behind us."

"So I gather. In any case, when I couldn't find you at Lady Keating's or at the tea shop, I decided to try Mivart's. No one had seen you here in days, but I took a chance."

"We just arrived a few hours ago," Hew said. "I was deciphering Baron's letters concerning the railroad accident in Carlisle."

Will raised a brow, indicating he didn't believe that was all Hew had been doing. "Baron has new information on Pennywhistle," Will said. "After reading your reports, he sent Duncan Slorach to the area."

"Really? His first official mission for the Saboteurs?"

"Information gathering, really. He's still waiting for his official mission."

"Perhaps Baron is waiting for a two-man mission so he might send Lucy as well."

"Why would he do that?" Will asked.

Lucy was Galloway's sister and another agent. Duncan Slorach had been half in love with her since setting eyes on her. He and Lucy had been competing against each other since their first days at the Farm, obviously trying to channel the sexual tension between them into useful pursuits. But Will, being Lucy's brother, seemed completely oblivious to the pop and crackle between the two whenever they were in the same room. Hew was not about to enlighten Will now.

"No reason."

"Spit it out," Belle interrupted. "What about my father?"

Hew closed his hand around hers. "We're coming to that. He's already said he doesn't know where he is or his condition. Our plan is unchanged." Hew nodded to Will. "What did Duncan discover?"

"Turns out just a few days before Duncan arrived, there was another accident. No deaths but several injuries. It was in the papers."

Hew shrugged. He hadn't been in any condition to read papers for most of the last week.

"The railroad sent a man to look at the damage and assess the sorts of repairs needed. By all accounts, the man had finished his work and was about to write up his report, when he disappeared. No one has seen him since."

"Curious."

"Not really," Belle said plainly. "Pennywhistle needs time to finish his excavation. By delaying the railroad's man, he also delays the repairs."

"I see you know something about the matter, Miss Howard," Will said. "But there's another possibility."

"What's that?"

"The man discovered something Pennywhistle didn't want made known, and Pennywhistle had him killed."

"What are the odds that if we searched Pennywhistle's property, we'd find his body?" Hew asked.

"Duncan would take that bet. I won't get into all the specifics in the report"—he eyed Belle meaningfully—"but the railroad man had no reason to run off, and there's some evidence of foul play. If we take the attempt on your life into account, it's too much for coincidence."

"More than one attempt," Hew said. "Someone wants me dead."

"If we can pin it on Pennywhistle, that would save us sending more agents to investigate. We'd catch him eventually, but if we could catch one of his men and force a confession…"

"I'm one step ahead of you," Hew said. "I'm to meet them at Hyde Park tomorrow night to exchange myself for Mr. Howard. I fully intend to set an ambush, though I hadn't worked out the particulars."

Will shook his head. "Baron wants you back at the Farm."

Beside him, Belle tensed.

"He sent me to tell you about the change in orders. Lady Keating convinced him your injuries are severe enough to limit your ability to succeed in a mission. I'm to take over."

"No!" Belle cried, in an echo of the protest in Hew's mind. "My father—"

"Miss Howard," Will said, turning a sympathetic gaze to her. "I assure you I will do all I can to return your father to you. I intend to make the rendezvous, but I think we need to take all the facts into consideration."

"What facts?"

"Although not independently verified, I think it highly likely there are rich mineral deposits on the land Pennywhistle sold to the railroad. He wouldn't go to all of this trouble without reason, and money is a powerful reason."

"My father has nothing to do with any of that!"

"Regardless, Pennywhistle and his men have now killed or attempted to kill multiple people. Other than Arundel and the railroad man, the others he's killed also had nothing to do with the land or the minerals. The man and those working for him are clearly ruthless and will stop at nothing to accomplish their aims."

Hew closed his eyes. He knew what Will was getting at. He'd considered the possibility himself.

"Then they must be stopped. We can work together to turn their ambush around on them. I just want my father back safely."

Will looked down. "As do we all, but Miss Howard"— Will met her gaze—"these men do not have finesse. They are brutes who only know how to do one thing. They weren't hired to negotiate prisoner swaps."

"You think he's dead," Belle said, her voice barely above a whisper. "You think they killed him and sent a message to meet in Hyde Park so they can capture Arundel."

"I think they intend to kill Arundel. They're killers. That's what they know. It takes planning and intelligence to carry out a prisoner exchange. They don't need Arundel alive. Easier just to lure him into the open and kill him."

"No," Belle said.

Will looked at Hew. "Baron wants you back at the Farm immediately. He'll have his doctors take over there, and I'm to take over here and in Carlisle with Pennywhistle."

"Hew." Belle looked at him with pleading eyes. "No!"

Will cleared his throat. "I'll meet Pennywhistle's men at the park and take them, if I can, kill them if I can't. I promise you, Miss Howard, the men who took your father will not walk free."

Belle wrenched her hand out of Hew's and jumped to her feet. "I don't believe it. I don't believe he's dead. How can you just give up on him based on an assumption?"

"I know it's not an option you want to consider. I don't either," Hew said softly. "But Will's reasoning makes sense. I've considered it privately. I think you have as well. Sweetheart—"

"Don't *sweetheart* me. You can run away if you like, but you can't force me to give up." She pointed to Will. "I will be at the park at midnight tomorrow, and I *will* get my father back or die trying."

***

Belle could not remain in the room any longer. She didn't know where she was going, but she would not stay here. Her father might already be dead, but the least she could do was to make every effort to rescue him if he were alive. He wouldn't have given up on her. And she hadn't thought Arundel would give up so easily on him—or her, for that matter.

"Belle, where are you going?" Arundel called.

She didn't answer. Instead, she flung open the door, startling Jenny, who was standing just outside. "Beg your pardon," Belle told the maid before starting down the corridor.

"Belle!" Hew's voice was closer. "Miss Howard!"

Belle shook her head and began to run. If she let him catch her, he would hold her and comfort her. She needed his comfort, badly, but now was not the time to feel comfortable. Her father wasn't comfortable. What had she been thinking? She'd been luxuriating at Mivart's while he'd been suffering. Logically, she knew that nothing she did or didn't do at this moment could help her father. He'd probably rather her be comfortable than hungry and cold...if he was still able to have any sort of preference.

No! She lifted her skirts and ran faster, pushing open a door and starting down what must be the servant's stairs as they were narrow and wooden. Arundel's voice faded behind her, but she continued to run. When she finally reached the first floor, she pushed through the groups of servants in the kitchens and work rooms until she emerged into the yard behind the hotel. Leaning against the building, she tried to catch her breath.

She would not allow herself to believe, even for a moment, that her father was gone. She would not give up on him.

She'd forgotten her hat in the room, so she pulled a soggy cap off a clothesline as she exited the yard. She pulled it over her head, arranging some of the hair so it covered the scarred side of her face. Then keeping her head down, she began to walk.

For a long time, she didn't know where she was headed. She couldn't go back to the shop on Fenchurch Street. Pennywhistle's men might be waiting for her there. Tears sprang to her eyes when she realized the place that had always been her refuge—the tea shop—was now dangerous for her. She thought she'd found another refuge in Hew Arundel, but she'd been a fool to depend on him. When would she learn that she couldn't rely on anyone but herself? Even a man who seemed to look past her physical defects couldn't be trusted with her heart. Her father was her heart. Her tea shop was her heart. Fenchurch Street was her heart.

Gradually, she realized where her feet were leading her. It was a long way to St. Katharine Docks, but once she understood that was where her body was taking her, she knew that was where she needed to go. She'd be anonymous there and surrounded by tea. That would be a comfort. She found a wagon heading in that direction and begged a seat in the back. The driver gave her a curious look, probably because she was dressed in ill-fitting but expensive clothing, then shrugged and nodded his approval.

Belle sat on the back of the wagon, watching all of London pass her by. It was late afternoon now, and men and women were hurrying to make purchases for supper before shops closed. The girls selling flowers and the boys selling fruit and vegetables were packing up. The flowers had wilted, and the produce would have to wait another day.

Belle was not very religious and rarely prayed. She went to church often enough to keep the others in the parish from knocking on their door and making accusations. But she prayed now. She prayed her father would be safe one more night and day and that she would see him the next night in Hyde Park. She would trade herself, if that was what it took, to ensure his freedom.

Finally, she and the wagon parted ways and she walked the remainder of the way to the docks. The ships had been unloaded earlier in the day, and the crates of tea, spices, and silks from the Far East were being moved into warehouses. The dockworkers looked at her a little longer than usual, a few calling out to her or whistling, but she ignored them. She ducked into one of the tea warehouses and strolled up the aisles, stacked seven and eight feet high with crates and bundles of tea. The scent was delicious and intoxicating.

She found a corner where she would not be easily spotted and sat, leaning against a sack of what smelled like Earl Grey. She could hide here. She knew the warehouse manager. If she were discovered, she would speak with him. No doubt he wouldn't like the idea of her sleeping in his warehouse, but he already thought her rather eccentric, considering that she insisted on seeing, smelling, and touching any tea before she purchased it.

Leaning her head back, Belle closed her eyes. The sounds of the warehouse and the dock were familiar to her, and they faded away after a few minutes. She'd occupied her mind with worries for her father for the last hour or two, but now her mind turned to the subject she'd been trying to avoid—Hew Arundel.

She really was a fool when it came to the agent for the Royal Saboteurs. She'd spent days trying to keep him alive, worrying that he'd die and she'd be blamed. She'd never thought that all that time, she should have worried that he was worming his way into her heart. Belle couldn't point to the exact moment she had begun to care for Arundel. Well, she knew the exact moment she had realized she wanted him. It had been when he'd stood up without his shirt and she'd caught a glimpse of his powerful chest. She hadn't known men could look like that. She'd wanted to touch him.

She'd wanted him to touch her.

And then he had touched her. She realized now that he had been delirious and probably thought he was touching his dead wife, but it had been enough to rouse a heat and desire in Belle that she hadn't known was buried within her. Once it had been ignited, the heat had simmered and burned until she couldn't resist its warmth.

She wished Arundel's hold on her was only physical attraction. Then she could have enjoyed what they'd done together in his hotel suite and moved on. Instead, every kiss they'd shared, every press of his fingertip, every caress of his hands or lips or—God help her—tongue seemed infused with meaning. When he touched her there, did that mean he cared about her? When he'd kissed her *there*, did that mean he loved her? When he'd given her pleasure—so much pleasure, more than she'd known she could ever feel—did that mean he wanted her for his wife?

No. It definitely did not mean that. He'd been clear that he never wanted to marry again and would not marry her. Belle had said she didn't want to marry him, but it was difficult to fall in love with a man and not want to spend the rest of your nights in his arms. And she *had* fallen in love with him. She'd fallen for his bravery, his strength, his determination. No to mention his intelligence, loyalty to country, and his vulnerability. If his former wife hadn't already been dead, Belle would have sought the woman out and killed her with her own hands. How dare she hurt Arundel like that? Belle never again wanted to see the pain he'd shown her when he'd spoken of his marriage. She would give anything to take that pain away.

And yet, here she was—not with Arundel but hiding in a tea warehouse. She peeked around the stacks surrounding her and out the open doors of the building. The docks were quieting, and the sky had darkened. Most work was done during the day, and most of the dock workers had gone home. But she knew from many visits over the years that the docks were never completely quiet. If the occasion called for it, men worked at all hours to move cargo from ship to shore and dock to warehouse, even though it could be dangerous to operate the cranes and move cargo in the dark.

Now was the time to close her eyes and sleep. Tomorrow she would figure out what to do about Arundel. She'd find some way to mute her feelings. She'd find some way to let him go. He'd never be hers, and she should simply take what they'd shared and be satisfied.

Tomorrow, she hoped, she would have her father back—or at least safe and away from his abductors. Or tomorrow she might be the prisoner.

Or perhaps she'd be dead.

Chapter Twenty

"She's gone," Hew said after bursting into the hotel room. Will still sat where Hew had left him, his head resting on the back of the chair, his eyes closed.

"I assumed that was the idea when she stormed out of the room." He lifted his head and gave Hew a sardonic look. "Some women run because they want to be chased. She doesn't strike me as that sort."

"I have to find her."

"No, you don't. You need to get on a train and return to the Farm. Baron has ordered me to take over."

"Baron can go to hell. I need to find Belle."

Will crossed his legs and gave Hew a long look. "What has happened to you? I thought you were wounded in the side, but perhaps you hit your head as well."

"I know I'm not acting like myself."

"That's an understatement. Aren't you the one who told me not to give up my career for a woman? Aren't you the one who told me women are the root of all evil?"

"I didn't say that."

"Pretty close. And now you want to run after a woman who, clearly, does not want to be chased. She's made it clear she will be at Hyde Park at midnight tomorrow. That certainly complicates things, but if I bring on another agent, I can probably have her intercepted and kept safely away. Nothing will happen to her, and if her father is still alive, which I very much doubt, then they will be reunited."

"I want to be there." Hew held up a hand at the look Will gave him. "It's not that I don't think you are capable. I know you are every bit as capable as me."

"Then follow orders."

"I can't leave her." Hew knew how that sounded, and he winced as soon as the words left his lips. "I mean...I *can* leave her. Of course, I can. I just want to see this through, make sure she's safe." Hew crossed to a chair where he'd thrown his coat earlier. He grabbed the garment and began to pull it on, wincing at the pain when he moved too quickly.

Will put his head in his hands. "I want to believe you are dressing for the train station, but I know better."

"I'm going after her."

Will spat an oath.

"I know what you'll say," Hew added, finally managing the coat. His wound burned now, but it wasn't so bad that he couldn't ignore it. "But I'm prepared to accept whatever punishment Baron doles out." He turned to look for his boots, inhaled sharply as his wound throbbed. He bent over to catch his breath and wait for the pain to pass and when he stood again, Will was beside him.

"I'll go after her," he said. "On one condition."

"I need to do this myself."

"You need to lie down. You may be feeling better but push too hard now and you could set back your recovery. That's the last thing any of us need."

"It's a risk I'm willing to take."

Will gripped his shoulder. Hard. "I said I'll go. Don't make me argue with you on this. I'm already annoyed that I'm disregarding orders and about to spend time chasing down a female instead of mapping out the area around the Serpentine Bridge in Hyde Park."

"She's not a *female*. Her name is Isabelle Howard, and I'd prefer to find her myself."

"You will drink a brandy and get into bed and sleep. She can wake you when I return her."

"Will—"

"Damn it, Hew. I have a wife. I understand how it is. That doesn't mean I have to like it."

Hew stilled. "This isn't like that. I'm not thinking of marrying her."

"The hell you aren't." Will held up a hand, cutting off Hew's protest. "We can argue that later—actually, you and she can sort that out. Save me time and tell me where you think she might have gone."

Hew hadn't thought that far ahead. Because his wound was aching more than he wanted to admit, he sat down and began to list all the likely places.

"No. No. No," Will said as soon as Hew mentioned each. Hew stared out the window. The sun had that golden color that precipitated late afternoon, the time when the fashionable families would be sitting down to dinner. The time when prostitutes and thieves would be waking and preparing for a night's work. The time when laborers would be counting down the minutes until they could go home to their families.

Laborers. Shop owners.

Hew lifted his head. "Dock workers."

Will eyed him, annoyance plain in his every expression and movement. "I told you I had one condition, and I think it's time I insisted you lay down. You're not making sense."

"I'll lie down," Hew said, shaking Will's hand off. "But I have an idea where she'd go—the St. Katharine Docks."

"Why there?"

"It's where most of the tea clears customs and where they've built all the large tea warehouses. She mentioned that she goes there to buy tea for her shop. She likes to seek out the most exotic blends and varieties."

"There must be a dozen or more tea warehouses."

Hew scowled. "Aren't you the son of the most renowned spies from the Napoleonic Wars? You can find a *female* in a warehouse."

"That was low, even for you," Will said, but his shoulders had straightened, and the lines of his face had deepened into determination. "I'll try the docks first." But his tone was the sort one would use to humor a small child. "Now get into bed."

"I'll get in after you've gone."

Will shook his head. "I want to see it."

"You can see my bare arse," Hew said, pulling his coat off and immediately regretting the quick movement. Finally, he lay under the bedclothes and listened to the door close as Will went out. The sun was lower now, casting the room into shadow. He supposed Will thought he was doing Hew a favor by forcing him to rest, but Belle had been sleeping in the bed, and the pillow sheets smelled of her.

He turned his head into the pillow and inhaled deeply, catching the scents of soap and cinnamon and woman. What the hell was he doing? Why didn't he just return to the Farm? After all the effort and time and sacrifices he'd made to join the Royal Saboteurs, now he would jeopardize his place for a shopkeeper who could take care of herself?

Except how was she to care for herself if her father was dead? Hew wasn't as certain of that fact as Will. Pennywhistle's men had proven themselves incompetent more than once. Not that he was complaining—he owed his life and Belle owed her shop to their incompetence. Better thugs would have killed him the first time, or if they'd failed, would have succeeded in burning Howard's Teas & Treats. These thugs might actually plan to exchange George Howard for Hew himself, rather than using the exchange as an excuse to attack.

Whatever happened, he didn't want Belle anywhere near the park tomorrow night. He wanted her safe. Hew closed his eyes and tried to ignore the voice that asked how he would keep her safe if he was in the north of England and she in London.

Hew rolled carefully on his side and clenched his eyes shut, willing sleep to come and, with it, the surcease of thought. Once he and Will had taken care of Pennywhistle's men, Belle would be safe again. Her father would be returned to her, or some other guardian—perhaps her brother-in-law—arranged, and she could go on doing what she loved—selling teas.

He could go on doing what he loved—working for the Royal Saboteurs.

You'll never meet another woman like her, his mind said even as he began to succumb to exhaustion. *Brave, clever, beautiful, brash...*

Impossible to clear his mind of her when her scent all but surrounded him. His heart had obviously not learned its lesson with Clara. He recalled the pain of Clara's betrayal, the shame of it, and the confusion.

She's not Clara.

No, she was nothing like Clara, but that didn't mean he could trust her or trust any woman. He'd vowed never to marry again, never to fall in love again.

You're already in love with her. You never loved Clara. Not really.

Hew opened his eyes. Where the devil had that thought come from? He had loved Clara. He'd been madly in love with her.

Hadn't he?

What exactly had he loved about her, he asked himself, staring up at the ceiling in the room that had gone dark now but for the flickering of the fire. He'd loved her beauty. He'd loved bedding her. He was like any other young man, randy and eager to sample the pleasures of the marriage bed. But had he really loved Clara, the person? Had he thought about her when he'd been at work? Had he ever worried that she might be tired or hungry? Had he even known what tea she preferred or how she took that tea?

Hew was ashamed to admit, even to himself in this dark room, that the answer to every question was no. He'd liked the idea of having a wife, liked the pleasure of a pretty woman on his arm, but he'd never really known or loved *Clara*. He'd never even understood her. Her tears and pleas were an annoyance. If he had listened to her, cared for her, he would have understood long before she'd run away that she was unhappy. How many times had she complained he worked too much? How many times had she begged to return to London for a few weeks or months?

A husband who'd cared, who'd thought of someone or something other than his own ambitions, would have listened to those cries, would have done what he could to accommodate her, would have put his needs second.

Hew had done none of those. The truth was, she had been an unfaithful wife, but he had been an uncaring, selfish husband.

And maybe, deep down, his own failings were the reason he didn't want to marry again. He feared he was a failure as a husband once and he'd be so again.

He'd tell Belle that, if she ever decided she wanted to marry him. He'd explain that he didn't want to fail her, as he'd failed Clara. Except he could imagine what Belle would say — "Do you think I'd allow you to fail me?"

No, she wouldn't. She'd smack the back of his head and tell him to straighten up. And he'd do it because — Goddamn it all — he loved her.

The admission seemed to lift a weight from his chest, and he was finally able to sink into a light sleep. Will would find Belle. Will would bring her back. She'd be safe. Hew would be safe too because Belle did *not* want to marry him.

And he didn't want to marry her…very much.

***

Belle startled awake when she heard the voices. The warehouse had been quiet for a couple of hours, and she'd fallen into a sort of sleep. She was too cold and too uncomfortable on the floor to sleep well, but she'd been dozing. She'd been resolutely *not* thinking about Hew Arundel or her father or her tea shop — the last of those being difficult considering she was surrounded by the scent of tea.

"I do know the chit," a man was saying, his accent rough and his voice a deep bass. "Well, don't know 'er, but I've seen 'er talking to the owner. Don't know why ye think she's 'ere. Everyone's gone 'ome for the night. I'm 'ere to make sure everything stays neat and tidy until morning."

"I'm sure you're right," a more cultured baritone voice answered. "I'll have a look about then leave you to make your rounds."

She heard the clink of coins.

"And thank you for your trouble."

She knew that voice. It was the man who'd come to the hotel, Arundel's friend. What was his name? Willoughby? A man with a name like Willoughby was likely to have his throat slit in a place like this. And yet, if he'd tracked her here, he must have some skills. Part of her wanted to call out to him. Perhaps he'd come for her because he had received some news about her father.

But she bit her cheek and shook her head, reminding herself this was the man who thought her father was dead. He'd given up without even the pretense of a fight.

She sank back against the bags of tea, making herself small. He'd have a look about and then move on to the next warehouse. It would take a man hours to search this place and to find her. She was a — what was the saying? — a needle in a haystack. She might as well go back to sleep.

"Miss Howard, we meet again." The light from a lamp illuminated her legs, drawn up against her chest. *Willoughby* stepped closer and the light shone in her eyes. Belle lifted a hand to shield her face.

"You found 'er!" the night watchman exclaimed, coming up the aisle at a fast clip. "Well, I'll be."

"Mr. Merrick, do you mind giving us a moment alone?" the saboteur asked, his voice like silk. "I promise we will be out of your way very shortly."

The watchman eyed Belle, who scowled right back at him, then gave a nod. "I'll be just outside."

"Thank you."

As the watchman's footsteps receded, Arundel's friend set his lamp on the ground and sat, rather awkwardly, on the ground. "You'll ruin your trousers," Belle commented.

"Oh, our friend Hew is much more concerned about such matters than I am, I assure you."

"I doubt that. A man named *Willoughby*?" She was being deliberately rude. "I imagine you dislike dirtying your hands."

"You'd imagine wrong, but I have no doubt you will realize your mistake soon enough and find out just how much a dandy Mr. Arundel can be. God knew we all had to suffer him brushing his coats out every night at the Farm. And for what? He'd just be crawling in the dirt again or dusting the coat with gun powder the next day."

"Shows what you know, *Willoughby*. Mr. Arundel and I won't be continuing our acquaintance."

"It's Will, and your entire attitude shows how little *you* know, Miss Howard. Who do you think fought me tooth and nail to come after you? Arundel isn't done with you. Not by a mile."

Belle didn't want to admit how those words made her heart jump. She tamped down the hope with the ease of long practice. "I think perhaps you don't know Hew Arundel as well as *you* think, Willoughby. He has vowed never to love again." She forced herself to meet his gaze. "I may not be pretty to look at." She touched her scarred cheek. "But that doesn't mean I don't deserve love."

Hew had taught her that. Her father and her sister had told her thousands of times that she deserved to be loved and cared for. They told her over and over that she was worthy, but only now was she beginning to believe it. The past few days had shown her she could do more than sell tea in a shop. She was so much more than the little mouse of a woman hiding behind a window on Fenchurch Street.

"And are you in love with him?" Willoughby Galloway asked.

"What business is it of yours?" She looked away.

"My God, but you are a trial, aren't you? I ask because if you love Hew and he loves you—"

"I told you, he will never love again."

"He's vowed never to *marry* again, Miss Howard. It's too late not to love again. Any fool can see he's completely in love with you."

Belle blinked then shoved Galloway back. He hadn't been expecting this reaction and fell over, almost toppling the lamp. Belle hastily reached to steady it, lest it shatter and set the entire warehouse on fire.

"What the devil was that for?" Galloway asked, righting himself and brushing his coat off.

"I don't believe you."

"Do you shove every person who tells you a man loves you?"

"No one has ever told me that before."

"No wonder," he muttered under his breath. "Believe me or not, just come back to Mivart's with me. I promised Hew I'd find you and bring you back."

Belle crossed her arms over her chest. "I won't go back."

"Of course not. I'm sure you intend to make this as difficult as possible."

"Why should I go back?" she demanded. She'd pushed him as more of a reflex earlier, but now she rather thought she wouldn't mind giving him a harder push or even a punch. "Hew is leaving and you think you can keep me from my father tomorrow night. Don't say it!" she warned.

He closed his mouth. Then he took a deep breath. "You should go back because Hew needs you. He's not as strong as he's pretending. He's in pain. The only way I got him to lie down was by promising to find you."

"You think *I* don't know that? I've been nursing him—or at least trying—for days."

"Then if you care for him at all, come back. We can work out the details later."

"We can work them out now."

Galloway's brown eyes seemed to blaze with anger, and she had a moment to worry that she might have pushed him too far. He took a slow breath. "It is a mystery to me how you have made it to the age of—how old are you?"

"As though I would own it to you!"

"Good—" He broke off and took another deep breath. He seemed to be breathing a lot. "I told Hew I would bring you back. What will it take for you to return with me?"

"You have to admit that my father is still alive."

"No. Try again."

"You have to allow me to go to the rendezvous with you."

"No."

"If you plan to deny my every request, then we are wasting our time. Good night, sir."

"Make a reasonable request, Miss Howard."

Belle thought for a moment. "Don't send Hew back to your Farm until after the rendezvous tomorrow night."

"I doubt he would go anyway."

"And if he says I can go to the rendezvous, then you have to acquiesce."

"Fine." He held out his hand. She stared at it.

"That was a quick agreement."

"He'll never allow you to get anywhere near Hyde Park. I told you, he's in love with you. He won't want you even in the vicinity of danger."

"You're wrong," she said.

"I doubt that, but out of curiosity, which part am I wrong about?"

"All of it. He's not in love with me, and he *will* allow me to go. I can be persuasive when I want."

"You can be demanding," he said. "That much I see." He held out his hand again, and she shook it.

Twenty minutes later they were in a hackney on the way back to Mivart's. Belle didn't know how she would persuade Arundel to let her go to Hyde Park tomorrow. Galloway was probably right. She would just demand it. After all she'd done for Hew Arundel, she deserved something in return.

Galloway had been blissfully silent for the last almost half hour, but she heard him take yet another breath and knew her luck had run out. "I haven't known Hew Arundel long," he said. "It will be a year in January, but I do know him well."

Belle didn't say anything, just wondered what Willoughby there, seated across from her, was getting at and wishing she had a cup of tea. She imagined it was because she could still smell it on her clothes and in her hair.

"You can't spend so much time in close quarters and not come to know a man well. He hasn't spoken much about his past. I know he's been hurt. I know he is reluctant to trust. And I also know, in spite of all that, he is in love with you."

"This again."

He gave her a rueful smile. "Yes, *this again*, as you so elegantly put it. You don't know him as well as I do."

She raised a brow.

"I don't want to know what that look insinuates, but I can tell you this. I have never seen him look at anything or anyone the way I saw him look at you. And"—he held up a finger before she could interrupt—"even more telling is that I have never seen him disobey an order. None of us disobey orders. We wouldn't have made it as far as we have if we were in the habit of ignoring our superiors, but Arundel, well, he is the sort who is by-the-book all the way."

"I hear words," she said, "but I'm not certain they have any point."

"The *point*," he said, through clenched teeth, "is that it speaks to his affection for you that he is willing to disobey orders and risk his place in the Royal Saboteurs. For a man like Arundel, that is a true mark of love."

"How romantic."

Galloway gave her the ghost of a smile. "What do you care for romance? You're a practical woman. I could see that within a minute of making your acquaintance. If you want to marry him, just tell him to get the license and call the banns. You seem to have no problem demanding everything else."

"I don't want to marry him."

"Bollocks. You want him, and you can't have him any other way." He gave her a wary look. "I don't make the rules. Talk to your neighbors if you don't like it, but you know as well as I that if there's any sort of perceived impropriety between a man and a woman, it's always the woman who pays. And I do believe you have a shop to keep open. You can't very well do that if people won't patronize it because you have a reputation as a scarlet woman."

"I'll never give up my shop."

"Then marry Hew or give him up. There's no other way."

She scowled at him.

"I'm beginning to feel some sympathy for Cassandra of Troy," he muttered.

Chapter Twenty-One

Hew didn't know how long he'd slept. He had been in a deep sleep and then he was wide awake.

Belle.

He remembered his wound a moment before he might have jumped out of bed and forced himself to lie still. He'd been in pain so long, he'd become numb to it, but now he allowed his mind to assess it. His side still hurt, but it seemed to be the dull throb of healing rather than the sharp pain of infection. He imagined all the soft parts of him that had been ripped asunder being knitted back together by that miraculous process that the human body employed.

All in all, he was feeling better.

Except for the lead ball in the pit of his stomach. That awful heaviness had weighed him down since the moment Belle had walked out of the hotel room. Logically, he knew she could take care of herself. She'd survived a quarter of a century without him. But she hadn't had Pennywhistle's men after her or her family. Not until he had stepped — very well, been carried — into her life.

It annoyed him that he'd fallen asleep without knowing if she was safe. He supposed he was weaker than he'd thought. It annoyed him even more that his last thought before falling asleep and his first thought on waking were of Belle.

Hew cut his gaze to the window. The heavy drapes had been drawn. He remembered looking out the window before falling asleep. Had a hotel maid done that or had Will returned? And if Will returned, where was Belle?

He pushed back the covers and began to rise when he heard a small sound and froze. His training took over, and he assumed a defensive posture. Someone or some*thing* was in the chamber with him.

The fire burned low, and the room was in shadow, but a quick scan of it didn't reveal any lurking threats. His gaze passed over the bedclothes and then went back again. He'd thought that lump was a pillow or covers he'd thrown back, but now he wondered...

Hew reached under the covers and moved his hand toward the lump, stilling when he touched warm flesh. Warm, naked flesh. His hand slid up what he now perceived was a thigh until it cupped the soft curve of a hip. A woman's hip, thank God, as this would have been rather awkward had Will been the one sleeping beside him. Careful of his injury, he leaned over and drew the covers down, revealing Belle. Her head was turned away from him, and he could make out the shadow of her hair on the pillow. More than that, he could detect the scent of tea emanating from her. She must have been at the warehouse, as he'd suspected. Will had found her and brought her back.

Thank God. The heaviness in his belly seemed to melt away…replaced by a heaviness a bit lower.

Where was Will now? More importantly, why had Belle climbed into bed with him? He might have chalked it up to concern for his wellbeing or even desire for comfort. Perhaps, knowing Belle, she remembered he had given her the bed and was determined to use it.

But that didn't explain why she was naked.

And in the wee hours of the morning, with a warm woman in his bed, Hew was not inclined to think too carefully about what it all meant. It had been years since he had slept with a woman. Years since he had woken with a naked woman sleeping beside him. Call it need, call it instinct, he slid back down and moved closer to her. He told himself he only wanted to lie beside her, but that didn't explain why he put his hand over her waist and pulled her closer. That didn't explain why that same hand moved upward to cup one small breast.

She made a sound of pleasure and snuggled closer to him, her bottom rubbing against his cock. His bare cock. His hard cock. He'd undressed before bed as well, leaving his robe at the foot of the bed for easy access when Will returned. But right now, he was naked; she was naked; and they were alone in a bed.

As much as Hew would have liked to continue fondling her, he wasn't completely delirious with desire. "Belle," he whispered. "Belle."

"Hmm," she said and snuggled against him.

"What are you doing in my bed?"

"Said I could have the bed," she murmured. He smiled. So he'd been partly right.

"Why are you naked?"

A pause as, presumably, she came awake and became aware of the situation. "Do you like it?" Her voice was low and still gravelly from sleep.

"I think you can feel how much I like it."

She moved her bottom, and he grasped her hips. "None of that or you won't be a virgin much longer."

"I keep telling you, I don't want to be a virgin any longer."

Before he could think what to do or say to that, she turned in his arms and threw a leg over him. Her warm sex pressed against his cock, and her mouth sought his.

The hesitations in the back of his mind fled, and he kissed her back. He'd been wanting this for so long. He'd been wanting her for so long. It seemed a lifetime he'd wanted her, though he'd only known her—what? a week? Hew couldn't remember his life before her. And he didn't want to imagine his life without her.

"Stop thinking so much and kiss me," she said, moving her lips to nibble his ear. "You are always thinking."

His hands were exploring her body, desperate to sample it before it was snatched away from him. She was so warm and the way she moved against him was so clumsy and, at the same time, incredibly erotic. She may not have ever done this before, but Hew already knew she would catch on fast.

God, he wanted to be the one to teach her—to learn from her.

"One of us has to think about the consequences," he said. "One of us has to stop this."

"It won't be me," she said, kissing his neck as her own hands began to explore. One skated down his back then found his buttocks and squeezed.

"*Belle*," Hew said in a warning tone.

She giggled and brought her hand around. He caught her wrist before she could take his cock in her hand.

"If we don't stop now, I won't have the willpower."

"Do you love me?" she asked, pulling back to see his face. "*Willoughby* says you love me."

Hew didn't think she could see him much better than he could see her. Her eyes glittered in the weak firelight, and only outlines of cheek, nose, and forehead were visible. But he could fill in the shadows with his memory of her. The tight line of her lips when she was angry. The fine brows above her deep brown eyes. The pink of her cheeks, especially the side that was scarred, when she was presented with a new tea.

Hew gathered her closer, still holding her wrist. "I do love you, Isabelle Howard."

"And I love you," she said, wriggling her hand free. "And that's all that matters in this moment."

He wanted to believe that. He *did* believe it when her hand slid around his cock.

"I know you don't want to ever marry again," she said, tracing a finger over him, seeming unsure what to do with him now that she had him.

Hew made a sound that was something like *Gah*. He wasn't quite able to talk with the way she touched him. There was something to be said for awkward curiosity.

"But you'll change your mind. You'll beg me to marry you, and I might even agree."

"Belle, stop." To his dismay, she did stop. Her hand on his cock stilling. "As much as I want you, I don't want to deceive you."

"I'm not deceived. You don't want to marry." She slid her hand upward. "But you'll change your mind, just as I have." Her hand slid down again. "Your friend *Willoughby* said something tonight that made me realize marriage is the only way we can be together. And you want to be with me."

"I do." God, her hand was driving him to madness.

"You will beg me to marry you," she said.

"I won't."

"And I will say no."

"What?" He tried to wrap his head around what she was saying, but his mind was having trouble focusing on anything but the way he was feeling.

"Ask me to marry you as much as you please. I'll say no."

"And if I tell your father about this." He moved his hips, thrusting them slightly. "He'll demand we marry."

"I knew it!" she said, pausing her movements and smiling down at him. "You don't think he's dead."

"Belle, I didn't mean—"

"Oh, shut it, Hew, and put this thing to some use."

***

Belle found herself on her back with Hew Arundel on top of her. She didn't know why he was finally persuaded. Had she aroused him to the point of no return? Had she finally convinced him she would not force him to marry her? She understood now that she wouldn't have to demand he marry her. His friend was right. He *wanted* to marry her. He just wasn't ready to admit it, and that was fine. She could wait. In the end, *he* would have to convince *her* marriage was a good idea.

He had already made several good points about the benefits of the institution of marriage, and then his hand slid between her legs, and she stopped thinking and allowed herself to feel.

His knee fitted between her legs and parted them, giving his hand more access. He had truly remarkable fingers. They slid over her slick folds, teasing and tempting her, until she caught his hand and pressed it where she wanted it.

He chuckled low in her ear, making gooseflesh pebble her skin, but he didn't move his hand. Instead, he slid his thumb over that part of her that needed him most, making her gasp and then moan in pleasure.

At the same time, she felt him at her entrance. His cock—hard and hot—had settled just inside her. The pressure of it was intoxicating, and the more Hew teased her with his thumb, the more she wanted that cock to go deeper. It did slide deeper, filling her almost to the point of pain. But then his thumb would incite some new sensation, and she'd forget the pain and beg for the pleasure.

Belle realized she was probably making an idiot of herself. She was mewling and begging and gasping for him. She didn't care. His own breath was coming fast and hard, his body rigid with the strength it took for him to hold back. She didn't want him to hold back, told him so, but he only murmured something about trusting him.

She did trust him. Would she be naked in bed with him if she didn't trust him?

Would she allow—*oh*. She couldn't think any longer as sensation took over. It was that same pleasure he'd given her earlier, and it rose inside her, blotting out every thought except chasing after the peak. She was dimly aware of her hips bucking and Hew trying to still them. She was also aware she made small moaning sounds, but she didn't care. The pleasure, when it finally came, overwhelmed her until she was swallowed by it. And that was when he pushed into her, melding pain with pleasure until she couldn't separate one from the other and didn't want to.

"Am I hurting you?" he asked, his voice low and husky.

"Yes. No. Don't stop," she said as she crested a final wave of pleasure and allowed herself to be carried away with it.

Gradually, she became aware of the pressure of him and the pain that caused...not a sharp stabbing pain but a dull ache that intensified when he moved. She thought she might like that movement—at some point. Not now.

She hissed in a breath as he moved again.

"I'm hurting you," he said through clenched teeth.

"Yes. Stop."

Instantly, he stopped moving. Braced on his elbows, he looked down at her, and she had a moment to wonder about his injury. Surely this was putting a strain on it. He began to pull away, but she wrapped her arms about his neck. "Don't move. Just stay like this," she said, pulling his mouth down to hers. The last vestiges of the pleasure were still coursing through her, and it was not so unpleasant to have him inside her, if he didn't move.

Her hands ran over his shoulders and his arms, all straining muscles and tight as a wire.

"Belle," he said, his voice ragged. "It's very hard for me not to move. I have to pull—"

"Wait." She wrapped her legs around him, and he groaned.

"You are killing me."

"This hurts you too?"

"Not in the way you mean."

She was torturing him. She should let him go, and she would have except she felt him throb inside her. He wanted her, and that feeling of being desired was something she hadn't felt before. When men showed interest in her, she always questioned it, always wondered if they'd seen her scars, if they could look past them.

She didn't have to wonder that with Hew. She knew he had seen the scars, knew he wanted her anyway, loved her anyway.

"Belle, I have to—" He moved inside her, and she winced. She contracted around him, and he gasped in a breath. "God, don't do that—"

She did it again.

With a groan he pulled out of her, and turned away, gasping as he seemed to find his own pleasure. She closed her legs, feeling the slight sting of pain, and then he was behind her, wrapping her in his arms, and kissing her shoulder. "I hurt you. God, I'm sorry. I shouldn't—"

"I liked it," she said with a yawn. "I think I'll like it even more next time."

"Next time? Belle, we can't—"

"This again?" Her eyes were heavy. "If you're not ready to beg me to marry you, then let's go to sleep."

She could feel him tensing, trying to think of what to say—something about giving her false hope or whatnot. She didn't care at the moment. She turned her head and kissed him. "Shh," she said. "Do you love me?"

"Yes," he said.

"Then that's all that matters. Now let me sleep."

***

Belle felt as though she'd slept for about five minutes before she was startled awake again. This time it was a loud, female voice, demanding…something.

She decided she didn't like hotels. Too many people came to call.

Hew was still holding her, and he hadn't been awakened by the noise, so she had to elbow him in the ribs—the uninjured side—to force him to release her. The woman was still speaking loudly in the next room, so Belle grabbed the first piece of clothing she'd found, which happened to be

Hew's dressing gown, donned it, and opened the bed chamber door.

The woman who had been making all the noise was standing in the middle of the outer chamber, dressing down a maid who was attempting to shoo her out. Judging by the tray on the table, the maid had brought tea and breakfast, and Belle's stomach rumbled at the thought of food.

She opened her mouth to ask who the woman thought she was but, at the last moment, thought better of it. Belle knew wealth and importance when she saw it. This woman was dressed in clothing that cost more than the shop made in a month. She was of medium height, taller than Belle, and had dark hair coiled and pinned under a fashionable dark blue hat. The hat matched her morning gown and the pelisse she wore over it. Her white gloves were spotless, the fingers of one wrapped about the handle of an ebony and gold walking stick.

She turned blue eyes on Belle, lifted the walking stick, and pointed it at her. "Who are you?"

"Belle," she said, somewhat distractedly. Belle couldn't help but stare at the woman's eyes. The color was lovely and familiar. Those eyes swept over Belle, seeming to take her measure rather quickly before making their final assessment.

"Belle, is it? Why are you wearing my son's dressing gown?"

"Your son?" Oh! Now the eyes made sense. This was Hew's mother. And this was not the way Belle had wanted to meet her, but then considering Hew's rank and her own, she doubted there would be any good way to meet his mother. The woman was unlikely to be pleased that her son had become attached to a shopkeeper. "You're Hew's mother."

"I am." She straightened. "Who are you? And where is he?"

Belle's gaze flicked to the maid, who was watching this exchange with avid interest. "Thank you for the tray. You can go."

"Yes, ma'am." The maid curtseyed and started for the door, dragging her feet in hopes that the argument between the women would continue. Once the door closed, Belle took a breath.

"Hew is still asleep," Belle said, to answer his mother's question. She pointed to the bed chamber door. "My father and I have been caring for Hew since he was stabbed."

"Stabbed?" Hew's mother seemed to sway, and Belle was glad she had the walking stick.

"Sit down, please." She crossed the room and motioned to one of the chairs near the fire.

The woman took the chair, quite gracefully, but her face had gone white. "I knew he had been injured. I didn't know he had been stabbed."

"Mr. Randall wrote to you?" Belle asked, going to the tea tray, selecting the Earl Grey Cream, and beginning to brew it.

"Yes, he said my son had been hurt and was being cared for, but that we should come as soon as possible. My husband has been ill with gout and could not come. I had to wait until the roads were passable. I—*stabbed*."

"Mr. Randall is married to the sister of my sister's husband," Belle said, thinking there was probably an easier way to say that. "Mrs. Randall went into labor at the same time your son was injured. Mr. Randall didn't know where else to send his friend, so he sent him to my father and me to care for at our tea shop. We've been nursing him."

Hew's mother's gaze lowered to the dressing gown again. "Where is your father now?"

"I wish I knew." She poured them both cups of the Earl Grey Cream, carried them to the grouping of chairs, and gave one to Hew's mother. "He's been abducted," she said, handing the other woman a cup.

"I don't understand."

"I'm not at liberty to explain," Belle said, sitting opposite her. "It has to do with Hew's work."

His mother let out an annoyed huff. "His work," she said, her tone dismissive. "That work will be the death of him."

"It almost was," Belle said, sipping the tea. Earl Grey Cream was not her favorite, but it was comforting and familiar. "He was badly injured."

Hew's mother took a sip of tea and eyed her over the rim. "I take it he has recovered." She sipped again. "What exactly is your relationship with my son?"

Belle shrugged. "I love him."

His mother's eyes widened.

"He says he won't ask me to marry him, but I think he will. I'll say no, of course. He'll have to talk me into it."

The woman coughed and set her tea on a small table before it could spill. "My, but you are a forthright young lady. I have the feeling if I ask what you were doing in the bed chamber with my son, you might just tell me."

"Just now, we were both asleep," Belle said. "I'm sure all of this must be a shock to you. I must be the last woman you want to marry your son. I work at a tea shop, and I think your son said you are the daughter of a duke."

"And yet you sit there and speak to me as though you are my equal."

Belle knew she should apologize, but she was too tired, had been through too much at this point, to care. "I imagine you won't be giving Hew your blessing to marry me then."

Hew's mother sputtered, and Belle thought this might be a good time to excuse herself.

"Allow me to see if he's awake."

She rose but just as she did there was a brisk knock on the door. This hotel was insufferable! She had more peace at her shop. The door opened, and Willoughby Galloway poked his head inside and spotted Belle. "Looks like you had a good night," he said, "despite having to be forced out of the warehouse at the docks."

Belle cleared her throat and glanced at Hew's mother. Galloway stepped inside, closed the door, then froze. "Er, Lady Eleanor."

"Mr. Galloway. I didn't expect to see you here."

"Er—I was sent to help Hew with the...with..."

"His work," Belle supplied.

"Yes. Er—how is Uncle Blue?"

Belle was rather surprised that Galloway seemed to know Hew's mother, but then she should have remembered that it seemed everyone in the upper classes knew each other.

"Ernest is quite well. I will tell him you asked. And your own parents?"

"Very well. If you see them don't mention me. They don't know I'm in Town, and there will be hell to pay if they find I didn't come and visit. In fact, I should go pay a call right now. Make everyone happy."

"Wait a moment," Belle said, not wanting to be left alone with Lady Eleanor again. "If anyone is leaving, it's me. I'll dress and wake Hew. He's the one you both want to see." Belle padded back into the bed chamber, opened the door, and found Hew already half dressed. He scowled when he saw her. "There's my dressing robe."

She might have scowled back, but the curtains had been partially opened, and she could see him clearly in the daylight. She had a quick flash of his broad chest moving against her breasts and those slim hips fitting between her thighs.

"That look is dangerous," he said. "It makes me want to forget about Will on the other side of the door and drag you back to bed." He crossed to her, took her shoulders, and kissed her. Belle wouldn't have minded Hew's suggestion in the least. She was half tempted to take him up on it. Until she remembered.

"Your mother is in the other room," she said.

Hew jolted backward. "What?"

"Your mother—"

"Good God." He began floundering about, searching until he found a shirt and pulled it over his head. "Why didn't you say that straightaway?"

"I was distracted." She gestured to his chest.

"Did she see you?"

Belle gave him a look.

"Of course, she saw you."

"I made her tea."

"Oh, God." He raked a hand through his hair.

"And then I told her I had my wicked way with you, but that I won't marry you until you beg."

"I hope to God you are not serious."

"About which part?"

He was dressed now and strode across the room, pausing before her. "We need to have a long conversation."

"Not unless it involves you begging."

"Belle!" He closed his eyes and took a long breath. "Not now. Get dressed and stay here. I'll be back."

And he went to the door, opened it, and said, "Mama! You're here." He closed the door, muffling his voice. Belle began to gather her clothing. She did intend to dress, but she would most definitely not stay here.

Chapter Twenty-Two

Hew was prepared for the sight of Will and his mother sipping tea in the outer chamber, but that didn't mean it wasn't a shock. They were chatting about his Uncle Ernest, the spy Blue, who Hew had forgotten Will knew. But then his uncle and Will's parents had worked together years ago.

His mother rose, and Hew went to her, kissing her cheek. She took his hands and looked at him. "You look quite recovered. In his letter, Mr. Randall seemed to imply you were half dead."

"Miss Howard was kind enough to nurse me back to health."

She released his hands. "Is that what you call it?"

Will cleared his throat. "I should go back to my room—"

"No." Hew gave Will a look that indicated he would throttle him with both hands if Will so much as tried to walk through the door. "Unfortunately," Hew continued, ignoring his mother's pointed comment. "They've suffered because of their kindness. Their tea shop was set on fire, and her father—"

"Yes, she said he was abducted. I assume you will fetch him back."

"I will."

"And do you have time to dress properly and take tea with me?" she asked. "Perhaps in the dining room downstairs?"

"Mama, I'm sorry."

She held up a hand. "Your father said there was no reason for me to hie to London as though I had a swarm of bees chasing me. I suppose I should have listened."

"I do appreciate your concern. I was badly injured."

"But you're better now." She lifted her walking stick from the arm of the chair, where she'd laid it. "I am happy for it, and to see you. It's been months and your letters are quite perfunctory."

"I'm not allowed—"

"No matter. Once you are done with this matter— whatever it is—you will come and visit? Your father has not been feeling well, and I think he will be cheered to see you."

"Is he still suffering from the gout? I'll come as soon as I am able."

The door to the bed chamber opened, and he turned and saw Belle step into the room. She wore the same clothing she'd worn yesterday, and she'd pulled her hair into a simple style, leaving some of it free to hide her scars. Hew didn't know why she bothered. Her scars were part of her and didn't take away from her beauty in the least.

"Bring Miss Howard with you when you come," his mother said.

Hew whirled back around. "What?"

"She says you will soon beg her to marry you."

"I won't." He wished he could take the words back as soon as they'd left his mouth. Instead, he closed his eyes then risked a look at Belle. She looked back at him, her gaze indicating she would make him pay for that. Later.

"Walk me downstairs and wait for me while the footman calls my carriage," his mother said. "You can spare that much time at least."

"I'll stay here," Will offered. "Don't forget to say hello to Uncle Blue, my lady."

"I won't."

Left without any other options, Hew took his mother's arm and escorted her downstairs. She commented on the carpets and the wall sconces until they stood in the hotel lobby, waiting for her coach. "I blame my brother for encouraging you in this...career," she said, giving Hew a direct look. "Your father and I wanted you to go to seminary. We were happy enough with you as a diplomat, though you were always gone for months on end. I think we knew even then where that would lead. And here we are, worried every day we'll receive word you've been killed."

"And then you received Mr. Randall's letter and worried. I am sorry, Mama."

"As well you should be, but I don't suppose it will change anything. You're determined to do this sort of work, just as my brother was."

Hew smiled. He knew how much his mother adored her brother and how proud she was of him, even if she didn't say so.

"I blame him for putting all sorts of romantic notions in your head. But I blame myself for the rest."

"The rest?" Hew frowned. "What do you mean?"

"Your marriage to Clara."

"Mama." Hew held up a hand.

"I know you don't wish to speak of her. You never do. I never should have encouraged that marriage. She was so young. You both were. I thought she would anchor you, but she had the opposite effect."

"She made her own choices, Mama. Those weren't your fault."

She cupped his face, tenderly, so tenderly that Hew wanted to push her hands away. He didn't want to remember

Clara or the pain he'd felt or the pain her betrayal had caused his family.

"But I knew better, Hew. I knew it wasn't a love match. I hoped you would come to love her, but I was wrong. I see that very clearly now. Very clearly."

"What do you mean."

"You never looked at her the way I just saw you look at that young woman upstairs."

Hew shook his head.

"Oh, don't think I am pleased with *that* match. Who are her people? It might be best if we don't look too closely. And apparently, she is in *trade*. Your father will not like it at all, so I won't tell him until it's done."

"There's nothing to be done. I won't marry again. She knows that." He glanced up, indicating his room above.

"And I've never known you to shy away from a challenge, and I don't believe for one moment that you will start now. Clara hurt you, but it's a scratch, a surface wound. Let that young woman bandage you up, as she did your physical injury, and then forget Clara. That's my wish for you."

"Mama, I don't think I've ever heard you speak so metaphorically."

"I promise not to make a habit of it."

The footman approached and notified her that her carriage was ready. She kissed Hew's cheek. "I do hope you are able to find Miss Howard's father."

"I'll find him," Hew said.

She smiled. "If anyone can, it will be you." And then she was gone.

Hew started back upstairs, not surprised in the least that Belle had won his mother over. She had a way of doing that. He didn't know how she managed it. She wasn't charming or witty. But she was genuine. Hew supposed that his mother could appreciate that as much as he.

He shouldn't have taken her last night—or early this morning. He'd known it was a mistake, and yet he'd done it anyway. And since it was a mistake, he should regret it more than he did. But it was hard to regret something that had been so pleasurable. It was hard to regret something he desperately wanted to do again.

But he wouldn't do it again because he didn't intend to marry her—despite what she said. He'd deal with that issue later. He'd make his apologies later, own up to his moral failures and weaknesses of the flesh. Right now, he had to find Belle's father.

***

"I liked her," Belle said after Hew had left with his mother. "She wasn't quite as arrogant as I'd imagined she'd be."

Galloway smiled. "You're not one for compliments, are you?"

"That *was* a compliment."

"Do yourself a favor and don't ever tell her that."

"Am I supposed to compliment her when she scolds me for thinking I'm her equal? As though she's better than me because of an accident of birth. I bet she can't tell a Ceylon from an Assam."

"The horror." Galloway paced to the window and pushed the curtains aside.

"Then you think her rank makes her better than me?"

"What I think is that a thousand years ago her ancestor fought on a battlefield and distinguished himself. William the Conqueror or some other king gave him a parcel of land and the title of the Duke of Ely, and he's passed it down for generations."

"Who's the duke now?"

"One of her brothers, I suppose."

"And do you think he would succeed on the battlefield?"

He turned to face her. "Absolutely not."

"What about me?"

"You're a veritable Joan of Arc. Don't worry. Given time, his mother will come around, if she hasn't already. Nothing wrong with adding some peasant stock to the bloodline once in a while."

He ducked, which was a good idea because she would have probably thrown her teacup at him if Hew hadn't opened the door at that moment.

He gave them both a look. "What's the matter?"

"Not a thing," Galloway said, smiling. Belle wiped the angry expression from her face and gave Galloway a look of challenge. Last night he'd agreed that she might go to Hyde Park if Hew said she could. Hew was about to say she could.

"What is your plan for today? I assume we'll go to Hyde Park and"—she gestured vaguely—"get the lay of the land?"

"You are not—" Galloway closed his mouth at one look from Belle. They both looked at Hew.

"What are you not telling me?" he asked, his tone wary.

"I am going to Hyde Park with you," she said.

"I don't think that's a good idea," he said.

"I agree," Will said. "In fact, the best idea is still for Hew to get on a train and Miss Howard to go back to wherever she came from."

"No one asked you," Belle said. "Hew, it's my father. I want to see where the meeting will happen tonight."

"I'll take the train tomorrow and take full responsibility for not following orders," Hew told Galloway. "As for Hyde Park...." He seemed to consider Belle. "I suppose there's no harm in you coming along. We won't be the only people at the park at this hour."

Galloway made a sound of annoyance, but Belle smiled at Hew. He seemed surprised by it and took a step back. "I feel as though I've missed something."

"Not at all," Belle said.

Hew went to fetch a hat and greatcoat. As soon as he was gone, Galloway hissed, "You haven't won yet."

"I'll be there tonight."

"I'll bring you a deck of cards so you might have something to do tonight, all alone in this room."

"We'll see about—"

Hew stepped back into the room and looked from her to Galloway. "What exactly happened at the tea warehouse last night?"

"We made a bargain. Miss Howard agreed to come back to Mivart's."

"And Mr. Galloway agreed to keep his opinions to himself. Now, let's go see where my father will be tonight."

***

The excursion to Hyde Park had been uneventful. They spent the majority of their time near the park's lake, the Serpentine. Belle had sat on the Serpentine Bridge while the two men walked across it, peered under it, and even rented a rowboat and rowed under it. Now they were back in Hew's chamber at Mivart's, going over their complicated plan. They'd been discussing it for hours, embellishing it, and now that it was after ten, they were almost ready to put it into motion. Belle had allowed them to plot and strategize until half past ten, and then disappeared into Hew's bed chamber, rifled through his trunks, and reemerged just as they were finishing up.

"You've made an exceedingly well-thought-out plan," she told the men, "But I have a better one."

Galloway gave her a look that said here-we-go. "It's far too late for a new plan," Galloway said. "We are leaving." He stood. "Now."

"I think we should at least hear what she has to say," Hew said. Then his eyes narrowed at the cape she wore — his cape — covering her clothing. "Unless it involves you somehow."

"Of course, it involves her," Galloway said. Hew looked at Belle.

She shrugged and smiled. "Mr. Galloway, didn't I hear you say earlier that simpler was better?"

"Perhaps," he said carefully.

"And yet, you have this complicated plan"—she gestured to the stack of balled-up paper where they'd tried to map out the strategy—"that requires precise timing and ambushing the ambushers and the moon behind a cloud—"

"I said it would be *helpful* if the moon went behind a cloud," Galloway argued. "It's not a prerequisite."

"The abductors have agreed to exchange my father for Hew," she said. "So why not just give them Hew? Force an exchange. My father starts on one side of the bridge and Hew is on the other. They meet in the middle and my father crosses to safety."

"And as soon as they have Hew, they'll kill him," Galloway said.

"Maybe they'll only think they have him."

"We thought about having Will act in my place, but there are two problems. First of all, there's nothing to stop them from killing Will."

"So don't give them Will." She unclasped the cape and let it fall away, revealing the men's clothing she wore beneath it.

"Bloody hell," Galloway said. "No, just no."

Hew's reaction took a bit longer. His gaze traveled over her body, clad in the coat and trousers she'd pinned to make them fit. "No," he said, slowly, shaking his head. "I won't have you put in danger either."

"They won't kill me," she said. "They'll know they've been duped, and they'll be so surprised that they have a woman, not the man they'd been after, they'll hesitate."

"They'll be angry and do away with you," Galloway said.

"Not if you jump out and overpower them first. Don't you see? If I'm on one side of the bridge, pretending to be Hew, then you two can hide on the other side. Once my father is out of their hands, you ambush them."

"She has a point," Hew said. "Our main problem with the plan was that we couldn't find a way to work together. This way, we can."

"I cannot believe you are considering this. What about the other problem?"

"What other problem?" Belle demanded.

"What if they don't bring your father?"

"They will," she said. "If they'd killed him, they have no leverage. I have no doubt they intend to kill my father and Hew, but they'll wait until after they have Hew to do it." She smiled. "That's when I yell *surprise* and distract them so you can step in."

Hew looked at Galloway, and Galloway swore. "I have to admit, it's not a bad plan."

"Not bad? It's perfect," she argued.

"It's not perfect," Hew argued back. "I don't want you in danger."

"And I don't want you in danger," she said. "So we're even. It's almost eleven o'clock. We'd better go."

***

Hew would have liked to argue further. The pit of dread in his belly felt heavier as soon as Belle explained her plan—mainly because it was a good plan. He and Will did need to work together, and a distraction would give them the perfect opening to attack. He just didn't want Belle to be the distraction. Galloway didn't think it would work because he believed Mr. Howard already dead but Hew agreed with Belle. The abductors had failed Pennywhistle several times now, and they couldn't afford to fail again. They had to get rid of Hew. His death would derail the entire investigation and give Pennywhistle the time he needed to either bribe the railway officials or excavate the minerals.

Hew hadn't argued further. There wasn't time, even if he had been able to think of reasons why Belle should stay behind. Instead, they stuffed the shoulders of the coat with extra fabric to make her look a bit larger and put her in boots and a taller hat. He still didn't think anyone would mistake the two of them, but if they were lucky, the darkness and the distance between one side of the bridge and the other would be enough to fool the abductors temporarily.

Now they walked through the dark park, taking a circuitous route to avoid being seen. Will walked in front, holding a lamp, but he had it shuttered for the most part. Hew walked behind, holding Belle's hand. Her hand was small in his but steady and cool. By contrast, his own felt warm and shaky. "You're not nervous at all, are you?" he whispered.

"I'm only worried for my father," she said. Then she surprised him by looking at him. "And you. Try not to get stabbed again."

He almost laughed. "You're the one in danger this time."

She waved a hand. "You won't let anything happen to me."

"You're right." Hew grasped her shoulders and turned her to face him. "I won't let anything happen to you. I couldn't live with myself if anything happened to you."

She smiled at him. "I do love you," she said and bent forward to kiss him. She wasn't used to wearing a man's hat, and it got in the way. He smiled, tipped it up, and kissed her back. The kiss was brief but there was meaning in it. They both knew the danger that lay ahead, and Belle couldn't be any less aware that this might be the last moments they had together.

"I need to tell you something," he said, resting his forehead on hers.

"This isn't the time for a marriage proposal," she said. "You'll want at least a quarter hour in which to grovel."

"Little minx. That wasn't what I wanted to tell you." Though he was increasingly beginning to believe that he would have to ask for her hand in marriage. The very idea scared the hell out of him but not as much as the idea of being without her. "Do you remember when I told you I was glad Clara died?"

She nodded.

"You argued that I wasn't. That I was hurt because I'd still loved her."

"And that's why it's taking you so long to trust me."

He gave her the ghost of a smile. "Yes, but I realized something else. I didn't hate Clara because she betrayed me. I hated her because she embarrassed me. I didn't hate her at all because to hate her I would have had to love her. I never loved her. I realize that now. I love you."

She took his face in her hands and kissed him. "Put that in your speech," she whispered. "The one where you grovel."

Will cut off his harsh rejoinder. "What the devil?" he hissed. "This is a mission. No kissing on missions."

"My apologies," Hew said, taking Belle's hand and starting forward again.

"The bridge is just along that trail," Will told Belle, pointing ahead. "Hew and I will cross down there at the bend. We'll circle behind and be in place before Pennywhistle's men arrive." He gave Hew a look. "But we have to leave now."

"Take the lamp," Hew said, handing it to Belle, "but keep it down and away from your face."

"Be careful," she said.

"You be careful." He wanted to kiss her again, but Will made a sound like retching and pulled him away.

"We will all be careful." Will pushed Hew forward, toward the rowboat they'd hidden among the bushes. Hew chanced one look back. But Belle was already gone.

Chapter Twenty-Three

Belle took a deep breath, set the lamp on the ground at the base of the bridge, and stepped forward. She stood straight and tall, trying to look larger than she was, though the other end of the bridge was quite a distance. She doubted the men would be able to make out many details when they arrived.

If they arrived.

She wished she had a watch so she might check the time. But she had no other way to measure the hour except to wait for the chime of the clock tower. She'd heard it mark the three-quarter hour. That seemed like ages ago. Seconds ticked by as she listened to the wind in the trees, the lap of the water against the bridge, and the occasional splash of a fish. At least she thought it was a fish. She hoped Hew was in position on the other side of the bridge by now.

She took another breath, resisted the urge to look over her shoulder, then gave in. The last thing she needed was for Pennywhistle's men to sneak up behind her.

The path behind her was dark and empty — she hoped — and when she turned back, four figures stood on the other end of the bridge. She recognized the thin, stooped figure of her father right away, and her heart soared. She'd known he wasn't dead! She would absolutely rub this in Galloway's face. She'd told him her father was alive.

"Arundel, that ye?" came a voice. It carried across the bridge, sounding oddly muffled. The abductors were most likely wearing some sort of covering over their faces to disguise themselves.

She'd been warned not to speak, so she raised her hand in answer.

"Let's make this easy," the voice said again. "Ye walk this way, and we send the old man that way. Try anything, and we shoot ye both. Agreed?"

Belle raised her hand again.

"Start walking," the man called.

Belle took another breath and began to walk. On the other side of the bridge, her father stumbled forward.

***

Hew watched Belle start across the bridge toward her father. Her shoulders were straight, and she stood tall. Still, he could see she was too short, too slight to be a man. Hew could only hope Pennywhistle's men saw what they wanted to see.

"Her father is alive," Galloway whispered. "She'll never let me live this down."

"No, she won't," Hew said, his heart pounding as he watched Belle take another step.

"I'm glad of it. Let's just hope he doesn't do anything to give her away when they pass each other. Once she's past the three-quarter mark, we go."

Hew agreed. Will and he wanted to strike before Pennywhistle's men had Belle in their custody. For that to work, the three abductors had to stay on this side of the bridge. If one of them realized they'd been tricked, they might race across the bridge, and then they could be gone—taking Belle and her father with them—before Hew and Will ever caught up. That was Hew's worst nightmare. He was trying not to think about it. Trying not to think about watching Belle carried away from him. His life without her. He'd been thinking too much about life without her these past hours.

He needed her with him. Wanted her with him—at his side, in his bed, back in her shop and selling tea. That's where she should be—not risking her life in the middle of the night

Belle neared the middle of the bridge just as her father looked up. He hadn't closed as much distance on the bridge as she, but Hew saw the way his step faltered. *Keep walking,* Hew pleaded. *Keep walking.*

***

Belle slowed slightly, giving her father a chance to catch up so they might pass the center of the bridge together. She was hungry for the sight of him. Was he moving slower than usual? Did he seem stiff? Bent over? She had to keep her head high and her steps confident. As he approached, she desperately wanted to reach out and take him into her arms, but she knew she must keep walking. He wouldn't be safe until he was on the other side of the bridge and far, far away from here.

She reached the center of the bridge at almost the same time as her father. Their eyes met, and she saw fear and confusion in his. She knew exactly what he was thinking—why was *she* meeting him on the bridge? She tried to tell him with her eyes that all would be well. Keep moving. Get to safety. She pleaded silently for him not to try anything now to "save" her. They passed each other, and she held her breath even as she reached between them and groped for his hand. He caught hers and squeezed, and she squeezed back.

There was a world of communication in that squeeze. She told him to trust her. He told her he was well. His hand trembled, and she knew he was as frightened as she. The touch lasted only a moment and then he was behind her, and she was moving toward the abductors on the other side of the bridge.

Hew had given her a hat and angled the brim over her eyes. She tilted her head now to use that same brim to shield her face. If the men realized too soon they had been fooled, all of this would be for nothing.

She had sixty paces left, then fifty-five. Her breath came in short bursts as though fighting through the constriction in her chest. She desperately wanted to peer over her shoulder and see if her father was safe and away, but she clenched her fists and resisted.

Fifty paces.

Dear God, what if Hew and Galloway hadn't made it to the other side of the Serpentine in time? What if they were still searching for their boat or still rowing across? What if she reached the other side of the bridge and no one came to save her?

Forty paces.

Belle didn't dare look at the men waiting for her on the other side. She was afraid to see if they suspected her yet. Meeting their gazes would only increase their suspicions, so she kept her face turned aside and shielded by the hat's brim.

Thirty-five paces. Her feet felt as though they were weighed down by lead.

Thirty paces.

For some reason her mind went to Hew. Of all the things she might think of in her last hours, she never thought she'd be thinking about the grandson of a duke who spent his days gallivanting about the land trying to protect Queen and Country. He didn't even know the first thing about tea.

And yet she loved him.

She hadn't wanted to love him. She'd fought it, fought the flutters of sensation that rose in her when she first saw him, when he first touched her. She really fought the growing feelings that took root when they'd talked and shared secrets, when he'd risked his life for her, when he'd finally given in and taken her in his arms.

Twenty-five paces.

He didn't trust women. He'd been hurt, his heart and his pride badly damaged, and yet she'd known, somewhere deep down, that he could still love. She'd known, perhaps before he had, that he loved her. And she loved him. She'd never allowed herself to love before because she too hadn't been able to trust. Now she was trusting him with her life and that of her father.

Twenty paces.

"What's this then?" one of Pennywhistle's men said, his voice carrying in the darkness.

Belle didn't dare look at the men. She continued walking, keeping her face in shadow.

Eighteen paces, seventeen.

"We've been bamboozled. That ain't the man we want."

Belle's foot hovered as she tried to decide whether it was better to continue or start running the other way. Now would be a very good time for Hew and Galloway to jump in.

Her foot lowered at fifteen paces—give or take—and she raised her face to stare at Pennywhistle's men.

"It's the pock-marked girl from the tea shop," one of them said.

"Get her!" another cried.

Belle didn't know why her feet wouldn't move. Her mind was screaming, *Go!* Her body was tensed to flee, and yet she stood locked in place.

***

Hew sensed Will readying himself to pounce. He imagined the man crouched beside him in the shrubs near the bridge was coiled as tightly as himself. He watched Belle cross the bridge and felt as though his heart was outside his body. He was too far away. He couldn't protect her. He should never have allowed her to risk her life like this.

"That ain't the man we want," one of Pennywhistle's men said.

"Now!" Will uncoiled and sprang forward.

Somehow Hew was right behind him, moving without thinking. Belle had halted on the bridge and looked like a startled deer. He couldn't believe she had made it this close without the men suspecting earlier. He wished she hadn't made it so close. She was practically within arms' reach of the thugs. A glance at the other end of the bridge showed her father had paused and looked over his shoulder. Just what Hew needed—for her father to play the hero and put himself back in harm's way. But there was no more time to think about Belle or her father because one of the thugs was turning to him now and Hew only had time to react.

He put out a fist, striking hard and fast. His hand met the nose of Pennywhistle's man, and he heard the crunch and felt the sharp reverberation through his body. His injured side gave a small twinge of protest, but Hew's blood was running hot now. He was numb to the pain.

Pennywhistle's man punched back, and Hew ducked, feeling the spray of the blood from the man's broken nose splatter on his cheek as he moved. To his side, he caught sight of Will engaged in hand-to-hand with another of the abductors.

But there had been three...

Hew's gaze went immediately to the bridge where Belle was now staring at him, even as the last of Pennywhistle's men approached her.

"Belle!" Hew screamed. "Run!"

She seemed to start awake at his words, noticed the approaching man, turned, and ran. Hew started to go after her, but the man with the broken nose jumped in his way. "Damn it," Hew growled as he swung and missed. This time the other man's punch landed in his breadbasket, leaving him momentarily breathless. He bent over and saw stars. The punch must have glanced off his wound. That was the only way to account for the fact that he was about to sink to his knees from a single gut punch.

His opponent, seeing weakness, grabbed his hair and jerked his head up. Hew stared into the other man's bloody face then squeezed his eyes shut, not wanting to see the blow.

Instead, the man released him. Hew fell forward and heard Will say, "I have this. Go after her."

Before Hew could argue, Will was pulled away and into another skirmish. Hew turned back to the bridge and saw Belle running for the other side with Pennywhistle's man right behind her. The pain in his side felt like an anchor he dragged behind him as he tried to reach her. He scrambled onto the bridge and watched helplessly as she stumbled to the other side and Pennywhistle's man reached for her.

***

Belle had tied her hair in a queue and tucked it securely in Hew's coat. Somehow in her mad dash for the other side of the bridge, it had come out. She saw her father up ahead. He had turned at the end of the bridge and was yelling for her. She reached for him then was yanked back by the head. Her neck twisted in pain, and she fell backward and onto the bridge. She knew she was hurt, but she'd been slammed on her back so hard, her ears rung and she was unable to locate the pain. She simply lay there, looking up at the moonless sky and trying to catch her breath.

"Belle!" her father called.

She tried to raise her head, tried to tell him to run, but nothing came out of her mouth.

"Run!" came the familiar voice of Hew. And then she was jerked upward like a rag doll and spun around so that the world turned on its axis. Except when she was able to make some sense of it, Hew was before her.

"Let her go," he yelled, still racing toward her.

"You want 'er? Come and get 'er!"

Pennywhistle's man thrust her aside, and Belle saw the flash of metal as the man pulled a knife out of his pocket. She heard the cock of a hammer and gasped. That was no knife but a pistol. She had to warn Hew, but there was no time. Head spinning and legs wobbly, she lurched forward, grabbed for the pistol and wrenched the man's hand upward. The shot went wild, the sound exploding in the park and startling sleeping birds from their perches.

She was knocked aside and then Hew and the abductor were locked in combat against the side of the bridge. Belle crawled away, grasped the bridge's thick stone railing, and limped toward her father.

Stupid man. Of course, he hadn't listened. He was coming across the bridge for her. She wanted to smack him. Instead, she fell into his arms and allowed him to haul her away from the water and the bridge, off the path and into the shadow of the trees.

"Daddy," she said, feeling the wetness on her cheeks as the tears ran down her face. She hadn't called him *Daddy* for years, but it seemed the most natural thing in the world at the moment. "You're safe. Are you hurt?"

"I'm fine. You, Belle? You fell hard."

"Just out of breath." She grasped him and hugged him tightly. Then she turned back to the bridge. She couldn't see it through the foliage. "Hew..." She tried to rise, but her father pulled her back down.

"Stay put. He can focus on the fight if he doesn't have to worry about you."

The sounds of men fighting echoed through the park and then she heard the splash of water and a muttered curse. Belle looked up at her father whose own face mirrored what she assumed was her frightened expression. "Was that Hew or...?"

Heavy footsteps approached, and Belle fumbled on the ground, reaching for whatever she might use as a weapon. Her hand closed on a stick, and she climbed to her feet, crouching low and brandishing the makeshift bludgeon.

Leaves crunched underfoot, a branch broke, and then she saw the shape of a man step toward them. She swung the stick, stopping short just as Hew's face came into view.

"That's not the welcome I'd hoped for," he said.

With a cry, Belle slammed into his arms.

***

The hours blurred together as Hew and Will dealt with the captured abductors, local magistrates, and several government ministers. Finally, as the sun rose, Hew left Will to deal with the last details and returned to Mivart's. He'd arranged a room for Belle and her father beforehand and had sent them to bed after Mr. Howard gave his statement. Hew retrieved his key from the front desk and started up the stairs to his room, wondering how badly the footmen and maids would curse him if he requested hot water and a bath this early—

"Mr. Arundel."

Hew turned and started at seeing Mr. Howard coming forward out of the salon area. "Mr. Howard. I thought you'd be in bed."

"I tried to sleep and couldn't. Belle is sleeping. I think she fell asleep as soon as her head hit the pillow. I checked on her before I came down."

"If there was something you needed, you could have rung for a maid."

Howard shook his head. "I was waiting for you."

Hew nodded, not really surprised. He gestured to the empty salon and led Howard to two armchairs near the hearth. "I had hoped to speak with you as well," he said after they were seated. "But I thought you must be exhausted after your ordeal."

Howard waved a hand. "I sat in a room for two days. I had little to do but sleep and think."

"I'll tell you honestly, sir. Mr. Galloway and I feared you were dead."

"I heard them discuss killing me, but in the end, they wanted me for the exchange."

"I'd be interested to hear what else you heard discussed. I want to tie your capture back to Pennywhistle and make sure he pays."

"I heard quite a lot about Pennywhistle, but I don't want to talk about him at present. What I want to discuss is why my daughter was walking across that bridge, all alone, toward three dangerous men." His voice, usually so quiet and meek, trembled with rage.

Hew took a breath. "I didn't want her to go. We both tried to talk her out of it."

"And yet, there she was."

"Sir, I think you know her better than anyone. There was no keeping her here. She'd made up her mind and devised a plan which, frankly, was better than what we had sketched out. Still, I take full responsibility for her being there, and I understand your anger. You must have been terrified."

"That doesn't begin to describe it. The only reason I haven't hit you is because I saw you were terrified too."

"I?" Hew reared back.

"When you came through the trees, the look on your face was abject fear."

"Ah." Hew shrugged. He didn't remember what he'd felt in that moment. He'd only wanted to see Belle and be certain she was unharmed. "Your daughter was about to brain me with a tree branch. That would scare anyone."

Howard gave him a long look.

Hew shifted and cleared his throat. "I actually had planned to speak to you, sir. I thought it might be best to wait until the morning, after you'd rested and had some time with Belle—er, Miss Howard."

"Speak now."

"Right." Hew had also thought he might have time to think what to say, or at least *how* to say what he must. But perhaps it was best to plunge right in and take the hits as they came. "I want to ask for your daughter's hand in marriage."

Howard's brows shot up. "Why?"

Hew stared at the fire, wishing it might swallow him up. "While you were away, we became rather close. Physically. Last night or perhaps the night before…" How the hell was he supposed to tell Belle's father that he'd deflowered her?

"The answer is no," Howard said.

Hew blinked. "What?"

Howard rose. "Good night, sir." He was halfway across the room before Hew found his feet and raced to stand in front of him.

"Why? I just told you I—er, I have to marry her. It's the only honorable thing to do."

"And do you think my daughter or I care about honor? That's a concept your class invented. If you want to marry Belle, you get her consent. I won't agree without it. But as it stands right now, I wouldn't agree even if you had it—not that she needs my agreement. She's an adult woman." He started away again but Hew blocked his exit. Howard glared at him.

"Why wouldn't you agree? I can take care of her. I'll treat her well."

"Like you did last night? Allowing her to put herself in danger?"

"Nothing like that will ever happen again, I swear to you."

"Bah." He waved a hand, dismissing Hew's assurances. "The answer is no."

"Sir!" Hew said as Howard walked away. "Sir, I swear to you I will keep her safe."

Howard kept walking.

"I love her."

Howard stopped. "Say again."

"I…" Hew swallowed. "I love her."

Howard turned around and Hew was struck by the smile on his face. "That was what I wanted to hear."

Hew closed his eyes, his heart thundering. He'd really thought he might lose Belle, and he couldn't deal with such a close call again tonight. "I didn't want to marry again. I thought I might love her without marrying her, but—"

"But then I would have to shoot you in the...foot?"

Hew smiled. "There was that. Also I realized that I love her, and with love comes trust. I never thought—"

"Young man," Howard interrupted. "Save all of this for Belle. I promise you will need every word to convince her to marry you."

"She's been telling me I will beg her to marry me for days now."

"That doesn't mean she'll say yes."

And with that, he did walk away, leaving Hew to sink down on a couch and stare up at the ceiling, feeling desperate and uncertain.

Chapter Twenty-Four

Belle had decided that the luxury of hot water and a bathtub was something she could become used to. She'd bathed and washed her hair and dressed in her own clothes as Hew had arranged for clothing from their flat to be sent. She didn't know how he arranged these things, but she was glad to be in her own dress. When she stepped out of her bed chamber, she found her father seated at the small table in the center of their suite at Mivart's. He had his own bed chamber and from the look of it, his own bath.

She smiled at him, crossed to the table, and kissed his cheek. "You still look tired," she said.

"I'm fine. I'm eager to go home and open the shop."

Belle frowned and sat across from him. "I'm afraid we still have a bit of work to do to make it ready. I'll hire a few boys and take care of everything. You should rest."

He buttered a piece of toast. "I'll rest when the shop is open again. The way you run it means I'm hardly needed."

"Nonsense. Half our customers come in to speak with you and ask for your recommendations.

He raised a brow. "And all of them take *your* recommendations and come back because of the tea you suggest. But if working in the shop is not something you'd like to continue—"

"What? Of course, I want to continue. There's nothing else I'd rather do, save buy the teas. But what's the point in purchasing the best tea if I can't share it with others?"

"Don't you ever want to marry?"

Belle stared at her father. He'd asked her this before, but there was something different in his voice this morning. "I-I don't know. But even if I were married, I wouldn't give up the shop."

"Not all men want a wife who works in a shop all day."

"No one is lining up at my door to propose."

Just then a knock sounded.

"Don't be so sure," her father muttered. "I'll get that," he said and rose. Belle watched him walk to the door. He opened it, murmured something to the person on the other side, then said, "Excuse me, my dear."

Belle watched him walk to his room then glanced at the door to see Hew close it behind him. She frowned. "I thought you would be on your way back by now. Mr. Galloway seemed to think Baron Keating had much to discuss with you."

"I do need to speak with him." He started toward her. "We'll need to coordinate with the Home Office and the railroads to take Pennywhistle into custody and charge him with sabotage, among other crimes."

"Don't forget arson."

He smiled. "I wouldn't dare, and I didn't dare leave without speaking to you first."

"Go on. You want to thank me for giving you the brilliant plan last night? I told you my father was alive, and I told you my plan would work."

He was standing beside her chair now, looking down at her. "I should always listen to you. You were right. About everything."

Belle opened her mouth then closed it again. She was used to acting more confident than she felt, used to putting on a brave face with young, handsome men like Hew Arundel. That was if they looked at her twice. And now Hew was looking at her quite intently.

"Do you know what else you were right about?"

Her heart had begun to beat faster, making her feel a little dizzy and lightheaded. "No," she said, her voice all but a whisper.

"You said I would beg you to marry me."

"And?" Her heart was about to leap from her chest. This was not happening. He was not about to propose.

"You were right." He sank to one knee and took her hand.

"What are you doing?" Panic crept into her chest and gripped her lungs so that she couldn't seem to take a deep breath.

"Your hand is shaking," he said. "And you look a bit pale."

"I'm hungry."

Hew nodded and squeezed her hand. "Is that it? Or is it that you aren't as sure of yourself as you pretended, and now that what you wanted is happening, you can't seem to believe it."

She tugged her hand out of his. "What I wanted?" She shook her head. "I never said I wanted to marry you. I said you'd beg me because one day you would realize the same thing I did."

"And what's that?"

"That you love me and want to be with me."

Hew nodded. "I did realize that. I also know you love me and want to be with me."

"In my weak moments, I might have said that."

"And in my weak moments, I told you I'd never marry again." He took her hand again, catching it and holding it tightly after she tried to evade him. "I was afraid. I can admit it."

Belle looked into his eyes. They were that dark velvet blue she so loved. Finally, she stopped fighting him.

"I didn't want to trust you," he said. "I didn't want to love you. But you tore down every single one of my defenses, and I think I loved and trusted you before I even had a chance to fight it."

"I disagree. You fought it quite well."

He smiled. "God, how would I ever live without you? I can't, Belle. That's the truth. Marry me."

She opened her mouth to agree, but her throat was so dry she couldn't seem to speak. Hew took that to mean he hadn't said enough.

"I know you have your concerns. I told you about my first marriage. I blamed the failure on Clara, but I was wrong to put the whole of the failure on her. I made mistakes too. I married for the wrong reasons, first of all," he said. "I never loved her. Not like I should have. But I love you."

Belle felt her heart leap into her throat. He'd said he loved her before, but not like this, not looking at her like he did now, not with his heart all but on his sleeve. His vulnerability all but broke her.

"You're the only woman I've ever loved. The only woman I believe I *will* ever love. Belle, you made me want to risk everything again. If you tell me no, I'll respect your decision, but please God, don't tell me no."

"I won't," she said, her voice cracking.

Hew seemed to crumple before her. "I understand. I—"

She tightened her grip on his hand, just as it began to loosen. "I mean, I won't tell you no. Yes, I'll marry you."

"You'll marry me?"

She nodded, and then she was swept up and into his arms. He was twirling her about, kissing her face, telling her he loved her. Belle adored every moment of it, but finally his lips met hers, and she grasped handfuls of his hair and kissed him back. He groped for a moment, sat on the couch, and pulled her into his lap, still kissing her. His mouth went to her neck, and he murmured words of love and praise. She was laughing and crying, telling him, "I love you too." Then she took his face in her hands and pulled back. "But don't think I will leave the tea shop. I'll never give it up."

"Good," he said. "I'd never want you to."

Belle felt her heart rise like that balloon she'd seen float into the sky once over Hyde Park when she was a young girl.

She'd marveled at how light and weightless it had seemed, and now she felt as though she could fly too. "Do you know what I want?" she asked.

"What's that?"

"Let me show you." She bent to kiss him again, and then there was the sound of a throat clearing. Hew jumped up, setting Belle on the floor and stepping away from her.

"Sir." He nodded at her father who had just stepped out of his bed chamber. At least Belle hoped he had just stepped out.

"I hope from what I've just seen that congratulations are in order?"

Belle ran to him. "He wants to marry me!" She hugged her father. He hugged her back.

"But do you want to marry him?"

She laughed. "Of course. I love him."

"Are you sure?" he asked.

She nodded. "I'd give up the Pan Long Yin Hao for him."

"Not the one from the Emperor of China."

"Yes. I love him that much."

He looked at Hew. "You're a lucky man."

"I have no idea what you just said, but you'll never have to give up the Long Pan—er, I'll never ask you to give up a thing. I'll give you everything you've ever wanted and more."

***

Belle had thought Hew was exaggerating in the heat of the moment. Didn't all prospective grooms pledge the earth and the sun and the moon as well? She should have known better. Hew didn't make promises he couldn't keep—though he sometimes took his time in keeping them.

First, he disappeared for three weeks. He'd told her he had to return to the Farm—wherever that was—and he'd be back in London to marry her as soon as possible. He'd arranged for Belle and her father to stay at Mivart's as long as they wanted. But Belle and her father were more than happy to return to their flat and Howard's Teas & Treats. The shop still smelled of smoke, but they worked tirelessly to repair the fire damage, air it out, and restock the teas and other sundries. Mrs. Tipps checked on them daily, and Mrs. Price helped with the cleaning and dusting. They tried to keep her from stocking. She tended to misplace items and then one found them in the oddest places later. As much as Belle wanted to dislike Mrs. Price, she had to admit, she was a helpful neighbor. And Belle didn't mind that there seemed to be growing affection between her father and Mrs. Price. After all, she didn't want her father to be all alone when she married.

If she married.

Almost three weeks after calling the banns, Belle still hadn't seen or heard from Hew. She put on a brave face but was beginning to think he might have been a figment of her imagination. That was until his mother stepped into the tea shop.

Belle dropped her dusting rag. "Lady Eleanor!"

"Ah," she said looking around, the feather in her stylish cap swaying with her movements. "You remember me."

"Of course."

Her father emerged from the back room just then, and she introduced him to Hew's mother. He gave her a courtly bow then said, "And where is your errant son? He seems to have disappeared."

Lady Eleanor's brows went up. "He said he wrote to you. He will be in Town tomorrow for the wedding." Her gaze swept over Belle's work dress. "Is that what you plan to wear?"

"I..." She was at a loss for words. "I didn't receive a letter." She looked at her father. "Did you?"

"No. Come to think of it, we've not received any mail for the last few days." His eyes met Belle's. "Mrs. Price!" they said in unison.

"I'll go find her," her father said.

"She won't remember where she's put it. She'll say somewhere safe." But he was already out the door and heading for Mrs. Price's house just down the street.

"I take it you haven't purchased a wedding dress?" Lady Eleanor asked.

"I have a blue dress upstairs."

"No!" Hew's mother shook her head firmly. "You need a new dress—a white dress. That's all the fashion now. We'll see my modiste. She will probably faint from the late notice, but I pay her a fortune, so she'll do it. Let's go. My carriage is waiting."

"I can't leave," Belle said. "The shop—"

"We have an entire wedding to plan in less than twenty-four hours, Miss Howard." Lady Eleanor clapped. "*Pressez-vous un peu!*"

Belle had no idea what language Lady Eleanor spoke or what her words meant, but she closed the shop and followed her into her waiting carriage. Twenty-four hours later, she was still reeling from the whirlwind of activity, and she clutched her father's arm tightly as he walked her up the aisle of a beautiful church in Hanover Square.

The wedding party was small. On her side were Mr. Dormer and her sister as well as the Tipps and Mrs. Price, who was wiping her eyes with a silk handkerchief.

On Hew's side, she saw his mother and his father, whom she had only met the night before. Willoughby Galloway had come as well and beside him was a lovely blond woman who must be his wife. And lastly—Lady Keating! Belle had smiled at seeing the baroness. How had she even known about the wedding? Lady Keating smiled back at her then looked toward the front of the church.

Belle looked too, and her breath caught in her throat. She'd forgotten to look at Hew. But there he stood—straight and tall, his blue eyes warm with admiration for her. It struck her then that she was really marrying him. He was marrying her!

Her heart began to pound, and she was glad her sister had forced her to eat that slice of toast this morning. She felt as though she might faint.

She clutched her father's arm more tightly, leaning on him until she was finally standing before Hew. He looked down at her, answered some question the minister had posed, then took her hand. He wore white gloves, as did she, but she could feel the warmth of his hand through the material. He squeezed her hand, and somehow she knew everything was right. This was right.

He was perfect.

***

Hew's parents had hosted the wedding breakfast at a rented town house. Now that it was late fall, not many families were in London, and they had been able to rent a large, lovely house. And yet, Hew rejected the offer to stay with his new wife in one of the many bed chambers. Instead, he took her to Mivart's.

He insisted on carrying her through the door of their room, and she gasped as soon as she looked about. "It's *our* room!"

He smiled. "I thought you'd like that."

"Mr. Arundel, I never would have thought you were the sentimental sort."

"I can be."

He nodded to the footman who had carried their luggage then used a foot to close the door behind him.

"You can put me down now," Belle said.

"Not here," he murmured and carried her straight to the bed chamber. He hadn't seen her in weeks, and he'd done nothing but imagine what he would do when he finally had

Belle alone. Hew set her gently on the bed and pulled her to her knees, cupping her face. "You look so beautiful," he said. Her cheeks reddened and she started to tilt her head to one side, to hide her scars, but he kissed her. "When I saw you walking toward me in St. George's, I knew I was the luckiest man alive."

"And when I saw you," she said, "all of my worries and fears floated away." She smiled. "I'd begun to think you were just a dream. Mrs. Price misplaced all of the letters you sent. My father found two, and I only read them this morning. You caught Pennywhistle," she said.

Hew reached for the ribbons of her hat and untied them, then found the hat pin and tossed the hat aside. "The Saboteurs caught him with the information your father and I provided, which included confessions from the men we caught." He nodded at her as he began to pluck pins from her honey-blond hair.

"Does this mean I am now an agent for the Crown?"

He laughed. "Retired. That was your one and only mission."

"Fine by me," she said and reached up to push his hat off his head. He freed her hair just as she began to pull off her gloves. Hew ripped his own off then ran his bare fingers through her silky strands. "Why did he do it?" she asked.

Hew removed a broach from her neck and began to unfasten her bodice. "Hmm?"

"Pennywhistle," she clarified. "Why did he sabotage the railway tracks and kill those people?"

"Exactly the reason we'd thought. A deposit of minerals had been found on his property and it extended into the land he'd sold the railway. He tried to buy it back and couldn't, so he decided to steal what he could. He needed time and a diversion."

"What will happen to him now?" she asked, the slightest tremor in her voice as he opened her bodice. Hew looked into her face, noted her eyes were large and a deep brown.

"A trial and hopefully years and years"—he kissed her neck—"and years of time in prison. But I don't want to talk about Pennywhistle." He kissed her again. "Or railways." Another kiss. "Or sabotage." He pushed her bodice off her shoulders and helped her shed it. "I have more important things to do."

"Such as?"

"Figure out how the devil to get you out of those skirts."

As it turned out, he didn't have to figure it out at all. With only a little help, she shed them easily, followed by her corset, and then her chemise. Hew had been shedding his own clothes, but when she stood naked before him, his hands trembled slightly.

My wife, his mind repeated over and over.

A bubble of fear rose in him, but then she reached for him, and the bubble floated away. This was Belle. His Belle. He could trust her with his life. Hell, she'd saved his life.

Hew shed the rest of his clothing and pulled her into his arms. Her warm body slid against his as he ran his hands over her, reacquainting himself with her every dip and curve. She kissed him, long and deep, and then they were on the bed, lips meeting and parting, hands stroking, bodies coming together. He was careful with her, but he needn't have worried. He didn't hurt her this time, only gave her pleasure. She gave it back, and after a while they lay spent in each other's arms.

Hew's eyes were closed, and he dozed, waiting for his strength to come back so he might ring for food or—Belle's favorite—tea. She rolled over, and he opened one eye to look up at her.

"How long do we have?" she asked.

"Until?"

"Until we can do that all over again."

Hew groaned. "Give me a *few* minutes to recover."

"I just want as much of you as possible. I never know when I'll see you again."

He rose up on one elbow. "You'll see me tomorrow and the day after and the day after that. I've taken a short leave of absence from the Saboteurs."

Her eyes widened. "You didn't have to do that. I wouldn't have asked that of you."

"I wanted to take a few weeks to spend alone with you, but even after my leave ends, I promise I'll always come back to you."

"And I'll always be waiting for you. You know that."

"I do," he said and cupped her face for a kiss. The kiss deepened, and he murmured, "I think I've recovered."

"Mmm-hmm," she said feeling the evidence of that. "But given that you've just told me we're not short on time, I'm in no rush. We should order tea." She began to climb out of bed. "I'll just tug the bell pull—"

He wrapped a hand about her waist and pulled her back down, his heart soaring as he heard her laughter.

"You'll have your tea," he said, gathering her into his arms. "Later."

About Shana Galen

Shana Galen is three-time Rita award nominee and the bestselling author of passionate Regency romps. Kirkus said of her books: "The road to happily-ever-after is intense, conflicted, suspenseful and fun." *RT Bookreviews* described her writing as "lighthearted yet poignant, humorous yet touching." She taught English at the middle and high school level for eleven years. Most of those years were spent working in Houston's inner city. Now she writes full time, surrounded by three cats and one spoiled dog. She's married and has a daughter who is most definitely a romance heroine in the making.

Would you like exclusive content, book news, and a chance to win early copies of Shana's books? Sign up for monthly emails on her website for exclusive news and giveaways.

Go back and revisit the first book in the Royal Saboteurs series! Beauty and the Thief introduces Hew and the rest of the agents. Here's an excerpt from Chapter One.

Bridget Murray consulted the small gold watch she held in her gloved hand and frowned. Nearby, the last train of the night blew out a burst of steam, sounding very much like an enormous, and rather impatient, horse. She looked about the deserted train station, her eyes roving over the same figures she'd observed the past forty-seven minutes. One lone porter sat on a bench, his eyelids half closed as he snoozed. Through the window of the small lounge, she noted the ticket seller beginning to gather his coat and hat. Bridget, in her dark traveling dress and old but still serviceable winter coat, stood between two columns, watch in hand and umbrella hooked on one arm.

Another minute ticked by. *Where was he?* The train would depart in twelve minutes. The rest of her charges were aboard, and she felt a twinge of unease at not being safely aboard, though she'd reminded herself several times that she still had plenty of time.

Baron wanted Kelly on that train, and Baron had asked her, specifically, to wait for the man. But she couldn't *make* this Kelly come to the train station. He knew the train schedule, didn't he? Surely, he did. Baron informed her Kelly had been given his ticket days ago. Whereas, she had held the tickets for her other passengers.

She looked at her watch again just as a gust of steam from the train ruffled her black skirts and momentarily deafened her. When she looked up again a man sprinted toward her.

He dashed down the platform, his greatcoat flying behind him, revealing dark, fitted evening clothes beneath. He'd lost his hat at some point and his chin-length hair flew back from his clean-shaven face. She might have retreated if not for the grin he wore. He looked like a man having the best night of his life.

She'd been struck momentarily immobile by his sheer masculine beauty. The way he moved, the way his eyes glittered, the way the wind whipped his hair back...

He was coming straight for her.

Bridget glanced at the train then the lounge, trying to decide which was closer should she need to flee. But even as she turned toward the lounge, the man, who was now only a few yards away, called out to her. "Are you Miss Bridget Murray?" His voice had a lilt she couldn't place at the moment, but she understood him well enough.

"I am." She shoved her watch into the reticule hanging from her wrist.

"Sure and I'm Callahan Kelly." He skidded to a stop before her and reached up to doff his hat. Finding it missing, he shrugged and gave her a sweeping bow. Oh, yes, he was handsome. That was undeniable.

Even more undeniable was the fact that he was trouble. One look into his gray-blue eyes told her that.

A commotion at the other end of the platform caused him to straighten and cast a look over his shoulder. Just then four other men tumbled down the far stairwell. A remarkably tall men led three burly men. They paused and looked about as though searching for someone. She sighed. "They're after you, of course."

Kelly hissed in a breath and stepped behind the nearest column, pulling her with him. "How long until the train leaves?"

"Eleven minutes." She peered around the column. The men had slowed, seeming to search, and moving in the direction of the lounge behind her.

"Too long." Kelly took her wrist and yanked her out from the columns and into the shadows at the back of the platform.

"Let go!" she objected as he pulled her into an archway built into the stone.

But instead of releasing her, he shoved her against the white tiled wall and pressed himself beside her. "Be quiet."

Bridget brought her foot down hard on his shoe, and he jumped back, a look of incredulity in his eyes. She straightened. "I don't know who you think you are, but I have not given you leave to touch me."

"Bridget—"

"*Miss Murray*, if you please."

"You'll be *Miss Murdered* if you don't shut up and step back."

She might be angry, but she wasn't an idiot. She could see the men who'd come for him were not the sort to listen to reason or, more importantly, to respect train schedules. She stepped back, pressing herself uncomfortably close to Mr. Kelly and dug out her watch. "Nine minutes until the train departs."

"We'll catch the next one."

She turned to face him. "You think trains to the Farm leave every day? I have strict instructions to be on that train no m—"

He cupped a hand at the back of her neck pulled her face hard against his chest. Two seemingly contradictory thoughts entered her head at that moment.

One, she wanted to hit him.

Two, he smelled remarkably good. She had the ridiculous urge to bury her nose in his coat and press her cheek against his warm torso. Instead, she shoved back. His grip on her neck held, and they stared at each other, nose to nose.

"Unhand me!" she hissed.

"My friends are just there." His gray-blue eyes darted to the side. "Once they pass us, we make a run for it."

She wanted to argue. She wanted to stomp on his foot again. She wanted a closer look at those eyes. Instead, she pressed her lips together and allowed herself to be gathered against his chest again.

Even she would be pressed to admit her current situation was a hardship. Besides the fact that his touch was doing strange things to her belly and making her chest feel tight, his plan was reasonable. Provided the men passed them in the next seven minutes, they'd have enough time to board the train and be away.

But seven minutes with her body flush against his, her breath quickening as her breasts were flattened against his chest, the hair at the nape of her neck rustling with each of his warm breaths. She clenched her fists, determined to bear the friction as he slid against her in an effort to peer around the wall shielding them.

"Miss Murray," he whispered in her ear, making her shiver. "We have a problem."

Truer words were never spoken. "What problem?" she whispered back.

"One of the men is standing guard just outside the station lounge."

Clearly, Kelly's plan must be discarded. The thug was unlikely to move in the next six minutes and she must be on that train. She could go without Mr. Kelly, but that would mean ignoring Baron's order to wait for the man. Baron wanted Kelly at the Farm.

She looked up, avoiding Kelly's unusual eyes. Her gaze rested on his lips, but those also proved too dangerous, and she settled on one of his dark eyebrows. "Do these men need to take you alive?"

"Sure and I don't know what you're hinting at, Miss Murray."

Irish. That was his accent. "Will they kill you now or do they need to bring you to their leader alive?"

"Alive, I expect, though they wouldn't mind damaging me, if you understand my meaning."

"Now who would want to hurt you, Mr. Kelly?"

He lifted a brow, which made her chest tighten a fraction more.

"I might owe their employer a pound or two."

They'd want him alive then. Dead men couldn't pay debts. In any case, there was no more time to waste. She held up her watch and palmed it so only a glint of medal showed. "Turn around and let me put my arm about your neck."

"Are you daft?"

"Don't try me, Mr. Kelly. Turn around."

He gave her a look of incredulity then turned and hunched down, so she could hook her arm about his neck. She pressed the watch to his temple as though it were a pistol.

"You can't think this will work," he muttered.

"Hello there!" she called, pushing Kelly out of the alcove.

The wide, muscular man standing by the column spun around, his small eyes widening. "Oy!" he called to his comrades.

"Is this the person you are searching for?" Bridget pushed Kelly forward. If she could move near enough to the train, they could make a run for it.

"Hand 'im over, missus."

"No, don't come any nearer. I have a pistol to his head, and if you come any closer, I will shoot."

"Oy!" The thug called again.

"They're coming back, lass," Kelly said under his breath.

"You won't shoot 'im, missus" The burly man moved forward. He had a vicious scar across one cheek, and his nose looked to be little more than a flat blob in the center of his face.

"I will. I've shot men before. Now, I want to board this train, and I am taking him with me."

The tall man approached, slowing to a walk as he assessed the situation. "You can't do that, madam." He was obviously the leader. His speech was slightly more refined. "We work for a very important man, and he needs to speak with Mr. Kelly. Immediately."

The train hissed out another blast of steam. Now she had two men between the train and herself. She couldn't look at her watch, but she knew she was almost out of time. "That's most interesting because I also work for an important man, and he would like to speak with Mr. Kelly as well. Perhaps my employer could speak to Mr. Kelly and then you could have him back. Now, if you would move aside and allow us to pass." She started confidently forward, pushing Kelly in front of her.

"I can't do that, madam." The tall man glanced to the side as the third large man joined them. "Hand him over, and I give you my word, you will not be touched."

"Get out of my way, or I give you my word that I will shoot him right now."

The tall man's eyes narrowed. "I think you're bluffing."

She kept her gaze locked on his. Bridget was a very good card player.

The train whistle shattered the tension, and Bridget jumped at the unexpected screech. Her hand opened, and she fumbled to catch the watch before it fell to the ground.

"Get him!" the tall man yelled.

Everything happened very quickly. Kelly pushed her out of the way as the three men rushed him. She stumbled over her skirts and went to her knees. She pushed up again just as someone called, "All aboard!"

"No!" She started for the train, but she couldn't leave Kelly behind. He had his hands full with the three men circling him. As she watched, he threw a punch at the flat-nosed thug, but it glanced off the man's cheek, doing little harm. The tall man grasped his arms from behind, but Kelly slammed his elbow back, and the tall thug bent double.

Bridget was used to seeing men who could fight, and she knew skill when she saw it. The enormous wheels of the train began to move, and she started for it. She could still jump aboard, but how to free Kelly to join her?

And if that wasn't problem enough, the fourth thug was racing toward them. He had his full attention on Kelly, and Bridget unhooked her umbrella from her arm and stuck it into his path at just the right moment. He went down hard and she closed in, bashing him in the back of the head with the umbrella's solid wood handle.

One down.

The train was moving in earnest now. She had less than a minute to jump aboard. "Mr. Kelly, we must go!" she called.

460 | *Shana Galen*

"I'm coming—" He threw a punch and missed. "—as fast—" The tall man hit him in the shoulder, and Kelly reeled back. "—as I can, lass."

"Must I do everything?" she muttered to herself. She dug in her reticule and pulled out all the coins she possessed. In one motion, she flung them onto the platform. As she'd expected, the men glanced at the dropping coins, and realizing what they were, dove for them.

Well, two of the thugs dove for them. The tall man turned back to Kelly, ducking his right hook.

The train was moving quickly now. She could see the last cars approaching. She began to jog to keep up. "Mr. Kelly, now would be an excellent time to board."

He feinted left then punched the tall man in the throat. Bridget turned away and, running now, grasped the stair railing, pulling herself onto the steps of the car just as the rearmost car passed the struggling men.

"Mr. Kelly! Now or never!" she yelled as the train whistle sounded for the last time.

Kelly grabbed the tall man by the coat, pulled his head down, and slammed his forehead against the tall man's. Bridget winced, but the desperate maneuver worked. The tall man stumbled away, and Kelly began to run toward the train.